ANGEL
DREAMS

An Angel Falls ~ Book 2

JODY A. KESSLER

Please visit:

www.JodyAKessler.com

Or sign up for the Newsletter

ISBN: 978-0-9862406-4-5

E book ISBN: 978-0-9862406-5-2

Edited by

J. Farrah & M. Hull

Cover Art & Design by

Laura Gordon

www.thebookcovermachine.com

Manufactured in the United States of America

First Edition

To Nancy and John.
Without you this novel would not exist.

Chapter One: Perks

Nathaniel

Life could go on without us. Leave us behind like a painting on a wall, a captured image of sunlight and trees and two people serene as the river winding its way through these mountains. We will exist in our own world and live as if we're the only two beings in existence. The appeal to stop time and extend this happiness to the end of eternity is as real for me as the illusion of time itself. If we could stay like this, the excitement, the newness, the pleasure of finding someone so fascinating, and so beautiful, and so perfect, would we leave the bounds of time to spend an eternal day together? Wouldn't anyone live out the best moment of their life forever, given the opportunity? I can't choose for her, but if I had the choice to change my reality, I would. Unfortunately, time is more powerful than the sun or the moon and I know our time is limited. How long do we have? Only time will tell.

Juliana wades barefoot in the rocky creek with her pant legs rolled up to her knees. I'm content to stay along the bank enraptured by her enthusiasm for the simple pleasure of enjoying the day.

"Come in, it's positively freezing."

She smiles at me and I can all but feel her little deviling pixies pushing me forward. *How can I resist that smile of hers?* I manage, but only because I want to see what else she will do to get me in the water with her.

"Very persuasive, but no thanks."

"It's not like you'll feel it anyway, or will you?"

Her emerald eyes meet mine with curiosity. They sparkle like the rippling water swirling around her ankles. "No, I can't feel the water when I'm like this," I say. Watching her response, I'm again surprised that it doesn't bother her that I am not a living breathing human like herself. She only has more questions.

"So if I do this," she bends forward and flicks her hand across the surface of the water sending a spray of droplets at me, "you don't feel a thing?"

"Nothing," I answer as the drops pass through me and land randomly around my feet.

"What about when you're solid?"

"Yes. When I manifest my body, I feel the water the same way you do. No, I take that back. I don't feel it *exactly* the way you do. When I was alive I didn't wade around in freezing cold creeks for fun. Are your toes still attached?"

"My toes are perfectly fine, thank you." She kicks some more water at me. "So you can come in here and you won't feel a thing."

"I prefer the land if it's all the same to you."

"Nope, not the same, you should come in, and with your real body. I swear it's not that terrible."

"Still going to pass." I give her a quick wink and a grin.

"Don't you want to feel the rocks under your feet or the silt between your toes?" She holds her hand out to me.

I shrug and shake my head. Feeling her hand in mine is the only real appeal of her offer. "You forgot to sell me on the algae and the leeches."

"Come on, nothing can hurt *you*. We're going over the hill so you have to cross eventually."

"Over that hill?" Her version of hill and mine are vastly different. "That's a mountain if I've ever seen one."

"Mountain, hill, tomato, tomoto. Yes, we're going up there."

"And why did the chicken cross the road?"

She gives me one of her beatific smiles. It's wide and brightens her entire being.

"Exactly. To get to the other side. Good to know we're on the same page."

Moving like a tiptoeing fox, she leaves the water and comes over to me. Her agility and gracefulness doesn't escape me. Everything about Juliana Crowson, more than I could have ever imagined, wraps itself around me and fills a need I didn't know was there. I reach out to brush my fingertips over the back of her hand. She looks up at me and I feel something in my chest expand. "You're a sly fox, you know."

Her nearness and those green eyes of hers make my voice alter somehow. It's low and rough, choked with feeling. Being with her has caused my entire universe to shift and, as far as I'm concerned, there is no going back. I've found someone who can not only see me, but wants me to stay around.

"Sly? No, I didn't know. You said foxes see things that others can't. I see you, and others cannot. What's that have to do with being sly?"

"Because, now I have to know where you're taking me. I was content to stay here with you all day, but now, I'm feeling the urge to go mountain climbing."

"Good. It's a surprise. Now will you cross this teensy weensy mountain stream?"

"Are you specifying in what form you would like me to do that?"

"Well, you said if you don't have a physical body then you could stay with me longer, so let's not push things. Any way you want."

Her smile turns to one of sweet innocence. I look up the steep incline on the other side of the creek and then down at her. Her stamina for prowling around the mountains is fascinating. We've spent most of the morning walking and exploring the area around our campsite, which is owned by her grandmother. She acts as if she's strolling through a city park instead of scrambling over rocks and climbing hills.

"Can't wait to see what's up there," I say.

The look she gives me tells me she's happy with my answer, but what strikes me is the depth to which her honest eyes penetrate my core. She doesn't even know she's doing it. She is a thief unaware, stealing my ability to function in this world without her. Breaking our brief connection, she bends down and hooks her fingers inside her discarded hiking boots. She stands back up and wades into the water, shoes dangling.

I follow her since she apparently knows the way and I like the sight of her walking in front of me with her raven black hair hanging down the length of her back. She stops on the other side of the stream and sits on a small flat rock to put her shoes back on.

"Is this side of the creek still your grandmother's land?" I ask.

"No. We're on National Forest property now."

"Aren't you worried about getting lost?"

She laughs. It's melodious and girlish and the sound makes me smile.

After tying her laces, she leans to the side and plucks a yellow flower from the rocky soil. She twirls the stem between her fingers.

"Is that funny?" I ask.

"Sorry. It's just that I don't think I could get lost if I tried. There's some kind of built in compass in me. I always know where I am, and where town is, and where my house is. Even if for some reason I couldn't get back to my car, I would know what direction the main road is with my eyes closed. It must be from growing up here."

"I'm glad you have a good sense of direction. Between the two of us we'll never be lost."

"Really? Do you have special global positioning powers or something?" she teases.

"Sort of," I answer in all seriousness. "I can see where we are from any angle if I want to."

Her teasing from the moment before suddenly dissipates as she asks, "How does that work?"

"I can move with my intent. I have to think something like, 'I want to see this entire mountain side' and then I'm doing it."

"That's it? Think it and it happens. Can you make things appear, ooh," she says as a rousing thought enters her mind. "Or disappear, like magic?" She wiggles her fingers like she is performing some magic trick in the air in front of her.

I feel my head shaking from side to side in bemused disbelief even as one side of my mouth quirks into a grin at her enthusiasm for my predicament. "Afraid not. I can move anywhere I want with thought and I can manifest a body for myself so people can see me. When I'm solid I can do things about the same way as when I was alive. It's not very exciting being an angel."

"I heard the *'about the same.'* I know how strong and fast you are. There are some perks to your job."

"You are the only perk I can think of."

"Shut up. I'm not a perk. And you said I wasn't your last case which means I wasn't connected to your last job. What happened? You still haven't told me the details."

She climbs to her feet and begins to hike over the mix of pine litter, bunch grass, and granite. As we make our ascent along a game trail I try to come up with the best way to tell her what happened.

"I think you must have bewitched me. I couldn't stay away from you and it caused me to make a mistake. That, and you were in so many life-threatening situations I had to assume you were mine to watch over, but you weren't."

It's the truth. I also know there's more to it. I screwed up worse than anyone like me should. It's hard to acknowledge my gross error, let alone say it aloud.

"I don't think it turned out so bad. I'm alive. And I kind of like you, so if you hadn't messed up then we wouldn't have met."

"You kind of like me?" I ask, digging for more detail.

"No, not at all. I only like hanging out with Angels of Death because it's so terrifyingly stellar."

She stops and turns around. Standing on the uphill side of me her eyes are almost level with mine. Her green and gold eyes flecked with rust disconcert me in all the right ways. "I'm not in the same position anymore," I say.

"Oh? Do angels get the shaft for messing up on the job?"

"Yes." My voice is betraying me again. It's difficult to speak when she stares at me like that.

"So you really aren't back to whisk me away to heaven, or wherever?"

"No."

She nods as if she understands completely and then turns on her booted heel, hiking away from me. "I thought you said this morning you already have a new case."

With her backside bouncing happily away from me it's easier for me to speak, but not by much. She didn't press me for the fine details of my mistake, which I appreciate. The truth is I was supposed to assist her brother, Jared, with his passing into the afterlife and I accidentally — well sort of on purpose — saved him. In doing so, I was taken off his case and another angel has been assigned to him. I can't do anything about it and I don't want to hurt Juliana by telling her what is to come for her brother, but she deserves to know. I have to find the right time to break the news to her, but not today. Not when we finally get a chance to be alone together.

"I do," I say. "But I don't help people after they die anymore. I have a slightly different role now."

A speculative look crosses her face before we move around an outcrop of boulders. Juliana turns to the rocks and then grips a jagged edge and starts to climb up the slanted face.

"So, do I dare ask, or is it against the rules to speak to the living about?"

"I can talk about anything. There are rules. Some are my own. Others are guidelines I'm supposed to follow."

She laughs and I have to ask again, "What's funny?"

"Supposed to follow? You're admitting it's okay to bend the rules."

"In my line of work, I have to stay flexible. But, I never break confidences and I can't tolerate abuse or liars. Those are my rules." What she doesn't know is that I broke the most important rule; don't interfere with a client's fate. The future isn't predetermined, but over the course of my afterlife, I've seen enough deaths to know when a person's life is over, it's over. The web of life is complete and to extend it for someone has far-reaching consequences, most of which are dire. What I've done to Jared is unforgivable, and yet I have been forgiven. The leniency was granted because I didn't know what I was doing until it was too late. What will be the price for such interruption? What will Juliana say when I tell her that Jared's time is running out? In the end will she blame me? I wait with shame riding on my back to find out.

Juliana climbs back down and faces me. "Confidentiality and honesty. Sounds pretty honorable. I can understand the bending part. I always find myself going against the grain and following my own rules too."

"Like what?" I ask, wondering what self-governing laws this nineteen-year-old vixen lives by.

"Well, for one, you can never leave your shoes under the bed." She flashes me a smile as I raise an eyebrow at her. "It causes nightmares," she explains. "And two, never walk on someone's shadow because you're stepping on their spirit. Which is pretty rude."

I nod my head at her in complete agreement although I have no idea where she is coming up with this stuff. "Anything else? I wouldn't want to offend from ignorance."

"Oh, there's a lot more. I have a small encyclopedia of rules and regulations about harvesting herbs. But that's where the flexibility comes in. Sometimes you have to go with what the situation brings."

"Agreed," I say.

Her smile widens, but I can see her watching my reaction. I've seen Juliana's superstitious behavior before. Like watching her cross her fingers and throwing salt over her shoulder, but now I have to wonder just how superstitious she is. Not that it matters. She's captured me in her web and I don't want to escape, I want to know everything about her.

"What about this?" The need to touch her, to feel the heat of her skin or the softness of her hair overwhelms me. I pull universal energy to myself and form my body, but instead of reaching for her, I bend down and pick the fragile stem of a plant I actually recognize. Holding it out to her she rewards my effort by giving me a sweet and tender look which makes my chest ache. She's beyond beautiful. "Do I offend you by picking this one?"

She takes the delicate green leaves. Her fingers are warm as they brush mine. She stares down at the petals. "This one is special. You're doing well. It's still morning, which is a good time to harvest clover. It has so many uses."

"Like what? Why is it special?"

She sits back against the granite and goes on. "My dad use to send me and Jared outside to look for four-leaf clovers when I was really little. He said if I found one, my most secret wish would come true. You know," she says, looking away and down the mountainside, "I could never find one." She shrugs and then lowers the tiny three-leafed stem to her side and looks straight at me.

The color of the clover reminds me of her eyes. I could stand here all day hypnotized by their color, but after a short silence, she tucks her hair behind an ear, and distracts me.

"My Grandma taught me everything else I know about how to use clover. It's edible and it makes a good tea for stimulating the liver and gallbladder."

"And, luck of the Irish, right?"

"Four-leaf clovers are lucky, and I am half Irish, that's true. But I think the herb affects me because of the memories of my family."

She averts her eyes and stares down at the green leaves in her hand once more.

Juliana told me about her father's death in a car accident when she was younger. "Did you see someone like me when your dad died?" It's out of my mouth before I realize what I'm asking.

Bringing up her past hurts was not my intention. I spend my afterlife talking to the recently deceased where communication has little boundaries and resolving emotional conflicts happens fast. I have to remind myself that everyday occurrences still affect her life. She has a past that includes pain and loss.

"I don't think so." She bites her lower lip and then changes her answer. "Maybe. I didn't really see spirits and people like you clearly until just recently, because of what happened at Castle Hill. It's a powerful place and I've changed because of it. When I was small, it was just a feeling most of the time."

"Do you regret it, Juliana? Your new abilities?"

"No." She shakes her head. "That's another rule; no regrets."

"That would be hard for me," I admit, and then go on to answer her question about my new angel position.

"Since Castle Hill, my cases are harder now. Before we met, I helped people adjust to being dead. I spent a lot of time answering questions and showing them the way across. Now I have to assess unfortunate situations and help clients who might be having thoughts of," I pause to find an appropriate way to explain my current situation. My new case is delicate, as if I'm walking on thin ice and carrying someone's life in my arms, while trying to keep us both from falling in. She wants to commit suicide. The first few days with my new client has given me a look at a grim reality. The magnitude of loss and waste of a life is far past pitying. Call it a gut instinct about this girl...and believe me, I know the idiocy of following my instincts right now. I had myself convinced Juliana was about to die and I've never been more wrong. My new case however, with my new duties, leaves the interpretation up to me. I want to help her, and not after she takes her life, but to do everything I can to help her find her way in the life she has now. She's young and there has to be a better solution. If only I can help her find it.

"What's the matter?"

"I apologize. I was trying to find the right way to explain what I have to do with my new case."

"So are you still an angel? Not some demon who stalks women for their souls," she teases.

"I don't find that very funny."

She turns back to the moss covered rocks behind her and scrambles up the sloped side, leaving me a spectator to her climbing abilities. She's good, confident in her grips and without hesitation. It's a short climb. When she reaches the top, she sits down and dangles her feet over the edge, watching me.

Her dark hair frames her face and shines like black glass. Her mouth looks soft and her eyes sparkle at me. This glimpse of such an innocent human moment almost paralyzes me. She is too fragile in a world full of danger. One slip on these rocks, or her comment about demons — there are real threats everywhere. I know she's joking, but anything could happen at any time, and she could be gone before we even have a chance to know each other.

"Yeah, Mr. Serious," she taunts. "Did I hit a home run or something?" She wiggles her brows at me like she wants it to be true.

"Of course I'm not evil. And yes, I'm still a helper." I forgo the climbing, relinquish my physical body, and lift myself up through the air to where she sits. Her eyebrows rise as I do, and by the time I'm next to her, they have completely disappeared under her bangs, leaving her with a look of wide eyed amazement. "I move with my intent, remember?"

"I've never seen anything like that before." Her brows lower and she looks to the mountain behind her rather than at my face. "What's wrong? I can tell something's up," she asks again, this time in a lower more solemn tone.

"Nothing," I automatically respond. She must have read my expression. I haven't been seen by people for so many years, I have to remember to control my face around her. That is, if I don't want her to know what I'm thinking. She rises and starts hiking away leaving me standing alone on the granite.

"I didn't mean to upset you by bringing up your job. Let's just forget it."

When you don't have a body, it is much harder to inflict pain upon yourself, but god if I could hit myself upside the head, I would do it on a regular basis. "Juliana, wait."

"No, we're almost there," she says, keeping her pace steady and not looking my way.

I move along staying close to her. *I'm an idiot. Fix this, Nathan.* "My case...is this girl. She wants to end her life because, and this is only what I've figured out so far, her home life is miserable. No. Miserable isn't a strong enough word. She's being abused in indescribable ways. That's not all I was upset about a second ago. I'm sorry. I want to explain, but it's difficult."

"Was it my joke about soul-sucking demons?"

I strain to hear what she just said under her breath but I think I got it. "Sort of. But, it's not what you think."

The ground levels out briefly as we cross a narrow road. Juliana hops over the ditch on the opposite side and ducks back into the trees. I look up and down the four-wheel drive track, seeing no one, but noticing fresh tire marks in the dirt. Amazed that we're not the only ones up here. I assumed we were in a remote area of the forest. I shake it off, and move to follow her.

The trees are thick, in size and in number. They surround me on all sides, blocking the sun, and leaving me staring through midnight green shadows. *Where did she go? I don't see her. Did I upset her so much that she would ditch me? No. She's not the kind of person to play petty games. I would know. She's more down to earth and real than anyone I've ever met. Don't call out to her. Keep looking. The trees are blocking my line of sight, that's all.* My previous fear that anything can happen at any moment to her human body is like a wasp buzzing in my ear, making me want to panic and overreact. The urge to protect her, to protect us, is overpowering but I manage to control my own imaginings. I close my eyes, listening for her soft steps on the spongy ground, but I hear nothing except the chirping of a songbird and the call of a distant raven. *Concentrate, and go to her, and quit worrying.* I could find her on the dark side of the moon if that's where she was.

"Ooowww! Oh, oh, oh!"

Life is never simple. How can I ever quit worrying when Juliana Crowson is on the loose?

Less than a half of a second later I find her lying flat on her back with her eyes squeezed closed. I create my physical body and throw myself down on the ground next to her. "Can you move? Speak to me. What's wrong? Please, are you all right?"

"Oh, holy saint mackerel, it hurts."

"Where, what? Can you move, love? I can have you to a hospital right now."

"A hospital?"

Her eyelids flicker open and then deep green sparked with bits of sun look up at me.

"Yes. I'll take you there right now."

A juicy tear leaks out from the corner of one eye and runs down over her temple making the clenching sensation around my chest implode. *Is this my fault? Can excessive worrying create your worst nightmare?* The need for action and security, to know she is going to be all right makes me start to lift her off the ground. I'll carry her to safety. I'll do anything I have to. The conflict between my brain and my hands is intolerable. Assess or react? When I see the slight twitching at the corners of her mouth, as if she may start laughing, I lean back an inch and take in more of the situation. She's cradling her hand over her stomach, but otherwise looks uninjured.

"The emergency room would be a little overkill for this," she whimpers.

She holds up her hand in front of me and I see the mother of all splinters in her index finger. I cringe at the sight of its jagged tail sticking out of her tender white skin. Looking down at Juliana's face I find her head is turned away and her eyes are closed again. In all honesty I don't want to look at it either. Seeing her blood, albeit only a few red drops, reinforces my overwhelming need to protect her. Her skin is turning red and beginning to swell. I want to take her pain and whisk it away like a Frisbee into oblivion. Straining for self-control, I ask again, "Can you move?"

"I think so."

All right. Realizing her situation is not life-threatening, the ability to organize my thoughts returns and makes speaking with an iota of logic come much easier. "Then why are you on your back?" I ask slowly.

"I tripped," she says, sounding embarrassed.

"We should get that splinter out," I say, somehow managing to find an appropriate response to her emergency.

"I know, but me and blood don't get along very well," she says, her voice shaking.

I close my own eyes for a brief moment. It looks as if I'm going to have to help her with this. It wouldn't be a problem to do it for anyone else, but to do it to her is worse than pulling my own splinter out. "I'll pull it out if you want me to," I offer reluctantly.

She looks up at me. Her eyes purposefully avoiding her hand. "Do it quick before I lose my nerve."

She covers her face with her free arm and then holds up her injury to me. Her hand trembles in mine and I feel like I'm about to amputate, which is absurd but none the less true. She clenches her fist, baring white knuckles, but leaves her index finger sticking straight out. *Now or never.* And then, with as much delicacy that is possible for my large hands, I grip the tip of the splintered wood and yank. Juliana's chest rises and falls in fast shallow breaths, but she doesn't scream. I throw the offending piece of splintered wood to the forest floor casting it away like a mortal enemy.

"It's out. Try to slow down your breathing."

Her arm lowers from off of her face and she pushes herself up to sitting. Small pools of tears threaten to escape her lower lids. Her brave face is more endearing than I can stand at the moment and I feel yet another shift inside of me for this bewitching girl.

"Can I try something?" I ask, feeling odd about having to ask aloud to help someone. Normally, I comfort people in total silence. They never know I'm there. "It can help," I add.

"Okay," she says as she watches me.

I place one hand on her upper back and the other at the base of her skull. Then I begin to pull the same energy I use to manifest my body from the universe and push it toward her. The tension in her shoulders and back immediately release and I can feel her calm down inside.

"Thanks."

"The wound should be washed out. Otherwise I would try to heal it."

"The blood will help cleanse it."

The ragged slash, about three quarters of an inch long, drips copiously.

"Is it very painful?" I have to ask.

"Actually, not excruciating...now. And I'll be able to do more for it when we get to where we're going."

"We're still going somewhere? I thought you were hiding from me."

Confusion flashes across her face. "You? What? No. I, well, I wasn't hiding. I got distracted." She gives me an almost bashful and embarrassed look and then directs her gaze at something near her feet.

A low growing plant with broad green leaves was the "distraction." Scuff marks in the dirt indicate where her heels had been digging in and where she had fallen back. She shrugs her shoulders at me.

"Was there something else? I feel like you're…I don't want to assume, but are you worried about something?" When I channel energy for a client, or someone who is grieving, I can feel layers of emotion. In Juliana, I would say there was more going on with her than an injured finger.

"I was trying to dig up some of the roots with a stick and it didn't work out so well. There was…I thought I felt something."

She pauses and looks away as if unsure, or unwilling, to continue.

"Were you afraid?" I ask tentatively. Fear was what I felt buried somewhere inside her. It was minor, but still there like the tail end of a passing undercurrent.

"From over there," she says and tips her head slightly, back toward the road. "I must be making it up," she says, shrugging and obviously not wanting to dwell on the subject. "Then my stick broke and attacked me. Vicious thing," she accuses, her gloom lightening to playfulness.

"Attacked? Well, you were being forceful with it," I say in the stick's defense. *If she doesn't want to share what was bothering her I won't push. When she's ready, she'll tell me.*

"Fair enough. Stick wins. Looks as if I won't be doing any more digging today. It's too bad. We're running low on devil's club roots at work."

"Devil's club? What's it for? Clubbing the devil," I say in jest.

"It's a general tonic, but Grandma Charlotte uses it for diabetes and sometimes arthritis. You know, she did tell me once that the Natives think the plant has strong magic. Warding off evil spirits and stuff like that. I don't know how they use it exactly, maybe it is a club. Feeling any ill will toward that bush?" She flashes one of her irresistible grins at me. It's a little shaky, but there. She will definitely live.

"You're hilarious, you know."

"I do keep trying, don't I?"

"Don't stop on my account." I pause and then offer, "I could get the roots for you. And I can do it without blood or pain."

"It's not that important," she says while staring at the leafy plant, disappointment clear in her tone. "I get sidetracked sometimes, and besides, I don't have anything to put them in. I can't believe I left my hiking pack in the car. And if I have to carry them the rest of the way, I may be tempted to whack you over the head to see what will happen."

"I knew the name must be fitting to the use of the thing."

Small bits of debris from the forest floor cling to Juliana's hair. I reach for a clump of moss and gingerly pull it free. Restraint has never been a challenge for me until I met her. My hand aches to touch the silky softness of her hair again.

"I know you must have some hidden dark side under all that perfection. Dark angel is the same as devil, isn't it?" She takes my cue and runs the fingers of her left hand through her long hair combing out the needles and dirt.

"I never said I was a dark angel."

"You didn't, but isn't that what some would call you?"

"What if I said yes? Why aren't you afraid?"

"Who says I'm not?"

Her green eyes are wide and clear and within their depths I would swear there isn't one minuscule speck of alarm when it comes to my presence in her life. "I say."

"I'm not afraid of you Nathaniel Evans. Maybe I should be, but you're not scary to me." All trace of her teasing has vanished leaving only serious calm to her words.

"I'm not the devil, or an evil spirit, or a dark angel. If you must call me something, then angel is probably the best. I guess. Nathan or Nathaniel is better. I help people after they die. I console and counsel. It's a job," I tell her with plain simplicity. "And I don't know much about depraved spirits, and I really don't want to."

"Well, that makes two of us. What little I know — that is real — I don't want to talk about either." She casts her gaze down and then starts to stand. "I was kidding, by the way. There's not a pinprick of wickedness in you. I could tell if there was."

She glances over to where the road is and her gaze lingers there for a second too long. *Does she sense something?* "Are you sure you're all right?"

She brushes her hand over her clothes removing specks of dirt. "Uh-huh," she answers, avoiding my gaze.

Images of our last encounter at Castle Hill fill my thoughts, and by the distress which flashed across Juliana's face, I'm guessing she's thinking similar things. When I had finally been able to return to her that dreadful day, it had been in time to see Juliana's brother, Jared, bare-knuckle brawling with a good-for-nothing scumbag methamphetamine dealer named Mason. Juliana sat on the floor half in shock and with clear red finger marks around her neck. I had been consumed with fear for her well-being, and no one else's. If she had not forced me, with those pleading eyes and her broken voice, to help her brother, I would have scooped her up and ran away with her. But I did help Jared, and what I saw was enough to change me forever. By the time I reacted, Jared was on the edge of no return, literally on the edge of an upper story windowsill of the castle. Mason had the upper hand in the fight, but he was not exactly alone. Someone — no, I correct, an evil spirit — was fighting within him. It was a malicious fiend, and it was horrifying. I saw it in Juliana's eyes, that she could see it as well. Castle Hill is a place I think neither one of us will ever be able to forget, and never want to visit again.

I reach for her left hand and she lets me take it. "I only want to keep you safe. Is that all right?"

She bites her lower lip and then looks up at me. "You can't be everywhere all the time, can you?"

"No. But for you, I wish I could be."

"Certain things are out of our control."

"That doesn't mean I have to like it, but I know. You asked me what the matter was earlier. This is it. I realized anything could happen to you and I can't control it. We have just started to know each other. It terrified me, and now this." I glance down at her red finger.

"Nathan. I, you...we just have to stay in the moment. This," She holds up her index finger showing me the swollen side and the drying blood, "is a perk of my job. Not a deadly accident. If anything does happen to me, or you, at least we knew each other. Even for a short time. Right?"

"Getting injured on the job is not a perk, it's a hazard," I argue.

Our relationship is just starting, so no. A short time is not good enough for me. When I'm with Juliana I can only imagine eternity together, not minutes. The way she stares at me, with caring eyes, and her kissable mouth, it's so innocent and alive. It makes me want to lock her away in a cell with both of us inside and never see any threat or harm come near her again.

"I want you, Juliana. I want to know you. I want to see your face in the morning light and be with you until you fall asleep at night. I want to hold your hand as we walk in these woods, not just today, but always. What I don't want, what I can't live with, is a collection of fading memories and a well full of regret." I watch her closely looking for any shift of uneasiness as I pour out my soul to her.

She looks up at me. Her face is open and the honesty I see echoes my own.

"We will know each other," she assures me, and then she seals her words by leaning forward on her tiptoes and brushing her perfect pink lips over mine.

Chapter Two: Reality Check

Juliana

"Come on. We're almost there. I want to wash this cut before it dries."

The crust forming on my right index finger is starting to crack and pull at the edges. It itches slightly, but I ignore it. The fingertips of my left hand trail lazily down the front of Nathaniel's shirt, reluctant to let this moment pass, but I make myself turn away from my new boyfriend.

How weird is that? Me, with an actual boyfriend. I've never wanted to assign that particular title to anyone before. Feeling a bit lighter of body and at the same time more befuddled in my brain, I walk up and over the last small rise toward my destination.

The spruce and pine trees thin out allowing the sun to shine down to the ground in patches of light. It plays with my eyes so I focus on the meadow grass popping up through the thick bed of needles and forest debris. Ahead, the forest opens up into a clearing. I look to where the grass is the thickest. Where it's long and bent over from its own weight. It's camouflaging a shallow channel where water runs through the tiny meadow. I listen for the trickle of water that I know is running beneath the mat of green grass. I hear it like the tinkling of distant bells, a fairy's song in the midst of this sacred place. I walk over to the teeny stream, and then turn, following alongside and moving toward its source.

I don't hear Nathaniel moving behind me. *Did he let go of his body?* When he is in spirit form he makes no sound, which is something I will have to get use to over time. Many peculiarities about my new — mhh-hmm — *friend*, will take time to adjust to. The first of which has to be how direct he is about his feelings toward me. I thought I was generally clear-cut with people but he makes me feel like a wishy-washy air head. *That Jules, come on, I'm worried about sounding light-headed, not the fact that the person I can't stop thinking about is a celestial being. For Gollum's sake, get your priorities straight.*

The warm tingle in my gut still whispers to me after one feather-soft kiss. Residual tendrils of disconcerting need swim around my lower abdomen and tickle my upper thighs. Is this what one brush of lips with this guy does to me? *Ridiculous — and so tempting.* Turning away from his warmth had taken all of my willpower, but it has to be for the best. *Doesn't it?* We need to take our time getting to know each other. If he's as serious as he says he is, then I have to be smart about this. I don't want to rush into anything and regret not taking the right steps with him. Too many people rush into a relationship only to find a cataclysmic end when they realize their "soul mate" is not the person they thought they were. I don't want to be one of those people.

We may not be a typical couple, but can't I at least pretend some things are normal for us, like dating? Yes, we should date, definitely do not want to skip this stage. Then again, maybe I should say damn it all and do what I want. Go with this crazy magnetic force and let Nathaniel Evans do whatever he wants to me, and me to him. The tingling sensation between my bellybutton and my pubic bone twitches at the thought. No. I'm not going there. We have known each other for what? A couple of weeks. And I only found out the truth about what he really is last night. Before that, I didn't know what to make of him, an apparition, a ghost, a delusion, a dream. It had all been very confusing. Even now I can convince myself I'm making him up. He's too perfect. If it had not been for Chris Abeyta, the shaman who also sees Nathaniel and knows what he is, I would likely be in a padded cell. No, Father Time has to be my friend in this, and we can use it to our advantage. I want to let our relationship grow and see what it turns into.

Aspen trees have taken up residence in this little nook of heaven. The trickling water is now visible and is nicely framed by the trees, mountain grass, and wildflowers. This place is timeless, a constant in an endlessly changing world. To the Natives this is a sacred place and for me it is fitting to enter in silence. If I was forced to have a church in my life, then this would be it, not necessarily this place, but nature in general would be my safe haven. Earth's Heart Spring could very well be the most holy place I've ever been, but anywhere there is untouched natural beauty is sacrosanct to me.

I still haven't looked back for Nathaniel. Instead, I'm letting my thoughts process. It surprises me how comfortable I am with him in these woods and even more surprised that I could mention my dad to him. I've never been able to talk about my father with anyone. With Nathaniel everything seems effortless. I wanted to share this quiet and peaceful place with him to see if he'll like it as much as I do, but as I approach the pool of water I see we're not alone. Odd as it is to see anyone up here — it's never happened before — it's even more bewildering to recognize the person. Coincidences don't happen. I stiffen, wondering what the universe has planned up its mysterious sleeve.

This spring is not often visited, mainly because people who come up this side of the mountain are usually seeking the more coveted hot springs nearby. The other reason, I would guess, is because it is not easy to get to. My grandmother Charlotte showed me the hidden trail when I was ten and then explained the significance of the water here.

It occurs to me that Chris may have been the source of the eerie feeling I had while digging the devil's club roots. No. Chris may be serious and a little intimidating but he's nothing like what I felt coming from across the side of the mountain. It was dark and cold. After staying up nearly all night with Nathaniel, my imagination must be taking advantage of my exhaustion. I shake off the remembered feelings and focus on what is before me.

Stopping next to the chalky white trunk of a mature aspen, I decide to go back and give Chris Abeyta his privacy. He's kneeling down next to the tiny pool scooping up some of the spring water with a jar. I can come back another time. Turning around with the utmost care to make as little noise as possible, it becomes inevitable — based on the laws of Murphy — that I'll make some loud intrusive sound. A twig snaps under my boot. I look over my shoulder to see if I caught Chris's attention. I did. Deep brown eyes stare into mine. At first his glare is cold and penetrating but then I see recognition pass over his features and it lightens him, as if the sun came out from behind a cloud to shine on his face.

"You don't have to go." Chris stands and screws on the lid of his jar.

I throw a glance over my shoulder, no Nathaniel, *thank God.* Chris has some rather frightening ideas about my boyfriend, and I would rather skip the whole introduction thing if I can get away with it. *Wherever you are Nathaniel, just hold back for another few minutes,* I silently plead.

"Hey, Chris," I say, slightly too loud, hoping Nathaniel will hear me. "Don't let me interrupt. I know this is a sacred place for the members of the tribe."

"You do? I would not be surprised, if it weren't for your previous ignorance at the Spring of Souls."

Chris is referring to my first experience and complete lack of information on the hot spring near Castle Hill, another ancient spiritual site for the local Native American tribe. "My grandmother told me about this one," I assure him.

"Do you need the water?" His eyes widen with what I think is concern. I watch the pale green and yellow energy of his aura expand in my direction as if he is actually reaching out to me. Touching, I think, that he cares I may be up here for my health.

Then I remember, he's an expert at reading my thoughts, at least from our previous encounters, and he *also* sees energy fields around people. He's the one who taught me to do it. I shut down all thoughts, like wrapping a wool blanket around my brain. It doesn't matter so much if he knows what I'm thinking, but it's a bit unsettling, and I like my privacy. Just knowing someone is capable of such a thing is the main reason why I don't want him doing it.

"Yeah, I do, but it's nothing major." I hold up my finger to display the ragged tear as I walk closer until I'm on the opposite side of the miniature pool from him.

Chris's eyes crinkle and he gives me a real smile with white teeth and everything. "You are practicing shielding your thoughts. Nice attempt."

"Thanks, Chief," I say flatly. "What good is it if you know what I'm doing?"

"Keep practicing and it will get easier, and less apparent." Humor plays on the planes of his flat oval face, but his teeth are no longer showing. "You must understand by now I am not the normal test subject for this exercise."

"I know. You can read me like I'm a first grader's school book." Mental phenomena, like mind reading and shape shifting, are apparently Chris Abeyta's forte.

"How are you trying to shield yourself? There are different techniques you can use and for different reasons as well."

"I don't know. I was sort of, well this sounds funny and kind of embarrassing, but I was imagining wrapping my whole head with wool."

"You don't need to be embarrassed. Your effort without prompting is something you should recognize as a quality in yourself. It is a decent place to start but try next time to shield your entire body and mind. Use a visual that is impenetrable. It can be anything that works for you, brick wall or bullet proof glass, it doesn't matter as long as you feel the strength of it."

"Thanks. I guess wool isn't exactly bullet proof. I'll keep your advice in mind next time I run into you." I give him a playful but still somewhat sarcastic wink. I mean honestly, when do I ever need to shield my thoughts from anyone? Hmmm, well maybe now that I know, it could come in handy in certain situations, like with my mom, or Jared.

"It is not only for thoughts. Sometimes protection is needed from the spirit realm or emotional attack." He's back to the Chris I remember, Mr. Serious Sourpuss.

I squat down next to the pool and dip my hand in the cold water and think about what he said. *Spiritual realm and emotional attacks. I can protect myself from these things?* "How does it work?" I ask.

"Have you ever been verbally assaulted?"

"Yeah." I remember all too clearly the episode with my brother at the dinner table. It had felt like an attack, leaving me shaken to the core, and brain-boggled. In fact, the fight was what had propelled me to leave the house and spend the night on Grandma's land last night.

"You do not have to absorb someone else's negativity. Try using the protection and notice if you do not feel quite so drained after fighting. As for the other, protecting yourself against evil is always good practice."

"I guess it would be."

"For sure," he agrees.

Chris's smile is back, not mocking or laughing at my expense this time, but a genuine kind smile. I smile back. He always surprises me when he acts more his age and not like the old grumpus he portrays so well. Not that I know his exact age, with his general temperament he could be anywhere from forty to one hundred and forty but outside in the sun I again have the distinct feeling he is closer to my age. Smooth red-brown skin, free of wrinkles, and shiny black hair without any gray. Twenty to thirties maybe?

"Have you always been a medicine man?" I ask, not holding back my curiosity.

He snorts out a small puff of air before he answers. "I believe so, but in terms of this life, more or less. My father has been training me since I showed an interest, which is before I can remember."

"Ever thought of doing anything different?"

"For a while I wanted to be a dinosaur. T Rex. Then I grew up and wanted to drive Formula One race cars. The questionable life choices passed by the time I was ten. At eleven years old I moved on to studying magic. I guess that one sort of stuck. Only when I was eleven, I thought it was all illusion and tricks, and now I know what is real magic and what is not."

"Yeah? So you're a magician of sorts," I say. The amount of words coming out of Chris is mind blowing. Oh, he of little words is awfully talkative today.

"No, I would never call myself a magician. I know the traditional medicines for the spirit, and a little of what our Great Earth Mother's medicine can do for the body. It is your Grandmother who knows how to heal the physical. She is a very wise woman."

He pauses and stares at me for a second. Then he breaks our brief connection and fiddles with the cap on his bottle of spring water as he continues telling me about himself. "I spent some time at university studying land management and conservation. You know, in case the Native Medicine could not pay my bills."

"Really? Where did you graduate from?"

"C.U. Surprised? Don't I look like a university graduate?" He teases and then goes on without waiting for me to answer. "I have not used my degree, but it is there if I need it. The last couple of years have kept me busy with Medicine work and the ghost hunting. People can be very generous when you get rid of whatever it is haunting them."

Couple of years and four years at school. That makes him around twenty-four. Smokin' frijoles, he *is* close to my age.

"*Whatever it is haunting them*?" I ask, quoting his words. I would do or pay just about anything to never see the ghost at Castle Hill again.

"I've dealt with some real boogers." Chris's attention becomes distracted and he peers over my head, eyes intent on the trees.

Is Nathaniel finally making an appearance? I look in the same direction. I don't see anything other than a mountain meadow and white aspen trees under the blue sky.

"Are you working today?" I ask, trying to keep our conversation going and hopefully take his attention away from Nathan, if it is him.

"This?" He lifts the bottle. "Yes. I need this for a ceremony."

The water inside his bottle refracts the sun's rays and breaks them into glints of rainbow colors.

"This is Great Mother's life force. Earth's Heart Spring water will bring displaced spirits back into their earthly body. It is strong medicine."

Displaced spirits sounds ominous, and way over my head, so I contribute what I know about this spring. "My grandma Charlotte told me to use it for diseases of the blood and circulatory problems, heart and spleen and such."

The lines around Chris's eyes and jaw soften ever so slightly as he watches me, which is good on one hand, but also a little disconcerting on the other. Does he consider me a friend now after our run-ins at Castle Hill? He did help me with an errand to release a girl's soul from being trapped on earth. Once you have done those sorts of things with someone, I guess that makes you friends.

"That, as well." He pauses, staring passed me again, and then asks, "Did you come alone?"

There's no point in lying to someone who can read your mind, now is there? Being a powerful shaman's friend may have some pitfalls. "No, my friend was somewhere behind me. I don't know what happened." No point in giving out names though.

"Did you come up here by motorcycle?"

"No," I say with questioning uncertainty.

Chris hops over the small pool close to where I'm squatted down. I rise, giving him a perplexed look.

"I saw a bunch of bikes on the south side of the mountain, near where I left my truck."

"No. I hiked up here from Grandma's land. I camped out last night."

"You like to go camping?" He asks me with his normal serious straight face, which is impossible to read.

"Yeah, sometimes."

He's standing so close. His aura of earthy colors blends with mine to the point where they almost cannot be seen as separate from each other. The chest pockets of his army green vest bulge with their hidden contents. I have yet to see him without a vest. It makes him looks like he is always on some kind of fishing trip. Cargo shorts, white T-shirt and hiking boots complete his look. Very typical Chris Abeyta.

Chris stares over my shoulder, looking suddenly distracted. I would have sworn he was about to ask me to go camping with him sometime, but he doesn't. Instead, he jerks to attention just as Nathaniel steps into view.

Nathaniel's smoky silver eyes focus on mine and the shy smile on his full lips is enough to turn my world upside down — or maybe that's already happened. My heartbreakingly beautiful view of him, and those perfect amber highlights shining in his thick chestnut hair, is blocked as Chris physically shields me. He spreads his arms wide and shifts his booted feet to a wider stance. Leaning to the side I watch as Nathan stops his progress in my direction. His attention is on Chris now. I can feel the tension shimmering over Chris's flesh like watching a heat wave roll over hot pavement. As I try to move around Chris, his arm locks into place like a closed iron gate. His hand grabs for my shirt and I immediately pull back.

"Chris, stop," I say, but he doesn't. His fingers have a handful of the fabric and he manages to keep me behind him.

Chris growls low under his breath. "When did he return to you?"

"It's not what you think," I try to explain. Somehow Chris shoves the bottle of water in his shorts pocket, has a firm grip on my waist, and is slowly moving us away from the spring.

"What you're doing isn't necessary."

"Don't be naïve, woman!"

I roll my eyes with exasperated impatience. I like Chris, as odd as he is, and I would also like for him to chill out and realize Nathaniel is not what he thinks he is. Chris believes he's a Shadow of Creator, or what I call an Angel of Death. Someone who comes to take back the lives that Creator has given. "Calm down for a second."

"We must leave. We should not anger him." Chris is making ground, albeit only an inch at a time through the grass.

"He won't hurt me. Remember, I told you once that he's my friend. He really is."

"No. You are being influenced."

"I am not." What I *am*, is losing my patience. "Let go of me."

"Nathaniel, will you tell him you mean no harm to either of us." I peer over Chris's shoulder to see Nathaniel's glare fixed on Chris.

"Juliana speaks the truth and she asked you to let her go." There's icy malice behind his words. I've never heard him sound so threatening before. Fear pinches me somewhere between my shoulder blades. What *is* my otherworldly boyfriend capable of?

If I were Chris, I would let go, but he doesn't. I pry at his fingers exaggerating the sincerity of my request. "Enough already! I know what I'm doing."

Chris stops tugging as he half turns to look at me. "Ha!" he snorts. "You do not understand the spirit world. Stop your foolishness before you injure yourself."

"She wants you to release her," Nathan says.

"Come with me now, Jules. Hurry," Chris urges.

Hearing the hardness in Nathaniel's tone, I get the feeling there isn't much time before he does something to stop Chris himself. I hold a hand up to Nathaniel to stay back. Chris will come around if he will just listen to me. "Surely not all spirits are bad. Can't you believe me on this? He's my friend."

Something like hurt and confused distrust passes over Chris's angry face, but his hand finally let's go of my shirt. He steps to the side and stumbles, going down on one knee.

"Yo jeez, are you all right?" I ask.

He pops back up. The muscles at his temples bulge as he clamps his mouth shut. Embarrassment followed by fury flash across his face. "I am fine," he growls through clenched teeth.

Stomping away, I hear him grumble, "If you have any brains in your head, you will stay away from the Shadow."

I blink rapidly at his retreating back trying to comprehend his hostility. His aura darkens and swirls around his rigid spine.

Seriously? What a goon. He doesn't understand.

I hear him continue to mutter as he heads toward an outcrop of boulders. "I tried to warn her. Ignorance isn't going to help anything…"

And then I can't hear any more. I've seen Chris Abeyta upset before. His naturally intense personality turns explosive. It's not something I'd like to witness again.

Take a deep breath and let it go. Better yet, take ten. After letting my nerves settle I brush my hair away from my face and look up into the eyes of two storms. His irises are as tumultuous as tornados, but their centers are a piercing black calm.

"He has no idea," I say feeling compelled to settle the waters even though Nathaniel has yet to speak. "Chris doesn't know you. He's overreacting. And, I'm fine."

"Are you?"

"Yes. He won't listen to me." The words fly out of my mouth even though somewhere inside I know I don't have to defend Chris.

"I knew he wouldn't hurt you, but it took everything in me to hold back."

"No, I'm glad you didn't do anything. He's sort of a friend, I guess, and I don't want it to get any worse. He thinks you're something you're not."

"He wants to be more than friends with you."

"Why would you say that?" I ask feeling suddenly annoyed.

Looking away from Nathaniel's angelic face, I stare into the slow moving current of Earth's Heart Spring. A bead of water bubbles up at a constant rhythm where the source comes out of the ground. No matter what the weather or time of day or year the water pulses exactly the same. I move closer to the pool suddenly needing to dip my hands in it and not wanting to hear Nathaniel's answer.

"I could see it in his face. Why don't you like him?" he asks.

His frank curiosity and absurd question is enough to infuriate me. I bite my lower lip and hold back my snide response. Placing both hands in the crisp water, I imagine all the unpleasant thoughts and feelings draining away. Why would the guy, who only minutes earlier, proclaim his love for me, then turn around and ask me if I'm interested in someone else?

"Chris Abeyta helped me when I was having nightmares. He also happened to be there when Mason was trying to kill me and my brother, after you...disappeared. So yeah, I kind of like him. As. A. Friend."

Nathaniel answers to my back. "You two would look good together."

"Are you freaking serious?" I stand up and whirl around on my heels. "What are you talking about?"

Nathan shrugs his shoulders and looks away at the trees. "He's right. I am a spirit. I have no idea if I'm harming you. I don't have to eat, or breathe, and I'm supposed to be working, not having a relationship. Marcus, I...don't know what he'll do if he finds out what I'm doing with you. Chris is who you should be with, not me."

"That's ridiculous."

"No it isn't. I'm a selfish jackass and I should leave you alone. I could be altering your future or who knows what. I can't ask anyone about it because I'm not supposed to be here."

"Of course you're changing my future! And I'm changing yours. Every encounter with anyone can change a person. No one has control over free will. You're being ludicrous, so stop it. I choose you too, you know."

Nathan turns even farther away almost putting his back to me now. "I can't hurt you. It would be more than I could stand."

"Nathaniel, you won't. It isn't in you. So please, don't ever tell me another guy is better for me. That's how you'll piss me off." I take another series of deep breath and then attempt to start over.

"Can we just forget it? Chris is gone. I brought you here to show you something. Come here," I say softly. I see his chest rise and fall. Even though he says he doesn't breathe, he still makes the motions of it. "Please," I add.

Moving slowly he eases down next to me on a patch of grass. Tentatively I reach over for his hand. He's solid and warm. He must have made his body in case it was needed for the encounter with Chris. I let my fingertips slide over the back of his hand and down his long fingers until I can hook my pinky around his.

He wears a mask of indifference, but I'm not fooled. Males try to hide their feelings, but I'm too sensitive, and it's always obvious to me when their emotions run on high.

"I'm not used to this. Forgive me, Juliana. For being a jerk."

"You've never had a girlfriend before?" I ask, teasing and trying to lighten the tone between us.

"I have, but it wasn't like this. You're," He clears his throat, "different. It feels different with you."

His voice is rough as he chokes this out. The words he used could have come directly from my own mouth. He's different for me too.

"It's like everything about you is a million times better and more intense than with anyone else."

"I've never felt this way before either," I confess.

He grips my hand in his, squeezing gently.

"Here." I tug him forward so he has to kneel. I dip his hand in the pool. "This spring is a direct connection with our earth. Like an open vein, her blood is the water. When we drink it, we can be healed of earthly disease or we can use it to help us remember what our purpose is in this life."

"How can water help?"

"It's not ordinary water. Do you want to try it?" I ask, not knowing if he can eat or drink. I haven't seen him do so before but he did say he's pretty much the same as I am in regards to the physical body — when he has one.

"It won't kill me. We already know that much."

Nathaniel's tone held the tiniest amount of bitterness, but he didn't linger on it. He plunges both hands into the water and swirls them around stirring up the fine silt from the bottom. We watch as it muddies the crystal clear water and then begins to flow out of the shallow pool.

"I had the idea that if you drank the water it would help you feel connected to the physical world again. Even if it was temporary."

Nathaniel lifts his cupped hands to his mouth and drinks. His eyes never leave mine as he takes it in.

"Thank you," he says as he lets his hands fall to his sides. He sits back again in silence, openly watching me with his intense eyes.

Feeling somewhat embarrassed now, I try to shrug it off. "Earth's Heart Spring is unique. I just wanted to show it to you."

"Don't do that. You were being thoughtful."

"Do you feel anything?" I ask.

"No. I have to be honest. What has an effect on the living, versus what I am, is different. I'm part of this world and I'm not part of it. The spring water doesn't make me feel any different."

"Oh. I..."

He interrupts me before I can finish stumbling out of my mouth. "You are the only connection to this earth that means anything to me. Being with you is better than anything I've ever dreamed."

It's inevitable, trying to prevent the color in my cheeks from flaring up at yet another proclamation of his feelings toward me. The thing is, I feel the same, only I can't say it the way he does. I decide to move quickly into another subject. Deflection can be a very useful tool in times of need.

Chapter Three: Glimpses

Juliana

"My mom came up here with me once. It was just the two of us. I asked her if she could see these little flashing orbs of light. They were almost like twinkling Christmas tree ornaments, but they kept moving around." I glance over at Nathaniel from the corner of my eye to see his reaction to my words. To my relief I see no disapproving judgments being passed.

"Wee folk?" he asks.

Nathaniel never presses me for more. He plays along like he doesn't notice my discomfort at his declarations toward me. It's another check mark for him on the positive side of the list in my head of all the reasons he is so amazing.

"Yeah. Fairies is what my mom said they were, and no, she couldn't see them. She seemed excited that I could see them. It embarrassed me in a way, and she could see it did, so she quit asking me about them. Instead, she told me about the fairies that live here. She said they protect this place and would protect all who have a kind heart that enter here. She said if you were to upset them, they may take you away to the fairy realm and enslave you until they tire of their game."

"Is that some sort of warning?" The mixture of teasing with blunt sincerity makes me glance over at him. His crooked half smile causes me to grow warm on the inside.

"No. I was wondering if you can see them. Being that maybe you are sort of like them."

I'm in unknown territory. Is Nathaniel Evans in the same category as fairies? Do all celestial beings see each other? Do they exist in harmony together or do they have no acknowledgement of each other at all? Maybe they dwell in completely different realms. All of this supernatural stuff is foreign to me. My problem has to be similar to someone finding out their IQ is off the charts. You would know you were smart but not necessarily *that* smart or what to do with it. It's the same kind of thing for me, not intelligence, although I do fair well enough in that department, but in paranormal skills. I've known, ever since I can remember, that I can see and feel things other people don't, but I had no idea of the extent of my abilities and I'm just now starting to figure it out. But what is really happening to me is that I have more questions than answers.

"Hmm," he hums a noise in the back of his throat while thinking about his answer. "When I was alive I wasn't aware of anything unusual or mystical, but now, I am."

Nathaniel picks a blue harebell out of the grass and holds it out to me.

I take it from him and ask, "Do you see anything here?" I hadn't noticed anything today, so far, but what I see often happens in quick glimpses that leave me questioning if it were real or not.

"Yes, and no. There's a calm to this place. It's similar to all hallowed ground and when the wee folk are present they have a distinct signature about them. But I should tell you I have only ever seen them twice, and not today." He turns his serious eyes on me and I want to drown in those thunderstorms.

"Why do they exist? I mean, what are they here for?" I whisper.

"Why are any of us here?"

I feel his stare penetrate me to the core. My skin feels like it has been stripped away, and for unexplainable reasons I don't care in the least. He can see me like no one has ever seen me and I don't want to hide from him. As much as part of me is dying to do so, another part of me likes the rawness of being exposed to him.

"Don't you know?" I ask, but it is a cop-out to an answer so I try again. "I could tell you what I think in the moment, but it will be a different answer tomorrow. Life changes so fast, and besides, I think we're not supposed to know some things."

"You're right. It's not until you leave the body behind that the answers are revealed. And not even then sometimes."

"The body is only a vehicle?" I ask, wondering if Nathaniel can answer something I have suspected for some time now.

"Yeah. And it's always changing. Let's add impermanence to our list of all things inexplicable, Jules. It's the only constant."

Being reminded about our growing list of perplexities of the human experience, I'm unable to stop the smile from creeping across my face. "And let's add the soul, too. It's as unexplainable as the rest of the list."

"Agreed," he says, and then pauses, staring at me with a new intensity. "You speak to my soul in a way I didn't know was possible. I'm here to experience you, Juliana."

I look down at the ground absorbing his words and fighting for control of the battle inside. Frantically excited and simultaneously frightened is a tenuous place to be. I can see myself being with Nathaniel forever and I even asked him for that very thing last night but I need to honor the pace of reality, and my reality is I want to get to know him over time. As it happens to be, emotions and brainwaves run on two separate channels.

"Your soul speaks to mine too, and I don't care where you're from, or what you are." Words flow out of my mouth that I would never have been capable of saying before we met. "You could be a Dullahan, or an incubus, and it wouldn't matter."

He leans close to me. "It would matter, but I'm neither of those things. I promise I'll never hurt you. If I did, it would be the end of me," he says with a low voice that purrs down my spine.

My head tilts to the side as if on command to expose my neck. He wields some kind of magic that has complete control of my body. "We should try to take things slow, okay," I manage to squeak out. I swallow hard forcing down whatever involuntary protest is about to betray me and confess I never want to spend another second without him.

He traces a line down the outside of my arm with a perfectly sculpted finger. Heat radiates from him leaving a hot trail over my skin.

"Juliana, if you're in my world then we can move at any pace you want."

His fingers stop on the top of my hand. "Thank you. It's important to me for some reason."

"Then it's important to me, gorgeous fox."

I feel my hand gently turn over and the tracing of a continual line around my palm. "I'm not part fox, you know."

"No, I don't know. I'll never be convinced otherwise. If I can be a Dullahan, which I very well may be because I don't know what one is, then you can be a fox. One that can change into a woman, and lives on the edge of multiple dimensions."

The melting butter sensation had made its way to my back and is creeping north and south simultaneously. In another minute I'm going to be a warm puddle. "An Irish Dullahan is a being that comes at night, he's headless, and forewarns of death."

"Ah, maybe that is what I used to be, but definitely not anymore."

His velvet rich voice caresses me from the inside out. I can feel his strength pulsing through his fingertips as he strokes my palm. His clean scent lingers in the air and I let myself drift away with the symphony of sensation.

"Sweet vixen, are you all right?"

"Hmmm?"

"Are you falling asleep?"

"No, why?"

"Your eyes are closed, love."

"It's fine. Please don't stop, Nathaniel." There it is again, a part of my brain notes, speaking without my permission.

He raises my hand to his lips and kisses the heel of my palm, then the inside of my wrist and up my forearm to the inside of my elbow. The top of my shoulder becomes his next destination and then along the edge of my collarbone. I want to protest — remember, taking things slow — but the jelly which my insides have turned into must include my voice box because recognizable sounds are no longer possible. Feather soft tickling on the side of my neck leaves me breathless, and all reason has now left the building. Somehow my hands have joined my betraying mouth and are doing things without my consent, like they have a separate mind of their own, even though I can still feel what they feel. Strong cords run up the back of his neck. The thick waves of his hair are soft and scrumptious between my fingers. My hand wraps around the base of his skull as he teases the underside of my jaw with his too warm mouth. My other hand moves over his muscular shoulder and down his back. He's so strong and so solid.

At some point I must have pulled him on top of me because I'm suddenly aware of the smell and feel of crushed grass beneath me. My ear is being nibbled and I can hardly breathe, not because of the weight of him, but because of the sheer excitement and the rush of blood pounding through me. It's taken my breath away. Turning my face to find his mouth, he's all too agreeable to meet me. My self-control has become as distant as yesterday's breeze.

"You have the most kissable mouth I've ever seen," he whispers and then proceeds to prove his statement.

Nathaniel is strong and gentle and urgent and tender. I send out a silent prayer to Father Time to let this perfect moment last forever. How did I not know kissing could be like this?

He moves to my throat and I whimper as he sucks gently on my oh-so sensitive skin. My hands find the planes of his chest and linger there relishing the smooth muscles.

Suddenly, cool air rushes over my body. The abrupt absence of his warmth is worse than the time I jumped in a frozen lake. My eyelids flutter open and focus on the azure blue sky overhead.

Slowly, I look around. He's not far away, only leaning on an elbow next to me.

"Don't hate me."

"Wha," I try, but find my voice uncooperative, melted honey seems to have replaced my tongue and throat. "I don't hate you," I manage. "In fact, it's the exact opposite. I even forgive you for what you said about Chris." I sigh deep in my chest and relax back against the ground and close my eyes again, holding onto the leftover pulsing deep in my abdomen.

"You said slow."

"Uh-huh. I did, and now I hate myself for it."

"That isn't entirely why I had to stop."

Silence fills the brief space as he pauses. I've never felt more relaxed in my entire life than right now, I think, as I absorb the warmth of the sun while drinking in his perfect scent and listening to his purring voice mixed with the quaking chatter of nearby aspen leaves.

"I have to leave soon. I wish I didn't, but it's my client."

"Really, that's too bad." His statement doesn't register. The kisses. His touch. The warmth from the sun. His husky voice adds kindling to the burning fire in my belly and tickles the entire length of my spine. At this point I'll say anything to keep him talking.

"So you're not mad?"

"Mmmh-hmm."

"I want to take you back down the mountain before I go."

"Go, why?" Now things are sinking in.

"Juliana, I want to stay. You have no idea how bad I want to be here with you, but I have been feeling the pull since your friend Chris was here. I need to check on her."

Turning my head to the side, away from Nathaniel, I open my eyes as if looking away will change what he just said. A floating ball of light hovers just above the blades of grass on the opposite side of the pool. It shimmers for a second and then disappears. I push myself up. Moving steals all but the faintest trace of the effervescence that had been flowing through my blood.

"Did you..." I turn my head slowly back toward Nathaniel. My eyes linger on the spot for any possibility of another glimpse. He nods yes before I finish the question.

"They're guardians and helpers," he whispers.

"Like you," I whisper back.

This time he shakes his head no. "Different job description. She's probably here to protect the water."

I nod like I understand even though I don't totally, and being that the fairy is already gone, I go back to the previous subject. "It's fine. We should go. Someone's life is at stake, isn't it?"

"Yes, it is."

"What do you mean by 'feeling the pull?' " I ask, as I stretch my arms over my head and realize my perfect moment is slipping away.

Nathaniel glances away from me and I notice a slight crease form between his brows before he answers. "When I'm needed, for my work, I feel it tugging at me. It makes me anxious. I have the choice to respond, but it's difficult to ignore."

"And then you just know where to go?"

"Sort of. I have to think about the person and want to go to them and then I move without any effort."

Starting to stand up, I change my mind and roll to my knees. I lean over to the water while I ask another question. "Does the pull on you vary by the situation or the person involved?"

"Both. Last night when you called my name, I knew you were not in danger, but I could feel the connection to you. My current case doesn't know I'm around, but I think it's urgent I find her."

Inspecting my torn finger, I had all but forgotten about it as I played with Nathan's chest and back. It's leaking blood again. Darting a glance over at his shirt I can see where drops and smears of blood mark the places where my hand had been. I grimace at what I've done. "Umm..."

"What?" The concern on his face as he watches mine is almost comical. He looks as if I just told him someone died.

Embarrassment flushes my pale skin, but I can't let him leave with streaks of blood on his sweatshirt. "My finger," I lift it up to show the ragged side. "I'm sorry. It's your shirt." I point at the mess I've made.

Relaxing visibly, Nathaniel looks down at his chest, particularly focusing on the area of his left nipple, where a dark rusty spot is. "Battle wounds. No worries." He closes his eyes for a second appearing to concentrate, but then opens them and turns those smoky gray eyes on me with a small mischievous smile. "I think I'll keep them. As a reminder."

"No. It's sort of gross," I say.

"No one will see it," he argues, "and then I can see exactly where your hands have been."

"No one will see it except for me," I correct.

"Ashamed of what you've been up to?"

I imagine the color in my cheeks blooming from rose to puce. Involuntarily, my gaze flicks down the front of his shirt to the hemline right below his belt and then back up to his face in time to see his small smile turn into a huge grin. There's a smear of dried blood near the lowest part of his shirt. Remembering the feel of his taut stomach sends another wave of heat to my face. What's worse than puce? Purple? I try to conceal my embarrassment by letting my hair fall forward. I hate that my fair skin gives me away so easily. I answer as defiantly as possible, "No," and then dip my hand in the water washing away the drying blood.

"If I could see all of the places on you where I've touched, it would make me happy. Like marking my territory."

He sounds so pleased with this idea that I roll my eyes. "Guys, I swear. You're like dogs. Now I know where that term came from."

"Do you want me to change my shirt?"

"Yes," I say to the water. "I really don't want to see my blood."

"No problem," he answers and I hear the rustle of him moving behind me.

With my hand as clean as possible, I stand up and turn around. Nathaniel leans against a tree trunk. The sweatshirt he had been wearing is now replaced with a plain white T-shirt. He looks down the length of my body and then back up again.

I should start wearing blush, then my cheeks would look the same all the time. "How did you do that?" I ask while assessing Nathaniel in his new shirt while ignoring the heat in my face.

"I can dress however you want, m'lady."

"Wish it was that easy for me," I say looking at my own grungy jeans and camp-smoked shirt.

"You're beautiful in anything."

I swear he knows how to tickle the inside of my ear with his voice. It isn't fair. He reaches for my left hand and we start to leave Earth's Heart Spring behind. A few steps away from the spring and a flash of sparkling light catches my attention. Thinking the fairy had returned, I stop to get a better look. Lying in the grass, reflecting the sun's rays, is Chris Abeyta's bottle of spring water. I bend down and pick it up, noticing the prairie dog hole in the ground next to it. It must have fallen out of his pocket when he tripped. Nathan looks down at my hand but says nothing about it.

"I can make it back down the mountain by myself if you need to go," I tell him as I become aware of the shift in the energy around him.

"Something is happening, but no, I'll wait until after you're back to your car."

He's so definite about his decision I know no argument will make a difference. I can tell he's anxious so I decide to speed up our pace.

At the edge of the aspen grove I spot a plant that will help my sore finger. I lead us in the direction, and as we pass the wild rose bushes I pick one of the pink blooms, being careful to preserve the petals. Handing the bottle of water over to Nathaniel I ask, "Could you hold this for a sec?" He takes it and watches as I walk and administer first aid to my finger at the same time. I pluck one petal at a time and lay them over the cut on the side of my finger until I have a tidy rose petal bandage.

"Will it really help, or does it just smell nice?"

"It's feeling better already," I say, and take the spring water back from him.

"I'm glad you know how to fix yourself. You seem to be accident prone."

"I am not," I defend, but as soon as it's out of my mouth I know it's not entirely true.

Nathaniel cocks an eyebrow.

Arguing my case, I say, "I'm easily distracted is all. I never have an accident when I'm paying attention."

He laughs, the sound is deep and velvet soft. "I think that's true for ninety percent of the world's population. All I'm saying is I get some relief knowing you can mend yourself."

"I love plants and what they can do to heal the body, but I really don't know much compared to what my grandmother knows."

"Don't underestimate yourself. I bet you know more than you realize. I had no idea you could put wild roses on a cut. Or that other stuff, the devil's hammer, whatever it's for."

"Devil's club," I correct. "Every plant in the world has a use to the human body because we are all made out of the same elements. You only have to know what to use it for. Memorizing everything is the hard part."

"So do you think there are plants that will affect me?" he asks as we pass around a spruce trunk the size of six people standing hand to hand.

"You know, I don't know. You're a spirit so I would say yes. Certain plants have an effect on the spirit, but that's when the spirit is inside a body, so I guess I don't know."

"I think we'll have to find out some time. You can experiment on me. Sounds good?"

"Okay," I agree with a smile. Suddenly aware of a change in the air, I say, "Hey, what's that noise?"

Chapter Four: Call to Action

Nathaniel

"Stay here," I tell Juliana.

"No way," she says, shaking her head at me.

"I'll be right back. I move faster than you, and I'm invisible, remember? Just stay back for a second."

Juliana presses her lips together in silent resignation as I disappear through the trees to see what, or who, is making the noise. On the other side of the narrow road, in a clearing, I see a handful of Harley Davidson motorcycles and find the source of the racket.

An engine rumbles as five bikers clad in an overabundance of leather argue over a deer carcass. No, not a carcass, the deer's alive, albeit not for much longer. Its panicked shallow breaths and inability to stand are a bad sign, but the tall, thin biker pointing a handgun at it is a clear indicator that its life is coming to an abrupt end.

"Shut up, Butch!" the man with the gun yells.

"You're a stool," Butch, a paunchy man with an excessive amount of black hair, grumbles back.

"Toad, or bar?" the gunman asks straight faced.

"Neither," Butch rasps. "A shit. You're a fat smelly shit."

"I'd watch who you're callin' fat and smelly."

Bang! Gunman pulls the trigger. The other three men watch unmoved, but Butch frowns through his bushy beard. The deer's suffering ends and the tall man glances away.

I would have left the five bikers behind and gone straight back to Juliana, except, she finds me first. Well not me, exactly.

"What are you doing? You can't shoot a deer this time of year!"

Six pairs of eyes turn on Juliana as she streaks out of the woods screaming. Her cheeks are flaming and she's brandishing the bottle of water like a club. I'm not sure what is going on in that pretty head of hers, but I'm in no way capable of understanding a woman on a mission.

"What did the deer do to you!" she screeches like a hysterical bat.

It would have been funny in any other circumstances, and I think two or three of the burly riders are thinking the exact same thing, but the one with the gun is not laughing, and neither am I.

"Whoa there, little lady," the tall blonde man with the gun starts to say, but he gets cut off by one of his bandana wearing cronies.

"Hey Eli, tell her why you just blew Bambi's brains out."

Eli glares over at the man and then turns his attention back to Juliana as if he might explain what has just happened. I can see something flickering behind his easy eyes and I would guess he's not an immediate threat, except for the gun he's holding. I move into the trees as fast as I can, so I don't suddenly appear out of thin air, and then I'm running back to Jules.

"You're not going to get away with this! Do you know the penalties for hunting off season?"

Juliana moves toward the motorcycles, looking at their back ends, for license plates, I would guess. The men all watch her and don't see me coming. Before I can catch up with her the hefty one named Butch snags Juliana around the waist and pulls her up next to him. She looks like a rag doll under his arm.

"What do you think you're doing! Let me go," she shrieks.

"Listen girl. Stay away from my ride."

"Put her down, Butch. It's a simple misunderstanding," Eli says. "Juliana."

The group turns to glare at me in unison. I notice there's no shortage of hair or black leather among them. I also notice hands reaching for unseen weapons as I rush over to her.

She's pale, more than normal, and I think she just realized she's one woman against five gnarly bikers. Butch backs up with Juliana under his arm. His glower warning me that he doesn't have to let her go and nobody can stop him. It would be true, if I were a regular human.

"Let the girl go. She loves animals. It isn't her fault," I say.

"Meddlesome bizzie is what she is. No sense at all under all that hair."

Butch has a raspy gruff voice and I can see the game he's playing. I don't think he is going to hurt her, at least not intentionally, but Juliana's waist looks as if she's being cinched in the middle.

I hold my hands up in mock surrender. "Get your hands off of her and we'll leave. No harm, no foul."

"Like hell. You can't just shoot anything in the woods because you feel like it. They have to pay for this. Look at her, she was nursing."

The three others behind us snigger at this and start to move toward their motorcycles as if the excitement were already over.

I look at the exposed underside of the doe and sure enough you can see the doe was still nursing. Anger wells up inside me, but as I see the large tears forming in Jules's green eyes I almost lose all control.

"Juliana," I attempt to warn her with a single word and a strong look. She frowns deeper at me and narrows her eyes. She's fighting anger too.

"Butch, is that your name? Put her down and we'll all put this behind us. I saw what happened and no one's to blame."

"You spyin' on us, boy?"

Butch's arm squeezes harder around Juliana and I see her grimace.

"I heard the noise and came to see what was going on."

"Uh-huh."

I look over to my left to make sure Eli is not advancing on me. He looks about as intolerant with this situation as I feel.

"Butch, quit playing around. We need to get out of here."

"Hey, you're the one who had to stop in the first place. Damn nature lovers," Butch spits out. He lifts Juliana even higher and plants a hairy kiss on her face. I think he was going for her mouth but Jules is struggling so much it landed on her cheek. "You sure are a pretty one though. One for the road, doll."

I move in to take Juliana by force but the biker places her roughly on her feet and shoves her over to me before I can grab him. Juliana lands heavily in my arms. Before I can get a decent grip on her, she whirls around and tries to go straight back for Butch, her claws extended and her intent to damage him obvious. I stop her.

"Ahh spunky." Butch's belly jiggles in a silent laugh as he turns for his bike.

"Let's go. Now!" I pick Juliana up and carry her far away from the bikers as fast as I can.

I hear Eli say behind us, "I have to take care of her before we go."

I hope he's referring to the deer.

When we're a safe distance away I set Juliana down and shake my head in disbelief. I look to the sky for staying power, patience, understanding, or anything that will keep my anger in check.

"He murdered that deer. How can you let them go? They have to be turned in."

"Unbelievable. Did you even stop to think for one second? You're still upset about the deer? Not the fact that you could have gotten yourself killed."

"What? Poacher's get away with murder. Who's going to stand up for the deer if I don't do it? Hmm, who?" She sounds irate, but her voice breaks slightly on the last words.

"You're serious aren't you?"

Juliana turns her back to me. I walk around to face her. She's hiding to the best of her ability under her hair again.

"Jules, you could have…" I start to say, but can't finish. Fear for her, and because I don't want to upset her further, stops me. She peeks at me through her hair and I see the tears in her eyes. It breaks me, and all my anger dissipates like evaporating steam. I engulf her with my body, wrapping my arms around her, and cup the back of her head in my hand.

"The deer. It's awful," she chokes. "I'm sorry. I know it's silly, but I can't help it."

"It's okay." I hold her close and let all the strain, and stress, and tension drain out of us both. When she stops shaking, I ask, "Juliana, when someone has a gun, could you—"

"I know," she interrupts. "I'm not smart." Her voice sounds stronger now, almost normal.

"I didn't know you were so fearless," I say.

"There's something wrong with me."

"No, there isn't."

She pulls back a little and looks up at me. "Yes, there is. Who would take on five bikers over illegal hunting? With this?"

She holds up Chris's bottle looking amazed and maybe embarrassed too. I give her a wry smile. She has a point.

"But, who else can feel and see the intentions of others? You knew he wouldn't really hurt you, didn't you?"

"Kind of. I'm still unsure of what I feel most of the time. I can't trust it enough, but that man — and don't misunderstand me — but he's a big softy on the inside. I bet my life on it."

"If you're unsure, then trust your instincts. And if you *know* something about someone, then also trust that."

She gives me a slight nod of agreement, but I see the uncertainty clouding her eyes. Even so, her anxiety lessens with every passing minute. Unfortunately, mine is growing. "Something's going on with my client. I have to go. If I don't, I may be too late."

"Oh! I forgot. Leave now. I'll be fine. My car isn't far from here," she says while looking down the treed slope.

"No. Let's hurry though," I say as the creases of concern on Juliana's face deepen.

The pull to be near Corrine is intense. I don't have much time if I'm going to try to make a difference for her. The strings which attach me to my clients are like mercury; fluid, dense, and seeming to yield to their own laws of physics. The closer she is to death the stronger the pull and now it feels as if a ship's anchor is dragging me away from Juliana into unknown depths.

My new assignment, Corrine, is my first case where I get to be involved before they die. Previous to her, I was supposed to help them adjust to being dead and transitioning to the afterlife. Now I get to detour my clients away from suicide. Since I'm new at this, I'm not completely sure what to do, but I need to try something. If I am not even with her and she takes her life, how am I going to explain to Marcus, my mentor, what I was doing, or why I failed at my first assignment?

Juliana's not done arguing with me. "I'll go straight back to my car. I promise not to tackle any more bikers. Just go, really. I've been on this mountain a hundred times. I'll be fine."

It's tempting. I stare into those emerald lagoons she calls eyes and the pull to stay with her is more overwhelming than the anchor yanking me away. "I'll come back as soon as I can. If you want me to."

"Of course I want you to. Now off to work. I won't be the one responsible for you screwing up your first case. The car is right down there." She points down the hill. "I'll be there in two shakes of a lambs tail."

"In this entire universe, how did I find you?" I lean in and kiss the top of her head while I give her a tight hug. "God, I wish I didn't have to go. Stay far away from those bikers."

"I will," she promises.

∞

Moving through the ether to be with Corrine takes me only seconds. I visualize her as petite, blonde, sweet-natured, and terribly desperate, while thinking her name and then I find her. She's on her hands and knees on the ground. Her head is bent low so I can't see her face. I look around for her tormentor, but see no one. She doesn't see me either. I move in closer and still can't figure out what she's doing. Her ribs move with the slight jerking motion of taking hard shallow breaths. *Did she already do something to harm herself? Is she overdosing on something? Did I wait too long?*

The scene looks almost exactly like the one I just left, middle of the forest in a clearing surrounded by trees and rocks with the sun shining down on us. Corrine is near a fire pit. The last tendrils of smoke curl into the air from a dying fire.

"Corrine, what's wrong? Can you sit up?" I ask, not expecting a reply. I haven't been able to get any response from her yet nor have I shown myself either. I've been waiting to see if I can help her without being in my physical form.

"Errrghh," she moans and then sits back onto her heels. She rolls over onto her side on the ground and wraps her arms around her middle. "Ehh," she whimpers.

Corrine, what have you done? My first glimpse of her, when Marcus changed my assignment about a week ago, Corrine was about to swallow a bottle of pills. Even though she didn't know I was there with her, I talked to her and channeled universal energy for her. She put the pills down. But now, by the look of her, I have to wonder if she has gone through with it. I don't see any pills, or bottles, but she's acting as if her insides are hurting. This may be the time to rush her to an emergency room, I decide. Marcus said it was my call. I can keep them alive or let them pass. This girl is younger than Juliana and from what I can tell she's not ready to die. She's only seeking an escape.

Escape from the very person who walks into the clearing. Her stepfather. Travis isn't a large man, but for reasons I don't understand he's capable of things that shouldn't be possible for someone so small. Like picking Corrine up off the ground and cradling her in his arms as if she weighs nothing. Travis stares straight at me with soulless eyes, or it appears he does, and then he carries my client away in his arms. Corrine whimpers against his chest.

"Silence," he orders.

There's a chill in the air around him that even I can feel.

Flustered by his appearance and even more so by his cold indifference to her pain, I follow at a distance thinking about what I should do next. This little man, all five feet of him, is the source of Corrine's misery, and I may be the only person, or angel, that has any control over what he's doing to her.

Chapter Five: Never Surrender

Juliana

Footsteps spike my curiosity. Single footsteps, one person, not the gang of bikers, I tell myself. Whoever is coming this way is close enough for me to hear. I duck behind some rocks and wait. Promises made are promises kept on my part, and I told Nathan I would stay away from leather clad deer killers. Although I don't think it's one of them, I have a gut feeling to hide anyway.

Thank you for good instincts. The steps come closer and then I hear low moaning. Female, or child, and in pain, it makes the hair rise on my arms and the skin on the back of my neck prickle with alarm. Two thoughts occur to me simultaneously. One, I must see if someone is hurt and two, don't breathe and pray he doesn't see or hear you. This second thought is so alarming that I do stop breathing and listen as the footsteps pass on the other side of my hiding spot.

The whimpering sound distresses me and I venture a quick look around the side of the boulder. I see a man, wearing blue jeans and a button down shirt walking away. He's carrying a blonde girl in his arms and has a pack slung over his back. There's something distinctly unnerving about this man, other than the fact of the moaning girl in his arms. It's his energy field. A black hole would be easier to stand next to compared to this slight dark haired man. Even as I finish the thought, I can feel him, and the prickles on my neck turn into stabbing needles. I duck back into my niche in the rocks as he starts to turn and look. I instantly put a field of protection around myself and the entire rock outcrop like Chris Abeyta advised me to do. The invisible shield feels like the Great Wall of China compared to the measly screen of protection I had tried earlier with Chris. Somehow, on another gut level, I'm entirely confident that it's working. The sound of his departing footsteps reinforces my certainty.

Where is he going? And why do I know her? My brain spins at a million miles a second as I process the image of the girl. It's the parakeet blue streak in her hair. Where? A quick intake of breath hits my lungs as I remember. Corrine, the timid girl who had come into work asking for me, and asking if I was a witch. I knew I had an uneasy feeling about her that day, but I was so shocked she wanted the services of a witch that I had turned her away, and now look at her. The soft sobbing carries through the air and is absolutely heart wrenching.

What should I do? I wish Nathaniel was here. Then one of us could do something for her. But who is that guy, and what is he doing with her? I have to try and help. I turned her away and this could be my fault. My gut feeling was so strong that she was is some kind of trouble, and I let her walk out the door at Native Naturals. I can't let her slip away again. The man isn't very big after all. I could take him. I just tried to stand up to a biker four times his size. *And look how that turned out. Shut up, Jules. I must be crazy again. Why else would I be arguing with myself? I have to do something, don't I? I couldn't help the deer, but maybe I can help this girl.*

I peer out across the forest floor and see Corrine disappear behind a screen of willows. They're headed toward the hot spring, I decide, or False Cavern. There isn't anything else up here. Looking down toward my feet I don't really see the gravel and dirt as I build up my nerve before following them. *I can always play innocent if he suspects something. The hot spring is a popular place.* I tread light and quick, scurrying after Corrine, and trying to keep out of sight.

Instinct takes over and leads me toward the caverns instead of to the hot pool. Very few people know the ground around here yields quartz crystals and garnets and the rock formations are a prime spot to find them. Moving without making a sound is nearly impossible when it comes to dry tree litter and gravel underfoot, but I attempt it anyway with mixed success. As I near the towering boulders, I listen and watch for any movement. Nothing stands out over the patter of my own footsteps until I hear a soft moan again.

"Travis. Take me home. I'm begging you. It hurts."

I stop pursuing and freeze. The voice is weak and filled with misery. There's no answering reply. *Oh god, what am I doing? Helping a girl in trouble,* I silently yell back. *Play innocent remember and don't think about the black void emanating from the creepy guy.* An enormous ponderosa pine grows next to one of the oddly shaped rocks and the path curves around them both. They'll be on the other side, I tell myself. I can feel them so close.

Pausing next to the tree, I take a much needed second to prepare myself for whatever I'm about to walk into. Someone grabs me from behind and slaps their hand over my mouth.

Having a heart attack at the ripe old age of nineteen is not a pleasant experience, in fact, it's downright terrifying. Barely able to grasp that I'm surviving, let alone that someone is whispering in my ear, I sort of register his words.

"Juliana, I'm sorry," he says.

I whip around and bury my face against Nathaniel's chest, gripping his shirt so hard my fingers ache. I will my body and mind to calm down. He backs up moving us farther away from the giant tree and Corrine on the other side of the rocks.

I swallow my stomach, lungs, and heart before I can speak. "There's a girl..."

"I know," Nathaniel says.

"What?" I whisper in a near panic.

"She's my client."

"What!" I ask again. The girl who was in my grandmother's store asking for help from a witch is his client? No way. Really? As I look up at Nathaniel's grave face, I know he's telling the truth. "We have to help her," I tell him, although the statement is obvious.

"I am. But *someone* showed up and distracted me."

"I know her," I say, and then continue on at his confused expression. "Sort of. I'll tell you later. What's wrong with her?" I hiss.

He shrugs and shakes his head. "I'm not sure. Stay back. I have to do this for her."

"No. I need to help."

"Nothing I say is going to make a difference, is it?"

"No," I say as I shake my head with emphasis.

Something like obligation toward this girl is making me react. I turned her away at the store and now she is in some sort of real trouble. My gut can feel it.

I see Nathaniel set his jaw with resignation and then he tips his head in the direction of where I think Corrine and the malevolent little man are.

Nathaniel takes the lead and I stay close on his heels. We inch along the edge of a towering rock and then pause as he peeks around its next corner. I feel or sense Nathan's body tense as he sees something. I'm dying to ask what is going on, but I stay silent not wanting to give up our location in case the dark haired man can hear us. Nathaniel gestures to a screen of scrub oaks ahead and on our right.

"Hurry," he mouths, and then we dart out from the cover of the boulder to the bushes. I catch a glimpse of Corrine on the ground as we move and no sign of the man. Nathaniel nudges me deeper into the scrubby trees until I am surrounded with the leafy branches.

He whispers close to my ear, "Juliana, if you care for me at all, please stay here. I'll get Corrine and then we'll leave together."

The desperation in his eyes makes me nod in agreement even though hiding is the last thing my soul wants to do. He turns to leave, but stops as we hear a bone chilling cry.

Animal, my brain tries to convince me, not human, but it still sends shivers of panic along my spine. I reach forward and part the branches giving me an inch of unobstructed view. Nathan leans in close and watches with me.

The slight man comes into view as he backs out of one of the rock cavern's openings.

It's not a real cave. The massive rocks have eroded away leaving passageways and tunnels and creating open ceilinged caverns. Veins of quartz run through the outcropping and crystals can be found if you have an eye for such things.

The chilling sound shrieks once more and as the eerie scream echoes off the side of the rocks, I see its source. He's dragging a fawn, still baby fresh with its white spots, by its leg. I clamp my hand over my mouth before I scream in horror and outrage. Nathaniel wraps an arm around my shoulders holding me close to his body to keep me from running out of my hiding place, or for comfort, I don't know which, but I suspect it's the former. I shrug off his arm and urge him forward. No one can see him except for me. Here is our chance to do something. He has to act now.

He takes my cue and relinquishes his physical body, melting through the bushes as I watch with anxious agitation and mind-numbing fear. As he moves closer, the man turns around and seems to look right at him. He says nothing however and then continues the last few feet, placing the struggling fawn close to Corrine. She opens her eyes seeing the baby deer and then squeezes them closed again. She lies on her side with her arms wrapped around her stomach. The fawn can't stand up. Something is horribly wrong with it, broken legs or spine maybe, I can't tell exactly. What kind of person is he? When he seems satisfied with the placement of the deer, he turns to Nathaniel.

"Go from this place. You have no power here."

Nathaniel stops, but only for a second. When he walked through the branches of the scrub oak I was certain he wasn't showing himself, but this man, with his hard eyes and sinister aura is clearly speaking to him. He bends down and picks up a branch off the ground. Still facing Nathaniel, he holds it up with both hands says something under his breath. Then he draws a circle in the dirt around himself, Corrine, and the fawn. Staying inside the circle, he kneels down next to the baby deer and reaches for his back pocket.

Nathaniel advances his position approaching the circle. The man doesn't even look up at him.

"Travis, I don't know what you're doing, but let me help Corrine."

I see Travis cut his eyes over to Nathaniel for a split second, but he doesn't stop. In his hand is a short silver dagger.

"Travis, stop."

"I command you to leave, Spirit."

Nathaniel's back stiffens, "I will not."

"Corrine, sit up," Travis orders.

"Noo," she faintly whimpers.

"It has to be now. Do it, you ungrateful tramp."

Travis looks up to the sky and then down at his watch, dagger still in his hand. He places it on the ground next to him and reaches over forcing Corrine up by her shoulders. She buries her face in her arms over bent knees pulled in tight to her chest. Travis picks up his weapon again and grabs the fawn by the back of its neck.

I close my eyes against the sight of him exposing the fawn's neck, sick with what I think is about to happen. But I can't take not knowing what is going on, however horrible, and open them again, focusing on Nathaniel.

"Corrine," Nathaniel calls.

She doesn't move or acknowledge him. He moves closer as if he's going to pick her up like he said he was going to, but then he stops short. Travis looks up and squints, his hatred turns to an indignant sneer.

"I told you to leave."

"Stop this madness!" Nathaniel yells.

Travis calls to the elements. "Wind, water, fire, and earth I give you the blood of the innocent. Yield to me what I desire."

He slashes open the mewling fawn's neck.

Black swirls creep in around the edges of my sight. I stay conscious by watching Nathaniel surge forward. He falls to his knees.

He pounds his fist against an invisible barrier as he rises to his feet and tries again.

Travis drains the deer's blood onto the ground and then he cups his hand under a stream of it.

"I give to you life blood in trade for quartz and bloodstones." He lifts his hand over Corrine and lets the fawn's blood pour over her head.

She screams as she scrambles to get away. Crying out again, this time from agony, she doubles over clenching her abdomen. Travis drops the deer and yanks Corrine to him. She pulls free, standing half bent over and unresponsive to her captor.

"Find the stones and then we can go home," he says.

When Corrine doesn't move, Travis's intensity escalates.

"Stop playing sick, you whoring twit. The sooner you do this the sooner we leave. It will take you only minutes. Stop refusing me!"

My stomach turns sour as I watch the fawn's blood drip from her hair in crimson rivulets. Nathaniel is unable to cross over the line drawn on the ground. I can't take feeling helpless so I scramble out of my hiding place, panic propelling me forward.

"Juliana, no!"

I dash straight for Corrine, yelling her name. She turns and sees me coming and by some miracle moves in time to avoid Travis's hand. She's out of his circle. I grab her hand and we run. Over my shoulder, I see Travis pursuing us, but as he leaves his ritual circle, Nathaniel tackles him.

"Go! I'll find you!" Nathaniel screams.

We flee away from the rocks and down a shallow slope through the forest. If we can keep up this pace we'll be to my car in almost no time. Corrine runs next to me, but she's clearly in pain. She grimaces and her arms are wrapped around her stomach.

"Are you okay?" I ask, between desperate breaths.

"No, but don't stop. He'll find me if we stop. He'll find me anyway," she gasps.

"No, he won't. My car isn't far," I say, trying to reassure her.

"You don't know him," Corrine huffs.

I didn't want to give her words any more power by dwelling on them so I point down the mountain and say, "Can you make it?"

"Yeah. But Travis will be there. Don't tell me where we're going," Corrine says as tears fill her soft blue eyes.

This girl must be brainwashed. Why else would she think Travis will know where we're going? And Nathaniel will stall him. There's no way he can find us easily. I look over my shoulder, watching for pursuit, but don't see them. *God, let him be okay. He is an angel after all. He couldn't get hurt. Could he?*

We run, stumbling over rocks and kicking up pine needles the entire way down. Corrine seems a little stronger now and is moving almost as fast as I am. When we reach the stream we run straight through, splashing water up to our shoulders.

"My car," I pant, as my blue Saab comes into view. I'm beyond grateful my camping gear is already loaded as Corrine runs to the passenger side as I circle around the trunk with my keys ready. My heart gives a lurch as I see a flash of movement. Could Corrine's prediction about Travis finding us at my car be true? No. It's Nathaniel.

He's holds his side and wears an unreadable expression.

"What's wrong?" I ask immediately.

"Not now," he says and gestures to the car. "We're getting out of here."

I yank the door open and Corrine and I climb inside. I look for Nathaniel, making sure he's getting in with us, but he's gone. Checking my rearview mirror, my heart flip-flops from surprise and I jump in my seat. My head hits the roof. "Ow!"

Nathaniel's in the back seat.

"Sorry," he says.

"That's all right. I'm gonna have to get used to it sometime."

"Get used to what?" Corrine asks through a mask of pain. Her arms are wrapped around her stomach and she is nearly bent in half on the passenger seat.

I look over my shoulder and Nathaniel shakes his head in dismissal. Corrine can't see him in the car with us. This might get complicated very quickly. "Never mind," I say, but Corrine is in too much pain to pay much attention.

As soon as the engine starts I throw it into reverse and whip the car around. We race down the dirt drive bumping along over wash boards and potholes that should rattle the teeth out of my head, but miraculously don't. Corrine whimpers only twice, but I can see her clenching her jaw and the stiffness of her back. She's hanging in there, but she looks wretched.

When I stop the car to open the gate to leave my grandma's property, I take a second to ask, "Are we headed to the hospital?"

"Nooo, just get me away."

"Are you sick?" I ask.

"No. No doctors. We need to keep moving. He's coming. I know it." She lets out an agonizing moan into her lap.

"Do you know what's wrong with her?" I ask Nathaniel.

"I think the emergency room is a good idea, whether she wants it or not."

He isn't looking much better than Corrine. He's still holding his side and his face is grim. "What's wrong?"

"Nothing, I said. Please, keep us moving." Corrine answers me instead of Nathaniel.

Out of the car and back in, back out, and back in again, to open the gate, pull through and close it again. It felt like ten minutes had passed to move twenty feet instead of the one minute it really took. I give Nathaniel the stink eye and will him to answer me, but he won't.

"Corrine, who's that man and what was he doing to you?" I ask, as we start down the dirt road toward the highway. *Maybe the police station would be a better destination.*

"He's my stepfather."

"Why did he kill the fawn?" Remembering the blood makes my stomach clench into a hard little peach pit at the bottom of my ribs.

"It was an offering. Ohhh," she moans and then says through clenched teeth, "He's a warlock. Don't talk about him. It gives him power."

I slow for a curve in the road and then slam on the brakes. My car slides on the dirt sending up a spray of gravel and dust. Corrine's hand slams into the dash bracing herself in time to keep from sliding off the seat.

An old silver BMW sedan is parked sideways across the narrow road.

I recognize Travis in the driver's seat as Corrine says, "He won't let me go. You can't out run him."

"How did he beat us?" I say in total disbelief.

"He's a warlock," Corrine answers, as if that should explain how her stepdad seemingly manipulated time and space.

With a surge of rebellion I add, "I sure as hell can try."

Nathaniel nods encouragingly and I yank the wheel around and try for another direction. Travis is blocking the most direct way to the highway, but I'm not going to hand over Corrine without trying something else.

I nail the gas pedal and take the first left watching in my rearview mirror for the silver car. It's not there so I press the pedal harder. I pray my memory isn't failing me as the road curves around trees and passes a couple of large expensive homes. As a cul-de-sac comes into view I yell, "Frickin' hell. I took the wrong road!"

"Can you walk?" I ask everyone in the car.

"Of course," Nathaniel says.

"I think so," Corrine whines, her pain obvious.

I park the car close to the ditch, turn off the key, and open the door all at the same time. "Let's go."

There's no houses at the end of the road so we dash back under the cover of the trees. Then we hear Travis's car coming. I jog toward the highway and continue praying that we can lose him again.

"Nathaniel, are we being crazy?"

"The highway's close. We'll hitch back to town. No, you're not crazy. We need to stay away from him."

"Who's Nathaniel?" Corrine pants.

I look over at Nathaniel, but he's not looking at me. He's looking back. A car door slams. Travis is coming. We pick up our pace letting the trees zoom by us.

"Jules, I can't stall him again. He did something to me. I'm—"

Nathaniel doesn't finish. His eyes search mine and his expression causes a fear so real as to be almost crippling. I stumble into a tree and grip the trunk feeling it's solidity against my sweaty palms. I regain my feet and force myself to move faster. *A warlock? Did something to an angel? What's going on? What kind of evil is following us?*

"There." I point ahead at the sunlight breaking through the pines showing us where the highway is. I glance over at Corrine. The agony on her face is worse than ever, but she keeps running.

We dash out of the trees and onto the pavement. The rumble of approaching vehicles echoes down the otherwise empty road. Corrine waves her arms as a couple of motorcycles round a corner. They begin to slow. More bikes follow, five in all.

The enormous stature and bushy black beard of Butch is unmistakable on his black and orange Harley. Corrine runs up to him as I begin to call her back. The tall thin one with blonde hair sticking out from under a bandana, Eli, I think his name is, pulls up close to me. They all stop.

"Corrine!" I scream. I doubt she can hear me over the hellacious noise from five motorcycles.

I see Butch nod his head at her and then he yells something over to Eli.

"Nathaniel, I can't do this."

"Jules, I don't think we have a choice. I won't let anything happen. Do you trust me?"

"I don't know. I mean, yes, of course, but please not these killers."

"Corrine, come back. We'll find another ride," I yell.

She gives me a confused look and then hops onto a tiny seat behind Butch. Eli is closest to where I huddle by Nathaniel.

He urges me forward. "Go, Jules. I don't think they'll harm you."

"But he has a gun," I protest.

"Travis does too," Nathaniel says and I hear the edge of panic in his voice.

"What?" I stare at his face and the fear in his eyes makes me swallow hard. Then I see Travis moving out of the trees, gun in hand.

"Juliana, now!"

Nathaniel is paler than before and for a split second I think I'm seeing through him. "Not him," I plead. Fear finally gets a grip on me and threatens to explode in an ugly emotional flood.

"Corrine. Get over here," Travis yells.

She starts to climb off the bike.

"No! Butch, go!" I scream.

Butch takes a quick look at me, then over at Travis approaching with his gun. Then he peels out, his motorcycle moving faster than it should with three hundred and fifty pounds sitting on top of it.

Two of the bikers shift into gear and zoom down the highway. The grumbling roar rattles my insides. I take a quick survey of my last two options. I can't get on behind this Eli. It would be like handing myself over to Travis. In my head, they're both deer murderers. In a panic I start to move toward the last guy, but then stop as I see something completely unexpected. The deer carcass is strapped to the top of a tiny trailer on the side of his bike.

"Get on or walk, but that fellar' over there don't look like he's playin' around," Eli yells over the thunderous rumble of the bike's exhaust.

"Now, Juliana. I'll be close." Nathaniel reaches over and pushes me toward Eli even though he isn't in his physical body.

Bang! I jump out of my skin as Travis shoots. Bark explodes on a tree not far from us.

I throw my leg over the motorcycle seat behind Eli The Murderer. The wheels begin spinning before my foot lifts off the ground.

Bang! Another shot fires. I check to see if anyone is shot. Everyone I can see is unharmed. Travis looks like a black demon with two laser-red pupils. I blink, not believing my own eyes, and check again. He's just a short man with dark hair, wearing blue jeans and a shirt. The black demon I saw is there around him, and not there. I don't understand it, but I swear he is the devil himself, incognito.

Nathaniel perches on the sidecar with the deer carcass almost comically, but there really is nothing funny about any of this. I turn my head staring at the back of Eli's leather vest and pray to every god I've ever heard of to let this end.

Chapter Six: Personality Disorders

Juliana

Hell on earth. That's where I've landed. Ear shattering, mind-numbing roaring has entered my skull, passed down my spinal column, and split me into two. I'm freezing wet from the creek water and being blasted in all directions by an unbelievable wind while hanging on for dear life. My rear end is planted to a leather seat, but I can't feel it because my butt is totally numb from vibration.

How many levels of Hell are there? There must be a lot because my current situation couldn't be described as anything else, and I would have sworn that running from an angry warlock was yet again another form of diabolical torture. The only thing which is even remotely comforting — I mean the most minuscule crumb of hope — is when I dare to open my eyes, I'm staring at a collection of crosses. Patches sewn onto the leather in various sizes and designs. I'm not religious and I've never been. Not that I have anything against it, but my parents raised me without organized religion, and I've never felt any need for it. That being said, somehow seeing this odd collection of crosses as the world blurs by my peripheral vision is helping.

I peek over the shoulder of my "rescuer" to look for Corrine and Butch up ahead. Huge mistake. Eyelids should never flap in the wind. Squeezing my eyes closed brings back some of the moisture, hopefully enough to be able to see again. Next I run my tongue around the inside of my cheeks to assure myself they're still attached to my face and by some mercy of heaven they are.

"Where you girls headed?"

Did I imagine the voice? Could it be the devil asking me if I'm residing in his lair of torture, or moving on at my leisure? I squeeze my eyes closed harder and keep the vision of the Celtic cross from the back of Eli's vest in my mind's eye. I like that one the best with its pattern of intertwining knots. For some reason it reminds me of my mom.

"I said, where am I taking you?" the voice yells.

Yes, Satan's minion, that must be it. I'm being escorted on a Harley straight to the blazing inferno of the underworld. Lead me to a place of no return. I'll miss you Nathaniel — we didn't get enough time together — but control of my fate has blown away with the wind.

"I know you're no mute, so tell me where you want let off."

The bike slows. Like from two hundred to one hundred miles per hour. Attempt number two is imperceptibly more successful as I peek behind us looking for Nathaniel and the others. Through wildly flapping hair I see them close behind. Nathaniel's face is strained, but he's not ruffled by the wind. No body to be ruffled, I remind myself. In this particular situation I'm ridiculously envious.

"In town," I squeak.

"Lady, you need to speak up. In case you haven't notice my ride is louder than a hurricane."

"Town. Anywhere!"

The bike rockets forward as he shifts gear and lays into the throttle.

"No! Wait. Next right!" I scream as I realize how close we are to my house.

He must not have heard me over the deafening roar because he speeds up instead of slows down. *God! How fast does this machine go?* Town will be fine too, I decide, but then I do feel the bike begin to slow. Daring another look, I see Butch and Corrine glide up next to us. Eli makes some hand gesture, which apparently means hit the brakes and turn right, because that's exactly what happens next.

Moving down the dirt road at a more manageable speed, I get a hold of my hair with one hand and take a few close to regular breaths, now that the wind isn't blasting through my nasal cavities at supersonic speed.

"Stop at the next intersection, okay?"

"Yes, ma'am."

Behind us, the others, including Nathaniel and the deer carcass, follow just out of range of the worst of the dust clouds. Eli downshifts and pulls to the side of the road at the corner of my street. Before he shifts into neutral I'm already sliding off the seat. This is a slight miscalculation on my part. The numbness of my backside from the outrageous vibration has traveled down my legs and into my heels. I stumble awkwardly — motorcycle legs — who's heard of such a thing? Before I fall down Eli grabs my elbow and steadies me. My feet find their grip on the earth and I jerk my arm free.

Eli raises both hands in surrender and gives me an innocent, although road rough and scratchy bearded, look from behind hazel eyes. I frown at him and look for Corrine and Nathaniel.

Nathaniel is behind me and a little on my left. Corrine is leaning over and wrapping her little stick arms around the giant, Butch, in an overly friendly hug. Eli cuts his motor and the rumbling ceases its assault on my innards.

"You girls need us to stick around for a while?" Eli asks me.

"No," I say with mild annoyance.

"That gun shootin' cowboy back there didn't seem all too friendly."

"I know. Thanks for the ride. We'll be fine."

"Sure you don't wanna go to the police?" Eli asks.

He has a slight drawl to some of his words. He's probably from the south, like so many other summer visitors around here.

"You? You want to take us to the cop shop?" I ask, as I look pointedly over at the dead deer. The only reason I'm not going to turn him into Wildlife Enforcement is because he saved us from Travis.

"You're misunderstandin' this—"

Eli gets cut off as Corrine steps between us.

"I'm Corrine. I'd really like to thank you. You don't know what you've done for me. You've saved my life."

Listening to Corrine speak blows my mind. She sounds different, all cutesy and innocent. She's even smiling and looking rather coy. She has her hands across her stomach, but now in an entirely different way than just thirty minutes before. All traces of her pain seems to have disappeared.

"It's only a ride," Eli says.

"You don't understand." Corrine takes a small step forward and places one of her tiny hands on Eli's thigh. "I had to get away from him. He's not right. He's a powerful S.O.B. I could thank you later, in private," she says low enough so his fellow bikers don't hear, but I do.

I watch in utter disbelief as Corrine's hand inches its way up Eli's leg toward his groin and her other hand moves to one of her breasts, fondling herself.

"Juliana, help her please," Nathaniel says.

"Corrine, we have to go. Now."

She turns an annoyed look on me and says, "I like these guys. You go."

Nathaniel says, "Something's way off. Try to get her to come with you, and sooner than later."

I couldn't agree more. I just met this girl, but Corrine is acting strange considering she just escaped her psycho stepfather and has dried deer's blood in her hair.

Eli's leather gloved hand stops Corrine's progress toward his crotch. "Corrine, you best go with your friends. I think they're needing you."

I take my cue and reach for her upper arm. "Corrine, you should get cleaned up. Your hair, remember?"

"Oh god! I Forgot. Of course you're not into me. I must look like a dirty troll." Her hand moves to her crusty hair. The parakeet blue streak was left untainted so she now has blonde, blue, and dark red. It isn't as pretty as it sounds.

"Unless you like that sort of thing," she adds with a flutter of lashes.

Pulling her back feels like moving a cardboard cutout of a person. She seems to weigh almost nothing. Eli's brows knit as he stares at her. I think I see concern in the depths of his greenish brown eyes, but I can only picture him with a gun in his hand, a heartless animal killer.

"You should call me sometime. I'd really like to thank you for your trouble," Corrine goes on.

"We need to leave," I insist and pull her another few steps away.

"You take care of yourself now, Miss, and don't give us a second thought. We do what we can," Eli says.

"You're so cute. Your leather is so hot. Maybe we could all go out together."

"Just shut up for a second okay," I snap at her.

"Bye. We'll be fine," I say again, keeping my hand firmly wrapped around Corinne's arm.

"I know you will be," Eli says to our backs with his slight southern drawl. "Your friend's watching over the two of you. Hey, what's your name anyhow?"

Processing his words is immediate, but comprehending them feels like working out pig Latin when I was seven. I turn to look at him one last time. Tall and lanky, covered in leather decorated with crosses. "Jules," I answer.

"Jules short for somethin'?"

This time I don't answer. I didn't really want him knowing my name at all. My eyes narrow and I hope he can see I still consider him a killer. He answers my flat expression with a serious look of his own.

"I think our paths may cross again, Miss Jules. Don't forget the love and light of the Savior will help you when you're in need."

"Yeah Man, thanks." I give him a half-hearted wave, which is really more of a wave off, and hurry in the direction of my house.

"Preaching, deer shooting bikers. Just what I ordered. Can I get a side of televangelist with that?" I grumble to no one in particular.

"I didn't know you could be so cynical," Nathaniel says.

"Yeah, well certain situations call for an adjustment in my attitude," I say back, not meaning to sound so snotty, but I've had enough of these bikers for a lifetime.

"He could see me."

"Oh?" I ask, remembering Eli's words, 'your friend is watching over the two of you.'

"He knew I was there, but he doesn't see me like you do."

"Hmmph," I snort. "Deer killing, savior loving, weirdo who sees spirits. Great."

"Eli messed up Travis's plans back there in the woods. I saw everything. Travis started the ceremony with the mama deer, but he took the baby when the motorcycles showed up. It was really awful. I told you they were nice. And you're doing it again," Corrine says.

"What am I doing?" I ask.

"Talking to someone who's not there. Travis does it too. Please tell me you're not like Travis. I heard you were a witch but I was hoping you were all like, white magic and stuff."

My hand runs over my scalp and my fingers catch in the thousands of new tangles in my hair. I look over at Nathaniel.

He shrugs and says, "I'm not sure if we should tell her about me yet. I'm confused about her behavior with Eli. I have some ideas, but it's nothing concrete."

"I told you before, I'm not a witch, and I wasn't lying. I know nothing about witchcraft and I'm sorry if it bothers you that I talk to myself."

"Uh-huh. Yeah, Travis never tells me everything either. I get it," Corrine says and then shrugs it off. "Where are we going anyway?"

"My house. The green one." I point up ahead on the left where our two story house sits nestled in the pines.

"Cool," Corrine says.

"She seems to be feeling better," Nathaniel says.

I nod in silent agreement with him. There's something distinctly different about this girl than there was an hour or so before.

"Corrine, does your stomach still hurt?"

"Huh? Oh. Well, kind of," she says, not making eye contact with me.

"What was going on earlier?"

"Hmm, cramps?" she says as a question. "Hey, can I use your bathroom? You know, my hair." She holds up one of her brown tinged golden locks for inspection. "That Travis, he can be such a bastard sometimes."

"Yeah, that's not what I'd call someone who spills fresh fawn's blood on me while performing black magic."

"He was preparing for some special moon ceremony coming up. An alignment or something? He uses me to get what he wants for rituals and sometimes to make extra cash. Then he usually buys cars he doesn't need. Like I said, he's an ass."

I bite my tongue, holding back any further remarks about her stepfather.

$$\infty$$

Nathaniel and I wait in my room while Corrine cleans up in the bathroom. My concern for his well-being quadruples as we settle into my space. He's trembling and his hand is clamped to his side.

"What happened back there?" I ask him tentatively.

"You mean with Travis?" he clarifies as he settles down gingerly on my velvet chair.

"Yes. I know something's wrong. You may as well tell me."

"He's more powerful than I gave him credit for. He wields dark magic and he's skilled at it."

"Corrine said he's a warlock. Do you know what that means exactly? What he's capable of?"

"Too much."

"What? Are you badly hurt?" I ask, and move from my bed to kneel on the floor in front of him.

"Don't freak out."

"Freak out? Why? What happened?" I feel all the blood drain from my face and fingertips. I didn't know it was possible to injure an angel. What sort of monster is Corinne's stepfather?

"Juliana, I can't show you if you are going to do that."

"What? I'm fine," I lie.

"You better lean back against the bed for a minute."

"No. What happened? Nathaniel, please. This isn't funny." Tingling in my pinky fingers alerts me to the level of stress I'm under. No blood flowing down my arms isn't a good sign. Leaning back against the bed helps. The feel of something solid behind me lets me hang on as the rest of the world drops out from under me.

"I'm not laughing."

"No, which is making this worse. You don't look right," I say. As I stare at him he looks like he is at the end of some tunnel. It's not my imagination, and it's not because of my stress. He normally appears like any other person to me, solid and real, but now he's dimmer and I would swear I keep seeing through him in places.

"I don't feel quite right either," Nathaniel mumbles while not meeting my eyes. "I may need to leave for a while. I'm so sorry, Juliana. I'm messing everything up again. Corrine is my case, not yours."

His apology unsettles me. He doesn't need to be sorry for anything. I press my palms against the wood floor to help me stay grounded as I divulge my side of things. "Corrine came to me when I was working at the herb shop. She may not have been in any of this mess if I had helped her when she asked. No, I have to help her too.

It'll be fine. We'll stay right here, in my house, while you rest. That's what you meant by having to leave, isn't it? You're exhausted and have to recover."

"I do. If it wasn't for Travis, I would never leave you two alone. Arrrgh! What have I done?" Nathaniel's hands moves to the front of his head hiding his anger and frustration from me. Lowering his hands, he gives me the most apologetic look I've ever seen. There's more pain and sadness in those smoky eyes than anger and I want to hold him and tell him everything's going to be perfect and he has nothing to worry about. I also know simple reassurances right now won't change anything.

He slides forward off the chair and kneels in front of me. His hand brushes mine and I can feel him in the most surreal way, like walking into cool mist. His radiating warmth is completely diminished. My fear peaks again, but I push it down to a somewhat manageable level.

"Nathaniel, show me what's wrong with your side," I whisper.

"Promise me you'll stay home until I come back. Travis is dangerous and Corrine is suicidal. I don't understand what happened to her after the motorcycle ride, but I'll figure it out. She may be manic. I should be able to return before she tries something again."

"Okay. I promise. Believe me, I never want to see Travis again. Now, tell me what he did to you."

Nathaniel's face hardens and I see him flinch as he starts to reach for the hem of his shirt. "I think it will heal. It's something else I have to ask Marcus about."

"Marcus is your mentor, right?" My voice shakes as I try to focus on his words and not on what he's about to show me.

"Yes. He'll know what I'm dealing with."

Nathaniel stares into my eyes and then he slowly lifts the left side of his shirt. We're both silent as we stare at the empty gashes across Nathan's left ribcage, or where his ribcage should be.

Ragged tears and empty space. "Nathaniel. Part of you is missing." My mouth is suddenly dry as baked sand. "How... bad... is... it?"

"Somewhere between acid and flames eating at the million exposed nerves of my soul."

"Eeea," I whimper for him.

He lowers his shirt and looks out the window. Deep bone chilling worry is somehow evident in his blank expression.

"You're sure it will heal?" I manage to say.

"No."

Before I can respond to this devastating admission, a piercing wail slices through the tension in the room and sends us scrambling to the bathroom.

Nathaniel disappears through the wall. I don't have time to be unnerved by this as I hear him call to me from inside the other room.

"Corrine. I'm coming in," I warn as I turn the knob. I've never felt dread before stepping into my own bathroom, but I do now. My eyelids close for a second before I can face whatever is going on inside.

"She's in the shower," Nathaniel tells me and by the look on his face it isn't good news.

"Corrine. Are you all right?"

"Noo," she sobs. "Help. Ooooh," she moans.

I pull the curtain back part way and peek inside. Corrine sits on the bottom of the bathtub curled into a small ball. With one hand I flip off the water and with the other I grab a towel from the bar. As I wrap her in the towel I see part of the problem. Thin watery blood washes down the drain, coming from somewhere underneath Corrine.

"Corrine, are you on your period?"

"No. I don't know. Yes," she says.

"Can you stand up?" I ask her and try to assist her at the same time.

I peer over at Nathaniel who has his back partially turned and is looking helpless and miserable.

"It's never hurt like this before," she tells me and then moans in agony as she stands up, steps out of the tub, and sits down on the toilet. She bends in half and buries her face in her hands and cries in pain.

Something dawns on me and I ask, "Sweetie, are you pregnant?" Her extremely straightforward approach with Eli was a bit shocking to say the least.

A sniffling reply is her answer, and then her shoulders shake before she finally says, "I...don't know."

Squatting down in front of her to try to see her face I ask, "Is it possible?"

Pale blue eyes meet mine through tender pink fingers. "I...don't know," she says again and buries her face.

She's so tiny, not so much in the way of height, but overall. I still think she must be around seventeen or so, but she hasn't begun to mature in the ways of a woman. She still has a young girl's body. Stick arms, bony collar bones, teeny wrists, and narrow hips. She may like older men, like those bikers, but she's still a girl.

The sound of fluid dripping into the bowl brings my attention back to the emergency in front of me. "Have you been with anyone and—" *Holy crap, I don't know how to do this.* I suddenly feel like my mother when she's dealing with young girls at her job. I take a deep breath and bite the bullet. "Have you had sex without using birth control?" I ask, while trying as hard as I can to sound gentle and nonjudgmental.

She doesn't answer this time, but breaks down further, sobbing and shaking.

After a few seconds of uncontrollable bawling she separates her legs and peers into the pot under her. "Aaahhh," she whimpers pitifully.

The pink flush on her face drains and leaves her ashen. Her hands begin to tremble.

I see a horrible flash of red under her. The entire bowl seems to be filling with blood. "I'm going to call an ambulance," I say to her and Nathaniel both.

"No!" Corrine yells. She grabs for the toilet paper and start to unravel some. "I can't go to the hospital. It's just really bad cramps. It'll pass."

Nathaniel says, "Could it be that simple?"

Looking to him and then back to Corrine and then back to him, I ask, "Have you seen her with anyone?"

He shakes his head no and asks, "Could she be having a miscarriage?"

I shrug my shoulders at him. "Corrine, I don't know what's wrong. Let a doctor look at you, please."

"Can't. No doctors. I'd rather be dead. I'll kill myself before I go to a hospital. I swear it's the truth."

I flinch at her declaration. That she could jump to such extremes so easily makes me sad for her. Is dying really a better option than going to a hospital?

"She's serious. It's the reason I'm assigned to her."

The towel around Corrine's shoulders starts to slip. I reach for it, but Corrine grabs the edges and holds it closed.

"It's already starting to feel better," she says, but I think she's lying. "Do you have any pads?" she asks.

Nathaniel moves closer to the door and says, "I need to step into the hall for a moment. Call me if you need me and I'll come right back."

"Okay," I say to Nathaniel. I wish I could step into the hall and let someone else deal with it, but he's having his own problems and a guy just doesn't get it when it comes to girl problems, angel or not. My brain spins for a couple of seconds. Mom could help, she's a nurse right? The obvious problem with that is, she's not home. There's Grandma, but how would I explain any of this? Wait, what about Grandma? What would she do? Lists of herbs run through my head like watching the crawl line on the national news. Is there anything I can do? Maybe if I could get a real answer out of this suicidal girl, then I could come up with a treatment.

Corrine wipes herself with the paper and I look away.

"Are you really feeling better?" I ask.

I see her tense slightly while avoiding my gaze. I don't want another appeasing lie. "Corrine, I may be able to help a little with the herbs I have, but I have to know what's wrong with you. Have you had sex with anyone recently?"

"I think so. And yeah, it feels a little better." She reaches for her clothes, so I bend down and grab the pads from the cabinet under the sink.

"You, think so?" I repeat, doubtfully. "Is it possible you may be miscarrying?"

"I guess," she says.

"You've never had cramps like this before?"

"No. You're talking about the herbs from the store where you work? I'd like that. I can't go to the doctor, Jules. Travis will find me."

"Certain herbs may help. Come on. You need to go lie down."

She finishes putting on her jeans and tank top. She's so tiny. She must be a size minus zero. Then I direct her to my room. Ariel, my cat, watches us enter from her spot on the bed. As we get closer to her, she flips out. Growling and arching her spine as the hairs on her back stand straight up. My eyes linger on her bottle brush tail, astounded by its odd shape, and then before I realize what she's doing, she launches herself at Corrine's face.

"Ariel!" I snap, as I grab her in mid-air and redirect her energetic leap toward the door. She lands with a thud and instantly turns around, coming right back at Corrine.

Frazzled and shocked by her behavior I yell, "Frickin' cat. Get out." I shoe her off with my hands and feet, only sustaining a couple minor scratches in the process. One last hiss escapes from her as the door shuts.

"I'm so sorry. She's never acted like that before."

Corrine gives me a look somewhere between indifference and annoyance.

"Will you rest in here while I go downstairs?" I ask.

She nods and then lies down on my bed curling up on her side. I glance quickly around my room looking for any sharp objects or other tools she might hurt herself with. Potted plants, blankets, pillows, and CD's are harmless, I decide.

Nathaniel watches us from the corner by my closet. He's fainter in appearance. *At this rate he'll disappear altogether. He better come back.* My hand reaches out to him as I leave the room, to feel him, to know he's still with me, but my fingers pass right through him.

"Downstairs," I mumble.

As I pass Jared's room I peek inside, assuring myself my brother isn't home. How can I begin to explain any of this? I don't want to, that's for sure. Then I fly down the stairs barely aware they're under my feet. Like this entire afternoon, I've been a part of every moment, but it's impossible to separate the feeling of the individual steps which have led me to this pandemonium, and panic, and strange girl, and devil-man shooting at me, and my new boyfriend fading into nothingness.

I don't understand the ability of my brain to multi task and I don't completely understand how I can feel fifty different feelings at the same time, but somehow I'm managing. Maybe I have a personality disorder, or maybe it's the people who can't handle chaos that are labeled with that particular diagnosis. Either way I have to come up with something medicinal for Corrine, say goodbye to Nathaniel — maybe for the last time — and or, talk him into leaving so he can heal. All this, and pray my family doesn't come home to find me talking to my invisible boyfriend while concocting an infusion which will keep Corrine from bleeding to death in my bedroom. Is this why people have mental breakdowns? Yeah, I don't have time to worry about that right now.

Chapter Seven: Ghosts and Goodbyes

Juliana

Digging through my herb cabinet yields very little, not because there isn't anything useful in there, but because my growing fear for Nathaniel's injury is distracting me, making it impossible for my brain to engage with my actions.

"Why don't you go? You need to take care of yourself right now," I say, as I walk over to the sliding glass door and put my anxious cat, Ariel, outside. She's acting so weird and I can't take her weaving around my ankles right now. She turns and attempts to get right back inside as I close the door in her face.

"I'm staying as long as I can."

Moving back to the herb cabinet, I look at the labels on the jars for at least the fifth time. "You're being silly. I know it hurts. You should take care of it sooner than later."

"It's going to hurt whether I'm here with you or not," he argues.

"Yes, but you said that you thought it would heal if you could go rest?" My hands fiddle with the jar lids in front of me.

"I also said I wasn't sure."

"The sooner you leave, the sooner you can come back," I say, using logic.

Nathaniel looks down at the countertop and doesn't answer.

"Are you worrying about—" I whisper.

"Everything," he admits, interrupting me.

He moves like a shadow. Standing in front of me, he closes his eyes, hiding the swirling emotions I can see there. His entire being shimmers like watching evening sunlight glimmer across the surface of a lake. I think he's about to leave me, which I said I wanted, but in truth I never want to be apart from him. He opens his eyes as his body becomes whole again. Pain sears across his face for a split second, but it passes as he searches my face.

"I have to do this one more time before I go."

"Nathaniel, don't. You're not strong enough."

"Shh, I have to."

He raises his hand and with gentle fingertips, runs them over my temple and brushes my hair back behind one ear. His caress continues, sweeping over the curve of my skull and trailing down my neck.

The heat rushing through me is instant. It warms my chest and makes me take a few deep breaths, which brings in his scent, clean and bright, and mixed with a hint of sweetness, like honeysuckles. His smell creates an urgency inside me, desperate to drink him in before he goes away. My head automatically tips upward, exposing more of my neck and making it easier for him to find my mouth.

He doesn't keep me waiting long and now I do drink him in. Passionate, urgent, then slow and soft, lingering and teasing. Over and over, I try to feel every part of his kiss and memorize it. I move in closer, wanting to feel all of him next to me. Then I remember his injury and have to hold myself back. It takes every last once of energy but I manage to not throw myself on him. I pull back first, afraid to death I'll hurt him.

He cups the back of my head not letting me get too far. Our foreheads almost touch as he stares into my eyes. The raging storm going on inside of him scares me, but I'll gladly ride through it with him for however long it takes, forever if need be.

"I'll be fine," I assure him. "And you'll be back soon."

Worry emanates from him. He doesn't have to say it, I can feel it.

"Won't you?" I ask.

He takes my hands and holds them to his chest. A sudden urge to cry chokes me. What if he's not coming back? I bite my lower lip. How does an angel get slashed open in the first place? How will he recover from it?

"Nothing can stop me from coming back to you, love. It's only that I don't know about this." He shifts his left side slightly and the creases of concern deepen around his penetrating eyes. "And I can't forget the last time I left you when I didn't want to. Things were not fine. You and your brother were almost killed."

There is a new weakness to his voice. He's draining the very last of his strength to stand here and talk to me. "This time there's no crazed meth-head chasing me. Now go. I promise, promise, promise, not to leave until you're back. Unless I absolutely have to," I amend, and then qualify it as I watch his expression change to one of severe disapproval. "In a life or death situation, I may need to leave the house."

Nathaniel starts to disagree, but he gets cut off.

"Who are you talking to?" Corrine asks.

Her pretty doll-shaped face is tinged with fear and uncertainty as she stands in the entrance to the kitchen. Nathaniel takes a slow step back as we both watch Corrine. I look at Nathaniel for an answer.

"She can't see me."

"What?" I ask him, totally confused.

He's still in his physical form. *What does he mean, Corrine can't see him? He's standing right here.*

Corrine answers me instead. "Who were you talking to?"

"My imaginary friend," I say slowly and then smile like I'm joking.

"Oh, right." She looks away staring out the back door.

"I thought you were resting upstairs while I make you something to drink," I say, trying to sound and look normal.

"My stomach is starting to cramp again," she says, and scrunches up her face.

"I have something that may help. It's outside," I add hurriedly as I have a flash of brilliance remembering a long ago conversation between my Grandmother and a customer about controlling uterine bleeding and a bunch of other stuff, including miscarriage, and what can be done to help. Taking another quick look at my two cohorts I make a split decision to try it. She refuses to go to the doctor and it may help. Chances of making her worse are virtually none, so it's the least I can do.

"I'll be right back," I start to say, but I get interrupted by the sound of the front door opening.

"Hello?" I call out, not able to see the front entry from the kitchen.

There's no answer. I look around the end of the wall between the living room and the kitchen and see Jared.

"Hey," I say, and then take a couple of steps back. The last time I saw my brother we had a full blown screaming fight and I don't want a rematch. Jared exploded in a rage, something he's never done with me before. The fight was the reason why I left the house in the middle of the night to go camping. Movement catches my eye and I peer around Jared and see he's not alone. A familiar looking tall black man with dreadlocks moves quickly out of sight and up the stairs. Jared doesn't follow his friend but comes into the kitchen. I check to see if Nathaniel is still showing himself, or not, and he's not. I let out a relieved breath. I'm not quite ready to explain him yet.

Unsure of Jared's feelings about our last run-in, I go back to my cabinet full of jars and pretend my feelings aren't still hurt. He was so unlike his normal self last night. If he's still acting strange, I don't want to talk to him.

"What's up, Jules? Mixing up one of your noxious teas?" he asks, and gives me an eyebrow wiggle and a half grin.

"Mmm-hmm."

"Hey, where's our car?" Jared asks.

He sounds like himself, spunky and full of misguided mischief. Apparently he's not holding a grudge about our recent clash of wills.

"Oh, well, umm, is there any way you can go get it for me? There was a situation and I had to leave it parked."

"Sure. Clue me in to where I can find it," he says.

"Hey, I know you. You're in Mostly Mayhem, right? You play a blue Gibson. I love the guitar. It really looks good on you too," Corrine says from the kitchen table where she sits tucked neatly into a chair.

Jared sees her for the first time and turns one of his heartbreakingly beautiful smiles on her. "Yeah. You've seen me play?"

"Sure, a couple of times. In different clubs. I think you know my brother, Patrick Dawson. And I'm Corrine."

Searching through the labels for raspberry leaves, I make my best attempt not to roll my eyes. Corrine is starting up again. I can feel and see the flirtatious tease coming out in her, like when she was talking to Eli. Her aura changes. It's sudden and unnerving. She has a darker aura, unlike any I've seen before, but when she was with the bikers, and now with Jared, her energy field expands and looks like what I can only describe as an eddy, dark and churning, and devouring anything that comes too close. And of course, my brother is eating up her attention like gobbling down gooey chocolate lava cake. This could get messy in a hurry. He has an endless appetite for adoration, especially from cute girls.

I look over to Nathaniel who is still managing to hang on. He looks as if he's worrying about the same exact thing I am. Unable to ask him my next question aloud without sounding like a psycho, I raise my eyebrows, shrug, and turn my palms up. His look of concern deepens and he shakes his head with uncertainty.

Dissatisfaction and a need for answers propel me to reach across the countertop for a scrap of paper and a pen and scribble down a question. *Why couldn't she see you?*

Nathaniel leans over and takes a look. "I don't know. I'll figure it out. It's a first for me. Something's way off. Be safe while I'm gone. If things get too strange, do whatever you need to, but please be here when I get back."

Both our attentions turn back to Jared and Corrine. *What's going on with her?* Nathaniel's worry is really starting to freak me out. And Corrine is acting as if the pain is gone again. Prickles on the back of my neck alarm me to the things in the room I don't understand. Grandma Charlotte would say pinpricks on the back of the neck mean someone on the other side is trying to protect you. A silvery chill passes down my spine.

"Patrick's your brother. Really? He's a sly kid," Jared says.

"Yeah. He can come through in a pinch when you need him." Corrine smiles a sweet shy smile and lifts her chest a little higher showing off her petite but curvy front.

Nathaniel steps in close to me and whispers in my ear. Even though I shouldn't be able to feel him in his spirit self, I think I do, like a disturbance in the air next to me. "As soon as I can. Don't forget me while I'm gone."

"Never," I whisper.

He bends down and gives me an angel kiss on the lips and then leaves the room.

"I have to run out to my garden for the ingredients to make the tea. You'll be all right for a minute until I get back?" I ask Corrine.

She appears perfectly content to flirt with my brother and doesn't acknowledge that I've spoken, but Jared hears me.

"We're cool," he says.

I slide open the back door and then turn back to my brother. Fresh air rushes passed me and the rays of the late afternoon sun warms my skin. "Shouldn't you go see what your friend is doing upstairs?"

"Is that code for leave *your* friend alone?" he says.

"No. But he's probably getting bored upstairs by himself," I say.

"You didn't tell me anyone was here," Jared accuses.

Playing innocent in front of the girl, that's Jared for you. He's all courteous and charming, and not wanting to leave the pretty little thing alone in the kitchen.

"Whatever, Jared. Hey, our car is over by Grandma's land. It's parked on Spruce Court. Do you know it?"

"Sure. I'll try to find a ride over. I need the car later tonight."

"Thanks, Jared," I say with sincerity. My brother is back. At least for right now he seems sane, and not high. I step onto the deck and start to close the door, and then I hear Corrine make an offer.

"I'll call Patrick. I bet he'll bring a car over. My stepdad has a couple of great cars. He lets Patrick drive them whenever he wants. Hey, I know where your car is too. We can ride together."

My eyeballs roll to the heavens. She can't go anywhere, at least until after I dose her with my noxious drink, as Jared so bluntly put it, and not until Nathaniel comes back either.

∞

Nathaniel

Marcus is here. Inside Juliana's house. Being torn apart by conflicting mental arguments is a precarious place to stand, but what choice do I have? Marcus is here, so on one side I don't have to worry about finding him to answer my growing pile of questions. Will I recover, or, am I dying? How do I defeat a demon? These are the first things I need to know. The other darker side is, that Marcus is here, with Jared.

Juliana's brother is the only case I've ever lost. The only good part is he didn't escape into the world of the tormented souls. Instead, he lived — also my doing — and he was taken away from me as my client. The problem was I got involved and saved the life of someone who was about to die, which is not acceptable when you're an Angel of Death. Because I saved him, albeit unknowingly, and fell in love with my client's sister — Marcus doesn't know that part either — I have been reassigned to a whole new set of clients.

I can interfere all I want now, as long as they're suicidal. I can choose to help, or watch her commit suicide, and then escort her to the afterlife. Believe me, if it was easy, then I would be finished with this case. But in my opinion, Corrine doesn't really want to die. How can I not help?

I should have known Marcus would take on my failure. He will stay with Jared and ensure I don't interfere, again. Juliana will never forgive me if I do nothing. Worse, I already feel like I'm failing. I am failing Juliana, the only person to whom it truly matters. Deceit isn't in me, it never has been, but how can I tell her that her only brother is running out of time in this life? How can I not tell her? I should've already and somehow I haven't found the time, or the words. She'll hate me and it will be my own fault.

"Nathaniel," Marcus says, as I step into Jared's dimly lit bedroom. "Do I want to know why my friend looks like he has been chewed up and spit out like bad meat?"

"No. Do I want to know how much time Jared has left?"

"No, man. Don't go there."

"Okay," I say, feeling a new level of exhaustion ripple through me like an aftershock. Sitting down on the chair by the desk is more for appearance than easing my pain, but I do it anyway. I watch my dread-headed friend and hide none of my discomfort from him. "Want the story or not?" I ask.

"The suspense is murderous," he says in his deep baritone, brows rising in anticipation.

∞

Juliana

The bittersweet fumes waft up my nose as I strain the pale infusion into a blue coffee mug. *May the angels and fairies bless these plants and may they do only good and never harm,* I pray silently over the cup in my hand. It's something I've never done before, but it feels appropriate, being as unsure as I am about what's going on with

Corrine's body. I grab my bottle of cramp bark extract from the cabinet to go with the shepherd's purse, raspberry leaves, rose petal, and licorice root infusion and then head back upstairs to my room.

"Still willing to drink this?"

Tears pool in the corners of her eyes. "Anything," she sobs. "It hurts so bad."

As I hand her the cup, my thoughts return to her bizarre behavior. Ten minutes earlier and no one in their right mind would have guessed Corrine was suffering in any way. Jared certainly didn't notice anything wrong with her and now that he's not in the room with her, she's back to whimpering. The urge to protect myself, the way Chris Abeyta was talking about earlier, gnaws at me, but I blow it off with the excuse that I'm just a little uncertain.

Opening the small brown bottle of extract, I squeeze one full dropper of the dark liquid and hold it out to her. "Take this too," I say.

She opens her mouth and I watch the extract disappear. She chases it with some of the potent tea and her face exclaims exactly how unsavory the flavor must be. The delicate muscles of her throat and jaw quiver as she tries not to gag.

"It's strong, but that's a good thing," I say.

"What's it going to do?" she asks.

"Help the bleeding and ease the cramping. I hope."

"You still claim not to be a witch? Your room doesn't look anything like I thought it would. No altar, or pentacles, or anything Wiccan."

Grinding my teeth really doesn't help anything other than keeping my mouth shut when I want to say something rude. "Still not a witch," I grumble through tight lips.

"You did say a spell over my drink though, didn't you?"

"No," I answer immediately.

She widens her large blue eyes at me in disbelief.

"I don't know any spells," I tell her flatly.

She shrugs and takes another drink. The little blessing and calling of the angels and fairies plays in my head like a recording. *It wasn't a spell for crying out loud. It was more like a prayer. And, how did she know?*

"Ooooh," Corrine moans. "It's not working yet."

"I can still take you to the emergency room. Let's go right now."

"No! I can't."

"Do you want to tell me why?"

"No. I'll be fine. I believe in your potion. It'll work," she says, sounding more determined than I feel for a positive outcome. She tips the mug to her lips and drains it to the last drop and then sets the empty cup on the floor.

Curling into a tight little ball on my chair she says, "My stepfather." An uncertain and fearful look passes through her eyes. Then she grimaces, her face contorting for longer than I can stand to watch, but the pain must subside because she continues. "He gives me valium, or dilaudid, but I don't really like taking drugs. They make me feel foggy and sick to my stomach."

"I don't have any drugs," I say, and then pause looking at her. "Should I call someone for you? Where's your mom, Corrine? Can I call her?"

The silence is heavy in the room before she finally answers.

"She liked herbs too, not Travis's pills," Corrine tells me as she stares out the window. She turns sad blue eyes on me. "I don't know. I think she's dead. Or maybe she's still in New Mexico. I haven't seen her in almost a year."

"Why is that?" I ask cautiously. As I watch her, an intense melancholy overtakes me. I shrink away, moving closer to my bed as if a little space between us can protect me from feeling her feelings. *Being empathic isn't exactly a joy ride.*

She doesn't answer. Another spasm grips her and she leans forward. "I have to use your bathroom again," she says with eyes closed.

Corrine's tiny body slips out of the chair. Bent nearly in half, arms wrapped around her middle, she rushes from the room.

Chapter Eight: Victims

Juliana

Alone, for me, doesn't mean lonely. Flopping back against the pillows on my bed, I take a few deep relieving breaths. When will Nathaniel be back? I wonder, and then I stop this train wreck of thoughts in its tracks. I have maybe a few minutes to myself and I will not waste it by dwelling on something out of my control. He said he'll be back as soon as he can. All six feet of him — gorgeous beyond description, thoughtful, intelligent, caring, and he gets me. Is this really happening? I thought relationships like ours only existed in fairy tales. Two deep breaths later and I tell myself, No, Jules. Take this minute for yourself. Nathaniel will be back and then I can focus on him, but for now, I need some time to process.

Rolling over to the side of my bed I grab my notebook and pen from the top of my trunk and then sit up, cross my legs, and hunch over the paper. Journaling always helps me express whatever it is that powers my being. What comes out on the page is a part of me, but it's not a conscious part. Jared and his band like my writing too. They've requested lyrics in the past and I'll surprise myself by looking over my journal and picking out segments I think might work for them.

I stare at the lines on the paper. My mind is unfocused. I have to tune everything out. Corrine in the bathroom. Worrying about Jared finding the car in some other way than I left it. *I didn't even warn him about Travis.* And Nathaniel's injury — which he never specified exactly how it happened. *Darn.* To clear my mind, I close my eyes and picture waves washing away footprints on a sandy beach. When the remnants of other people's existence are erased, I begin to scrawl whatever comes to me.

Truth lives in the depths of a black life.

Whisper licks of fire and flame.

It touches my soul and steals my hope.

Buried alive up to my eyes.

The tide is coming, heavy and high.

Say goodbye till the day you die.

Leave all you know in your shattered bones.

She'll eat you, and then she'll be you.

I slam the notebook closed and brush it off my lap. Embracing darkness is not part of who I am. It never has been. Through all my heartache, my dad dying, my mom working all the time, my brother choosing to do drugs, I've never felt anything evil inside of me until maybe just now. I stare at the cover on the book, now lying innocently on the floor, and shiver with revulsion. *What was that!*

Being alone in my room was, for a minute, a welcome treasure. I wanted to feel its comfortable familiarity, but for the first time, it's not there. Reaching for my purple comforter I pull it up around my shoulders, making a cocoon, and tell myself I'm imagining things again. There's nothing different, or out of place. This is my home. I've slept here since I was a baby and it has always been safe. So why does something feel inexplicably terrifying?

No answer comes. Instead, I hear Corrine call my name. Anxious to leave my room and the cold eeriness crawling over my skin, I hurry to the bathroom door across the hall.

Tapping lightly with the back of my knuckles, I say, "Corrine?"

"Come in," I hear weakly.

Expecting a repeat situation from earlier, I brace myself for more blood and cramps, but instead I open the door to Corrine sitting on the edge of the bathtub holding a razor blade. The tender white skin of her left wrist is exposed.

"I don't understand what's wrong with me," she says, and I see trails of tears running down her now pallid complexion.

"You're just having a hard time right now," I say trying anything that may help. I really don't know enough about her, but I can't let her kill herself in my bathroom.

"If I'm dead, it will stop."

"What do you need to stop, Corrine? Maybe if you tell me then I can help." I take a tentative step forward.

"No one can help," she says, and lowers the blade to her skin.

"Corrine, you called me in here. Some part of you must not want to do this," I reason out loud.

"No, I didn't!" she screams.

"Okay, okay. It's going to be all right. I can help you find your mom, would that help you? I'll do whatever I can, but don't hurt yourself." Corrine's hand is shaking and I'm afraid she'll slice herself open, either by accident, or on purpose, but somehow it's going to happen.

"My mom, she was...and he," she sobs, and her head droops lower, the tears falling fresh. Her hand with the razor lowers to her side. "I don't think you can help me. I don't even know what's wrong."

"I can try," I say, and take another step forward. "Can you try telling me what it is?"

"I want to see my mom so bad, but I can't leave my brother alone with him."

Him, has to be her terrible stepfather. Leaning over, I grab a tissue from the box and hand it to her. She places the blade down and takes it. Mild relief gives me some false security that, at least for now, most of the threat of her cutting herself has passed.

"You can't just walk away from someone who is...a part of you," she sobs into her wadded up tissue.

"I wouldn't leave Jared for anything," I confess with absolute honesty. "But Corrine, is it him, your stepdad? Is that why you're so sad?"

Where is Jared? Surely going to get the car doesn't take that long. Some help right about now would be desperately appreciated.

She shakes her head no. "He's horrible. Travis uses me. He does wicked things for fun, but he won't hurt me. He needs me too much."

"Well, what is it then? I won't tell anyone if you tell me," I promise, not knowing if keeping her secrets will make any difference. Picturing Corrine in my mind, I can see her walking a line as thin as the razor's edge. On one side is sanity and on the other is insanity. She wavers to both sides like a drunken tight rope walker trying to find the balance point. *Falling down can happen to the very best of us. Can't it?*

She goes quiet as she picks up the razor blade, toying with it between two fragile fingers. The bathroom is darkening by the minute as gray light from the one small window above the shower filters into the room. Unbelievably, the day has gone and evening is already here.

"It's her fault," Corrine says in a breathy whisper.

"Who?" I ask, and a chill — which has nothing to do with the end of the day's warm temperature — whispers down my neck and across my bare arms. *Warnings from those who have passed, my Gram's voice says again.* I back up toward the door a couple of inches.

"She likes to do things. Then I can't remember afterwards," Corrine says, and she sounds like herself again. Nasal and choking on misery, but not the previous horrible whisper. "It has to end. I don't know what else to do."

Corrine holds out her wrist.

Her hopelessness weighs down the room like we're being smothered in wet concrete.

"Please. Give me the razor, Corrine."

"You really want to help?" she sneers, as if I don't mean it.

"Yes. Just give it to me. Let me help."

"You don't want to help me! Go away!"

"Put the razor down."

"Leave me alone!"

"No!" I yell back feeling out of control. "Stop this. We'll find you some help."

She doesn't stop. She runs the blade across her wrist and a line of crimson, instant and terrifying, wells up.

Human instinct kicks in and I know she won't die from this cut. I can tell it's not very deep and she went the wrong direction, cutting from side to side rather than down the length of the vein. I grab a towel with one hand and her wrist — the one holding the razor — with my other hand. The blade falls to the floor with a tiny plink and then I wrap the towel around her wound.

The stunned look on her face and the horrible pallor of her skin has me more concerned than the actual bleeding.

I swallow hard trying to put the image of her blood somewhere where I will never ever recall it. "Sweetie, everything's going to be okay," I say, although for myself, I'm unsure. My heart races like that of a hunted rabbit, easily a million beats per second. My nerves are firing like bolts of electricity, causing every cell in my body to shake, but somehow I get Corrine's wrist bandaged and ease her out of the bathroom. "You're all right. Everything is going to be fine," I hear myself saying over and over.

We sit down on the edge of my bed and I keep my arm wrapped tight around her bony shoulders. How long we sit, I'm not sure. My room is totally dark before either of us come out of the stupor. As I feel some sort of life moving through her, my thoughts begin to return to some kind of normalcy. *How can I get her some help? I'm not equipped to handle a suicidal maniac.*

"Jules?"

"Yeah?"

"I need help. I don't want to die," Corrine whimpers into the dark.

"Please live," I say, and give her shoulder a light squeeze. "I'm going to call for help now."

"You can't. Please. I won't try anything again. Just sit here with me."

Then she breaks down, sobbing, and I wait, feeling numb and unsure of who to call or what to do. With some relief, I think she sounds saner. It's odd because I keep thinking she's just a girl in a messed up situation and could use a little therapy. Then she says something that makes me think she needs serious professional help, and locking her away may be a feasible option. At least she's admitting there's a problem. *That's a step, right? Crazy people don't admit they have a problem, do they?*

Corrine's head tips over to rest on the top of my shoulder. When my shoulder is soaked with tears, I feel her shift a little. My back is so tight from not moving that my muscles are beginning to burn. I want to turn the light on, or even better, go to sleep and let this day pass away.

Sounds on the stairs tell me someone is home. There's a click and then yellow light casts a slanted rectangle across my floor. A spark of hope that it may be Nathaniel is extinguished as I hear a door open and then close. Jared's bedroom door. Corrine shifts again.

"I like your brother. He's luscious. Too bad he's *your* brother," she says emphasizing the word "your" like it's forbidden.

I stiffen, more on the inside than physically, because my back and arms couldn't get any more uncomfortable. Something in her tone sounds different again, but it's hard to be certain because she's so stuffed up from all the crying. Call it my sensitive nature, but I suddenly want to get far, far away from Corrine.

Her hands fidget in her lap. I lower my arm from her shoulders and lean slightly away, but Corrine moves with me.

"Do you want to sleep on the blow up mattress tonight?" I ask.

"I don't think I'll be able to sleep tonight."

"Oh?"

"I feel like going out."

"Your stomach's not hurting anymore? You should have some more tea. I think I'll go get it." I start to stand.

"Wait," she says, and places a hand on mine.

I try to slide my hand out from hers and get up, but her grip is unyielding.

"I really have to thank you, for everything," she says in her strange breathy voice, and then she turns to me and wraps her tiny spaghetti arms around me.

Returning the hug, I give her a quick squeeze and then try to pull away, but she doesn't let go.

"I want to get the tea, okay? I think it's helping."

"It is helping. I feel tons better."

Her hand travels to the back of my neck and I pull back harder, but I can't move. Her arms feel like steel bands. How is this little body holding me? It's not possible.

"Corrine. Get off!"

"Almost," she hisses.

Then teeth sink into my shoulder and I scream. My cry is muffled as she slams her wrist over my mouth. I jerk back with all my strength and she falls over me. Throwing my head to the side, I thrash and claw for my freedom, but she's like an angry pitbull, attached to me with vise-like jaws. I can taste her blood in my mouth. It's the wrist she cut. With sickening disgust, I realize she had been taking her bandage off.

Her teeth finally unclamp from my shoulder and her arm is away from my face. Less than a millisecond later, I throw her off with as much force as I can. She bounces across the floor with tiny thumps. She's so petite. How had she been able to pin me?

Grabbing my stinging shoulder, I roll off my bed and onto my feet screaming, "You freaking bit me!"

I run into the bathroom leaving Corrine on the floor mewling pathetically. Slamming the door behind me, my fingers shake as I turn the lock. I catch a glimpse of blood streaked across my cheek and onto my lips in the mirror. Bending down, I rinse my mouth under the faucet, spitting and spitting into the sink. It doesn't begin to satisfy my need to erase the copper taste of her blood and the fear of what may be in her blood. Panic makes my movements clumsy and erratic, but it doesn't stop me from trying to erase the taste and feel of Corrine from my memory. Whipping my head back upright is a terrible mistake as the room begins to swirl and melt around me. Ignoring the swimming images in the mirror and holding onto the countertop with one hand I open the medicine cabinet and grab the bottle of disinfecting mouthwash. I twist open the cap and pour the burning liquid into my mouth again and again and then I swallow some hoping it will continue to work on the inside of my throat. With my mouth on fire and my stomach turning circles with disgust, I whip off my shirt and grab the bottle of rubbing alcohol, the bottle of peroxide, and the bottle of disinfectant, and begin to cleanse the bite wound. There are small smears of blood around the swelling crescent shaped marks. She broke my skin, that evil little minx. Pouring the rubbing alcohol on my wound brings tears to my eyes and I scream as silently as I can as I rub at the marks with a towel. I scrub at my flesh until I am close to passing out. The queasiness in my gut is rising, but I swallow my bile and switch to the peroxide.

"Jules! What's going on?"

I attempt to answer, but a rush of dizziness makes me clamp my mouth shut, afraid vomit will be the only thing that comes out. Setting the peroxide down, I reach for the disinfectant, continuing to cleanse the F-ing bite. The bottle is heavy and I barely manage to open the cap. Then I feel myself sinking to the floor, my eyes close against their will, but I slosh the cool liquid onto the top of my shoulder anyway.

"Jules, open the door."

"J, not feeling—" I can't finish the words, but I manage to open my eyes and look at the lock on the doorknob. It seems impossible to reach that far. Somehow, my arms are no longer connected to my brain, along with my speech, and my reason.

The bathroom spins around me. Black shadows move in and fill the confined space. How odd, I think, as I stare at the light. It's bright, but the darkness is taking over the room.

The door rattles as Jared tries to force it open. It has the peculiar effect of looking like it's falling away from me. How strange, I think, as the door gets smaller and the light in the bathroom gets darker. *No*, some part of me realizes, I am falling, not the door.

Blackness folds around me and a terrible rushing feeling seizes the inside of my skull, as if my brains are being shoved out of the way. It takes complete control, pushing me to the far corner and then penetrates down my spine like tendrils of fog moving in off the water. I collapse fully onto the floor, feeling distant and smaller than a grain of sand.

"Stand back, Jules!"

A shudder of the walls accompanies a crack of the doorframe and then the door rams into my feet.

Jared hovers over me, shaking my leg, and asking half coherent questions. "What the shit, Jules? Do you think this is funny? What's wrong with you?"

"Help me up," I garble, noticing instantly the sound of my voice is different.

He grips my elbow and hand and lifts.

"What happened?" he asks, and the fear in his deep brown eyes is penetrating.

"I think I blacked out," I say, and there's an echo of myself talking. This is quite disturbing, as if I'm talking through a microphone from the far corner of the world.

As soon as I'm on my feet, Jared turns his head, but leaves one hand on my arm for support. With his free hand he reaches for my discarded shirt lying on the edge of the sink.

"Here. Put this on," he says.

I grab it from him and notice part of me is intensely gratified by his discomfort at my partial nudity. I don't put my shirt back on though. I look down at myself and take in my purple cotton bra over high round B cups and my smooth stomach below. Narrow hips and long legs fill in my jeans. My hand finds the curve of my waist and I brush down the length of my side. Part of my brain is telling me I have nice skin, pale as milk, and perfectly soft. Fascinated by my body, I had forgotten about my brother standing awkwardly next to me.

"Get dressed. Are you feeling better now?" he asks as he moves into the hall, keeping his face averted.

"No," I say. "Better than all right. My body is amazing." I'm so much stronger than the frail little girl in my bedroom, and much curvier. Yes, this will do. We will have so much fun. *What? Where did that come from?* Fear tightens the already present knot in the pit of my stomach. I can't explain what is happening.

He moves out of sight but not completely away from the door. "Jules, should I call Mom?"

"Don't. I'm fine." *What is coming out of my mouth?* I want to tell him the freaky girl in my bedroom bit me and I feel strange, but instead I tell him *I'm fine?*

"I don't think so, Jules. You should tell Mom what just happened."

"You're totally right. I'll tell her later. Hey," I slip my shirt on so I can talk to him without the discomfort — even though I like it — and then I follow him into the hall. "Did you say you're going out tonight?"

"Yeah?" Jared answers with a deep questioning look printed in the lines on his forehead.

"I want to go," I say. *I can't believe what is coming out of my mouth.* But even worse is that I can't stop it.

"No, you don't," he says with a huff of contempt.

"Yes, I do."

Just then movement by the stairs catches my attention as my cat Ariel appears on the landing. Her green eyes meet mine for a split second and then she's rushing me with all of her claws extended and a hiss that curls my toes. Before being shredded to bits, I sidestep the cat and give her a swift, booted sweep into the bathroom. As she slides into the tub I slam the door closed. Then I have to work at getting it to latch after Jared's forceful entry. "Why do we even have a cat?" I say with disgust.

The look on Jared's face is one of utter disbelief as he looks first at me and then to the closed door. Hissing and growling emanates from within and a gray paw, claws extended, scratches at the floor.

"You both need medical attention. Sooner than later," Jared says with conviction.

"Never mind that. I'm going with you, and if you don't take me, I'll tell Mom you're shooting up meth."

"Crap, Jules! You wouldn't."

"Try me."

"We're going to The Edge," Jared says as a mild warning because he knows I dislike the crowd there.

"Perfect," I say, and unexplainably it does sound perfect right now.

Chapter Nine: Danger in the Wild

Juliana

"I need to hit up an ATM before we go in. I'm low on cash," Jared says.

"They're not gonna' charge you to get in," I say as I pull into the parking lot of The Edge nightclub. Jared and his band are a local favorite here and cover charges don't apply to him.

"It's not for the door, Jules."

"Whatever, shithead," I say, not really caring anyway.

Something like a knee bumps the back of my seat, not once but three annoying times in a row. Turning, I see Patrick, Corrine's brother, staring out the window, his hood pulled up over a mop of shaggy brown hair. He shifts again and I feel a strand of hair pull out of my head.

"Will you stop squirming around back there, asshole?" I bitch over my shoulder at him.

"What?" he says, matching my snotty tone.

I glare at him and then turn my attention back to parking the car.

Jared and I followed Patrick to his house to drop off his car, a BMW. They used it to retrieve my Saab. In Patrick and Corrine's driveway I recognized Travis's silver BMW and felt mixed emotions. Confusion already reigning over my night, I didn't dwell on either the fear of Travis inside the house, or the déjà vu that I had been there before. Then Patrick jumped in with us for the fifty minute drive to the club. My need to get out tonight and find a more stimulating environment is the only thing that seemed to matter. I did register Patrick calmly saying his dad wanted Corrine to come home as soon as she was done screwing around, but the message filtered into one ear and lodged itself into a place that held very little importance.

"Hey, I know him," I say, as I recognize Chris Abeyta walking into the front entrance of the club.

"Hmmph," Patrick snorts from the back seat, clearly unimpressed.

I ignore his uncaring — who-gives-a-crap — grunt and open my door excited to go inside. Normally I would arrive at the clubs with Jared and his band. We would enter from the back, set up the equipment, and I would hang around listening and watching from the shadows until the band finished and Jared was done flirting with all of his groupies. I've never had the urge to mingle with drunks and swim through the sea of testosterone and pheromones. Tonight, ripples of eagerness course through me at the thought of dancing with some cute guy. The thought is instantly followed with disgust. I hate when slimy men hit on me. *So why does it sound so intoxicating now?*

Patrick climbs out and I hear the thump of the car door closing. He shuffles up next to us, still hiding in his oversized sweatshirt and stares down at his shoes as we wait for Jared to finish his transaction at the cash machine.

"Why are we dragging this baggage around with us?" I ask, and tip my head at Patrick.

"Nice, Jules. What's up with you?" Jared asks. "You're sort of a rag tonight."

Another snort escapes from the hooded Patrick and then Jared continues. "He's cool, so lay off."

"So when you say cool, you mean he's hooking you up with drugs," I say back.

"Keep it up, Sis," he warns, and gives me a dirtier than the floor inside The Edge stare.

"I know how you operate these days. See you losers inside." My heeled boots tap sharply against the sidewalk as I leave them standing under the neon lights.

Raging drumbeats assault my eardrums as I enter the dark club. The crowd is more interested in drinking than listening to the band play, based on the number of people milling around by the bar rather than by the stage. As the song pounds on I can understand the need to medicate with liquor. It's atrocious at best. I sincerely hope there will be a huge improvement with the next band, or I may have to shoot myself.

Looking around the drab nightclub for anything of interest I catch a dark haired cutie checking out my long legs and short skirt. I know I should run in the opposite direction — this would be my usual M.O. — but instead I throw him a demure smile and find myself walking over to him and his friends.

"Nice boots," he yells over the music as he stares at my twenty eyelet boots with buckles and heels.

When I originally bought them, the heels had looked cool. It had become an obvious mistake after wearing them only once, and they have sat on my closet floor ever since. Now they were perfect with my one and only short skirt and a black tank top.

"Nice tattoo," I say back, and let my finger brush over the partially exposed tattoo on the side of his neck. "What is it?" I ask, as I tug his collar open to see more skin.

He likes me. I can feel the heat in him building. His blood moves to places unseen and very warm. My excitement blooms knowing how easy it is to reel him in. His eyes travel up the length of me until he looks me in the eyes.

"What's your name, gorgeous?"

"Jules." I don't care what his name is as long as he keeps feeding me. *What! Jules, walk away before you regret this.* I hear myself telling me to leave, but I don't. Panic seizes a portion of my insides like a deer in the headlights. I should scream or cry out, *"What is happening to me!"* but instead I keep talking like everything in the world is a perfect fuzzy peach. "Is it a snake?" I ask, and lean in closer to the guy.

"It's a snake if you want it to be." His dark eyes travel down to my chest for a second and then back up.

I want to be repelled by him, but instead I'm turned on. His aftershave is tart and it tingles inside my nose. It's yet another previous turnoff that now has me curious for more.

"Here alone?" I ask, as a short haired guy with eyes magnified by the farsighted lenses of his glasses watches me.

"Dave? You gonna introduce me or what?" the one wearing glasses asks as he checks out my tiny outfit.

He's not as cute as Dave, but he is nonetheless showing interest in me, so I turn to him and smile. "It's Jules. You guys like doing the group thing?" I ask. Let them assume what they want about it.

The one with glasses smirks and I can imagine all too well the images floating through his baseball shaped head.

He leans in close and asks, "It depends on what you're talking about."

Tipping my head up at an angle so my words are aimed toward his ear I say, "I like you and your friend. We should all get to know each other better in the back."

I lower my eyes, feigning coyness, but in actuality I'm absorbing the energy of this horn-ball's rising heartbeat and he doesn't even know it. I sneak a peek at Dave and then the two of them, with sparkles in their eyes, practically trip over each other as they simultaneously offer to buy me a drink.

With devilish delight I accept. "I'm up for just about anything."

A shot of something dark with a dab of whip cream floating on the top appears a few minutes later.

"It's called a blow job," Dave's friend tells me.

"Yummy," I say, after I down the creamy coffee flavored alcohol. "Is that what the two of you like?" I tease.

Dave swallows hard and it thrills me that I have rendered him speechless. He holds up a beer in front of me. I take it from him and let my tongue lick at the rim of the bottle where a little head of foam is peeking over the edge.

"I said, did you guys take shots too?" I have to yell over the insulting music. If I get them excited too quickly it may not fulfill my needs. *What! What needs?*

Two heads nod in unison as they hold up their beers in a mini salute.

"Great. Let's go to the back. This band is terrible."

I grab Dave's free hand and pull him through the crowd toward the back of the club where there's a smaller more private room.

"Juliana!"

Leaning in close to Dave, I try to ignore whoever is calling me. I let my breasts press up against Dave's arm as we squeeze through the crowd by the bar. The feel of his muscular upper arm is doing something incredible to me which I can't explain. My body gets a rush from the contact and I need more. *What is happening! Get away from these two. Do it now.* But I can't leave them. I physically can't make myself walk away. *This is crazy.*

"Juliana."

Someone steps in front of me, blocking my way.

Chris Abeyta stares at me stony faced. "Interesting. Running into you here."

"I come here. You don't," I say.

"Family obligations carry their own weight."

"Yeah? What family?" I ask. Chris looks amazing, different than I've ever noticed before. There's a power around him which has me fixed. It's not his size, he's average in the height department, but the air around him is brewing with a dense and magnificent energy. It's sucking me in and I'll gladly go.

Dave sticks his chest out an inch and says, "Excuse us, Bro. We're in the middle of something."

Chris looks over at Dave and his overeager friend and then back at me without replying. He continues where he left off. "My cousin Philip is in the band. He wanted some moral support."

"Very nice of you," I say, and let go of Dave's hand. "I don't want to insult your family but they're horrendous, all but the drummer. Which one is your cousin?"

Chris's gives the slightest nod, eyes softening almost imperceptibly. A silent laugh ripples through him, crosses the few inches between us, and penetrates me with his inner strength. My breath catches for a mere second, but it's enough. I must have him.

"You didn't insult him. Philip is the drummer."

Dave and his friend lean in to talk amongst themselves and some decision seems to pass between them. "Hey, gorgeous," Dave starts.

Before he can fully interrupt, I tell them both, "I'll meet you two in the back. Can you give me a second? This is a good friend of mine." A peck on the cheek as an incentive, and a few flutters of my lashes, and the two boys move off toward the curtain sectioning off the back room. They looked like they were pouting, but they left, and now I have a new toy. *Goody.*

I take a long swill of my beer, my eyes never leaving Chris. I'll take one of him over ten of Dave and his friend anytime. "Don't you want a beer or something? It could help lighten your mood."

"I'm in a great mood," Chris says straight faced. He ignores my suggestion for a beer and asks, "Where's your other friend?"

"Oh you're downright jubilant, aren't you?" I smile at my own joke. Then I lick my lips looking at Chris's mouth. Soft lips, not too big or too small, and no noticeable four o'clock shadow.

"Did you lose The Shadow for good?"

He wants to know about Nathaniel. A stabbing sensation somewhere in the vicinity of my heart makes me wince at the thought of my Nathan. I desperately want to tell him he will be back very soon and everything will be fine, but my voice is overridden as I hear someone who sounds like me but isn't me say, "Gone forever." The ache hardens, but I'm unable to do or say anything about it.

Reaching one hand forward, my fingers run along the edge of Chris's vest. "Why do you always wear a vest?" I ask, as my fingers brush his undershirt. I can feel his smooth chest underneath.

He watches me with stern eyes that match the hard line of his mouth. Chris has the ability to keep his feelings buried deep, but I can feel faint ripples of pleasure moving through him with my touch.

"Will you come over here with me?" he asks, and starts to walk toward a less crowded area by the wall.

More privacy is exactly what I want. The powerful Native moves with the stealth of a jaguar. Anticipation for what's to come excites me in places I didn't know existed. I chug the last of my beer and set the empty bottle on a table then move to follow my prey.

"Has anyone ever told you how impressive you are?" I say and take his hand in mine. The same compressed energy I see around him flows out of his hand and gives me a rush. I bring our hands up by my face and give the tip of one finger a taste.

His eyebrows rise, but still no smile. "Jules, what have you been doing since I last saw you?" he asks, while I play with his hand.

I move in closer to his body and let the back of his hand rub the front of my skirt. My other hand is under his vest. "You didn't answer me about your vest obsession."

"I will tell you why I wear a vest if you tell me what you did today."

"Playing hard to get, hmmm?"

"Not likely, Juliana."

I feel him pull away slightly, the frown on his face hardening. I decide to change tactics. "You dropped your bottle of spring water. I saved it for you. It's in my car. Would you like to go outside and get it?"

Chris nods and then leads me to the exit, letting my fingers stay entwined with his. We leave the barrage of noise and step into the relative stillness of the dark parking lot.

"You're always so serious. I could help lighten your mood." I say as I walk him over to my car.

"I think I can help you out as well," he says.

"I know exactly what you can do for me," I say, letting every insinuation flow out of me with my words. Stopping next to my car, I turn around to face him. I lean forward wanting his mouth on mine worse than I've ever wanted anything. He leans in and I can see the smoldering fire in his black eyes. Our mouths are about to touch when he turns his head. I kiss his neck and then wrap my mouth over his pulse and suck. Salt and heat penetrate my being as I get a small teasing taste of him. He steps back forcing a clear boundary between us.

How can he stand there so calm and silent? My heart races with the thrill of being so close to my goal. "Do you still want your bottle?"

"Yes."

"Will you get in the car with me?" I ask, and step closer to him again. "I need you," I whisper into his ear. "Right now."

"Why don't you follow me to my house?" he suggests.

"No. Here is good." *If we hurry then I can go find Dave and his friend, I think, and my night will be even better. Noooo! I don't want this! You do. Admit it.*

"No, this is not the right place," he says.

"You're not a prude, are you? It'll be fun, I promise." I stroke the front of him as a token of what I'm offering.

"Come with me to my house," he tries again. "There is already someone inside your car."

"What!" I spin around ready to burst into flames because my plans are being interrupted.

The windows are slightly foggy but I can make out Jared and two others.

"Juliana, come with me now," Chris says in an almost demanding tone.

His hand squeezes mine harder and now all the previous heat pulsing through me drains away to be replaced by repulsion. Fear grips me with multiple conflictions. I want to go with him desperately, and yet I want to murder him with my bare hands, which makes me even more afraid.

"It's all right, Jules. Come with me now," he says straight into my eyes and the penetrating force coming out of him is like looking down the barrel of a shotgun, commanding and terrifying. Suddenly, I feel like I have to follow him, even as I want to run away. *Help me,* is what I want to say, but the words won't come out.

The car door opens and Jared steps out in a cloud of smoke and skunky smelling steam.

"What's up, Jules? Friend of yours?"

"No," I manage to say.

"Your sister isn't feeling well. I'm sure you've noticed," Chris says, as he relinquishes my hand.

"Yeah, man. I have noticed," Jared agrees. "Hey, do I know you?"

Backing up, I feel rigid like the freezing gears of a seizing motor, both mentally and physically, but I manage to open the car door and slip inside, landing on someone's lap.

Patrick complains with a few expletives as he wiggles out from under me. I raise my arm protectively as one of his boots narrowly misses my face as he slips between the two front seats and into the back.

A moment later, Jared folds himself onto the other front seat and closes the door. Staring at the floorboards is all I can do to hold it together. Uncertainty and rage boil through my bloodstream but overlying everything else is fear. It's the fear that has me frozen. Part of me, the real me — Juliana Katherine Crowson — is fighting and losing, and I am terrified. One second I feel like myself and the next I'm saying or doing something that isn't like me at all. Jared's searing gaze bores a hole in the side of my head, but I can't explain to him coherently what's happening to me. If I do nothing, then at least I'm not harming anyone, including myself.

"It's a private party," he tells me.

The two others in the back seat are quiet as gravestones as they wait to see what happens next.

Having no control over one's body and only minimal control over one's mind is literally a petrifying experience, and exhausting. I want to sit here and never speak or move again, but I know that's not going to happen. Whatever is wrong with me wins this inner battle again as I hear my answer to Jared. "I'm ready for a party. The club sucks tonight."

"Too bad, Jules. Get out."

"Too bad, Jared, I'm staying. Seriously, I need something to take the edge off. Chris is intense."

"Chris says to—"

"I don't care what the crazy bastard has to say," I interrupt before Jared can finish.

"He took off, but he wants—"

I stop Jared mid-sentence, turning to the guys in the back seat. "Help a girl out and let me take of hit off your pipe. I know one of you is holding."

Two sets of uncertain eyes look to Jared. I give Jared the most 'I dare you to object' look I can in the darkened car, and he responds by gripping his good hand around the steering wheel.

"What do you think you're doing?" he threatens through clenched teeth.

"Do you think you're the only one who's allowed to party and have a good time? Shit Jared, just relax."

Reaching my open hand into the back seat I wait for one of the numbskulls to give in. It takes about a second for a small pipe and a lighter to appear.

"Thanks." I flash them my brightest smile and then turn to Jared in triumph.

"For Christ's sake, Jules, at least bend down so you don't get us busted," he says.

"No problem."

"You're gonna hate yourself," he warns.

"Thanks for the concern," I say, sarcasm dripping, and bend down low in my seat so the flick of the flame is below the level of the dashboard.

Pungent acidic smoke burns a path down my windpipe and into my lungs. I hold in the hit as long as I can, letting the drug absorb into my bloodstream. The used smoke rushes out of me in a long grayish-green gush. I take another long drag off of the pipe, already feeling the effects begin to mix with my buzz from the two drinks I had inside.

"Incredible, Jules," Jared spits out. "Don't bogart the bowl."

"Let me have one more and then I'll leave you alone. To your private party," I say testing his patience.

"Pass it over."

I do and wait for one more turn, enjoying the rip roaring rush which has taken over my senses.

"Your sister is wild. Does she even know what she's smoking?" Patrick says from the back seat.

"It's doing a fucking good job. That's all I need to know," I say, noticing my tongue feels too large for my mouth.

"When did you start cussing?" Jared mumbles.

"Shut up. I'm going back inside. Thanks, J."

How I made it back into the club is beyond my comprehension. I think I flew, but I really don't remember.

Dave and his friend are foremost on my mind, but The Edge is teeming with fresh young bodies all tempting me to come and play. A different band has replaced the previous dead meat on stage. My ears perk up. The bass drum pounds inside my bones and draws me to the dance floor like a bee to nectar. I start to move to the beat and then let the melodies guide me.

Tricky half-licks and the upbeat tempo have me rolling and jumping with the crowd. Some beefcake moves up next to me and I press myself into him, feeling the length of his body against mine.

We begin to move together to the music and I slowly inch us over to the closest wall, wanting to get a more private feel of him.

"Hi. You like the band?" he asks.

Brawn and brain together are a rare combination, one not to be found here, but I don't care, he's male and virile. "Yeah, terrific," I yell back at him.

"You're cute," he says.

"You too," I say, as I let my hand slide down his back and onto his tight round ass.

"Hey, there you are," someone yells close by me.

I ignore it, and lean up to my new friend, sticking my tongue in his mouth. He kisses me back, a sloppy, wet, beer-tasting kind of kiss.

Pulling back, I want to wipe my mouth, but refrain from doing so as the muscle bound goof smiles down at me.

"We've been looking for you," the same voice says.

I feel fingertips on the top of my shoulder. Looking back, annoyed, I find Dave and his friend staring at me.

"Dave! Hey, there's no need to glare. I've missed you too."

Spinning on a heel I throw an arm around him and pull him in close to my overheated body. "God, you're cute," I say and kiss him too.

I feel his surge of territorial instinct kick into overdrive as he returns my gesture, more to make a point to the new guy than because he wants to kiss me on the edge of the dance floor. Dave is so much better at it than Mr. Beefcake behind me, firm and soft, and sucking slightly at my tongue. I groan into his mouth. When the kiss ends I'm mildly disappointed.

Big brawny guy looks as if he might throw a punch so I try to make everyone happy. "There's no need to pout, boys," I say and climb onto the nearest tabletop and begin to dance for all three of them and the couple of guys whose table I confiscated.

My skirt is short and my top is tiny and I'm fully aware of the attention being flung my direction. I'm eating up their desire, and I can feel my energy growing by the second. Trying my best to make my private show as interesting as possible, I swoop down close to the table and swirl my hips as I ascend. My hands move over my body, feeling my curves. When I'm satisfied I have every male's full attention, I let myself get lost in the excitement, the blur of faces, and the pounding rhythms.

It shouldn't have been a surprise when I'm completely caught off guard as someone grabs me around the middle and pulls me down from the table.

"It's time to go," he shouts.

"Jared! Put me down," I shriek, and then buck at him like a wild rabbit in a snare. For all of my struggling, he won't let go of my waist. Jared towers over me, and most everyone else, but I keep up my fight anyway. There's a slight pause as my boot contacts his shinbone, but he doesn't relinquish.

Four or five guys circle to my defense, but Jared manages to keep them at bay as he drags me to the door. I see the bouncer nod agreeably to my brother and I know my fight is over. *Damn him.*

"You're out of control and we're going home," he says, as he carries me to the car.

"How dare you! I was having a good time."

"Yeah, you're having a great time ruining my night!"

"Screw you, Jared. I wasn't doing anything to you."

Jared pops open the car door and drops me unceremoniously onto the seat. "I'm not sorry for keeping you out of trouble, so shut your trap, Jules."

"I'll find my own ride home!" I say, and try to open the door, but he has it locked.

Jared reaches over and grabs my arm. "You're coming home. And yes, I can make you."

"Damn you, Jared Crowson. You're going to Hell for this."

He rolls his eyes and shakes his head as he starts the car and pulls out of the lot, heading for the highway. We have about an hour drive back to our house. *Oh goody.* Pouting in the front seat isn't helping me solve my problems, but an answer miraculously lands almost in my lap.

Jared's friend, someone I don't know, leans forward from the back seat and is messing with the stereo knobs. Having been consumed with my own pity, I didn't even notice Patrick and the other guy are still with us. I climb between the two front seats and squeeze myself between them. Patrick takes one look at me and decides to switch places, almost kicking me in the stomach this time as he tries to get up front. I'm not overly insulted. Patrick repels me anyway — which I can't explain because he's cute as a button although a little grungy — but for some reason I know I have to stay away from him. Besides, the other guy with me in the back seat is much more my style.

"Hi there," I say, as I slip my hand over the top of his thigh. "Still have the pipe on you?"

Chapter Ten: Invisible

Nathaniel

5:50 p.m. To my complete and total relief Juliana is sound asleep in her bed. In the other rooms in the house I find Jared — thankfully still alive — taking a shower in the bathroom. Patrick, Corrine's brother, is also here. He's in Jared's bedroom with Marcus, my mentor. As for Corrine, my suicidal client, she's curled up on the couch watching television and looks frazzled, but not any worse than when I last saw her — except for a bandage on her wrist. Juliana can fill me in on that small detail later. The important thing is everyone is here and breathing.

I prayed they would stay safe inside the house until I could get back. It's the reassurance I needed to keep me connected to this world. I would have died — again — if anything had happened to them while I was healing. I did recover some. The rest period I was forced to take helped heal the damages from the demon attack. The wound on my side is raw, but the open tears are sealed and the searing pain is mostly gone.

Questions circle my mind like cars racing around a track. This is the one consistent activity in my life since I met Juliana. Questioning everything, and worrying I'll lose her, even before I had her. Longing to speak to Juliana and ask her why she's asleep in the early evening almost makes me go mad with the need to wake her up, but I have to wait. She'll wake on her own and I'll be right there when she does. The rounded mound of her body under the bedspread rises and falls with each breath. There's nothing I wouldn't give to lay beside her and feel her breathing peacefully next to me. That will also have to wait too, I tell myself. I don't want Marcus to know the extent of our feelings for each other. At least not yet.

A surge of exhilaration, contentment, and a happiness I've never known rushes through me as I remember the entire night and the day we spent together. Juliana knows what I am and she didn't ask me to leave her alone. It's difficult to believe she wants to be with me as badly as I want her, but she says she does. I'll take any time she will allow me to be with her, a second, a minute; eternity wouldn't be enough.

Before temptation or selfishness get the better of me and I wake her, I leave Juliana to rest in her bed and move across the hall to Jared's room.

Marcus looks me up and down as I enter. Heavy drapes are closed to the evening sun, casting the room in a navy blue hue. Patrick sits on the floor between the bed and the stereo reading a magazine and listening to music. The track playing is edgy and full of drums and guitars. My mentor appears fixed between keeping an eye on me and peering outside through a crack in the curtain panels.

"You look much improved," he says.

"You could say that," I agree. "How're things around here?"

"Funny you should ask," he says and then looks away, watching out of the window again.

"I take that as in not the ha ha sort of funny." *Does he not want to tell me something? What's going on?*

"Jared's sister, she's unique. Isn't she?"

"What happened?" I ask, jumping ahead but trying to sound as casual as possible.

He will not approve of our relationship and he has the power to change everything for me. He already has — in some ways. It is the reason I ended up with Corrine as my client instead of Jared.

"Have you seen Corrine?"

"Yes. She's downstairs. I saw the bandage on her arm. Were you here?"

"Sorry, man. I didn't see it. I saw her after it happened. I think she slept while we were out last night." He glances between me and the window again, making me wonder what has his attention.

"You and Jared, you mean?" I ask.

"Yeah, man. We all went out. Jared, Jules, and Patrick. We picked up another kid, but he left a while ago. Your Corrine stayed here."

Digesting what he just shared with me feels like I swallowed a pile of rocks. Juliana went out with her brother last night after I left. "Corrine stayed here. The rest of you went out," I say numbly.

"She has a way of knowing things, doesn't she?"

"Corrine has a difficult home life. Her stepfather is a warlock, and apparently wields demons for fun. He uses her for selfish personal gains, but I haven't learned enough," I say, like an automaton as I attempt to digest the boulders Marcus has just fed me.

"Not Corrine, the sister, Jules. She's a troublemaker when it comes to confusing the fates."

"What?" I ask. *Confuses the fates? Knows things?*

"Didn't you say she can see the likes of us?"

"Yes."

"Well isn't that interestin'?"

"What, Marcus? What happened last night?"

"Jules had quite the late evenin', but the strange part is, when it comes to her brother, she seems to know how to prolong the boy's life."

"What are you talking about? Didn't she see you? Did she talk to you?" I force my voice to stay calm. I'd like to scream at the top of my lungs so the entire neighborhood can hear, but I can't lose it right now.

"I thought I was going to have quite the mess to deal with last night. Car accident. You know how those go. And four teenagers and all, but somehow she got Jared to pull over just in time. I don't even think she meant to do it. Funny. Is that what I said earlier? Yeah man, it was funny how it all played out. And now I'm still hangin' around."

"How? What was happening that she made her brother pull the car over?"

"These kids and their drugs. It's something I'll never get used to seein', the way they pollute themselves. Why can't they understand life is the ultimate high and drugs are the poison?"

He shakes his head in disbelief as he remembers.

"Drugs?" I ask. He has to be talking about Jared. Juliana doesn't do drugs. But if Jared was driving and there were drugs in the car...?

"I'll say one thing for sure. I'm glad I was already dead to be along for that car ride."

"Marcus."

He gives me a look at the tone of my voice and then continues with his story. "Sorry man, I forget Jared was your case first. Funny that we're workin' together again. Our circles run small. It happens for the two of us more than anyone else, don't it?" he muses.

Closing my eyes to try to find patience in the void of blackness behind my lids only helps while they remain closed. "Yeah, funny," I say flatly. "Please Marcus, what happened last night?"

Is Juliana all right? Is she sleeping off some terrible injury? God! How do I make someone speed up the conversation when they have all the time in the world?

"They were getting high while driving back from the city. This is after they had been partyin' till late last night. Jules and Jared were bangin' heads about what was goin' on in the back seat. And you know, words were exchanged. Jules and this other kid wanted to be dropped off somewhere in town, but Jared was refusin'. Jared was hot with his sister. I mean smokin' around the collar. She yanked the wheel and he slammed on the brakes. Swervin' onto the side of the road. He missed colliding with an enormous bull elk. Man, the timing was absolutely unreal. It's good that your Corrine stayed here. She's a frail little thing. Don't think she would've handled it so well."

"They were getting high? In the car, and arguing? And they almost crashed?" I try to clarify what I just heard, but none of it makes sense.

"If fight is equivalent to two atom bombs explodin', then yeah. If my sister was actin' in such a way I would've been mighty upset too."

"Acting how? If you were with them, why didn't she see you?" I ask, trying to put it all together.

"Not sure, but she was…"

Marcus's eyes roll up as if he is trying to see the words forming inside his brain before they come out of his mouth. Two large fingers drum on the point of his chin as he tries to find the best adjective.

If Marcus could see the pressure building inside me right now, he would move this along a little faster.

Movement behind me distracts my focus as Jared leans against the doorjamb of his room and interrupts our conversation. His hair is still wet from the shower and pulled back into his customary short tail.

"Hey Patrick, you ready?"

Patrick hits the stop button for the music and climbs to his feet. "Let's roll," he says as he shrugs his shoulders and then adjusts his baggy clothes.

"We're rollin'," Marcus says. "Ride's here. I'm glad you're back, man." He leaves his place by the window and follows Jared and Patrick.

"Wait," I say. *What about Jules? What in the world was going on last night?* I have to find out, but my anxiety is too close to the surface and I don't want my mentor to see it. Marcus turns his melon sized head to me with questioning eyes.

"You know how it is. Stay close to the client. Catch up with you another time."

"Yeah," I say.

Watching the three of them leave reminds me I may never see Jared walk this earth alive again. His time is close. Marcus said Jules saved him from a car accident last night. How many more close calls can he have?

She'll never forgive me for this. For not telling her Jared was my last case, that I know he'll pass soon, and for not being able to do anything about it. My silence shames me. It's like a bone deep bruise. Eventually it will rise to the surface and show itself, but the damage is already done. *How will I be able to face her? I have to tell her. There's no more stalling on this subject. It will only be worse the longer I put it off.*

Checking to make sure Corrine is still on the couch, and without any sharp or dangerous objects nearby, I see her nestled into the cushions and staring glassy eyed at a rerun of some sitcom. Juliana Crowson is foremost on my mind, so I quickly return upstairs. I hesitate by her door, not wanting to wake her, but wanting to be there when she awakes. I decide to peek inside like I did earlier.

Strange does not begin to describe what it's like to have to remember she can see me when I'm not in the physical. After I died, it took years to remember that people couldn't see me and to let go of common human courtesies because they're irrelevant to an invisible angel. With Jules, I'm relearning to pay attention again. I can't watch her unseen like with everyone else. Well almost everyone else, I correct. Her odd medicine man friend, Chris, he also sees me. Unlike Jules, he doesn't like what he sees, making the situation altogether different.

I'm hesitating, I realize. Her brother is the most important person in her life. Is it fair to tell someone in advance that their closest relative will no longer be a part of their life? Of all the countless loved ones I've assisted over the last twenty some odd years, who of them would have wanted to know when their mother, or father, or husband, or wife, or sons and daughters, was going to leave them forever? Who would really want that burden? Knowing exactly when time was going to run out? No, there's no simple answer to death, or time. Like the individuality of every soul that has ever crossed my path, there isn't only one answer to satisfy them all. My truth is there can't be any secrets between Juliana and me if this is going to last.

She's sleeping when I peer through the door. I go over and sit on the edge of the bed and wait. Gravity doesn't have a pull on me so she shouldn't feel me sitting next to her. She shouldn't, but then again, she shouldn't even see me, and yet she does. I run over and over all the ways I might tell her about Jared and none of them make me feel any better about what I have to say.

Her face is turned toward me, and framed with her dark hair. I catch myself staring at her pale skin, so satin smooth. There are faint lines of old scratches across her forehead. My eyes wander to her lips. They always do. They're exquisite. If I have ever had to describe anything with that word, her mouth is it. Lush and perfect, and God, the way they feel is indescribable.

"No one has ever had this effect on me before," I whisper to her.

I came to her in her sleep before, and she said she remembered our conversations with full clarity. Could I tell her something as important as this in her sleep? Would that be the route of a coward?

"I came back to you," I start over.

She rolls over onto her stomach hiding her face under waves of hair.

"Do you want me to leave? I've asked you the same question so many times, but it's difficult for me to accept I have someone as perfect as you in my world."

I see her chest rise and fall in a deep breath like she so often does when she's processing something important. It encourages me to keep whispering to her.

"The first time I was in this room," I say, thinking about the moment when I made the worst, and best, mistake of my afterlife. It was from the first glimpse that I couldn't stop thinking about her; when I was supposed to be doing what Marcus is doing now. This may be the only way I can explain what is coming for Jared. To start at the beginning. "I only saw you," I say.

"Jared was in here, playing his guitar, and I thought maybe you knew I was here, but I wasn't certain. You didn't see me the way you see me now. Something changed for you at Castle Hill. I hope you don't regret it, because you see me Juliana. The real me."

"I want you to know that whatever happens in your future, I want to be a part of it. But you must promise to tell me when you've had enough? I love you enough to walk away if I'm bringing you despair."

She stirs after I say this, rolling again, this time onto her side. I wonder if I've gone too far and awakened her. One of her hands brushes the hair out of her face and then settles half curled under her chin. Her eyelids flicker and I can see the orbs shifting under the thin skin. She frowns and then her eyes squint up tight. Her head begins to shake slightly against her pillow as if she's struggling with a bad dream.

Concern that I'm the cause of her distress makes me shift closer to her.

"I'm sorry. I'm an idiot," I whisper.

Her head shakes no and a whimper escapes from her throat.

"I'll leave. Sleep, love."

I start to stand. I can wait downstairs with Corrine. She jerks to a sitting position, with her gaze cast down.

"No," she calls out, but doesn't look up.

"I didn't mean to wake you. Forgive me."

She looks down farther hiding completely beneath her hair.

"Was it a bad dream?" I ask.

She still doesn't answer as she turns away and faces the wall by the bed.

"I'll see you downstairs whenever you're ready."

This appears to upset her further and she begins shaking her head again. She raises her hands and she presses her palms against her temples.

Worry and fear grip me like a monster. "What's wrong?" I form my physical body and reach out to her.

"Juliana, what is it? Please say something."

Then as if nothing were wrong at all, she drops her hands to the bedspread and throws it back, exposing her body. She's wearing a blue tank top and I get a glimpse of the white flesh around her hips and a flash of black under-things.

Stepping back from sheer surprise at her change of reaction, and a need to give her some privacy, I turn my head, staring down at the floor. We're new at this, but she has always had a sense of modesty, which is rather cute and innocent. I like that about her. God knows I want to see her in nothing but a thin clinging T-shirt, but out of respect I look away.

"I'll wait downstairs," I say.

I hear her slide out of bed, on the far side next to the wall, and then the soft padding of her bare feet. No reply.

By the door I hesitate, "Juliana? Do you need anything?"

Then, as if I'm drowning inside a sinking ship, there's intense pressure on me from all sides. Drowning in the Arctic Ocean with nothing but ice over my head would be heaven compared to what I think is happening right now.

She doesn't answer. I hear her take a deep breath, heavy on the exhale. I sneak a look at her. Her back is to me as she stands by the window. Straight black hair nearly to the curve of her backside and those long legs are even better than I had imagined.

She turns to look at me over her shoulder. I'm caught, but God, it's worth it. Creamy flesh, long and slender, and curving in all the right places. Only it's not worth it. She stares through me. Her eyes pass over the doorway where I stand and then move onto something else. She sees me not. Death inside death. Who knew? It's over. The gift of having time together is gone. Just like that.

No!

I will not accept this. In as little as a few hours apart, she no longer sees me. *What in God's name happened last night!*

"Juliana, I'm right here. I promised I'd return. What's going on, love?" I take a desperate step forward.

Her shoulder twitches once as if shaking off a pestering fly, but she shows no other response to my desperation.

Walking across the room makes no difference, and as I step in close enough to touch her, she sidesteps away from me and moves to stand in front of the closet. No other expression on her face could be worse than one of no acknowledgment at all. I could take anger, or tears, or her telling me to go straight through the nine circles of Hell with a one way pass, but to be completely ignored is worse than I could ever have imagined.

Her hands move over the clothes hanging in front of her, searching for something to wear, while completely unaware to the fact I'm standing right behind her. I close my eyes and try not to wither.

I can never give up. I have to know what happened to change her. Can someone lose the ability to see angelic beings overnight? What could cause such a thing to happen? Is she sick? Marcus said she was doing drugs last night. This information directly from Marcus is the only way I would believe it. Jules hates drugs, and she hates that her brother does them. *Juliana was doing drugs last night. Is this a side effect?* Has her mind been altered by the toxic effects of the drugs? *AHHHHHH!* I scream inside, and then I slam my hand onto my forehead. How can this be happening?

I relinquish my body. She can't see me. I must conserve my energy.

"We'll figure this out," I tell her. She doesn't turn to look at me. It causes another wrench in my chest, as if clamps have just been tightened around my heart.

Juliana takes a black shirt from a hanger and then pulls a pair of shorts out of the dresser drawer. I place my back to the wall and turn my head respectfully as she dresses.

Marcus may have more to tell me when he returns. And there's Corrine as well. She's been here since I left. It may be time to introduce myself to my client.

Juliana walks past me and out the door. She was three inches from me, and not a flicker of recognition. I've become invisible to the one person who matters. A hole the size of the moon takes the place of where meaning and happiness lived inside me only moments before. *No,* I shake my head in denial. *We will figure this out.*

Chapter Eleven: Faces of Fear

Nathaniel

Downstairs I watch as Juliana makes nice with Corrine. It's awkward and unsettling between them, but I can't explain exactly what it is. Let's just say, Corrine looks like a mouse trapped in a corner facing a pair of green cat eyes, Juliana's eyes.

"Did you get enough rest last night, sweetie?" she asks. "Eat anything?"

"Yeah, I ate. Jared said to help myself. I hope it's okay," Corrine says.

She's tucked into a small ball on the couch and watches as Juliana slips on some shoes by the front door.

"You should come with me to do an errand. It won't take long. I'm sure you're ready to get out of here for a little while, aren't you?"

Juliana squats down to tie the laces on her tennis shoes. Her eyes flick up to watch Corrine as she waits for an answer.

"I'm still not feeling too great. You know the bleeding from yesterday. It's better but not gone. Can I wait here for you?"

"The fresh air will be good for you. Come with me. All you have to do is sit in the car anyway. Not a big deal," Jules says. She stands back up and takes a few steps toward Corrine.

Corrine shrinks back into the cushions and, oddly, I get a similar urge to move away.

Where is she going and why does she want Corrine to go with her?

"Come on. You can't stay here by yourself. My mom will be here any second and I don't want to have to tell her why you're here. She won't like it," she adds with an edge of irritation.

I get a distinct impression that Juliana is lying about her mom. *The Juliana I know isn't a liar. Nothing feels right around here.*

Corrine's pale blue eyes stare out the front windows for a second and then she unfolds her knees and inches off the couch.

Her tiny body looks even more fragile today than I remembered it being.

"Sure. Let's go," she says.

The blank expression on Corrine's face, although somewhat solemn, looks like a mask of indifference, but I suspect she's really freaking out inside. I wonder if my face looks the same as hers.

∞

"Where did you say we're going?" Corrine asks.

"I have to stop by a friend's house," Juliana answers.

She turns the corner from one dirt road onto another. Corrine's hand curls into a small tight fist around the armrest on the door panel. I'm not sure where we're headed either, but by Corrine's physical response she seems to have an idea.

With more than a little desperation, I sit in the back seat and make myself stay silent. Neither one of them can see me and I need to play my cards right if I'm going to approach Corrine. For now I have to observe and pick my time to make another appearance with care. The last thing Corrine needs is to be shaken by an unexpected appearance from an Angel of Death.

"Why would you bring me here?" Corrine asks with despair in her tiny voice.

Juliana slows the car as we pull down a narrow driveway toward a desolate looking house. Now I recognize it. This is Corrine's house. There's nothing really wrong with this place from the outside. If it wasn't for the cars, it would look uninhabited. The curtains are all pulled shut and grass has taken over the flower beds. Not one sign of life is to be seen outside the house, not a trash can, or a lawn chair, nothing personal. As for maintenance and up-keep, I don't think anyone has done a thing to the place for the last twenty years.

Jules parks next to the two BMW's in front of the house and shuts off the engine. She turns to face Corrine.

"He told your brother last night that you needed to come home, so I brought you home." Corrine shudders and her somber blue eyes fill with tears. Juliana doesn't seem to care. "Go on. He knows we're out here."

Corrine doesn't open her door, but sits still as stone, blank faced and unblinking at the small brown house. Juliana climbs out and comes around to open Corrine's side.

"You do live here, don't you? It can't be that bad. I'll even come inside with you."

Corrine moves as if her spirit has already left her body. A hollow shell on legs. My heart aches for her. After getting her away from her maniacal stepfather, I thought there was definitely some hope for her mental well-being, but now Juliana has driven her straight back to him.

"It will never end. I told you he would never let me leave. He always finds a way."

"Well, he is your father," Jules says coldly.

"Stepfather," Corrine mumbles.

When we enter through the front door, Travis is nowhere to be seen. A chill passes through me as I stand at the entrance. I've been here before, of course, with Corrine but we mostly stayed in her bedroom. My hesitation comes from the fact that I haven't been back here since he attacked me. Or should I say, the thing he was wielding attacked me and shredded my side into raw agony. The house has a new nightmarish quality. And I have a much clearer understanding of what Corrine has been living with.

We don't see Travis Dawson in the bleak living room, but like the smell of day old fish, I can feel his presence lingering from somewhere inside.

Corrine ignores the two of us and settles into the corner of a gold-brown couch. I suspect the couch and the other hodge-podge pieces of seventies looking furniture came with the house. Juliana sits on the opposite end and the two of them could be playing a game of who can be the quietest the longest.

Before I can decide whether or not this is the most bizarre, or the most terrifying situation I've ever been in, sounds from the hallway alert me to Travis's whereabouts. Quickly, I step into the kitchen and out of sight of the hallway. I'm still able to hear and see most of the living room — including Juliana on the couch. If anything happens, I want her in my reach, whether she can see me or not. I don't want another battle with a demon, but I'll protect her and Corrine at any expense to myself. Previous to our encounter by the rock caverns, Travis seemed to have no interest in me, and if it were up to me, I would keep it that way. Unfortunately, I don't think that's the case any longer.

"Glad you made it home safe, my little seeker," he says.

The condescending sneer in his tone makes me want to wring his neck.

"Cook dinner tonight. Patrick will be home later and you two need to eat."

There's a silent pause and then Travis interjects. "Did you hear me, Corrine?"

"Yes," she says without emotion.

"Good. Now, are you going to introduce me to your friend? Your mother would frown on such rude behavior if she were here."

"Where is my mom?" I hear Corrine ask.

"Where is my mom?" Travis mimics in a horrible grating impersonation of his stepdaughter. "I'll tell you where. She lives with Satan in the pits of Hell."

He laughs as if he's told some hilarious joke. "Now stop keeping me waiting. Who is this beautiful friend of yours?"

No one should ever have to deal with a parent as disturbed as Travis.

"Travis this is Jules. Jules, Travis. I think you met yesterday."

Jules turns wide appraising eyes to the opposite side of the living room where I can't see. The corners of her wide precious mouth turn up slightly. "It's my pleasure, Travis," she says.

She moistens her lips with the tip of her tongue. I have to close my eyes to the sight of her staring at the nefarious man with a hint of what, *seduction?* It can't be, but what else can I possibly call that look? A retching sensation, something I'd forgotten about in this afterlife, turns my stomach into a heaving knot. I would vomit now if I could. Corrine's petite voice interrupts my anguish.

"Can I go to my room for a while before Patrick gets home?"

"Of course. You look tired. Try to rest. We still have to finish our excursion."

I open my eyes and see that Jules doesn't follow Corrine.

Can a person taste rising bile when they don't have a body? Yes, yes they can.

A door closes, and then Juliana stands up. She moves out of my line of sight.

"So Travis, have anything to keep a girl entertained while her *friend* takes a little nap?"

"I'm sure we can manage some form of entertainment for you, Night Siren."

A tinkling laugh escapes from Jules which sounds like her, and yet doesn't sound like her. It is her voice, but it's not a sound I've ever heard her make before.

"Hmmm, I like that. What else will you call me?"

"I can think of a few choice suggestions, but first let me have a look at you."

The laugh again. "I wondered if you would recognize me."

The bile that has risen now sinks to the pit of my stomach and churns with some unknown substance. The effect is unsettling to say the least. *What happened to my Juliana?*

"It's not bad. Quite the opposite really. I'm loving the change," Juliana says.

"It's not as convenient though," Travis says.

"We'll make it work. I'm starved. Think you can help a hungry girl out?"

The sound of bodies moving alerts me, the rustle of clothes and footsteps. *Are they moving into the kitchen?* I look around trying to plan my next move in case Travis decides I'm unwelcome. It's a square outdated little room and there's nowhere to go. Slipping through the wall may be my best option, but when neither appear, I decide to sneak a look around the corner into the living room.

Juliana sits straddled legged over Travis's lap. The fabric of her shorts is stretched tight, showing way too much skin. Travis reclines back against the cushions taking in the view with the smuggest look on a man's face I've ever seen.

The urge to kill him propels me out of the kitchen and straight for the weasel. I don't even think about what I'm doing. He'll never look at Juliana that way again. I feel my hands reach for his throat and eyes simultaneously, but before I can lift her out of my way and fulfill the primitive need to murder, the front door rattles and Juliana slides off of Travis. In one fluid movement she twists to the side and sits down on the couch, feigning naiveté.

Travis likewise composes his rat face and we all watch as Patrick and Jared shamble into the room.

Similar to watching court proceedings, both parties' facade of innocence is obvious to the extreme, and yet no one says anything that may shatter the fragility of guilt lying just under the surface.

"What are you doing here?" Jared asks, not hiding his disapproval.

"Nice to see you too, brother," Juliana says.

"I mean it, Jules. What are you doing here?"

"What are you doing? No wait, let me guess, you're—"

"Leave," Jared interrupts. "Go home."

"That's hilarious, Jared. I was about to tell you the same thing."

Marcus, who is standing outside, raises two wide brows at me. I disappear from my awkward stance in the living room and reappear outside next to him. While I regain control over my emotions, I half listen to the bickering between Juliana and her brother. Jared's intrusion is an overwhelming relief compared to what I was just witnessing between her and Travis.

"Here we are again," Marcus says.

I grunt, a noncommittal sound which is neither implying nor approving.

"Going that well, is it?" he asks.

This time I shrug.

By the face he's making, I have to think he doesn't believe it's going all that well. At this point I don't think composing my shattered mind into an intelligible reply is a real option, so I frown at him and elect to say nothing.

"This place is what some would call a devil pit. Nasty little party going on inside. You feel it?"

I have to take a second and focus on his words before I can answer. "Yeah, maybe," I conclude.

"Oh, it's him all right. He's brought it to this house. That devil wielding man in there. I won't step a foot inside if I don't have to. Jared best get out of here before he crosses over, or something may try to take over his body. I don't need a mess like that today. Hey, man, your injury. It was this evil sucker, wasn't it?"

I give Marcus a sharp quick nod, and then lean to the side for another look. Travis is just a man. A man who plays with dark things and uses his stepdaughter as a tool. He's a monstrous little man that Juliana is attracted to. *What did he do to her! He has to be to blame for this.*

Jared stands in front of his sister on the couch, insisting she get off her butt and go home. She doesn't budge. Travis cuts their squabbling short by standing up and hissing something I don't quite catch.

"Dad, yeah. That's why he's here," Patrick insists.

"The two of you come with me. I'll show you what I've got," Travis says to Jared.

Then the three of them start down the hall, leaving Juliana on the couch.

"What? The girls aren't allowed to play with the boys?"

"No way, Jules. I swear you better stay out of this," Jared calls back.

"Really Jared? You can't hide anything from me. I know what you're about, and you better share it with me too."

"Fuck, Jules! Forget the whole deal. I can't watch you do this. You're not getting high ever again. Not after last night."

Jared turns around and walks out the front door nearly walking straight through Marcus and me. We sidestep out of the way and then Patrick staggers out after him. Marcus gives me a salute. "I'm off." He follows the boys across the yard and off into the trees.

Neither Patrick nor Jared acknowledges our presence. Why would they? I have to wonder if Juliana inadvertently saved Jared from something horrible again. There's no way of knowing for sure, but Jared is still breathing, and that's what matters.

Inside, I see Juliana move from the couch and toward Travis who is standing at the far side of the living room.

"I still want to play," she says, and the foreign sound of her voice gives me a chill that could freeze the sun.

The creep smiles at her. It's a menacing and self-serving grin. It haunts me and crushes me with fear, even as I clench my fists.

"This way, Siren. I have the perfect game for us."

"You're not mad about *my brother* are you?"

The way Jules's voice inflects on 'my brother' sends another shot of ice down my back. She's not done though.

"Self-righteous prick. How dare he dictate what I can and can't do."

"Forget him. You can have whatever you want. Jared will be back. When you're not around, he'll finish our deal. Come. You'll like what I have for you downstairs," Travis says as he walks down the narrow hallway.

Scared senseless to let her out of my sight, I move back into the house, staying not far behind. Travis doesn't look back at either of us. *How can this be happening? What if Travis tries to attack me again? And why is Juliana putting up with this freak?*

As Travis turns the knob on the last door in the hall, she leans her face close to his ear and says, "Is it naughty, or nasty?"

The cool smile returns to Travis's thin mouth. His dark eyes meet hers for a brief and intimate moment before he opens the door and steps out of sight.

Chapter Twelve: Binding

Nathaniel

Juliana and Travis head down a darkened staircase. The concrete block wall on my left is painted a dark color, brown or black, I'm not exactly sure which, but it has succeeded in its job to suck all traces of light out of the air. The Light, both metaphysically and physically, is gone from this basement. The feeling of being sucked into a cold abyss, surrounded by watchful, hungry beings is overwhelming. About half way down the stairs, I hesitate, Marcus's description of a "devil pit" sounds in my ear. Even he will not enter this space. Only for Juliana do I keep moving.

They move around the corner when they reach the bottom, and as I follow, I hit a wall. It's the same invisible shield that kept me from getting to Corrine when Travis was spilling the blood of the fawn. It burns me to touch it and I shy away. Now trapped by the bottom of the stairs, I feel helpless as I watch Travis lead Juliana to the other side of the room.

Black candles are lit, giving off just enough light to see the room. Dark fabric covers the ceiling and hangs down like drapes over the walls. Travis stops in front of an altar. It's large, like a bureau with a lot of different sized drawers and cubbies. There are shelves above and to the side. He lights a few more candles and I can see it's an old piece of furniture, intricately carved and has a marble top. He opens and closes drawers removing small items and then searches a shelf for something. Juliana moves up behind him and places her hands on the back of his hips, spinning him around to face her.

"It would benefit you not to interrupt," he says.

"I don't really care right now. I'm starving."

She steps in even closer to him and places her mouth over his, kissing him. Her entire body is pressed up against him in a way that makes me want to kill again.

"Why?" I ask the air, and then complete my frustration by making a declaration. "I can't do this!" I hit the invisible barrier keeping me from entering the room with my fist and it changes nothing other than leave my knuckles burning.

As I make my way up the first couple of stairs, I hear Travis speak and it halts my retreat.

"We will have time for that later. Back off for a minute, Siren."

"You're no fun. Let me play. Since the little mouse is out of the way, I can finally get my hands on you."

"I am the epitome of fun. Let me work on securing your body. I don't have to help you, you know."

"I didn't ask for your help either. You'll do it anyway. I know how much you get off on this crap," Jules says.

"I'm the only one who is powerful enough to bind your little soul. Don't you forget it."

"Well, Mr. Dawson, you think very highly of yourself. Don't forget, I'm the one who chose. And I'm the one who already made the switch," Juliana spits the words back at him.

She doesn't even sound the same anymore. If I couldn't see her mouth moving, I wouldn't believe it was her at all.

"We made an arrangement to use Corrine. Why did you break it?" Travis asks with evident anger.

"She was having problems that didn't interest me. I wanted something new, and it's pretty spectacular, isn't it? These curves are so much better than that sniveling little girl's."

With this, Jules runs her hands over herself. Her left hand lingers on her breast. My eyes close involuntarily. *This is not the girl I knew yesterday.*

"This new arrangement doesn't please you? I can have you any way I want now. And, I do need your help. She's much stronger than Corrine. She was fighting me earlier. I won't have her doing it again."

"Let me make one thing clear, Siren."

My eyes open. Juliana and Travis are only inches apart. I'm not sure which of them is making me feel more ill.

"I will have *you*, when I want. You will never touch Patrick. And don't forget, I can be rid of you whenever I choose."

A hissing sound, like a very angry, large cat escapes from Juliana's mouth. It makes the hairs on my body stand on end. Travis smiles with wicked pleasure.

"Stand in the circle," he says. "Face west."

"First, one more kiss. Seal this new deal."

"Don't you ever get enough?"

"Never," she whispers.

Rage, repulsion, and terror rip through me. I have to turn away as Juliana leans in to meet him. *The bastard! What has he done to her? It isn't her. It isn't her. It isn't her!* Like a mantra, I repeat the words. *How can I get Juliana back? How?*

"Enough," he says. "To the circle. Now."

"So bossy. Would it hurt to be nice for one second?"

"I want you out of here before your brother comes back. He has money for me, and I need it to buy another Beamer. Don't pout. You can come back after he leaves."

"Cars. Why are men so fascinated with them?"

"We can ride them when we want, and they don't whine or tell us what to do."

"Whatever." She waves a dismissive hand as she moves to the center of the room and turns to the west wall. "Fix me up, Mr. Dawson."

"Stop this. Don't touch her again, or I'll kill you," I say from the stairs.

Travis stops looking in an open drawer and turns his head to stare at me.

"I mean it, you son-of-a-bitch. Don't go near her."

His cruel smile returns. Insidious evil oozes from the warlock like stench from a putrid swamp. He narrows his eyes at me and then returns his focus to the altar. He chooses two small boxes and places them on the altar and then slides the drawer back into place. Next he opens each lid and lines them up neatly above each box. From another drawer, he removes something small and white, and another candle.

"Apparently, Siren, we have an unwanted visitor."

"What are you talking about?" Juliana asks.

"It's nothing to worry your pretty head about. No more than a nuisance. But I will seal the space in a different way than I would have if it were not here."

With one of the boxes in his hand, he moves around Juliana in a wide clockwise circle sprinkling the contents of the box over the already visible circle on the floor.

At the bottom of the stairwell, I stand burning, and unable to pass the barrier this warlock has created. "Juliana, love, stop this. Please," I beg.

Travis continues to make a continual circle around her with the dark powder. When he's finished, he puts the box down and picks up the white object.

"Take this, and draw another circle inside my own, Siren. Do not lift the chalk, and connect the ends. Start here and end here," he says while pointing to a specific spot on the floor.

"Juliana Crowson, come back. Move away from him now." She walked straight into the basement and could leave if she wanted to.

Her shoulders twitch as if a shiver has moved over her. Then she looks over to me. I could swear her eyes meet mine.

"He's evil, Jules. Come with me."

She screams and I stumble forward. Fire passes over me, a burning flash of heat rolling over my skin. But where my feet should be, something solid stops me. Looking down, I see a line of gritty powder. It's stopping me from entering his accursed space.

Juliana's scream stops and she begins to shake her head, jerking from side to side. Her hand reaches up as if to stop her own violent twitching.

The voice coming from her is not Juliana.

"Do it now, Travis. I want this over with."

Juliana is still holding the side of her head and the shaking eases somewhat.

"It must be done in order if you want it to work," Travis growls.

"What are you waiting for then?"

"Draw the circle. I'll do the rest."

He moves to the altar and picks up another of the boxes and the unlit candle. With these in hand, he squats down in front of Juliana. He lays out five small whitish objects in a smaller circle and places the candle in the center. Careful to step over his lines, he returns to his supplies on the altar. The smallest circle on the floor, I can now see are bones. Animal or human, I don't know, but the knobby joint ends are unmistakable.

If I can't find a way to stop this madness, I will have failed myself and Juliana beyond repair. I pull energy from the universe and manifest my body. Travis's attention turns my way as I do it and he watches as I try to cross his line again. The pain of touching this barrier is like being stripped of skin by a red hot blade, one piece at a time. Travis smirks as I pull back, and then he continues to ignore me. Juliana hasn't looked at me again.

There are angry welts on my hands from attempting to cross his invisible wall. It fuels my determination.

"Leave. Her. Alone."

"Light the candle, Siren," he says. He stands outside of the circle and hands her something.

She bends down over the candle and then I hear the flick of a match followed by a yellow and blue flame. The wick on the candle flares bright and then settles to a soft glow. The pale skin of her hands and forearms catch the light and cast shadows across her face, making her appear dark and unholy.

"Damn Corrine," Travis spits out. "I still need the garnets and quartz."

"Can't you do this without them?" Juliana complains.

"Yes, but we need your blood instead of the garnets."

"Let's use blood then," she says.

The twisting wrench in my stomach heaves afresh with the sound of the near excitement in her voice over the prospect of using her own blood. Juliana hates the sight of blood. She would never do this willingly.

"That's my girl. I have just enough quartz. Corrine *will* find me more precious stones later."

"Get on with it, will you? Give me a knife already. I thought you said you were in a hurry."

"Silence, hell cat. I will tell you when to cut."

He reaches under his shirt and pulls up what looks like a cross on a chain. The end of the cross slides out of a miniature sheath producing a tiny dagger.

Dipping the blade in a basin on the altar, he whispers over it. "With the water from the stones of the dead this blade will be cleansed."

Then he turns back to Jules and hands her the knife. "You must put three drops of blood from each of your thumbs into the melted candle wax. Then drip blood onto each of these stones. There are six of them. Move clockwise around the circle until you are facing the candle again. I will call the demons to assist the binding. Do not interrupt me as I cast."

Travis moves around the circle placing a quartz crystal at six points around the circle. As Juliana is about to stab the end of her left thumb, her body begins to shake and her feet stumble. Her foot slides over the chalk line on the floor. Travis looks down at her foot. I see his jaw harden and his spine stiffen.

"You've broken the seal. Maybe Corrine was a better match after all, you incompetent wench."

"Screw you, Travis. I told you she's strong."

"This is the one time I'll fix it. Get some control over her, or forget it."

The powder on the floor. She's broken the seal. Lord! It's worth a try. Why didn't I think of it sooner?

With all the power I can manage, I bend down and blow on the line before me. Forces unknown to me must be assisting because a howling wind escapes from my mouth. The gust circles around the room, causing the drapes to flutter and the candlelight to flicker madly. Half of them extinguish, darkening the room further. The dirty line, which is keeping me from Juliana, scatters like ashes in the wind. Juliana falters, collapsing to the floor. I plunge forward. You would think that hesitation would be the more intelligent course of action, but no one has ever accused me of having too many brain cells. Death is a barrier I've already crossed, so how much worse can it get?

Juliana sits on the floor with her knees hugged into her chest. Her body is shaking violently.

"Juliana, get out of here!"

She doesn't respond. I am whole. I am physical. Why can't she see me?

"Now, love. Go!"

Just as I'm about to lift her up, she digs her heals into the floor and pushes herself backward. She slides across the hard floor until her back touches a wall. I don't have time to react to her rejection. Travis's movement from over by the altar distracts me.

"What did you do to her?" I scream.

"This does not concern you."

"Not good enough. What did you do!"

Sounds reach me through the floorboards overhead. Someone's moving around upstairs.

"Corrine! Down here," I yell.

"No, no," Travis says in a patronizing tone. "I don't think so, angel. You've disturbed my life enough. It's time for you to go away."

"I haven't even started, you despicable little bastard."

Approaching this small guy, I'm not sure if I want to throttle him or bash his face in. Both have their appeal. He backs up a step, but otherwise, looks undisturbed. It infuriates me further.

"You know what?" I say, and stop advancing on him. "You can fantasize in your slice of Hell all you want. Just leave Juliana alone."

He narrows his eyes at me, one of his favorite expressions. It only serves to enhance his impersonation of a mad rat about to attack. I turn my attention back to the one who matters, Juliana. She alternates between watching Travis and burying her face in her knees.

"We're out of here," I say.

"She won't go," he says to my back.

My molars grind with hatred for this man, but I will not lower myself to his despicable level. I squat down in front of Juliana.

"I'm going to carry you out of here now."

Behind me I hear Travis moving. I glance over to make sure he's not about to stab me in the back. He pulls back a piece of fabric. It slides to the side, revealing a large mirror above his altar.

"I release you. In the name of the unholy, enter now, my Night Terrors."

In a stream like black smoke, they come out of the mirror and into the room.

I bend down to pick Juliana up. Now would not be soon enough to get us out of here. She's shaking all over and cowers away from me.

Before I have my arms around her, something attacks me from behind, wrapping me in an immovable cloak. Immediately I relinquish my body and slip from its grasp by twisting to the side.

The thing is all black, very tall, and desperately evil. There's a man's tortured face somewhere inside, but it's mostly hidden in shadow. There are others in the room. They circle around, never holding perfectly still. Some of them hover like ominous clouds over my head. I get a distinct impression they're waiting to see what this big one is going to do before they move in on me. I think I've angered it, and it comes at me for a second time. Avoiding its grip, I slide out of its path, and then not wanting to be cornered, I duck past it to the opposite side of the room.

This freak show game of cat and mouse is not what I had planned for today. I cut my eyes over to where Travis is. He's watching the play from his altar and looks self-satisfied. He's the one who brought this on and he's the one who can stop it.

"Call off your dogs, Travis."

"You need to learn some respect," he says.

"Respect for what?" I say incredulously. I dart out of the demon's grip again.

"For the powers you know nothing of. Consider this your free lesson in demonology."

"What is the matter with you?" I don't know how long I can keep this up. When the thing touched me I could feel my energy draining almost instantly. If it touches me again, I may not have enough life force to even save myself, let alone be any help to Juliana, or Corrine.

"Your ignorance is laughable. How dare you enter my sanctuary and make judgments over me."

His anger is rising, his tone is growing louder, and there's a new fire behind his eyes.

"You're pathetic. A weak man who gets off on playing with himself in the dark," I say trying to make him as angry as I can. With every maneuver I try to move closer to Juliana. It isn't working though. The demons are nearly as fast as I am. The basement isn't large enough and there are too many of them.

From upstairs, I hear footsteps again and now there are voices. Someone other than Corrine is up there.

"An angel that has no power. That is what is pathetic. Let's see how you handle this," Travis says. "Night Terrors, shred him to pieces."

Every shadow in the room closes in on me. As a last resort I had been planning on leaving by disappearing and then reappearing in another location. It is how I normally travel anyway. This calls for a last resort plan, I decide. Picturing the cars outside of the house, I expect to be there instantaneously, but nothing happens. I try again, but I can't leave. Through the wraiths encircling me, I see and hear Travis laughing at me.

The demonic creatures grab at me. They are everywhere, above, below and all around. I feel myself being torn apart. Sick hungry joy emanates from them as pieces of my soul are being ripped away.

"Marcus!" I yell as loud as I can. Maybe my mentor is within earshot. If he is, then at least someone will know what happened to me. "Downstairs!" I scream to whoever can hear me. Please help Juliana get away from here, I silently plead as I lash out against black razor edged shadows.

Nearby, I hear her sobbing. It fuels my efforts to escape from these evil beings. I fight back, trying to find any opening but there isn't one. With the last ounce of my will, I call for help. "Heaven help us! Pure light and love find us now!"

The shattering of pure brilliance is an explosion in the room, radiating from my core. The dark beings shriek and pull away. I hear thumping on the stairs of descending footsteps. Then a male voice calling, "Jules? Jules, where are you?"

The light is complete. It is everything, and everywhere, blinding me and encapsulating me. I am no longer a separate being from this light. I am the light and it is me. Odd as it sounds, the feeling is not entirely disturbing. There's a faint memory of being torn to pieces, and it still hurts, but not that bad. Below me is a dark and heavy place, and the impulse to be away from it is so strong. Stronger than anything I've ever felt before. But this encapsulating sun is guiding me to someplace far away. I think I want to go. It has to be better than the memory of the pain. Do I have a choice? I let it lead me farther away. My last clear thought before giving in completely to this radiant luminosity is simply, goodbye.

Chapter Thirteen:
Cleansing Blood and Bone

Juliana

"Jules, what are you doing down here? Get off the floor."

When I'm unable to respond to him, he shakes my shoulder.

"What's the matter with you?" he says, as my head bobs like a broken doll's.

"I, I, umm, I…" The shaking and sobbing is uncontrollable. The ability to speak and cry at the same time isn't possible. I hide my face from my brother and let the tears fall into my lap. Misery at its best is unbearable, but at its worst, it's debilitating.

"You gotta get out of here, Jules. Patrick's dad doesn't look right. I'll help you up."

Managing to nod my head at Jared takes every bit of my determination. A part of me I don't recognize is desperate to crawl over to Travis's feet and beg him to let me stay here and finish what we started. Jared moves to my side and awkwardly tries to lift me to my feet with his working arm. His left hand and arm are still in a cast from the incident at Castle Hill, but he manages. My body resists his efforts even as my mind wants to go with him. There seems to be no way of controlling the shuddering violence coursing through me. As I stand, I have to lean on Jared. The sobs continue as he half drags me across the basement.

I take one last look at Travis as we start up the stairs. He's standing in front of the oval mirror with his back to me. His full attention is on his hands as he makes a measured pour of some liquid into a basin on the top of the altar. Wracking sobs blur my vision, but I can see that the mirror doesn't reflect Travis's image. Its surface is empty of any reflection. The feeling coming from the mirror is dense and icy. The demons which had come into the room had exited the same way. I'm afraid if I stare at the mirror too long, I'll see them. And they will see me. I turn and bury my face against Jared's side.

As we leave the house, I have to hold the sides of my head again to help control the shaking. The urge to stay here almost overpowers me and I have to force my feet forward. Releasing my head, I cling to Jared like a life raft saving me from stormy seas.

"Get a grip already, will you?" Jared says.

A few feet from the house, I lose it altogether. Pushing Jared away, I fall to the ground in a heap, sobbing and clawing my way back toward the house. The gravel scratches my hands and the side of my leg, but I don't care. Part of me wants to hide in the car and escape from this nightmare, and part of me needs to get back to Travis. He can fix my pain. He's the only one who can stop this battle inside.

"What the hell happened to you, Jules? I'm taking you to Mom. Where are the car keys?"

"She's fine," Travis says from just inside the front door. "Leave her. We have business to finish."

The sound of his voice encourages me and I begin to climb off the ground. Jared grabs my upper arm and helps me to my feet. He doesn't let go as I start toward Travis.

"Get off, Jared," I manage to say.

"I'm gonna have to come back later," Jared says.

"It will not be here later. You're not my only buyer, Jared. Give me the money and I'll bring it out to you."

"Whatever, dude. Look at my sister. Did you give her something? What were you doing downstairs?"

"I gave her nothing. She's a girl," Travis says as if this is an obvious answer.

I hear the change in his tone as he tries to influence my brother's reasoning by softening his voice.

"You still want the hashish, don't you? Help me out, and take it off my hands. There's a car I need to go look at. I'm supposed to be there tonight."

"Yeah, Jar. Let's go back inside," I say, suddenly feeling stronger and less out of control.

Jared looks from me to Travis and back to me. "What's up with you, Jules? You're acting really strange. Even for you."

"Shut up. My blood sugar's low."

He's giving me the dad look. One eyebrow is so high on his forehead it's almost comical and the other one is down in derisive speculation. The bulge of his jaw muscle is what really makes him look like my dad though. I give a half-hearted tug on my arm to free myself. His grip doesn't slacken. The longer he touches me the stronger and less freaked out I feel. I want to go inside. Jared can buy his drugs. Then Travis and I can finish what we started.

"Did you smoke something with Travis?" he asks me.

"No," I say, defending myself. "If you're going to though…"

"No way. You were crazy last night. We're leaving."

"No. I'm not done."

"Yes, you are!"

Jared forces me to the car and stuffs me inside. He comes around to the other door and then climbs in.

Travis walks over to the car. He stops in front of the hood, staring at Jared. "If you leave, don't ever come back here."

I turn in my seat to watch my brother's reaction. His good hand clenches the steering wheel, the knuckles turning white with strain. The bulge on the side of his jaw hardens even more and I wonder if he is about to crack his teeth. He drops his gaze to his lap for a second and then he reaches across his body and slams the door.

I open my door to get out, but Jared is quick as he reaches over and slams it closed too, narrowly missing my foot.

"You're not even supposed to be driving with your cast on," I say.

"You weren't so concerned yesterday."

"I left something inside," I lie, and reach for the handle again.

"Jules, open the door again, and regret it for the rest of your life."

His right hand opens and closes on the shift knob between us as if flexing his muscles fuels his determination.

"What do you care? I need to grab something inside," I try again.

"You, you, you. What happened to you, Jules? You're being a selfish little snit. I'm taking you to Mom. You don't even care how you've screwed up my day."

"I haven't done anything. In fact, I want you to buy the hash. I could use a good buzz right about now."

"That's it," Jared says, and turns on the car.

Damn. I left the keys in the ignition.

Travis had already gone back inside. The void left by his absence is an empty cavity inside my chest. The feeling is unreasonable and unexplainable. Suddenly, everything that happened in the basement rises up to the surface and the pain is back. As Jared backs out of the drive, the misery takes hold of me. It cinches my chest and constricts my throat. The building pressure behind my eyes lets loose and the tears stream out. Something terrible has happened. I know it in my soul, and yet I don't know what it is exactly. I've lost something precious, not something, more like some... Jared barges in on my nearly completed thought.

"Cut the crap. Seriously, Jules, the tears aren't going to work on me. You can save it for someone who buys B.S."

"Jared," I choke out in total agony. Inside, I'm desperate to tell him something awful has happened, but I just can't get it out. My head begins to vibrate and convulse. I have to hold myself by wrapping my arms around my head as tight as I can. It barely helps.

"Something's wrong with you. Really wrong." He stares hard at me, his brow furrowed with concern.

All I can do is sob and weep, and try to keep my head from coming off.

Jared shifts the car into a higher gear. "Change of plans, Jules."

∞

Clack, clack, clack. The sound hammers on the inside of my skull. He does it again, wood smacking against wood. It's so close to my head that I bury my face deeper into Jared's shirt trying to muffle the intrusion. He's pounding on someone's screen door while cradling me against him. The edge of his cast digs into my back as we wait for someone to answer. The noise and discomfort seem trivial though, compared to the pain swimming around inside me.

I hear the inner door swing open, but don't bother to look. Jared can ditch me anywhere. *What difference does it make?*

"Good. You're here. Bring her inside."

Jared steps over the threshold.

The male voice commands, "You, stay outside."

Jared mumbles, "Huh?"

"Forget it. We'll deal with it later. Follow me?" the man says.

Jared settles me higher against his chest. My foot bumps into something solid, probably a wall, as he carries me through the house. "I thought you were kidding last night."

"I thought you were too high to remember what I said."

"Nah, I remembered. Didn't think it was real though," Jared says.

The other voice is familiar. I'm afraid to look at who it is. It's as if every time I'm near any men, I become something totally different. I can't control what I'm doing, or saying, and the need to be near them is overpowering. If they want me sexually, I'm completely lost. At least with the crying and the shaking, I can feel the real me — as miserable as that is. Even being near my brother, I start to morph into someone unrecognizable.

"What has she been doing over the last twenty hours?"

"Pissing me off," Jared says bluntly.

"Obviously. But what else?"

Before I hear what Jared has to say about my behavior, the man interrupts.

"Put her down here. Then don't touch her unless I say to."

With a gentleness so unlike his earlier treatment of forcing me into the car, he lays me down on a stiff surface. The room we're in is brighter and the light penetrates through my lids. I turn my head away from the sound of their voices and then cover my face with my hands. The uncontrollable shakes have stopped, but the sniffles continue to make my chest heave.

"Why can't I touch her?" Jared asks.

"She feeds on male energy. You carrying her has strengthened her. Look at her."

The feeling of their visual inspection irritates me. *How dare they treat me like a specimen.*

The man's voice is familiar. And so strong. Not in tone, but more like Travis's. It's an inner strength. My hands slide back and my eyes begin to flitter open. *Who is talking about me when I'm right in the room? Some arrogant asswipe, that's who.*

Recognition comes in the next instant. As does violence. The surge is so compelling my body jerks upright.

"Noooo!" I shriek. "You get away from me!"

Scrambling off the cot my eyes search for a way to get out of the room.

Chris Abeyta, the medicine man, steps in front of a door, blocking my exit. "I think we'll have to restrain her," he says to Jared.

"Are you serious?"

"Unfortunately, yes. And it's not going to like it," Chris says.

"It? I thought you said she's been captured by a she-demon."

There's a hallway across the room and to my right. I'm in his sunroom and workroom. Organized clutter is everywhere. Chris stands between me and the back door. *I'll go the other way then.*

Chris anticipates my plan.

Before I take my first step he says, "Get her back on the cot, Jared."

"I'm not sure I can tie up my sister," he says.

I take that as my cue, and sidestep toward the hallway. Jared doesn't grab me, but he does move in front of me.

"Jules, convince me you're not possessed and I'll consider moving."

"Christ, Jared! I don't know what you're talking about. Move it, or I'll castrate you in your sleep."

It's the wrong choice of words. I guess I should have thought this through a little better. He body blocks me, lifting me off my feet, and over his shoulder. I pound on his back and kick at his nuts for the two seconds it takes for him to dump me back on the cot.

He must know I'm not going to stay here because he forces me onto my back and then pins me down with his good hand and the weight of his body.

"Stop fighting, Jules. You have to get this thing out of you and Chris is the only one who knows how."

"I'll never forgive you for this, traitor. You don't know a thing about Chris. He's wants to hurt me. He's a psycho, Jared. Let me out of here."

"It will try everything to get you to do what it wants," Chris says.

He's across the room, grabbing what looks like a dog leash and some kind of strap from a shelf by the door.

"I know. Hurry up, man. She's kicking my ass over here."

Chris ties me down to the cot. It's crude and unbearable. When Jared takes a step back to inspect the makeshift restraints he looks straight into my eyes and shakes his head as if he doesn't quite believe what he's seeing.

"I don't know what you are, but you're not my sister."

I narrow my eyes into slits and stay silent. If I could rip his throat out with my bare hands, it would not be satisfying enough.

Wiggling under my restraints, I realize the straps aren't very tight. With a little effort, I could probably free myself. I just have to wait until they're not hovering.

"Jared, will you stay to help, or should I call someone?"

"Err... I would, but I don't know what I'm doing."

"Right now I need you to make sure she doesn't go anywhere. I have to prepare many things for tonight and I will not be able to do that if she keeps trying to get away. Think you can manage?"

"Yeah, no problem. I can totally do that." Jared looks down at his big hands and then runs them over his scalp of thick hair.

"How could you?" I hiss at him, trying once more to inflict guilt.

Instead of answering, he moves toward the foot of the cot and sits down on a wooden chair. "Man, how did this happen to her?"

Chris rummages through a wood box and then sets a couple leather pouches on a nearby table. He moves across the room and opens a tall cabinet, peering inside. "That's what I'd like to know. I spoke with her at Earth's Heart Spring in the morning and she was fine. Then last night at The Edge, she was already infected. So maybe you can tell me. What happened yesterday?"

"She was making tea, or something, when I got home. She had a friend with her. Corrine. I'd never met her before. I wasn't really paying attention to Jules. Corrine was, well, she's kind of cute. Hey, Jules needed me to go pick up the car yesterday. I can't remember if she told me a reason why, but it was strange. She left it parked on some random street."

"Was she herself, when you saw her making the tea?"

"I thought so. She did say one thing that was strange. She said I had a friend waiting for me upstairs, but there wasn't anyone. Could that have been this thing inside of her? Would she have seen it in our house?"

As they talk about me my anger calms somewhat. It settles somewhere inside of my limbs, like a fire just under the skin. In its place, the despair I had been experiencing earlier rears its hideous face and begins to eat at me. The emptiness of a terrible loss —

which I can't fully explain — seizes me. My eyes fill with tears again. The lump in my throat is nearly suffocating and I swallow hard against it. I close my eyes to help me shut out the inevitable flood, but it doesn't stop the tears from leaking out. They flow over my temples and into my hair. *Is this insanity? Does a crazy person know that they're insane? Or is it illusive, like trying to capture the wind? I need this uncontrollable behavior to stop.*

The distinct smell of sage smoke burns a path up my nostrils. The fiery feeling under my skin, where the rage had planted itself, alights and makes me scream.

"Jared, this may get very difficult. I will need you through the entire night. If you cannot follow my directions exactly, then I will call someone else to help. Your Grandmother Charlotte may be more appropriate for this."

"Grandma? No. I don't want her to find out about this. Jules won't want her to know either. It's...I've never heard her scream like that. It's freaking me out, but I can handle it."

"It's not her. Keep reminding yourself and it will make what I do to her easier."

"Right," Jared says, but sounds unsure.

"You said Jules told you she saw a friend of yours?"

"Yeah, but then there wasn't anyone," Jared repeats his earlier answer.

"That wasn't the she-demon. Succubus is probably the term you are more familiar with. In our tribe, we call them she-demons. They need a body at all times or they will starve to death. It would not be waiting around for an opportunity to attach itself. It moves from one person to the next."

"A succubus? That's what it is? Yeah, I've heard of those. Damn, Jules *is* screwed."

"Yes, something along those lines. How long has she been upset like she is now?"

"She's either been screaming, or crying, for maybe an hour."

"I believe it's Juliana crying, not the demon. It is a good sign. She is fighting its hold on her from the inside."

The words I hear have two effects on me, overpowering anger, and relief. Understanding and comprehension provide the relief. The rage and the desire, the need to be with men, is not coming from me. It's the will of the succubus.

"I need to look in your car," Chris says.

I can hear the questioning tone in Jared's, "Sure, man."

"Don't touch her, or talk to her, while I'm outside unless she tries to get up. And keep this burning for me. The she-demon hates the smell and the feel of the cleansing smoke."

Chris is back within a couple of minutes. Although the pain and misery is still acute, I think my eyes can no longer produce anything wet. I blink hard a few times and then let my swollen eyes focus on Chris and the room that has become my prison.

He's holding the bottle of spring water that I saved for him from Earth's Heart Spring. In his other hand he carries a bunch of wilted green leaves still attached to their stems and gnarled roots. I watch him put everything down on the workbench.

In front of him is a west facing window. The last remnants of the evening sun give his red-brown skin a luminous quality. I take it as a sign, although I have no idea if it's a good one or bad. By the time the sun sets and rises again, he's either going to save me, kill me, or both.

"Jared, do you know if Juliana has been injured in any way since I last saw her. What kind of tea was she making yesterday? Did it smell medicinal?"

"The tea? Yeah. All her concoctions smell like medicine, but that wasn't it. Hey, I forgot to tell you something. Probably because I'd been smokin', but I think I know when this happened to her. It was last night. I heard some strange sounds and I felt this weird vibe in the house. So I went to check it out. Jules was in the bathroom. She wouldn't answer me when I asked her if she was all right. I busted the door down and found her on the floor. Her shirt was off, and that's when I saw it. Come over here. I'll show you."

Jared stands next to the cot and points at the top of my shoulder. He reaches down and brushes my hair to the side. I know the bite mark is easy to see with my spaghetti strap tank-top on. The fierce heat of anger ripples over my skin as they stare at me. I'm completely helpless, strapped down and laid out like the frog I once dissected in science class. I want to scratch their eyes out with my fingernails. *God, what's happening to me? I don't want to hurt my brother, and yet I do. This is madness.* My nails dig into the canvas at my sides and I turn my head to stare at the rough boards of the wall on my left.

"It is a clean wound, but I can see blood was drawn. It would be enough, I think," Chris says.

"What do you mean?" Jared says.

"The demon would enter through the blood and take over her body."

"Is Jules…I mean, will she…be okay because, I need her to be all right. You know?"

The stress in Jared's voice makes me feel stronger. The thing inside me likes his suffering. I shudder at the realization.

Chris doesn't answer. "I have preparations to make. Why was there devil's club roots in your car?"

"Devil's what?" Jared asks.

"The roots? I found them in the back of the car while I was looking for my water. You didn't put them there?"

"No, no idea."

"Hmmph," Chris huffs. "Keep the smudge pot burning for us while I prepare."

"Yeah, sure. Hey Chris, can I ask you another question?"

There's a silent pause between them, and then I hear my brother continue.

"Did this happen to her because she *sees things*?"

"I see them and I have never been possessed, so I say no. But because it is your sister, then maybe I'll say maybe. She needs training."

I hear Chris move to the other side of the room and Jared returns to his chair. The light in the room is fading to gray, the corners deepening. It will be night soon.

Had I known that I could actually be more uncomfortable I would have kept up my attempts to escape this awful smelling room. By the time I realize I am thirsty, have to pee, and I'm starving, I'm already so miserable that these minor inconveniences are only icing on the cake. I guess the feeling of my soul being broken and the burning rage under my skin is holding most of my attention.

In Chris's darkened workroom, Jared looks as if he's asleep in the chair. He rouses himself every so often to keep the smudge pot burning. Shifting and rustling sounds from outside the screen door grab my attention. Starlight and the distant glow of a neighbor's window provide the only light coming into the room. Chris's eclectic mix of tools, boxes, leather bags, and various animal and bird parts have lost their definition to the dark. I stare at the back door trying to see beyond the mesh screen, but there are only shadows shifting around like restless ghosts. The sounds continue and then I see the unmistakable flicker of orange flames. The smell of burning pine dilutes the weedy smell of the sage and gives me some minor relief.

One of the larger shadows move around the fire, making the light fade and brighten alternately. Then something, or someone, moves in front of the door blocking the flicker of firelight. It seems impossibly huge, too wide and too tall. Instinctively I want to move far away from it. Then a voice fills the night.

"Come outside," it says.

Jared stands up as if he's been waiting to leave and slips outside. If I have any opportunity to take my leave, this is it. I struggle against the leashes. One is across my lower ribs and arms and the other is strapped down just above my knees. I dig my heels into the canvas, pushing my body upward. Then I bend my upper body as far to the left as I can while inching my right arm out from under the strap. All I have to do is get my elbow to slip under the restraint and I will be as good as free.

The sound of rattlesnakes makes me jerk back to the middle of the cot. I bury my hands under my legs trying to make myself as compact as possible. The rattling enters my ears and makes my nerve endings scream. I'm stuck here and there are snakes coming for me. Gooseflesh breaks out over my entire body and cold sweat seeps from my pores. The thumping of my heart roars through my blood as I think I hear snakes slithering across the floor. The rattling grows louder and blossoms into layers of bone chilling sound. Suddenly, it's as if the room is full of the venomous snakes. My lungs begin to ache for air. The fear had paralyzed me and I hadn't been breathing. I close my eyes willing the incessant noise to stop and make myself take in oxygen. It's a slow and painful process. Most of the air feels trapped in the back of my throat. My nails dig into my palms as I focus on each breath. *Breathe in, force the air out, and repeat. They must be underneath me. If I don't move at all, they won't know I'm here.*

My heart continues its erratic pounding rhythm. It seems to only be circulating blood to the upper half of my body. My feet are tingling and the numbing sensation is growing toward my legs while my head feels like it has become a pressure cooker.

But pressure can only build for so long and then something has to give. In this unfortunate circumstance I'm deathly afraid my sanity will be the first thing to go. That, or my heart may give out. As I'm about to take the plunge from the precipice of reality into the depths of the unknown, my heart begins to slow. Lucidity is still far, far away, but the release valve has opened. My pulse becomes near to regular, but then as I realize it, the beating moves into every cell of my body, all the way from my hair follicles to the tips of my toenails. I feel like I'm standing next to a massive drum, THUMP-thump, THUMP-thump, THUMP-thump. In my mind I can see my blood pulsing to the beat. At least the rattlesnakes sound as if they've moved to the far side of the room.

Snakes and I have an uncomfortable history. And although I don't care for them much, I think the best way to deal with snakes is to leave them alone, and they will give you the same courtesy. This irrational paralyzing fear is not me. *It's not me! Holy Mother! The thing inside me is afraid of snakes, not me.* My eyes fly open at the realization. *I need to be separate from this thing. Please make this stop,* I plead and beg, but no sound escapes my lips. *It*, has control of my body. *It* has control and I can't stop it. Tears well up once again and I close my eyes against my helplessness and fall into the unseen pounding rhythms, letting the sound carry me into darkness.

Sensing movement nearby brings me back to the surface. My eyes flicker and I see a ghost leaning over me. My already straining breath catches in my throat, making me choke. I try to shrink into the cot underneath me. His face is ash gray with a black band painted across the center in an attempt to conceal his eyes. It almost works, but the firelight reflects off the surface of his eyeballs like tiny mirrors. Even with the eyes, I'm not entirely sure it's alive, or if it's something undead. But there are two sets of black eyes staring down at me. As I take in this ungodly beast, I see it's part man and part animal. The animal's face lies above the top of the man's head and its long furry body hangs down his back. The second head has a long muzzle, erect ears, and, thin slits for eyes — as if it's narrowing its gaze at me. *Coyote,* a distant part of my brain says.

In his hands, he beats a drum. Its surface is covered with waving lines, chasing one another around and around. *More snakes.* The beat gives them life, as if they're dancing to some terrible haunting song. My heart matches the beat. Its pulse is inside me, relentless and penetrating. But my eyes are glued on the snakes. The fear and paranoia of their scales and their venom convinces me that they are going to slither off the drumhead and come for my restrained body. The rattling starts again, this time from the corner of the room. An illogical fear convinces me the snakes are everywhere, on my left, and the right, above and below. The straps holding me to the cot are the only thing keeping me from exploding into hysterics.

Then this man-beast begins to chant. Low tones at first, mixed with the yipping and barking of a coyote. The song ends with the distinct laughing sounds of the trickster canine. I think I can feel the panting of the dirty animal breathing on me, sickening me with its musky scent. Then a new song begins, full of loud, long, calling chants. I tear my eyes away from the drum and focus on the window, wishing I could escape into the night and away from this nightmare.

The smoke from the sage continues to burn me from the inside out. The pungent scent is mixed with something else, which only intensifies the sensation of fire moving through me. With desperation I want to stop breathing, but this only works for a few seconds before I have to inhale another burning acid lungful. Soon, I will be dry and crumbling on the inside. On the other side of the window is cool clean air. I want it desperately. A shift in the glowing firelight from outside darkens the room to near black, then lighter, then darker, as if men move around the fire ring. For a second I wonder if Jared is out there. Then anger overtakes me. I'm furious he's allowing this torture.

When the glow from the fire returns, I look hard to my right trying to find my disloyal brother in the room. I don't see him. Instead, I stare at another tall figure. It's wrapped in some kind of fur giving it an enormous presence in the room. I never see its face because it's holding a snake about two feet from my face.

Panic overwhelms me at last and I start to buck and thrash at my restraints. I have no doubt now that if I don't get away from here, I'm going to die. The slow smoldering burn, running like a grass fire under my skin, or the snakes will be my end. My vision becomes unfocused and the room flashes in shadowed images. The coyote, the snake, the black eyes, and the windows glowing faintly orange swim in circles around me. Chanting assaults my ears and baffles my brain, making it impossible to protest or scream. The pandemonium seems to go on forever until I'm completely lost in agonizing vertigo.

At some point I think I'm having visions of Native Americans dressed in fur robes and wearing headdresses of animals and feathers. They seem to be concentrating on helping the looming furry beast and the snake. I continue to battle against things I don't understand. Somewhere inside, I know no one should ever have to endure this, and I also know I'm not going to win.

My eyes close to the visual torture. The inner darkness behind my lids provides no comfort. It allows my other senses to heighten, and for me to focus on the searing heat which is taking over my insides. The burning smoke has penetrated the inside of my limbs and is moving slowly to my core. The agitation of listening to the unseen rattlesnakes in the room makes me feel like I'm being bitten by a million fire ants simultaneously. Strangely, only a small patch of my abdomen seems unaffected by the burning. With all my concentration I try to stop thrashing and focus on the one part of my body that's not in anguish. Below my ribs and in the center of my belly is one spot where the painful sensations stop. Out of curiosity, my hand moves to it, but I can't reach because of the straps. As I concentrate on my stomach, I feel streaks of something heavy, yet fluid, moving to my center and collecting like a pool of molten lead just underneath my navel.

Hands grab my shoulders and push me against the cot. They feel strong and solid and mildly reassuring. A familiar voice says something I don't quite comprehend. He speaks again.

"Juliana, it's time to drink."

"Drink?" It comes out as a raspy question. The lead weight in my gut isn't painful, especially compared to everything else going on, and a cold drink sounds better than anything I could ever imagine. The hands lift my head until I'm partially reclined. The hard edge of a glass presses to my lower lip and my dry burning mouth opens to take in whatever he's offering. It's tepid and tastes bitter, but it's not totally unpleasant.

"Finish it," he says.

He stands mostly behind me so I can't see his face, only the glass and part of his arm and hand are visible. I swallow the last dregs of the tea and then he lowers me back down. Aware that I'm at least half free — I never felt him remove the strap — it no longer matters all that much. Exhaustion and pain are the only two things in my universe. I turn my head to the side and look to see who had brought the tea. The coyote man watches me watch him. Behind him to the left and right are the others. Four of them, distinguishable and eerie in their own right. Each one has his face painted and they all give me the distinct impression of being a visitor from the past. My coyote man sets down the glass and picks up his drum. The beat he plays is heavy and rhythmic. My blood and bones pulse with the reverb. The sounds, and the smells, and the supernatural looking men, are inside and outside of me. They are above and below, like an inescapable dream. A numbing stupor takes a hold of my brain and I'm fixed like a mummy in her tomb. He continues his endless chanting. My head turns slowly to stare at the ceiling, but I see nothing. The pounding of the drum and his repetitive song lulls me deeper. The tea he gave me must have some calming effects. It helped soothe my raw burnt throat, but the rest of my body is still on fire. All but my core. The heaviness there is growing larger and is beginning to swirl. I take notice of the odd changes going on in the pit of my belly, but then I find myself drifting off to unconsciousness.

∞

A piercing scream wakes me from my strange coma. Quickly, I realize it's coming from my mouth. Something is stinging my belly, like a wasp sting, it's sharp and excruciating. I suck in my breath and instinctively try to get away. Hands press me down, keeping me from rolling off the cot. My head bends forward looking for my assailant. My shirt is pushed up to expose my ribs. The few inches of skin showing seem to glow blue-white in the darkened room. Two puncture marks show clearly against my pale skin. In the near dark, my blood looks black as it beads up into two tiny spots. But neither the stinging nor the blood is nearly as terrifying as the large snake hanging over my stomach. It writhes with anger and then drops down on top of me.

"Aheeeey! Aheeeey!" I scream and scream with primal outrage and absolute fear. I thrash to get the snake off me, but there's nothing I can do to move under the weights holding me down. The snake moves over my stomach. The weight of it is surprising and its scales are smooth and warm. My eyes move to the coyote man standing over me. He has an oval dish in one hand and a thick smudge stick in his other. The smoke billows out of the glowing end, surrounding him, the other Natives, myself, and filling the entire room.

He speaks an ancient language. To me it sounds like a prayer. A prayer for my soul, for surely this is the end of my endurance for torture. I think I black out again, but somewhere in the far reaches I become aware of his strange words coming to a stop. My eyes open to see the coyote man set the oval dish and the burning stick down on a nearby table. When he turns back to me, he steps in close to where I lay. His hand passes over me three times, shaking a rattle, from my head to my feet.

"Oh Great Spirit, Grandfathers, and Blessed Grandmothers, I ask for your protection from the underworld, and from the spirits of darkness. Our Great Mother Earth has no home for you, she-demon. I command you to leave this body. I command you to leave this body. I command you to leave this body. With the help of the great feminine serpent, you must leave now. Take nothing that is not yours and never return here. Be gone!"

His hand suddenly appears over my face and he smears something over my mouth. It feels thick and gritty. I press my lips closed, afraid of getting it inside my mouth. The next thing I know my stomach turns, clenching and roiling like a sea of angry vipers. I look to see if the snake feels it moving like I do. It lies motionless in a wide circle around my navel, as if in anticipation for attack.

Then, like a great vacuum, the weight inside my gut starts to suck upward and out of me through the bite marks in my skin. It rises in a thin black stream above me and floats in front of the coyote man. The snake lifts with the black streaming cord and wraps itself around it, in a strangling hold. The painted coyote man is quick as his hands release the rattle and then wrap some sort of cloth bag over the snake and the shimmering cord. One of his hands reaches down and he wipes a finger over my bite mark leaving a smear of the same thick substance that is over my mouth.

"Wrap her up, and bring her to the door," he says.

Then like a shadow he glides out the back door. If I had not heard the screen door slam closed, I would have thought I dreamed it all because reality could never be this unbearable.

Reassuring hands guide me to sitting and then I feel my head, shoulders, and back being enclosed with a large fur cape. Jared steps in front of me and pulls me to my feet. I collapse forward onto him, but he doesn't let me fall to the floor.

"Jules, I got you. Come on."

With my feet dragging, he pretty much carries me the short distance to the door. The bristly hair of my covering tickles my neck and shoulders, but Jared is careful to keep the huge fur wrapped around me. I don't understand why I have to wear it, but I seem to have lost control of every part of my life.

The coyote man stands next to a fire on the patio. The others, who are not of this world, stand with him as silent witnesses. My coyote shaman holds the bag, containing the snake and the succubus inside, over the flames. When he sees me watching, he releases it into the fire. The other Natives, which I realize all look like medicine men, move to encircle the fire. Maybe they know Jared and I are watching, because there is just enough room between two of them for me to see the bag burning amidst the glowing coals and licks of flame.

The thin cloth bag evaporates in seconds, leaving what looks like two black snakes writhing. There's a penetrating evil essence emanating from the struggle and I know it's not coming from the snake. The battle is horrible, twisted, and dark as the succubus burns and suffocates in a fiery death. My overwhelming fear of the rattlesnake is gone, but the image in front of me is etched in my mind forever. The shamans begin to chant and tighten their circle around the fire, obstructing my view.

The disgust and horror causes the hollow feeling in the pit of my stomach to switch to cramps. I watched the thing that was inside of me burn. Either that, or I'm dying of snakebite. At least the burning sensation under my skin, which has been tormenting me for God knows how long, is gone. But don't be fooled. Misery doesn't begin to express my current state of being. My stomach gives a last wrenching lurch. Not sure what else to do, I stumble out the door.

My hands hit the patio table as I start to fall. Jared grabs me around the middle.

"Hey, I'm not sure you're supposed to be outside," he says.

"Urrrg," I moan. I can't even speak, my stomach hurts that bad.

"Jules, wait. You okay?"

"Nooo."

I slip to the side out of Jared's grip and stagger into the yard. The familiar crush of dirt and grass and pine needles underfoot gives me the tiniest bit of courage to keep going. Jared keeps the scratchy fur wrapped around my shoulders. The shadows deepen as I move away from the firelight until I find a thick tree trunk to lean against.

I squat down and let my left shoulder rest against the crackling bark. The next thing I know, my stomach heaves. With as much effort that my body puts into empting its guts, very little comes up to show for it. Small whimpers come from somewhere inside me. Apparently my body can cry for itself, because I don't feel the urge to cry right now. Death would be my choice, if I had one. I feel Jared's hand on the back of my head as he strokes my hair. He even makes little consoling sounds.

"Dear God, let me die," I moan. My stomach isn't finished. Moving with near panic, I half stand and try to push Jared away. At the same time I try to work at the button on my shorts. As more dry heaves ruin my diaphragm and tear up my throat, I get my shorts and underwear down to my ankles and let my bowels and bladder take their turn at unbearable cramps and excruciating humiliation. My brother becomes a saint in that moment as he stands by me and holds up the giant fur pelt like a screen.

"Tell me if you need anything," he says.

What I need is to curl up in a tiny ball and disappear, but I don't say so. After the gut wrenching stops, my body is so weak and shaky I don't even have the strength to pull up my shorts. I manage to inch away from my mess and fall to the ground. Pine needles are as comfortable as anyone would ever need to leave this earth, I decide. Jared catches me before I get to rest my head on the ground. He uses the fur pelt as a sort of sheet to keep me covered and I feel his hands tug my clothes back into place. Jared carries me to the house. I look up at him as he cradles me against his chest. His jaw bone is strong and defined yet delicate. His nose is long but fits his face beautifully. His eyes sparkle even after being awake for hours upon hours. *My brother will always be here for me.* In my short life, I always thought this was so, but now I really know for sure. *He's got my back.* Behind him, the eastern sky glows fuchsia and creamsicle orange. It's the beginning of a new day.

Chapter Fourteen: A New Reality

Juliana

"Juliana, I want you to wake up now."

I hear the voice, but I'm seriously inclined to ignore it as long as possible. *Go away and I'll promise not to bite your head off,* my inner voice tells him.

"You do not stand a chance at getting your teeth into me. Now, will you open your eyes for one minute? Then, I will leave you alone."

Chris. How does he always know what I'm thinking? If I wasn't half out of it and as weak as a hatchling I would be annoyed that he's still reading my mind.

"Whaaat?" I groan, and keep my eyes firmly closed. The sunlight in the room is glowing bright under my eyelids and it's about as comfortable as being stabbed with pins. The thought of facing the brutal rays is torture enough, let alone actually doing it.

"Sustenance. You must have some, Juliana."

Sure enough, the faint smell of food teases my senses. My nose wiggles and my dry mouth somehow salivates. I turn my head away from the sound of Chris's voice. Sleep wins. I don't want anything else right now. He doesn't accept my rejection. He props me up and shoves thick cushions under my back and shoulders. I hear, or maybe feel, him sit down near me.

Before I open my eyes, I do a quick survey of my body. All burning sensations are gone. My stomach is feeling somewhat better, no churning gut, only hollow like a carved out pumpkin. The fragile and empty feeling inside my core is also inside of my limbs, making me feel like a shell of myself. My eyeballs feel heavy and sunken. Put all this together, and my mental picture confirms that I must look like a ghoul. *Maybe my looks will scare Chris off.*

When I dare to peek over at him, he resembles his old self, Mr. Serious Sourpuss. It's mildly comforting. And to my great relief, he's no longer half coyote. He wears his usual vest. A navy blue one, with a beige T-shirt underneath. He holds a mug of something to drink. Before he hands it over, he shows me a wet cloth. I examine the room behind him. His friends, the medicine men, are nowhere to be seen. Neither is Jared.

"For your face," he explains.

My fingers move to my mouth. The grit is still there. I take the washcloth and wipe my lips. When my skin feels smooth, I hold the dirty thing up for inspection. There are dark smears on the terrycloth.

"Charcoal?" I ask. My voice is hoarse and barely able to make sounds.

"Yes. From burning the sacred wood."

Chris takes the damp towel from my hand and replaces it with a mug of warm tea. My hand automatically lowers to my lap and I stare at the liquid with suspicion. The last thing he made me drink caused me to be violently ill. At least I think it was the tea.

"It is nutrient rich and I added some mint for your stomach," he says.

"Hmphh," I blow the sound out through my nose.

"Don't trust me?"

"No." I continue to stare down at the cup rather than look at Chris. Inside, my soul feels drained, like I'm exposed and vulnerable to everything and everyone under the sun and the stars.

"You can trust me. Then again, people who say that are often the ones who you should not trust. The medicine you drank before was supposed to turn you inside out and this one is supposed to bring things back to normal."

Lifting the cup to my nose I give it a tentative sniff. Peppermint is the main ingredient with something else, which I can't name for certain. I cut my eyes to the side, looking to see if he's still watching me. He is. Not having the strength to argue with him, I take a sip of the warm liquid, barely enough to wet my mouth. It's excellent, warming, and cooling from the mint, and it's sweetened with honey, which will help my raw throat immensely. I take another drink.

"Thanks," I whisper.

"I did not think it was terrible, and there's more in the kitchen for later. When you are ready for food, you will eat this."

On his lap, is a small plate of food, which I didn't notice before. There are three small servings of what I think is corn, dried cranberries, and some kind of roasted meat.

He continues, "Before the day is over, eat all of this. Remember to have gratitude for the food."

I feel my eyebrows rise in questioning uncertainty. The entire contents of the meal would fit in the palm of my hand. I don't think it will be a problem, except I'm not hungry. I look away from the food and to the windows. It's already late in the day. The sun is still above the trees, but in the western sky. *How long have I been sleeping? And what's with the gratitude?*

"Your spirit has been under the control of another. Then you have been burned from the inside. I am trying to help you put all of your pieces back in place. The food will help you feel connected to your physical body again, and having gratitude for it will help your mind connect to your body. In a healthful way."

"You burned me?"

"Not with fire, but in a way, yes."

"I felt like I was on fire. Is it gone forever?" I ask.

"The she-demon is gone, but you are not completely in the clear. You must stay here for some time. Where you are protected. Until your strength rises your spirit is compromised. Especially you," he adds.

"What does that mean? *Especially me.*" I take another drink of the tea and watch Chris over the rim of the cup.

"You need guidance. I don't think this is the best time to get into it, but I will say this. You are sensitive and open to other dimensions and the things that live there. This attracts them to you. You should stay here while you recover."

I let the mug rest in my lap and lay my head back against the cushion. "How long?" I ask.

"I am not sure. Are you willing to do what I ask?"

"I don't know," I answer, not willing to commit to the unknown.

"Drink, eat, and rest. The hardest part is behind you," he says and I think I hear a softening to his tone.

"That doesn't sound unreasonable," I concede. Then it occurs to me, "Is Jared still here?"

"Yes. He's asleep on the couch in the front room. Do you need him?"

"No. I was just wondering if he was still here with me."

"He's going to stay while I make a run to Earth's Heart Spring. You could use more of the water." He looks down at my mug of tea. "Again, it will help you connect to your body."

"So if I eat and drink this stuff, then I'll quit feeling like a dog turd?" I ask. The uncaring, broken, hollow shell of myself lying here, needs to be a thing of the past. At least I can acknowledge that much. *It's a step, isn't it?*

"Dog turds are in your past," he says. "I'm going now. Try to eat, then rest. There is food and tea in the kitchen if you want more. For today, you can only have this food. It is pure and has its own medicinal value. Understand?"

"Mmm-hmm," I hum and nod my head at him.

"One last prayer before I leave," he says and then places the plate of food on the nearest workbench.

Chris takes a small pouch from a pocket of his vest and opens it. He faces the north wall and takes a pinch of whatever is in the leather bag and puts it in his mouth. In his native words he says the prayer. I don't understand the exact meaning, but I watch as his aura expands and glows brighter. He turns to me and takes another pinch. I see the tiniest amount of something pure gold, a powder of some kind as yellow as the sun, between his fingers. Chris reaches forward and sprinkles the mystery powder over my head as he completes the prayer.

I could be imagining it, but my hollowness suddenly feels the tiniest bit fuller.

My eyes close and then before I can thank him I hear Chris leave the little sunroom. Instantly, I start to nod off, but I force myself to wake back up. *Drink your tea, Jules.* Finishing the drink soothes my throat and stomach and I'm mildly disappointed when it's gone. I reach over and place the empty mug on the chair. *Later, I'll eat it later.* My hand grabs at the cushions behind my shoulders and pulls them out, letting them slip to the floor. *Sleep please, that's all I need.*

As far as I can tell, not much time has passed. It's still daylight, but I can tell the sun is farther west. Maybe an hour since Chris left. His tea and prayer apparently lifted my spirit because I feel ten times more alert than I did before. The tea is also putting some unwanted pressure on my bladder, which I suspect is the real reason I'm awake. Can I move, I wonder? I guess I don't have much choice in the matter. I roll to my side and push my body up to sitting, letting my legs rest over the side. I see the plate of food still sitting on the workbench near me. *Yeah, yeah, I'll get to it.* The wood floor is warm and reassuringly firm beneath my feet. *Let's see if my legs are as firm. Baby steps, right?* They hold as I shuffle out of the sunroom and into the main part of Chris's cabin.

I find the bathroom almost immediately on my right. It's small, and clean, and very bachelor-esque. There's no decorations, one towel on the bar, and smells of cedar scented soap. After I finish with the necessities and wash my hands, I don't return to my cot. I head down the short hallway passed a closed door and into the living room and kitchen.

Jared is asleep on the couch like Chris said. He's curled up on his side with his back pressed to the couch cushions. His long legs are bent and his knees hang off the front. A lock of his hair has escaped from his ponytail and hangs down over his face. I want to brush it back for him, but not at the risk of waking him up. *My brother is an angel. He's an annoying, beautiful, frustrating, charismatic, pot-smoking angel. What would have happened to me if he hadn't forced me to leave Corrine and Travis's house? The answer is unimaginable. Thank you, brother. I owe you.* I turn and leave the room, letting Jared get some rest. His night was almost as awful as mine. Almost.

Angels and she-demons? Really? What is happening to my summer? My life?

At the back of the house, I take a look at my small canvas cot. An icy shiver crawls over my skin starting along my spine and then working around to cover my entire body. My eyes shut involuntarily. I want to believe all the images swimming around inside my head from yesterday and last night are just from a vivid dream, but I know it was all real. That thing, the evil soul-sucking succubus, had attacked me and wedged itself into my life. It had control over my body, and most of my mind, and it was planning to stay for a long time. Chris and his pals had forced it to leave. Actually, it was more like they had made my body so completely uninhabitable that she found the one spot — somewhere underneath my bellybutton — which wasn't quite so painful for her, and then Chris gave her a way out. Lifting my shirt, I peer down at my stomach. Last night I was sure I had been bitten by a rattlesnake, but if I had, then I would not be standing here right now. A smear of the same gritty charcoal is just above my bellybutton. Rubbing the black smudge away, I do see two tiny puncture marks. I push my shirt back down and look up. All the blood in my head drains and must be pooling somewhere near my big toes because I suddenly feel like I'm going to fall over.

Reaching for the nearest solid object, my hands grab the back of a chair. I bend forward and rest my forehead on the back of my arms. *Breathe,* I tell myself and force the air to move in and out. *Right now, you're okay. Keep breathing. There's no snake, and you're not possessed. Jared is in the other room and you're going to be all right.* When I run out of reassurances and realize my arms are beginning to tingle from the circulation being cut off, I very slowly raise my head.

The tall cabinets, rough plank shelves, and workbenches are all neatly organized and very Chris Abeyta. There are various tools around the room, and lots of jars and pots. Some are empty, but most are filled with anything from screws and nails to beads or dried plants. On the largest workbench is the wing of a large bird, wood stems, chunks of carving stone, and a bunch of wilting green leaves. More jars line the back of the workbench. Furs, bones, feathers, and drying plants hang from pegs on the walls. I recognize the braids of sweet grass and bunches of artemisia and maybe a few others, but my brain doesn't want to focus on plants. It feels too much like work right now. The sunroom looks like the workshop of someone who likes to dismember nature.

My eyes are continually drawn to the world outside. The south and west facing walls, from the waist up, are almost entirely square panes of glass.

The sudden urge to be outside is startling. I need air and sun more than anything I can ever remember needing. Chris said to eat the food today, but he didn't say to stay inside. I notice the small plate of food I'm supposed to eat. I frown at it. After not eating for such a long time, I'm not sure I'm capable. I sidle around the chair and pick up the large brown fur that has been my cot companion, and for some unknown reason, I wrap it around my shoulders. Before stepping out the back door, I pick up the plate of food. Maybe it will be more appealing outside.

On Chris's back patio, I settle into a chair and make a nest for myself. The evening sun shines through a break in the trees. It warms my face and hair and provides me with a kind of nourishment all its own. After drinking in the light, I force myself to try the food in front of me and then remember after a couple of bites, to express gratitude for the sustenance. At first, the act of chewing feels foreign to me, like I had forgotten the most basic act of survival, but after my saliva glands begin to work again, my stomach is more than appreciative for the food. To my surprise, I eat every morsel of the simple food, including the meat which I almost never eat, and catch myself staring at the empty plate. *Thank you for the wonderful food,* I say internally. *May it keep me healthy and strong. And, thank you Chris for providing the meal. And thank you for everything you've done.* Emotions swell up inside me as the enormity of what Chris has accomplished rises up afresh. He forced a succubus out of me and saved my life. At the least, he saved me from a life I wouldn't want to live.

The she-demon's possession of me was more horrifying than there are words to describe it. I could feel everything she felt, and desired. And what she most desired was lust, and greed, and domination. She had absolutely no conscience. That part of its personality is strangely exhilarating — which is terrifying. I got to experience total self-absorption, and to act on it in the most inappropriate ways. *Holy crap! What have I done?* The memories from my night at the Edge are clear, and foggy, in my mind. Even though she was controlling my body, I remember almost everything. But there are blank spots, breaks in the conversation, and empty voids, like missing pictures in my memory. I would have to guess the cause of this is because of the hash I smoked, but I'm not sure that is the only reason I can't remember everything. I'm also fairly certain the hash was laced with some unknown substance. Extremely potent is describing it mildly. No one, except my brother and Chris, will know it wasn't really me dancing on the table and kissing those guys. And after we left... *Oh jeez, after we left the nightclub, I... I was totally ripped. Jared's friend? I don't even know him. What did I do? No. What did I try to do? Breathe, Jules. She's gone now. That's all that matters. Chris pulled her out of my body and burned her in the fire. I must move forward and let the past be behind me.* It would be great advice, if I could listen to myself and actually believe it.

This experience has created a shift in a corner of my mind and I'm afraid I won't come all the way back from it. She did things with my body I would never have done and some things can't be taken back.

A depressing sadness adds to all the other emotions swirling around in my mind and body. I blink hard a few times realizing I've been staring at the empty plate in my lap for a long time. Reaching over from my chair, I place the dish on a table and then lean my head back against the chair. The openness of the sky overhead makes me want to escape into it and sail away on the next passing cloud. Only there are no clouds.

I will never be able to face Nathaniel again, not after what I've done. *What kind of girlfriend am I?*

Wait!

Where is he? Why haven't I seen him? And how long has he been gone? My brain twists and turns and wrings itself out trying to figure out how long it's been since Nathaniel left me in my kitchen. *Think, Jules.* But time is an enigma to me right now. I can't grasp exactly how long it's been. Oh Mother, what if he didn't survive from his injury? Here I am pitying myself, and he may not be alive. I mean he's not alive anyway, but he's not here either. My eyes close. Now I can't even face the sky. Then I find that even the inner darkness behind my eyelids is unbearable. I force the tears to keep away. I hate crying and God knows I've done enough of it lately.

But why? What was I bawling about yesterday? The lack of control was one thing, but there was something else. I can feel the truth of it. Something else had me wracked with misery and sobbing until I couldn't cry even one more tear. The memories I want to retrieve are as elusive as catching starlight. The succubus controlling me must have had something to do with it, I decide, as regret, shame, and an emptiness, which I cannot justify, take hold of me and won't let up. To my utter dismay, my eyes start to leak from the corners. I wipe away the evidence with the back of my hand and then shake my head from side to side. Sitting straight up in the chair, I open my eyes and face my reality. *It's what people do, right?*

I have a visitor. I shut my eyes again and turn my head away. My hair falls over part of my face. *Why do things like this have to be a part of my reality?* I take a deep breath, not wanting to deal right now, but of course I will. *What choice do I have? Sometimes, life really blows.*

He sits on a bench to my left, near the edge of the patio. His ankles are crossed and his large hands are clasped loosely in his lap. He's not really staring at me, I don't think. It looks more like he's watching the cabin. Multiple things about him make the hair on the back of my neck bristle with alarm. It should be his size. He could easily be considered a giant in some countries, but that isn't it. I'm used to being around really tall males, just look at my brother. Nope, what worries me about this man is that he isn't alive. Well, I should clarify. He probably is alive in some way. But, I would bet money if I were to throw a rock at him, it would pass right on through, like he wasn't there at all.

"Hey," I say.

Maybe if I take a direct approach with the members of the mystical world, it won't be as terrifying. Nathaniel isn't scary after all, I remind myself. I reach over, tightening the fur robe around my shoulders.

"Hello, Jules," he says. His eyebrows rise a tiny bit and he turns his massive dreadlock covered head my way.

Wow, deep voice, a part of my brain acknowledges, even before I realize a millisecond later that he knows me by name. *Lovely, he knows who I am.* When in need, I find sarcasm becomes a trusty old friend. "Since you know who I am, may I ask who you are?" With some success, I think I'm controlling the shake in my voice. *What is he doing here?*

"Ah. I am a friend, and it is my pleasure." His bright and lively brown eyes close in a slow blink as he gives me the slightest bow. "I was told you can see us. You did not say anything to me the other night so I was uncertain, but now I see it is true. Did you know your kind are very unusual?"

"Yeah, I know," I say flatly. I want to ask him who told him I see *'things,'* and what does he mean by *the other night*, but I don't. If I learned anything about dealing with beings of unknown origin, such as she-demons, it is to be overly cautious.

Chris once told me, one way I could tell whether or not I was seeing a real person, or a dead one, was that the dead don't have an aura. This is how I knew the man on the patio with me is not made of flesh and blood, no aura. Although as I continue to stare at him, he does have an energy field of sorts, but it's not human, more like Nathaniel's. The realization startles me further. *His glow resembles Nathaniel's.* He's an Angel of Death, my brain informs me. The field of light around his body — or rather where his body should be — is mostly clear, but radiant, and if I had to give a name to the color it would simply be white with a hint of gold. People, living people that is, have energy fields full of different colors. He definitely looks different than a "normal" person. I press my back hard against the chair, instinctively trying to get away from him, if only by an inch. *If he's here now, does that mean he's here for me? Did getting possessed by a succubus cause more damage than Chris could repair? I feel awful. Could I be dying?*

"What are you doing here?" I manage to say.

"I'm gonna ask your forgiveness for not answerin'. At least not yet. You should be resting. Last night was taxing, wasn't it?"

"Yes, it was," I say. "But why would you care if I'm well rested?"

"Believe it or not, I'm hanging around to ease suffering, not cause it."

"Is there any way I can make you leave?" I ask. When I first met Nathaniel, he thought he was assigned to escort me to the afterlife. That my life was ending after nineteen and a half years. He actually tried to keep me alive, which he wasn't supposed to do. In the end however, he made a huge mistake and another girl, Ashley Johnson, had died. "Oh my god," I blurt out.

The Angel of Death, sitting nonchalantly on the bench, gives me a questioning look at my outburst.

"I've seen you before," I say. "The night Ashley Johnson had a seizure, by the Spring of Souls."

"I know."

"But I didn't know what you were at the time." I wonder if I should just walk away and see how far I can get. He has to be here for me. Why else would he be here?

He frowns. The change that transforms his easy going features to one of anger and frustration is phenomenal and a little spike of fear clenches my insides.

"No, no. I don't mean to frighten you. That night upsets me still. I have not lost a client in over a century. It's distressing and I'm not used to being helpless."

Swallowing his statements takes some effort but I manage, and then say, "We helped her." He blinks at me a couple of times so I make an attempt to explain. "She, or her soul, I don't really understand it all, but Chris and I went back to the Spring of Souls at Castle Hill, and I saw her leave this world. It was...well, I don't really have the words, but it felt right."

"You? And the shaman man? Released her soul. Really? Well, that lightens me. I thank you. Your shaman is something special. A good soul is what he is."

The angel's facial features soften to his previous look of good natured humor.

"Wait a second," I say as the wheels in my mind continue to turn with vigor. "You were assigned to Ashley? Do people usually have two angels when they die?" I was under the impression

Nathaniel was hanging around to help Ashley after she passed. Nathaniel and Ashley were both by Forge Creek when we first met and then again at Castle Hill.

"What?" he asks. One of his large hands rubs at his chin as he contemplates what I just asked. "Two of us? No. On occasion, we will assist each other if we need to."

"So you came because Nathaniel was a little distracted and not paying close enough attention to Ashley?" I ask trying to sort this all out in my mind.

He looks mildly confused as he attempts to answer me. "Ashley, no. Ashley's death was sudden. I often get the harder cases because I have more experience. Sudden changes in fate can be more difficult. For the deceased, but also for the families."

His answer sinks in slowly as if the workings inside of my head are trying to operate in a pool of quicksand. My next words come out rather slowly. "Are you telling me Nathaniel was not assigned to Ashley Johnson?"

"That's correct. I was. Now I'm here to take care of someone else."

My head drops and I stare down into my lap, breaking eye contact with this angelic being. My fingers rub at my temples as if massaging my brain will help me process better. I try to make sense of what he has told me. "Someone else?" I ask tentatively.

"Mmmh-hmm," he answers simply.

The brain massage isn't working. I look over at him expecting a pointed look to confirm my suspicions that I'm near to death, but he's no longer looking at me. He's staring at the sky, or Chris's cabin, or who knows what. His large fingers absently scratch at his stomach over his linen shirt.

Nathaniel wasn't Ashley's escort to the afterlife. Then what was he doing there? He said it wasn't me, so he either lied, or he's not telling me something. Either way, he's a liar. *That's impossible.* Part of me immediately starts to argue. I would know. I'm never wrong about people. Nathaniel is a true and honest guy if I've ever met one.

He's almost too easy for me to interpret. He's also moody, intense, and overprotective, but I accept that about him. Nathaniel is the most straightforward and sincere person I know. I would bet my life on it, or would I? What was he planning to do? Continue to save me from my death so he could sneak in a kiss here and there? Rescue me from danger and illness until I became an old lady? The idea is ludicrous. Something is wrong. *What am I missing?*

Nathaniel neglected to tell me something, and that makes him a liar. If he loves me, like he proclaims, then he would have told me. Is this the end then? I can't be with someone who can't tell me the truth. If there is no honesty in a relationship, there's no relationship. And where is Nathaniel? Do I even want to see him again? The growing pain in my heart tells me some piece of me isn't ready to walk away from this relationship.

"Are you hangin' in there alright?" my strange visitor asks.

"Huh?" I say stupidly. At first, I think he's some kind of mind reader like Chris, but then I shake myself.

"You've been through an ordeal like no other these last couple of days. I'm asking if you're handling it okay."

The snarky reply is out of my mouth before I can stop it. "Is this your way of preparing someone for death, because I have to tell you, it's more than a little strange. I would think you would try to give me a heads up about what's coming, and to 'follow the light,' all that kind of woo-woo crap. I mean, if I'm dead, what does it matter?"

Confusion crosses his broad face and then is replaced by a look I can't read. Then quite unexpectedly, his mouth spreads into a wide grin, his chest heaves, and a deep chuckle rumbles out of him.

I can't watch while he finds something rather hilarious. "Oh, dear," he says between gasps. "Jules, oh my." He laughs some more, his hand slapping the top of his thigh.

I begin to wonder if he's going to fall off the bench. His face is one of sheer mirth. I frown, not finding any of this funny whatsoever. I may not have the most grand and important life, but it's mine, and I thought I would have at least a few more years. He covers the front of his mouth with a fist and coughs. Then he clears his throat.

"I apologize," he says, taking on a more serious tone. "Ah, but it's only you remind me of being young and innocent and what a delight it is to be alive. I work all the time you see, and I very rarely speak to my clients before they pass on. When I do, it's usually not a joyous occasion. You surprised me." His smile is huge. The gap in the center of his white teeth seems to glare at me.

I grimace deeper. He likes talking to me because I can see him, and I'm still alive. Oh happy-happy-joy-joy for me. My head shakes side to side with utter disbelief.

"Let me set one thing straight for you, Jules."

His now sober demeanor catches my attention and I stop my next sarcastic remark.

"I am not sitting here for you, young one. Your time will come to pass someday, but it's not in the near future. With the exorcism, I'm sorry about that by the way, and the loss of Nathaniel, I thought maybe you could use a companionable ear. If I am mistaken, forgive me, but I thought the two of you have been makin' friends with one another. He was also a good friend of mine. Nathaniel is gone, but he is also still alive. We will meet up again in another life, I am sure. As will you, if it's in the highest good. As for the other, it is truly unfortunate. What a wicked creature she was. Taking over your body like that. You're one lucky girl to have someone around like your shaman man. He probably saved you a heck of a lot of heartache and trouble."

I hear words coming out of the angel's mouth, and I know it's processing inside my head, but the part I can't quite get past are the words "loss of Nathaniel" and "Nathaniel is gone."

I'm not sure if time has just stopped, or my heart did.

"You in good health over there?"

"What?" I breathe out.

"Looks like you're about to fall over."

"I, um, what?" I manage to garble.

The confused expression mixed with concern on the angel's face makes me try to find a more coherent statement. It doesn't really work. "Nathaniel. Where is he?" I mumble.

Deep creases line the angel's face as he watches me. "He moved into the next level of his afterlife, Jules."

I'm speechless. Not only because I'm unsure what he means exactly, but because I also know somewhere deep inside that it's not good. That it's abysmal.

"To be frank with you, Jules, I was wonderin' if you saw what happened. You were the only one there, besides that demon-loving sucker, and Lord knows I won't be speaking to him about it. Jared and I came in too late, but I saw enough to know Nathaniel passed on."

A long silence fills the space between us, and in those countless seconds my world is suddenly tilted, and I'm left standing a little off center, turned around, and upside-down.

"I didn't see," I tell the angel. "The succubus..." I say and then stop. "Will you excuse me?" I rise from my chair, amazed that I'm capable of moving at all, but my body somehow knows what to do.

"Would you like some assistance? You look whiter than a swan."

My body feels hollow again and I seem to float toward the back door. I don't answer him but I suddenly feel someone take my arm and guide me to the house.

"I've been asked to stay outside, so this is as far as I go," he says as he opens the door for me.

"Okay," I say automatically.

"Jules, I think your shaman man will understand if I step inside to help you while he's away."

"No. Not necessary," I murmur.

"If you change your mind, it would be my pleasure to assist you. Call me by my name and I will come. I am Marcus. It is so simple. So please, anytime or anywhere, you are a friend of my friend, and these last few days have been as strange as they come. Call for me. I'm close by anyway."

My head jerks in acknowledgement of his words and then I step away from his almost overbearing presence. The door clicks closed behind me and I'm alone in the sunroom. I look over my shoulder to make sure I didn't just imagine the whole bloody rotten conversation. The angel, Marcus, sits on the bench, watching me with his wide brown eyes.

In this odd state of numb, I don't feel my body move, but then I'm lying on my side on the stiff canvas cot facing the wall. An engorged river of thoughts floods my brain. The debris swirling around is bulky and doesn't belong in the water, but there it is anyway. It's creating an immense amount of pressure on the sutures of my skull and I don't know how long I'll be able to handle it before the floodwaters burst and tiny bits of brain matter explode onto everything. The morbid side of my personality smiles at the thought of Chris walking into his sunroom to find his recently recovered patient missing her head. But in truth, I wouldn't want him to have to clean up the mess, so I better keep the maelstrom contained. On the other hand, a quick and morose ending to this misery called life would be welcome right about now. It just seems easier than having to deal.

My Nathaniel — I already think of him as mine, which is weird but true — has passed away. What does that even mean? He wasn't exactly alive to begin with. And if he's gone, where did he pass away to? Heaven, Hell, the Great Cosmos? What happens to an angel when they die? I have no freakin' idea. It's one of a thousand things I don't understand about my otherworldly boyfriend. If a friend of mine were to confide in me about a mysterious new boyfriend and she told me even one of the things that has happened between me and Nathaniel, I would shake her by the shoulders and scream that she run away and never look back. What has happened to me? Why can't I walk away from this guy? Not that it matters now. Nathaniel is gone, right? At least according to Marcus he is.

An enormous weight presses on my chest as the reality of the situation dawns. He is really gone. *And I know when it happened.* Marcus said I was there. Me and Travis. In the basement. I couldn't see him but part of me knew. I knew it and I couldn't do anything to stop it. Heavy-hearted, my breath hitches. The increased pressure is unbearable and my head does explode after all. It's not in the way I had imagined, however. A stinging sensation, like razor burn, creeps in around my eyeballs and causes them to leak like mad. The wood grain on the rough-cut boards of the wall blur into a swimming brown mess. I throw my arm over my eyes to hide. My lungs finally give in to the unseen weight of sadness and push a heaving sob from my lips. My core shudders from my pubic bone to my throat in a wrenching swell of emotional vomit.

This is ridiculous! I hate crying. No, let me be clear about this, I detest crying. I force myself to turn over and then push my body into a sitting position. My fists rub angrily over my eyes trying to erase all evidence of my vulnerability, but the tears carry on, so I keep wiping them away. *So what if I fell in love! So what if I didn't get a chance to experience what lasting love is! So what if I may never find anyone else again! So damn what! People lose the loves of their lives all the time. It happens every day. Think about all the wars and the sickness on this planet. I'm not special. People live with all sorts of pain, and so can I. Even if it's a monstrous, gripping hole full of what-if's and if-only's.*

"Hmm-hmm," I hear a quiet clearing of the throat.

I cup my face with open palms leaving only the tip of my nose sticking out between my fingers. My hair falls forward as I bend my head down. With effort, I manage a shaky inhale and wait for some courage so I can face my brother, but I can't find any. Jared eases down next to me. The canvas creaks and the metal frame groans under our combined weight, but it holds. I don't look at him. He wraps an arm around my shoulders and squeezes me in close. To my relief he doesn't say anything. The smell of burnt sage is strong on his shirt, but underlying that, he smells familiar, like our home, and of the laundry soap we use, and also his own unique Jared smell.

Swallowing my sadness feels similar to having a pill stuck in my throat, but this pill is the mother of all pills, bigger than a walnut and bristling with thorns. I force it down, and then my eyes finally quit leaking. My hands lower to my lap, exposing my face, which feels puffy and tender, but I still don't have the balls to look up at Jared.

After I've watched the shadows of the window frames move across the wall with the setting sun do I realize that I've been sitting here for a long time. Once I have the conscious thought of time passing, my back cramps. Shifting my body slightly, prompts Jared to do the same. I feel him lengthen his spine and then he straightens each of his long legs, one at a time. His left knee pops loud enough to startle me. We don't move away from one another, but only stretch a few inches and then settle back into our grooves on the canvas.

The silence in the room is starting to become its own entity. It hovers near my ears and is daring my voice to chase it away. But I stay silent, unable to think of one appropriate thing to say in the moment. Saying, "my angel boyfriend died," aloud is more than I can do.

"So, who are you today?" Jared forces the silence to leave the sunroom first.

Did I hear him right? I let myself look up at him just long enough to meet his chocolate brown eyes for one second. His face is completely serious, except for the tiny crinkle of mischievousness at the corner of one eye. I look away, but only because I'm embarrassed about how awful I must look right now.

I feel him shrug his shoulders. Then he says, "I thought Chris exorcised you, but he obviously screwed it up because my sister, Juliana Crowson, never cries. Well, at least not in front of people. So, who are you?"

I listen to his taunting and don't comment.

"Okay, how about twenty questions? I'm pretty awesome at this game. Are you the Lady of the Lake?"

I shake my head at him in incredulity, but he takes it as an answer no.

"That's one, but I'm not going to need all twenty. I think I've got it. You're a bean-sidhe, right? No, I take it back. Yo! This is it."

The excitement in him grows and so does his tone. He's getting louder and more animated with every word.

"I've figured out who's taken over your body this time. You're one of the muses. The inventor of tragedy, Mel something. Go ahead and confess, so I can win."

I gnaw at my lower lip, trying not to succumb to his whimsy. He leans forward slightly and looks over at me. I give him a pitiful look that hopefully says I'm not in the mood for games.

"I'd like to have my sister back now," he tells me. "So the sooner we can get Mel to leave, the better."

"I think you mean Melpomene," I squeak. My voice cracks and sounds worn out.

"Ah, so you do admit it," Jared says.

Using my pointer finger, I make a cross over my chest. "Swear to God, I am not — hmm-hmm," I clear my throat, and then continue. "No longer possessed by anything, or anyone."

Jared seems willing to accept my declaration. His hand rubs my back, a little too briskly, as if to say, 'Good, now let's move on.' Then he confirms his gesture by asking, "Chris still gone?"

I don't really feel like making small talk, but I answer Jared's question and it helps redirect my pain. "He went to Earth's Heart Spring for more water."

"Yeah, he made you some crazy smelling drink with it."

Jared rises from the cot, stretches his long skinny body from fingertips to toes, and then turns and looks down at me.

"Hey, why did you have that bottle of water and all the plant stuff in the car anyway? Chris was shocked to find exactly what he needed in the trunk."

Thinking and making my tongue work simultaneously is challenging so I answer in multiple sections. "I, um, I had the water because he dropped it and I wanted to give it back to him. And what plant was in my car?" This part of the question isn't finding an answer no matter how hard I try to come up with one.

Jared walks over to the workbench in the sunroom and picks up a limp stem of some large plant and tosses it at me. It lands on the cot next to me, a wilted and lank dead thing. I recognize it anyway. I pick it up and toss it back across the room where Jared snatches it out of the air.

My brain works furiously at putting together the missing pieces. I had tried like heck to get the devil's club roots out of the ground with a stick, but instead I gave my finger a nasty splinter. I look down at the scab. I know I didn't put the plant in my car, so that leaves only one explanation.

"Nathaniel," I say aloud. "He must have gone back and gotten the roots for me."

"Nathaniel's not the name of the succubus, is it?"

"No," I say mildly exasperated.

"Just checking. I haven't ever heard you talk about *Nathaniel* before."

He wiggles his brows at me as he says Nathaniel's name, adding his own silent innuendo.

In spite of my grief, I feel my cheeks flare with embarrassing heat. *Damn my fair skin.* "Chris treated me with devil's club? I've heard it could be used for spiritual issues," I can barely say these last words, but I choke them out. "I guess I didn't really believe it. Shows you what I know." I can't meet Jared's eyes as I attempt to stay off the Nathaniel subject, so I stare out the window instead. The Angel of Death, Marcus, is kicked back in one of the patio chairs with his feet propped on the table.

Staring between Marcus and Jared, my head turns very slowly back and forth. I think I do at least three double takes. Something is happening and threads of understanding are slowly weaving together. My eyes finally land on Jared. He appears to be entertaining himself by perusing the contents on top of the workbench. The fingers of his good hand fiddle with a string of multi-colored beads. I just now notice he's not wearing the sling over his casted arm like he's supposed to be. The small detail registers in my mind, but doesn't carry near the weight of my other epiphany.

"Jared?" I whisper.

"Yup?" he answers as he lifts a long black feather from a clay bowl, turns it over, and then puts it back.

"Is there someone outside?"

His focus moves to the window in front of him. After a brief perusal of the yard, he turns to me and says, "No. Why? Did you hear something?"

His level of concern appears to be about as worried as if I just heard the pizza delivery guy ring the doorbell.

"Jared, do you see anyone on the patio?" I ask again, this time slower.

Now he's starting to catch on. First his eyes shift to the window and then his head rotates to follow.

"Jules? Do you see somebody out there?"

"Answer me first."

"No, Jules, I don't see anyone."

Jared takes two steps back from the workbench.

"Is there anyone else in this house?" There's a noticeable shake to my voice.

A crease of apprehension makes Jared's brows knit, and his normally wide and soft mouth hardens a little.

"No. Not unless Chris is back. Hey, do you need to lie down or something?" he asks.

I shake my head, now incapable of forming words. *No. Yes. I mean no, I don't want to lie down. And no, no, no! Marcus is outside waiting for someone and that someone isn't me. God please. Please, this can't be happening. Marcus is here for my brother.*

Jared comes closer to me. "Can I get you something...like tea?"

I must look really ill if Jared is offering to bring me tea. In fact, I do feel off. There's an itching sensation in the center of my head and it's growing like a swarm of angry bees.

The last thing I remember, other than a million bees, is Jared's perfectly cut face hanging over mine and his low timber voice calling my name.

Chapter Fifteen:
Learning to Say Goodbye

Juliana

"Jared," I call out.

My head smacks against something hard. Reaching up, I feel smooth glass, and the edge of a, a what? Another jarring bump causes me to bonk my head again.

"Ow." My eyes flutter open and I'm in my car, staring out the window. The streetlights along Route 160 are lit even though it's still light out. We're heading east on the highway, and for all the life in me, I have no idea why. I hold the side of my head where I hit the car door and turn to my driver.

"What the hell, J?"

He must not have heard my previous grumble because his eyes nearly pop out of their sockets and he yanks the wheel, sending us into the median.

This sends me bolt upright in my seat as I look around for other cars, curbs, or signage we are about to crash into. Jared corrects and puts us back in our lane. As I look back to see the dust cloud he's stirred up in the turn lane, I let out a loud, "Bejesus, F-ing, criminy," and grip my chest.

"Learn how to cuss, damn it," Jared orders. "It sounds like this. Fuck Jules, you scared the shit out of me."

I can feel his eyes boring into me, but I'm temporarily frozen in my seat and can't respond. What he doesn't know is I didn't scream because of the near accident, but because of the man sitting in the back seat of our car.

I take another look over my shoulder at Marcus. "I don't like cussing," I say.

"He's takin' you to the hospital," Marcus tells me.

"The succubus had a dirty mouth," Jared says. "Don't you remember? She must've really screwed with your head."

"You're kidding," I burst out, directed at Marcus's words, not my brothers. "Jared, pull over."

"Yeah right. You're going to see Mom."

"Jared, stop the car. You have no idea what's happening. Stop, now!"

One long curved eyebrow rises. The look makes me think he is not only patronizing me, but he also feels sorry for me. The car doesn't slow down.

"This is the part where I tell you if you try to prevent the future from happenin', it's gonna worsen the overall effect of the upcoming situation," Marcus says calmly from the back seat.

His meaning is all too clear and a frozen knife rips a path down my spine, opening a wound which should never exist. He's letting me know if I try to stop my brother from dying, it will make things more painful. For Jared, or for my family and myself, I'm not sure, but I suspect it's probably both.

"You've been passed out for like an hour, Jules. You need to see Mom, or a doctor. Be thankful I didn't call an ambulance."

"An hour? No way," I say, shocked by this revelation. How out of it am I? I don't feel too terrible, now. I got overwhelmed. *It happens.*

"It's been less than ten minutes," Marcus corrects.

"I'm tired, and, none of that even matters right now," I say while trying not to panic.

Jared shifts the car into fourth gear and then third as he gently applies the brakes and steers into the turn lane for the hospital. "Okay, so maybe more like twenty minutes. But, so what? I couldn't wake you up, Jules. I'm taking you to Mom."

"J," I start, and then look over my shoulder at Marcus, "I promise not to pass out again. And, I swear to God I'm not going to take one step into that hospital. Mom doesn't need to know about any of this. Once the story comes out, I'll have to tell her what you were doing at Travis's house. Do you really want her to find out about that?"

Jared parks our car in a space near the main entrance to the hospital, where our mother works inside as a nurse. He cuts the engine and turns to face me.

I can see his jaw moving as he grinds his teeth. Jared is attempting to control his anger. I should shrink back in my seat. He can be a fierce rival when he wants to be, but I have to hold my ground. I press down the lock on my door and then meet his stare with my own stubborn defiance.

"Blackmail may have worked once, but I'm not falling for it again. You don't have to tell Mom anything. And if you do, I have plenty to share with her about what you've been up to. Let her look at you, and then I'll take you home, or back to Chris, or wherever." He pauses for emphasis. Then, in case I'm not taking him seriously, he adds, "Jules, I *can* make you. Remember the slutty table dance? I carried you out of the club with one good arm."

The fingers on my right hand twitch with a need I haven't felt since I was about thirteen. It's the uncontrollable urge to rip Jared's hair out for being a bratty little brother. Since I'm past that stage of my life, I take a deep breath and realize this may not be the worst place to be if someone may suddenly keel over. The thought stops me cold. Jared's Angel of Death is sitting behind me this very second. He's about to leave me forever. I feel my eyes flood with instant tears. Turning away from his deep brown glare, I open the door and slam it closed behind me. I rub my knuckles over my eyes while trying to hide under my hair and then walk around to the other side of the car. Jared is turning the key in the lock. As he turns around, I throw my arms around him in a fierce hug.

"You're my brother, right?"

Jared stands still, his arms pinned to his sides, as I press my cheek against his chest. He's too skinny, but still very strong. He smells like every childhood memory I have with him in it and his heart beats reassuringly under my ear. I don't let go of him until he says something.

"Did you flip your wig? Get off."

"I will, but please do something for me. Please," I say.

"What, Jules? You're acting freaky again."

"Stay by me. Promise me, Jared. Stay right next to me, okay."

He finally manages to shrug me off, but not before I feel him lightly squeeze me back.

"Okay."

I take a deep breath and then say, "Here we go. Mom's probably busy. And I'm fine, you'll see." With that, I walk straight into the hospital, Jared and Marcus by my side.

"Hi, Mrs. Baker," I say, as I wave at the receptionist. I point a finger down the corridor where my mom's station is and ask, "Can we go see our mom?"

Mrs. Baker turns her attention from the computer monitor and tips her head down an inch to see us from over the frame of her gilded reading glasses. She nods with approval, but her stern upper lip doesn't look happy to see us. I think Mrs. Baker is the kind of person who's not overly fond of the younger generation, but she doesn't stop us from passing by the desk.

When we get to the nurses' station, my mom's co-worker, tells us Mom is busy with a patient and she will let her know we're here as soon as she sees her. She suggests we go take a seat in the waiting area at the end of the hall. Actually, this is sort of perfect. I mean, how much danger can Jared really be in, sitting inside a hospital?

As I round the corner, expecting to see some nice padded chairs and a coffee table covered with boring magazines, I'm nearly struck down by my own ignorance. Sure, Jared may be safe in here, but I never thought for a second there might be dead people in the hospital. *Duh*.

Six sets of eyes look at us as we enter the small waiting area. I gasp with the shock of seeing so many of them together. The woman breaks eye contact first. She looks grief-stricken so I don't stare at her for more than a second. She needs privacy right now, and if I were her, I wouldn't want to be stared at if my eyes were shadowed and red, which I'm sure mine are. A small boy with sandy colored hair sits on her lap. He buries his face against the woman's chest when our eyes meet. These two are not the problem; they're breathing the same air I am. It's the two men who don't have an aura around their bodies, and look tense and upset, that made me gasp. They're dead. I know it, and so do the two angels in the room. No, make that three angels in the room, including our tail, Marcus. No doubt, *he* is fully aware of who is living and who isn't.

"Oh, Marcus, you couldn't have chosen a better time for an entrance," the angel with the blonde hair says.

She turns away from the mixed group of the living and the dead and walks straight over to us. She's gorgeous and exudes otherworldly power. The other one, who I would guess is also an angel, although she has a different color about her aura, sits down in the chair next to the woman and child.

"Miss Harmony, you've got it backwards. It's always my pleasure. How's everything?"

"Not well. I've run into an upset."

Jared plops down into the farthest chair away from the woman and her child. He slouches down in his seat and sticks his feet far out in front of him. His long legs take up half of the waiting room. Jared has no idea about any of the drama going on in the room.

I, on the other hand, want to get far away from this scene. I gaze down the hallway with longing, wishing I could escape, but I don't want to draw any extra attention to myself. All I need is a plausible excuse. My best efforts at ignoring a room full of dead people fails as I can still hear the conversation between Marcus and Harmony.

"They each have their own agenda. It's a complicated mess," the angel, Harmony, is saying. Then her tone changes and she says, "Oh Marcus, have you heard about Nathaniel?" she asks.

"Yes. It's…well, it is what it is. I would have helped him if I could have, but I was too late. I will miss working with him."

Now, instead of trying to block them out, I strain to hear every word.

"You haven't heard the latest news, Marcus. Nathaniel has been—"

Jared nudges my ankle with one of his size fourteen shoes. "Sit down, Jules," he says in a low voice. He tips his head to the chair next to him.

I missed it. I didn't hear what she said about Nathaniel. *He has been what?* I glare at my brother and try to hear the rest of what they're saying but they have moved on to something else.

I glance over at Marcus and Harmony and then back down the hall. Unfortunately, I also see, and hear, the two dead guys in the room. One of them is saying, "Tom, go away and leave me alone. She's my wife and I don't want to hear another word out of you."

The one, which I presume to be Tom, argues back. "You can't make me leave."

"Want to see me try?" the first one says.

"Jared, we need to leave okay?" I ask with desperation.

"We already did this, Jules. Mom is going to look at you before I take you anywhere."

"I meant, let's go sit somewhere else," I say. The two dead guys behind me sound as if they're about to start brawling.

I hear Marcus say behind me, "They can't hurt each other. Could be the best thing for them."

"Just chill, Jules. Would you sit? You look like you're about to hurl."

Just as I'm about to start begging Jared to move somewhere less crowded, Tom, the dead guy, says, "He's my son. I don't have to leave if you don't."

"Of course you have to bring that up. Being the sperm donor doesn't give you any rights. You're an asshole of a brother, you know that."

I turn my head just in time to see Tom take a couple of steps backward as the first guy comes at him.

"Ahh! Excuse me," I say, and jump out of the way before I'm about to get stepped on.

Someone who doesn't have a body cannot really step on someone who does. I realize this too late of course. Jared gives me a queer look — something he's been perfecting lately. Blood drains from my face and pools somewhere below my ankles.

Tom and the other man stop their about to be fight to stare at me.

"You can see me?" he asks.

I don't want to answer, but I feel my head shaking no.

"She can see us, Tom."

The first man steps around Tom and walks right up to my face.

"You can help me. Please, my name is Carl Davis and this is my wife and son. Oh Jesus, this is exactly what I needed. You have to help me!"

My head continues to shake as I stumble away from the dead man. I trip over Jared and fall in slow motion. First my knee bumps his leg, then my hip hits the floor, and last my upper body sprawls across the carpet.

"Bravo, Jules. Twenty points for style, ten for gracefulness," Jared says. He reaches down and helps me to my feet.

Marcus, Harmony, and the other angel encircle Tom and Carl.

"She is not here to assist you, Carl," the other angel, an elderly woman with dainty bones and pale green eyes, says.

"Listen to your mom, Carl. She knows what's best for you," Harmony says.

Carl pays little attention to any of them as his watery brown eyes fix on me.

Grabbing Jared's sleeve, I leave the room, stretching the cotton fabric of his T-shirt to its limit. "Come on. Now," I order.

Carl darts out of the group and blocks my path. Tom follows suit, and the two of them effectively create a ghostly barrier.

Their mother, also a member of the undead, attempts to speak some reason. "Leave the girl alone. We will figure this out. Please, boys."

Meanwhile, I spin around, release Jared's shirt and then grab a hold of his good hand, and make my best attempt to yank him to his feet.

"Fine. If it makes you happy, we'll go sit somewhere else," Jared says.

But I can't get away.

"Please, her name is Gayle. Just tell her—"

I cut Carl off by saying, "I have to leave now."

He goes on, "Tell her, the accident, the whole thing was Tom's fault."

After this statement, Tom looks like he's going to explode. The elderly lady/angel steps between me and her two dead sons. I take that as my opening and, with Jared firmly attached to my hand, I slip through a narrow gap left by her running interference. Jared passes right through Carl and it makes me shudder, but he looks as if he felt nothing at all. As I rush around the corner and into the corridor, Jared and I almost have a head-on collision with Marcus and Harmony. They're both in the physical now. Marcus is even more overwhelming with a body. He's at least as tall as Jared, which is impressive at six-foot-four, but Marcus is built like a bodyguard.

My breath catches in my throat as I try to dart around the angelic pair. Carl and his mother continue to bicker behind us.

"Pardon me, Jules," Marcus says.

"No problem," I say, as I pull Jared in close to me.

He doesn't move to the side, however, and there's not quite enough room for us to get by.

Harmony looks at me wide eyed. "Hello," she says.

Kindness radiates out of her, not only because the sound of her voice is like a warm sunny day, but also because of her open and welcoming expression.

"Hi," I say with a little too much apprehension. I tuck my hair behind my ear and look down at the floor. *I wish they would move out of my way.*

"Do not fear what is out of your control, Jules," she says to me.

Looking up, I find her smiling kindly at me, eyes so bright and with a depth of understanding and recognition that I feel an electric shock zing through me. *Who is this angel?* Disturbed, I take a step back and am unable to speak.

"My friend is having some trouble. We're gonna make it right, and then I'll be back later," Marcus says.

"Um, yeah," I say.

"Take care now," he says, and finally steps to the side.

"Nice to meet you," Harmony says to my retreating back.

If I could run away and not look ridiculous, I would. As it is, I also have a hundred and seventy pounds in tow, and he's in no hurry.

"Who was that?" Jared asks, once we are out of earshot.

"No one," I say.

"Sure, Jules, try again."

"Jared, can we please go home now?"

"Nope. Mom, remember? And who were those people? This time, tell me."

We're in sight of the nurses' station. In desperation, I glance over at it. I'm not sure if I want to see her there, or not. I definitely want Jared to see her. It may be his last time ever. I swallow hard. She's not there.

I halt our retreat, let go of his hand, and close my eyes for the space of a heartbeat. Then I look Jared in the eyes and say, "J, they were, those people, were not people. I'll tell you everything if you just let us leave."

Jared cocks his head to the side and peers down at me with skepticism.

"We're running out of time. Can you please trust me on this?"

Something clicks inside him. I see the change in his energy field and feel him make up his mind about something.

"Yeah," he says, then adds a condition, "But no more passing out."

"Fine," I agree quickly, and follow with an exasperated, "Thank you."

We turn to leave. I'm determined to get Jared out of here and far away from Marcus. Even knowing it's a futile attempt, I have to try to save my brother from death knocking at his door. As I rush past the nurses' desk, I hear a familiar voice call out.

"Hey, what are you two doing here?"

Mom already looks preoccupied and tired even though it's only the beginning of her shift. There's a slight shadow under each of her eyes and many loose strands of hair hanging down around her face. She smiles at us and then goes immediately to her desk and bends over a chart to scribble something down.

I say, "Just wanted to see you. It's been a couple of days."

"It has been, hasn't it? Everything okay?"

"Mmm-hmm," I make a noncommittal sound. I hate lying and try to avoid it whenever possible.

Jared and I stand on the opposite side of the high counter and watch as our mom moves to the computer and types in some information. It only takes her a minute and then she looks up at us.

"You look really busy, Mom. We'll leave you alone so you can work. Sorry to bother you," I say.

"No, wait. Don't go. I am busy but we can go get some dinner together in the cafeteria. Oh jeez, that's why you're here, isn't it? I'm sorry kids. I've been meaning to go grocery shopping. There's nothing in the house. I'll give you some money if you want to go pick up some things." She bends down under the desk and reappears with her purse.

"No, no, it's not that. We're fine. And besides, I have my own money."

"Oh, that reminds me. Your grandmother called. She left a message, wondering why you didn't come into work."

Work? I don't even know what day of the week it is. My life is falling apart. "Crud. I hope she's not mad at me."

"I don't think so," Mom says as she walks around her station to come stand by us. "I think she was just checking to make sure you were feeling well. You're not sick are you?" Her hand automatically rises to my forehead. "You look different," she says scrutinizing my appearance. "What's wrong?" she asks and I can hear her mother instincts kicking in.

I bite my lower lip as I come up with the best answer that's not a lie, but also doesn't tell her anything.

"Jules had an upset stomach," Jared says.

"But it's totally better now," I add.

"Are you sure? I could have a doctor look at you. You're here anyway."

"No, really, it's okay. Actually, I need to get home. Come on, Jared."

"Well, if you change your mind, it's no problem. And, here," She hands over some money. "So you can get some dinner."

"No, no" I say, and shake my head refusing the cash.

"You have to eat. Get something healthy. Especially if your stomach has been acting funny."

She stuffs the bills into my hand.

"Thanks." I lean in and give her a hug, and then I remember. "I love you so much, Mommy."

After I let go she gives me a slightly surprised look mixed with uncertainty and pleasure. I nudge Jared forward. "Give Mom a hug J, and tell her you love her."

He takes a step backward instead of forward. Jared isn't one to openly display affection toward his family members, even though I know he loves us. He gives me the crazy look again.

"Do it," I demand, and surprisingly, he does.

"I love you too," she says. "Now, be safe, kiddos."

Chapter Sixteen:
Thumb Screws Preferred

Nathaniel

Dying was a curious event. My second death, that is. Painful is not the word for what happened to me. It lacks in intensity to the thousandth degree. Travis and his demons are expert at what they do. His soulless monsters tore me apart, bit by bit. They were efficient at their task and I suffered for it. Now I know. Now it's too late. Should I feel fortunate to have another chance? Can I call what I have become another chance? I'm no longer an angel, and I'm no longer dead. The powers that be have granted me another pass. If I succeed, then I'll be reinstated to my last position. If I fail, then I'll be stuck in this strange limbo. The other side will not be there waiting for me. And the other side was not an unpleasant place to be. It was freedom at last, but I pleaded to return. My case needs me. She'll commit suicide without my intervention. That was my argument. They let me come back, but with restrictions that I didn't fully grasp before asking to return.

In the meantime, I've been hiding on top of the clothes dryer wallowing in self-pity, in the dark, by myself. Not hiding exactly — no one can see me after all — but the closet felt like as good a place as any for a ghost like me. I hear the two of them as soon as they enter the house. My uncertainty eats at me like battery acid. Will Juliana be able to see me like this? If so, will she listen? Do I have the courage to go through with this? Will she forgive me for not telling her sooner? Would it be easier if she doesn't forgive me? It is a risk I am willing to take. She couldn't see me at all the last time I was here, but I would wait until the end of time to speak with her once more.

I will help Corrine. I wasn't lying when I practically begged to return to what I left behind. It's just that I didn't mention Juliana and Jared Crowson to those who have an effect on my future. After I have a chance to speak with Juliana, then I'll find Corrine and do whatever I can for her. Will Travis's demons attack me the moment I enter the house? In some ways I hope they do. It would be a welcome distraction from the misery I'm about to face.

"I call the shower first," Jared says.

I don't sense Marcus's presence near, but that doesn't mean much. All the comforts that come with the title of Angel of Death have been stripped from me, like knowing where my fellows are without seeing them. All but the ability to move from place to place with thought. Marcus will undoubtedly find *me* if he's in the house. I've never completely understood the extent of his angelic abilities. I only know he's powerful, and he's a master when it comes to death, dying, and the afterlife.

Someone walks by the closet. I think it's Juliana. Her steps are lighter than her brother's. The kitchen is near and I think I hear the refrigerator door open and close. Passing through the wood door, I'm reminded that I'm not myself anymore. I round the corner and see Jules standing behind an open cabinet. Shock, then grief, grips me by the throat rendering me speechless. She has that affect on me, cutting off necessary life support when I'm in her presence. She's in every way beautiful and when I'm near her, I only want more. More of her thoughts, more of her smile, and more time with her. Like a coward, I leave the kitchen before she sees me. *In private, I'll tell her what I have to say. I have to. Then I'll leave her alone.*

It quickly becomes apparent Marcus isn't inside the house. He should be here. The meaning of this doesn't escape me. Jared may have some time left. It could also mean Marcus had something come up which required his immediate attention. Time without my mentor nearby is a precious and rare gift since Jared is here. If I had an ounce of intelligence in me, I would get this over with as soon as possible, or I may be explaining everything twice, once to Juliana and then again to Marcus. He could be here any second.

Juliana walks into her darkened bedroom and sets down a coffee mug on the large brass-trimmed trunk. Her hand reaches under the edge of the lampshade, and with a tiny click, the room is filled with soft yellow light. She doesn't see me standing in the far corner of the room near the window. I've become a ghost, barely there, existing like a shadow of what I was. She's preoccupied with her stereo and CDs. I watch as she takes her time picking the exact right music to fit her current mood. Repetitive piano chords blend with distorted guitars and a haunting bass flow from the speakers. Juliana turns and sits down on the edge of the bed and then lies down flat on her back, eyes closed. She's wearing the same clothes from when I last saw her in Travis's basement. I thought at least a day had passed, but maybe not. Time isn't the same after you die. When I'm not with the living, time has little importance and even less influence on my surroundings. What could she have been doing? Will she even know I'm here? She couldn't see me at Travis and Corrine's house.

"I promised I would come back to you."

Her entire body jumps off the bed and flies toward the door. An ear piercing yelp escapes from her mouth and then stops almost as soon as it had started. Our eyes meet only long enough for me to see recognition in them and then she cuts me off. She stands with her eyes closed for so long I begin to worry for her. Her hands hold the front of her chest as if to steady her pounding heart.

Just as I am about to say something, she finally speaks.

"I thought you died," she whispers.

Her green gaze flicks up at me and then down to the floor. Her curtain of black hair falls forward covering most of her pale face.

"Travis's unholy creatures," I say with detectable disgust, "they changed me." I take a step away from the window wishing none of this had happened. Wishing — no — yearning with my soul to hold her close and protect her from all the unknowns of the world. "It's different now. I didn't mean for it to happen. You were...I tried to help. I'm sorry. I failed."

She looks up and finally lets me see her. She is gaunt, hollow cheeked, and bleary eyed. The vitality, which normally radiates from her, is missing. "You're not well," I say.

My misery swells as I take in her appearance. She's rumpled, exhausted, and maybe sick.

"I'll be all right," she says, unconvincingly. "You're...what do you mean, changed?"

"Juliana, I didn't come back to talk about what happened. I'm only here to tell you about your brother. Then, I can quit hurting you, and go finish what I started."

She looks out into the hallway where we can both hear the low din of running water in the bathroom. Slowly, she reaches over and closes the bedroom door. Then she walks over to her bed and sits down again. She slides her back up against the wall and pulls her knees to her chest.

Her green eyes look like the heart of the forest. The gold flecks in her irises are like the sun shining down through the branches. At least this part of her appears the same.

The strain in her voice is obvious. "Tell me what happened to you," she says.

I could almost convince myself that the worry I see on her face is equal to my own, but I can't let myself get distracted. I have to get through this. The pain in her life is my fault and I have to put a stop to it. Only, my news is going to hurt like no other pain in the world.

"Jared," I start, and then move back to the window, looking out, as if the night were not black and all the world was out there to see. "I've made two mistakes. The first one was the day we met. I chose to follow you instead of Jared." I pause, hoping she hears every word clearly. "The second one, I'm trying to fix right now. I should've told you before, but I didn't. Jared's time is coming to an end, Juliana, and there's nothing anyone can do about it."

The silence is long. The soft music coming from the speakers is the only thing keeping the room from cracking with tension. I want to escape right through the wall, to let the night take me from her, but leaving without letting her retaliate would be another insult to the injuries I've already inflicted on her.

Juliana finally speaks. Her words are definite and pained. "It's my fault," she says.

"Of course it's not." *How could she even think that?*

I hear her move off the bed, but I don't have the guts to face her. Not yet. Then she's standing next to me by the window.

"I know about my brother, Nathaniel," she tells me and the misery in her voice makes me believe that being torn to pieces by demons wasn't a severe enough punishment.

From the corner of my eye I notice she's wringing her fingers. I don't think she's finished so I wait in silence for my verbal punishment.

"But you...what's happened to you. Is my fault."

I turn and look down at her. Can she see the hurt and the guilt I feel? Her hand rises to my chest, and ever so slowly, she tries to lay her fingers on me. They pass through the air as if I'm not here.

"Can you..." Her mouth tightens and the fear in her eyes deepens the color to a darkened forest. "Your body? What's wrong with you? This happened in Travis's basement, didn't it?" She keeps her hand hovering near the front of where my shirt should be. "I couldn't see you. But somehow I knew when this happened. This is my fault," she says again.

Her sadness shreds what little resolve I have left. "It wasn't really you acting that way. I didn't understand at first, but I know now something else was controlling you. Travis's binding ceremony couldn't be allowed. You would've been gone forever. I would do it again, Juliana. I don't regret not letting that evil spirit take you."

Huge tears fall from her gorgeous eyes. She lets me see the first of them and then she looks down, hiding beneath her lashes.

"Did you see me...were you at the bar?" she asks.

The tears continue to fall down her face like a solemn rain, drenching us both with sorrow.

I shake my head, not sure what she's talking about. "No. I wasn't at any bar. I came back here, to your house, like I said I would. You were sleeping. I couldn't understand what was wrong."

She turns farther away from me, staring down at the floor. Her hand moves to brush away some of the tears.

With my answer, I sense a mix of relief with something else. My not being at the bar seems important to her so I continue. "I found out about the succubus after." I pause, seeking the correct words to explain to her. "Few earthly things cross over with a person's soul when they pass. But I had to know about you, Jules. I passed into another level of the afterlife and you were still with me. As long as the soul is willing to know the truth, then the answer is always there. That's how I found out. After death, the answers come like the ease of breathing air when you're alive."

My arms ache to reach out to her. But I have nothing physical to offer her anymore.

"I dreamed you were here Nathaniel. The day after I...she took possession of my body. I heard you. I think I saw you sitting on my bed. Why? How is it possible? Can you tell me why I can see you in my sleep? Can you tell me why I know you're not the same now as you were before? Can you tell me how I'm able to talk to someone who isn't alive? Why can I see these things and not be able to protect myself from...it?"

She stops herself before saying the words succubus, or evil. The pain from her experience is tangible in the room. I am as much to blame for what happened to her as the succubus. How could I have been so ignorant? The questions are gnawing away her insides. It troubles her that she can't understand or explain what she sees, or knows, or feels.

"You want a simple answer and there isn't one. You were born exactly the way you were meant to be. For the last twenty-three years I've been trying to figure out why I was chosen to help others cross over. You helped me understand that if I'd never become an angel, I wouldn't have met you. There's a purpose for everything, even if we can't see it."

I know how special she is. I know how rare her abilities are. But she's the one who has to accept who she is and my answers are not hers.

Soulful eyes search mine, connecting us for a heartbreaking moment, and then she breaks the tie and changes the focus from her to me. "Are you still an angel? What have I done to you?" she asks.

"It doesn't matter. What matters is what I've done to you. It's unforgiveable."

"I disagree. I've met Marcus, and I know what's coming for Jared. Now I need to know how you came back. Please tell me."

"It won't work for Jared. My case is different because of what I was," I say. I close my eyes so I don't have to watch as I shatter her hopes.

"Damn it. I'm not asking because of Jared. You were clear about the fact that nothing can change his future. Tell me about you."

Juliana's never been angry with me before, but she's pissed off now. Color flushes her cheeks. This is what I deserve. Having to explain myself. It's not what I expected, but who gets the luxury of choosing their punishment.

"I'm like a ghost, except I have a responsibility to fulfill. I've been granted one last attempt to fix things for Corrine, but I've been stripped of all my powers. If I succeed, and she finds her will to live, then I'll be reinstated to my old position. If I fail, then I will be lost to eternity, like this. I'll be an outcast from everything. I pleaded and argued and begged for another chance to help Corrine, but I came to see you first, because you are everything to me. Now you know what happened. I'm worthless beyond description for letting you get involved in this, and not telling you sooner about your brother. I am sorry, Juliana. I can't continue to hurt you. After tonight, you'll never see me again."

I start for the door, my humility and grief greater than it has ever been. She doesn't try to stop me as I drift away.

As I'm about to leave the room, she asks, "My brother?" Her voice catches in her throat, but she gets through the rough spot and keeps going. "Is there anything, any way at all?"

"You can keep trying to give him more time, but I've never seen or heard of anyone cheating death for very long."

∞

Juliana

Dead on my feet. *Oh God, save me — what an awful expression.* Choosing which tragedy to deal with first is like picking the rack before getting smashed in a head crusher. Simple times, right? During the Inquisition, I would have been tortured to death for being a witch. Corrine seems to think I'm one and Ashley Johnson's favorite accusation would have had me condemned a year ago. But no, I live in the twenty-first century, and all I have to worry about is keeping an Angel of Death from taking my brother to the afterlife, staying away from soul-shredding demons, and try to figure out what just happened between me and my ghost/angel boyfriend, or ex-boyfriend. Drawn and quartered, thumb screws, a decent flogging? Do I know anyone who would be able to help a girl out? Would anyone be willing to torture me so I can escape from my supernatural woo-woo problems? Yes, dead on my feet would be preferred right about now.

Stop daydreaming, Julie. I always hear Gram's sweet voice when those three words enter my head. I really don't have the time for daydreams anyway. Time is what it always seems to come down to. The mysterious illusion of time has become a blight in my life. Why is there never enough of it?

"Hey, Jared?" I tap on his bedroom door lightly with my knuckles.

"Aye," he answers.

The blue light bulb in his lamp is on, filling the room with deep shadows highlighted in cobalt. The smells of freshly washed body and aftershave waft around the room. Jared sits on the end of his bed holding his guitar. The cast on his left hand and arm won't let him play, but he looks like he's attempting it anyway. Guilt, sadness, grief, longing, desperation, the whole gamut of emotions ripple through me as I see him holding his one true love and lust.

"I'm about to collapse," I start to say.

He interrupts. "Do you need to go back to Mom?" he says, looking worried as he sets his guitar down and stands up.

"No. I didn't mean it like that. I'm just exhausted. Sit back down," I say.

He does and I do too. I cross my legs into a pretzel, grab one of his pillows, place it in my lap, and hide my hands under it.

"Make yourself at home, why don't cha'?"

"This may take a while," I say. My shoulders droop with resignation.

Jared picks up his Gibson by its slender neck and places the guitar back in position. The fingers on his right hand immediately start to pick and strum. "Go sleep, and we'll talk later."

"No. I have to say it now because it affects you and once I'm asleep, I may be there a really long time."

I tell him everything I can think of that he doesn't already know. How I met Nathaniel and who and what he is. Who Marcus is and more importantly, why he's hanging around. And much more. Jared listens and asks very few questions. Before I leave his room I make him promise me he will: 1) stay home until I wake up and, 2) wake me if he needs anything.

"I swear I'll figure something out, Jared. I just have to rest first, okay?"

His brows are knotted with concern, but he gives me a nod of acceptance.

"Do you want me to sleep in here? Would that make you feel better?"

"I, err," he sits up taller, stretching his back, "I think I want to be alone."

Slowly, I slide off his bed. My legs feel stiff and much older than nineteen years. The reluctance to leave his side is painful. How can I go sleep? What if he doesn't make it through the night?

I console myself by giving him a huge hug and a small kiss on the top of his head.

"Would you get out of here already? You're stinking up my room." A half smile plays around the corners of his mouth.

I notice the smile doesn't reach his eyes as it normally does. I feel awful inside and out, and after everything I've been through I probably smell worse than I look, but I'm too tired to even shower. "Night, J," I say as I step into the hall.

"Night, Jules. Don't let the bed bugs tickle your toes, or your nose," he says to my back.

It's what our dad use to say to us when we were little, and after he died, we kept it up as a way to remember. I'm not sure when we stopped saying it to each other, but it's been a few years. I blink hard, making an attempt to shut off the tears pooling around my eyes, but it's impossible.

Chapter Seventeen: Fantasy and Reality

Juliana

Waking up from a long night's sleep can be an event in and of itself. Most mornings, my consciousness takes its lazy time to come to the surface. What keeps me lying around for longer than necessary is recalling fragments of my dreams. They're explicit in detail, and most often baffling to try and make sense of, but I will lie in bed and try to piece together the scraps even if I can't understand their hidden meanings. Then after the warm fuzzy feeling of being cocooned in my bed wears away, I make myself get up and embrace the day.

Last night, I think I was in a coma for most of the passing stars, but at some point I began to dream about the airport. I've been to only a few airports in my life and the one in my dream, I didn't recognize. None the less, I was in the airport, and I was rushing, *of course.* I was in an absolute panic to catch my plane. The anxiety over missing my flight was enough to make my heart pound and my eyeballs bulge. There were too many people in this airport and my suitcase was too heavy. Every step I took, there was someone who needed something from me, or someone else keeping me from my gate. Directions to the restroom, what time is it, please have your luggage checked at customs, can you hold this for me? Finally, I ascend an escalator that is too long, and too high, with too many passengers blocking my way, but it eventually leads me to the door of the plane. I board and as I'm about to take my seat, I see Jared sitting between Nathaniel and a man I think I know, but I'm so distracted by Nathaniel that I ignore my brother and the other man, as Nathaniel's gray eyes lock with mine. The gloomy sea of misery on his face makes me catch my breath. His face is still gorgeous, but the new lines of stress stand out like fresh blood of a recent roadkill on the highway. All I can think of is how am I going to help him. Nathaniel doesn't deserve this pressure. None of this is his fault. He breaks our connection first as he turns his head to stare out the window.

I look to my brother who doesn't see me. He's animatedly bobbing his head and smiling as he talks to the man next to him. With shock I realize the other man is my father.

"Dad!" I say, but he doesn't look up.

As I try to make my way down the aisle, I'm stopped again, this time by a flight attendant.

"Please take your seat, miss. You're holding up our departure," she says in a tone that is partly authoritative but mostly bitchy.

She's full body blocking me. I try to ease around her anyway, but she points to a seat on my left and says, "Right there. Sit down and fasten your seatbelt. It's going to be a very turbulent flight."

"Umm, I just need a second," I say.

"Nooo," she draws out the word, giving it an extra syllable.

I don't sit down in the offered seat. "My seat is back there," I argue.

She huffs at me as I push past her. Jared and my father still haven't seen me standing only feet away. The aisle stretches on as I try to get to them and can't.

"Jared, Dad," I call. And when they don't look up, I say, "Nathaniel?"

The plane begins to take off, even though I'm still shuffling down the aisle toward the three men I care about more than anything else in the world. No one seems to notice. "Hey, wait," I say and turn to look toward the cockpit but we're in the sky already. The dropping sensation in my stomach tells me we're climbing in altitude and climbing fast. I stare at the cockpit door, which is open, but I don't see anyone. As I wonder who's flying this thing, I'm aware that the entire plane is missing all of its passengers. Everyone has disappeared. I spin around to check on my brother and dad, but they're gone as well. Only Nathaniel is on the plane with me, and he's now standing right in front of me.

"Come on," he says and holds out a hand to me. His face is still serious, but the fact that he's speaking to me at all is encouraging. Without question, I take his hand. It's strong and warm as it wraps securely around mine.

"We don't need the plane, Juliana."

As he tells me this, the plane disappears, and we begin to fly through the night sky. First there is weightlessness, followed by a rush of confidence. I let go of his hand and begin to spin, flip, soar, and dive, anything I can imagine to enhance this freedom from the confines of my body. Nathaniel flies next to me, but he's more subdued, foregoing the aerial tricks. He laughs at my enthusiasm and his smile sends jolts of bliss through me.

"Oh my god, this is so incredible," I say.

"I'm surprised you haven't flown before," he says.

"I think I have, but every time is amazing."

"You're amazing," he says.

"I'm not. I'm just having fun," I say as I soar straight ahead and then tuck and roll into two perfect summersaults, finishing on my back and begin to backstroke like I'm in an endless pool with only the heavens to guide me.

"What are you doing here?" he asks me from somewhere over my right shoulder.

"Swimming, and flying. You should try it. This must be how a penguin feels in the water," I say, feeling buoyant and amazing.

"Are you a penguin tonight? It fits. They're the supposed experts of slipping in and out of their body."

"What are you talking about?" I say, and laugh. "Like, out of body experiences?"

"Penguins soar underwater like a bird through the air, but they can also jump straight out of the ocean and onto the land. They leave one realm and enter another with perfect ease. Like what you're doing right now."

"Is that what I'm doing?" I ask, feeling a little heavier suddenly.

"You tell me, water bird."

I ignore his implications about me being out of my body. I don't want to lose this perfect moment of freedom. It's the best feeling in existence and I'm not willing to let go of it yet. I do a quick loop around him, enjoying the movement and the wind in my hair as it flows behind me. Then I float over next to him, and stare down at a disturbance.

"Hey, look over there," I say, distracted by the view.

A circling mass, almost like how I would imagine the beginning of a tornado would look like, is far below us. Nathaniel tenses.

"What is it?" I ask. Wanting to know both what I'm seeing and why Nathaniel is suddenly so grim.

"I don't want to talk about it."

"Why?"

Nathaniel shakes his head as an answer. I find that completely unsatisfactory so I decide to move closer and take a look for myself. Diving through the cool night air is exhilarating. The stars become an audience of light, watching my back as the ground rushes up to me.

"Juliana, stop. Just wait."

I pull up at his plea, hovering in the midnight air. My eyes, however, never leave the scene below. I recognize where I am. I've traveled on that highway through the town below since I was born. It's unmistakable. I'm flying over my own town. The high school roof is almost directly beneath me. The swirling eddy of dark clouds, which is neither water nor wind, is close by. I try to pinpoint exactly where it is and it doesn't take me very long. The streets look different from a bird's eye view, but I recognize the way. I can clearly see Cemetery Road and the turn off to the gates, and then nothing. The eerie mass of gray and black is over Hilltop Cemetery.

Falling down usually happens so quickly that you don't have time to think about it. More often than not, by the time your brain has a chance to consider the fall, you're more worried about what just took you out and how bad it's going to hurt, than the actual fall itself. When you're dreaming, a fall can go on for a lifetime, complete, breathtaking, endless fear, as you contemplate hitting bottom. This is what I experienced before a hand snatched me up, like gripping a small child's arm as they stumble over a crack in the sidewalk, and protecting them from the inevitable pain.

I grab onto Nathaniel, clinging as if my life were in serious danger, and bury my face against his shoulder. "My dad's buried there," I choke out. "What is it?"

His hand strokes the back of my hair, his touch more calming than any touch should logically be. My heart stops pounding and returns to normal. Then I'm aware of the ground under my feet. No crash, no splat, no shattered limbs, nothing actually. The earth is solid and yet I don't really feel it. I can feel Nathaniel though, and I can see everything around us. We're surrounded by pine trees. They're tall and their branches look sharp against the night sky.

"Your dad's fine, Juliana. I promise."

"How do you know?" I ask.

"I know," he says with a finality that leaves no question to his sincerity.

"How?" I ask again. I can see the edge of the abyss overhead not far from where we stand. It's so ominous it should be a cliché, but no less scary for the fact.

"I was over there with them. He's the worst kind of man, Jules. Don't make me tell you what he's doing. Please believe me, it's not a Crowson grave he's disturbing."

"Disturbing? He, who?" I whisper into Nathaniel's shirt.

"Travis. Travis and Corrine," Nathaniel whispers back.

"Is this a dream, Nathaniel?"

"I wish it was," he says.

"You're supposed to keep your mouth closed when you pass by a cemetery," I say.

His hand stops on the small of my back, holding me close. "Why?"

"Spirits can steal your soul through your mouth if you don't."

"We didn't pass it yet," he says.

And then I wake up.

A little moan escapes from my lips as I roll over and hide my face under my arm. Dreams like that should be illegal, forbidden, eighty-sixed, exiled, whatever. To have pure elation followed by life-threatening fear, wrapped together with a ghost telling you it's not a dream — *no thank you.* I lean over so my head is hanging off the side of the bed and look for shoes. Shoes under the bed could explain this dream, but of course there aren't any. *I wouldn't set myself up like that. Would I?*

I flop back over and stare at my sparkly popcorn ceiling trying in vain to distract myself from all the mixed emotions and images from the dream and then I'm aware of movement by my right foot. Before I have a chance to see what it is, *it* bites my big toe.

"Aaaaye!" I yank my foot away as my head pops up to see Ariel, my cat, jump off the bed. She slinks over to the door. The end of her tail twitches with contempt as she rubs herself back and forth against the doorjamb.

She watches me watch her. Her impatient body language is telling me very clearly she wants food, and now isn't soon enough. I've had Ariel long enough to know that if she doesn't get fed promptly, she will exact her revenge in one of a thousand different annoying ways. I reach under my head and toss my pillow at her. I'm rewarded with the sound of cat's claws scratching the floor as she bolts, but I know this is a temporary retreat before she makes another attack.

At least she's not trying to shred me to pieces, like she was before, when I was possessed. A second later I realize that I — well not I, but the succubus — had locked Ariel in the bathroom and had left her there. *Oh my God. My poor cat. I hope she was okay. I wonder who let her out of the bathroom?* Making amends, I slip out of my bed and leave my bedroom to go give her some kitty-crunchies. I also leave the dream and all the feelings that go with it tucked away under the covers. *Illegal, definitely should be against the law. If I could, I would turn that dream into the authorities for disturbing the peace.*

Ariel attempts to trip me when I reach the bottom of the stairs. It confirms my suspicions about her empty food bowl. Running in front of my feet, when I'm not looking, is her favorite form of getting my attention when she's hungry. Instead of booting her lightly in the backside for trying to break my neck, I bend down and scoop her up. She doesn't protest as I cradle her against me. We round the corner to the kitchen and I spy her dish on the floor. To my relief she does have water.

Suddenly, and without any forewarning, a multitude of fragrances bombards my senses. My nose lifts slightly in the air, trying to distinguish the difference between the spiciness of whatever is steaming out of the Crockpot on the counter and the sweet cinnamon smell coming from a rectangular pan on top of the stove.

Absently, I put Ariel down on a nearby chair and let my hand glide over her silky back and down her tail as I watch Jared stuff some sort of pastry into his mouth.

While he chews, he half smiles at me. After swallowing, he says, "Mom went shopping, and she cooked too." He puts the last enormous bite into his wide mouth and then reaches over and takes another cinnamon roll out of the pan.

"She made your favorite? Did you ask her to?"

"Nope. I just got up and all this was here. She's in bed asleep. I haven't even talked to her and there's a lot more," Jared says, nodding toward the refrigerator.

I reach into the lower cabinet where the cat's food is and pull out the bag of dry crunchies. Ariel gives me her sickly sounding meow that sounds more like "merrrrp," and then reaches out a paw to make a scratch on the bag. When I stand back up, I see Jared scooping out whatever it is in the slow cooker.

"Want some?" he asks.

"What is it?" I ask, but my stomach definitely does. A grumbling and clenching of my gut leaves no doubt that I'm hungry, probably famished.

"Breakfast casserole."

"Yes, please," I say, and then swallow as my mouth waters.

While Jared grabs another plate, I move to the fridge, looking for some juice to go with breakfast. A large plate of fruit greets me when I open the door. Strawberries, cantaloupe, sections of mangos, kiwi slices, raspberries, and blueberries, all call out to me with their vivid colors and delectable sweetness. I grab a new container of OJ with one hand and the fresh fruit platter with the other and go set them on the table.

"Mom must have felt really bad about not having any food in the house. I can't believe she did all this," I say as I reach for two glasses from the cabinet.

"I don't know what's up, but I'm not gonna jinx it by questioning her," Jared says as he brings two plates of casserole over.

"Should we go wake her and see if she wants to eat with us?" I ask. The gratitude for all this food is nearly overwhelming as I stare at the colorful feast in front of me.

"Nah. She already ate. Look at the dishes by the sink," he says.

"Wow, this is so...exactly what we need," I say.

"Yeah," Jared agrees. "It's been a crazy last few days."

As we chow down on Mom's Monterey jack, green chili, and egg casserole, I begin to think about all that has happened and what still has to be done. I reach over for a cinnamon roll, thinking that the food is fueling my overworking brain. The icing oozes over my fingers. I step over to the counter to grab a napkin and I see Marcus sitting on our back deck. His presence only adds to my burning brain cells.

"J, do you know Patrick and Corrine's mother's name?"

"No. Why?"

"Just everything that happened with Corrine. It's kind of important. Do you think you can find it out for me?" I ask. "And without Travis knowing," I add.

"Yeah, I'll call Patrick. It shouldn't be a big deal. Just a name, right? Are you gonna tell me why?"

"No," I say as I pop berries into my mouth. Ideas are filling my mind and I can tell there's no going back from here.

"You're never allowed near that family again, Jules. I mean it. And if I'm on house arrest, so are you."

So Jared is taking our conversation from last night to heart. "I'm going to do a little research is all. And you're staying close to home for obvious reasons." I couldn't help myself, my eyes immediately move to the huge angel chilling in one of our deck chairs.

"He's outside?" Jared asks.

"Yes."

"Should we invite him in?" Jared asks.

I can't tell if my brother is serious, mocking, or being sarcastic. I answer with all seriousness. "I think he's comfortable outside." I actually think Marcus is treating me and Jared with some thoughtful consideration by giving us some privacy. Most people are not aware when an Angel of Death comes calling, so it doesn't matter if they're in the room with their client. But Marcus knows I see him, and for now, I think he's staying out of earshot.

I take my plate over to the sink and as I rinse off the residue I hear a loud slap followed by a thump. It makes me turn my head toward the sound. Jared grips the dining room table and then his hand whacks his upper chest. He's heaving slightly, but no air comes out of his mouth. My hands drop the plate with a clatter and I run over to him. He grabs at his throat and his face is starting to turn a deep reddish color.

"No, Jared. You can't!" I don't know what he's choking on, but he's not going to choke to death in front of me.

"Stand up," I order. With my mind instantly made up about the order of things happening in my universe, he stands, as if he also knows I mean business and nothing is going to get in my way. Moving with a certainty I feel in my bones, I climb onto the chair behind him. Because he's so much taller than me this is the only way I can wrap my arms around his chest. I can feel the panic surging inside him as he struggles for air. Locking my hands into position, I heave and thrust, trying to force the food out of his airway.

Nothing happens. The edge of panic is like a knife at my throat, but I know this is going to work. Jared can't leave me yet. There's more he has to do before he's allowed to die. Marcus steps into the room, walking straight through our glass sliding door. I shoot him a dirty look; a warning to stay back. My brother will not die in our kitchen.

A gripping shudder passes through Jared and a tiny bit of fear stabs me in the gut. I release my hands from around Jared's chest and I stare straight into Marcus's deep brown eyes. I raise my right hand high over my brother's back while leaning precariously in the chair and then whack my brother as hard as I can.

A chunk of red flies out of Jared's mouth and across the kitchen. It hits the refrigerator, sticks for a second, and then slides to the floor leaving a thin pink streak.

At first I'm afraid that I smacked a piece of Jared's insides out, but then I see that it's a strawberry. Marcus's expression looks to me to be somewhere between interested concern and mild amusement, with maybe a little disbelief in the mix.

"Killer fruit. Never would have guessed that in a million years," Marcus says.

I ignore him. Then without realizing I've moved from the chair, I'm in front of Jared urging him to sit down.

He stumbles away from me until he hits a wall. He slips down it until he's sitting on the floor. Jared is breathing hard and it makes him cough a few times. His color is returning to normal, but his entire body is trembling.

As I squat in front of him, I have to continually push aside the screaming fact that anything can happen and how am I going to stop it?

"Mmh-hmm," Jared clears his throat between taking huge swallows of air.

My eyes search his face as I watch him struggle for normalcy. I know part of me is trying to memorize everything about him, to take in every minute detail of him and store it somewhere safe and always retrievable. It's been a problem to recall the details of my father when I want them, and the fear of not having perfect memories of Jared is unbearable. Stop it, Jules, I chastise myself. Jared is right here. You don't need to memorize anything. And yet my brain keeps taking pictures and putting them away in that forbidden vault. The strands of his black hair hanging over his eyebrows, the ultra-long lashes framing his sparkling brown eyes. His wide mouth and his sculpted cheekbones. There's so much life inside him. How can it be extinguished so easily?

"Don't worry, Jules," Jared croaks.

I wonder if he was just reading my mind, but then he continues.

"I won't eat another strawberry ever again."

∞

Later in the afternoon, after a shower, nap, more food, and a long session writing in my journal, I decide to start putting my plans into action. Downstairs at the computer, I find Corrine's mother with little difficulty, thanks to the internet. As I stare at the name, Laura Petit, on my computer screen, I have a moment of doubt, no, in truth, I have about a hundred hiccups of hesitation about what I'm planning. Laura Petit's address is in Taos, New Mexico. I find a phone number for her on another webpage and jot it down on a scrap of paper. *Could this really be her? How is it that she is only a few hours away and Corrine doesn't know it?* I decide I will try to call, and if it works out, then it works out, and if it doesn't, then it doesn't, but at least I tried.

As I click off the internet, I hear Jared coming down the stairs. There's nothing distinguishable about his jeans and shirt, but he has an air about him that I recognize. Disturbingly, he smells of aftershave and plans.

"Hey, thanks for finding out that name for me."

"No problem," he says.

"What's going on?" I ask. My defenses are already up as I watch him. His fingertips pick at invisible guitar strings next to his leg and his face is a mix of false innocence and determination.

"I can't stay shut in the house forever," he says.

"We've been home for," I look at the time on the corner of the computer monitor, "like nineteen hours," I say with audible disbelief that Jared is already antsy to get out of the house, especially after all I told him.

"Jules, maybe you can't understand, but I'm not going to sit around and wait for something to fall on my head. Christ, I almost choked on a berry."

Jared's agitation increases as he tries to explain what's going on inside him. I know from past experiences the more emotional he is about something, the harder it is for him to find the correct words. He stares down at me. The side of his jaw bulges as he clenches his teeth. His dark chocolate eyes are hard and soft. He's determined, but I think he's also silently pleading with me to understand and not make this harder for him.

"Stay home with me and Mom, J. We can watch a movie, or work on a new song. Anything you want."

Bringing up his music is a mistake. I can see it as his strumming fingers stop their constant movement and he hides his emotions by looking down at the floor. He shoves his good hand in his pocket. He's been suffering at home with a broken hand while his band is on their very first tour. Now he knows about Marcus, and has realized touring and living his dream may never happen. The ache I feel at this realization is more painful than I would have ever imagined. *Jared has so many dreams left to fulfill.*

We both hear a car pull up in front of the house. His shoulders shrug half-heartedly.

"I'm out. Later, Jules," he says without looking at me.

Jared takes a couple long strides over to the front door and he pulls it open. I move to follow him outside, not sure if I should force him to stay with me, or just let him go. Marcus follows behind.

"He has a valid argument, doesn't he?"

Marcus's low tone seems to vibrate into my senses, filling my ears and my head clear to the brim. I shoot a glance at him as he moves to step around me.

"He wants to live his last moments. Can you blame him?" Marcus says as he follows Jared off the front porch.

"Yes," I answer with a pout.

"Say goodbye, Jules," Marcus tells me.

I shake my head in stubborn refusal and absolute denial that this is the last time I will see my brother.

Standing in the driveway, Marcus turns and gives me the slightest of bows, mostly with a small nod and a slight sway of dreadlocks. Then he catches up to Jared with super-human speed, or maybe it's just his super long legs. The two of them climb into a black BMW parked at the end of the drive. The recognition of a BMW causes a spasm of fear, but then I have to calm myself as I remind my brain that Travis's beamer was silver. I squint to see who's driving the car and it's not much better. Patrick Dawson, Travis's son.

As the sleek black car pulls away, Jared gives me a single wave with his un-casted hand. I return the gesture and then silently plead for his safe return.

Who am I pleading to? I'm not totally certain, but if it's to God, then so be it. I will start praying everyday if I get to see my brother alive again. I watch the dust clouds churn from the tires as they make their way down the street. When I no longer see the car, I realize I'm watching another familiar vehicle driving toward me.

Chapter Eighteen: Boundaries

Juliana

He parks his truck behind my car, but doesn't immediately get out. The engine stops and the relative quiet of our mountain neighborhood returns. A Steller's jay squawks somewhere over my head and then I hear the distant caw of a raven. Chris Abeyta leans over and grabs something off the seat next to him and then opens his door.

I would really like to scurry inside the house with my tail between my legs and hide in the nearest corner, but it's way too late for that. *How could I forget to call Chris? I'm a horrible, selfish, no-good, thoughtless, piece of dung. And here he is, at my front door. Yay.*

I do my best to not squirm under the self-imposed pressure. It's so unlike me to forget about someone. The instant heat of embarrassment pulses through me. I'm sure my cheeks are flaming. As he walks over to me, I manage to say, "My excuses are lame and inadequate, but I still owe you an apology."

He stops at the bottom of the steps. "Accepted," he says, straight-faced as always and impossible to read.

The Steller's jays in the branches overhead multiply to at least a half dozen. Their raspy call surrounds us like a chorus of sickly sirens. I look up trying to pinpoint just how many of these little bosses are yelling at me and then the sound ceases, and they're all simultaneously quiet. Then one of the large blue and black birds jumps off a branch and swoops down in front of me, landing on the wood railing of the porch. The large crest of black feathers on his head flexes and stands at attention as he eyes me dubiously. These birds are impressively intelligent, and they're smart enough to know to keep their distance from unpredictable humans. Slightly unnerved by his close proximity, I step closer to my front door. The jay lifts his beak, lengthens his throat, and then puffs up all his feathers. The next thing I know, the bird is screeching at me. He imitates the sound of a hawk exactly. A smile of surprised wonder takes over the corners of my mouth as I stare in amazement. Only a couple of seconds pass, and then the jay lifts off the railing, but he doesn't fly away from the house. He comes straight for the front windows of the living room.

"Watch out," I gasp, but it's unnecessary. The jay sees the glass and makes a swift and hard turn left, now heading directly for my face. I duck, feeling the wind from his flapping wings ruffle my hair. I stay crouched down longer than necessary, startled and watching the feather dust float in the air.

"He came to tell you something," Chris says, as I straighten up.

I sneeze and a tiny fluff of down feather drifts past my nose. "Yeah? Is he saying beware of the wildlife? He almost took my eye out."

Chris climbs the few steps up to the porch. He shifts the furry bundle under his arm and his almost black eyes meet mine. He's unblinking and looks as stern as always. I've come to know by now that his serious face doesn't mean all that much. He's a master at revealing nothing he doesn't want to. I, on the other hand, have what some would call a glass face and, oh how I wish I could learn Chris's trick.

"A jay will present itself when you need to learn about power. Using your power, or someone else using theirs against you. The jay bird knows how to acquire the forces of Great Spirit and of the earth, and to use it. Pay attention right now to figure out the message he brings."

The dream instantly comes to my mind. It was so real feeling. I had been flying and then I was falling to the earth. Nathaniel was with me. Being with him always overpowers every other feeling inside me. His strength is not just physical. He has the power to wipe away all of my reason, to turn me into a girl who is absolutely carefree, and something else too. I struggle to remember the exact feeling, and then it hits me. I'm so happy when he's around. The joy inside me when he's near is unlike anything I have ever felt before. Happy. I didn't know I was without it, until he entered my life and I could really experience it for the first time. The change he brings out in me should set off alarm bells. I've always sworn I wouldn't let anyone change me, but it feels so right when we're together, like I am powerful. *Except we're not together anymore.*

My stomach clenches at the realization. He said he wasn't going to see me again. Except, what about last night, in my dream? Was the dream real? All of it, or part of it? What about Nathaniel? He told me I was like a penguin, able to move from one realm to another. Can I travel in my sleep? I think I did that very thing last night.

But penguins and squawking jays? A bird that can use the powers of the earth and of Great Spirit, like flying between heaven and earth — with an angel to keep me from falling. Is that the message? Am I supposed to use my power to find joy? Are angel dreams the path to my happiness?

"Can people leave their bodies when they sleep?" I ask, half absent in my own thoughts. Then I shake myself and try to focus on Chris.

"Of course. It is a matter of the person doing it on purpose, or by accident."

"What if I'm not sure?" I say.

"Learning to master your dreams is a skill worth practicing. The dream world is a powerful place. Your jay may be a reminder to pay special attention to a dream perhaps?" Chris says as a question.

"Maybe," I say aloud. *Definitely,* I say to myself, not wanting to share the details of my dream with Chris — my shaman friend disapproves of Nathaniel's presence in my life.

"Why did he call out like a hawk?" I ask.

"They're great imitators. Smaller birds think a hawk is near and they will find cover, letting the jays come in and eat all the food. He's telling you, 'do not be fooled by someone.'"

"Hmm," I ponder, thinking back to my dream. Nathaniel wouldn't try to fool me, would he? No. My gut knows the answer. He was as surprised to see me as I was him. Nathaniel's not the one. Then my thoughts flicker to my plans about trying to help Corrine reunite with her mother. Could I be fooling myself into thinking I can make a difference? Images of the faces involved, Corrine, Patrick, their mother — whose face is unknown — Nathaniel, and of course the insane stepfather, Travis, flash and then die like sparks from a fire. The pieces won't come together, but the itching sensation on the edge of my subconscious is real enough. By now I should know better, but I shove the warning tingle aside.

"So, do you want to come inside?" I ask with a little hesitance. I know it was wrong of me to leave Chris's house without a word or note of explanation, but really, what does a shaman do for follow up care?

"Inside, or out here. It is up to you. Your treatment was not complete, Jules. The spirit needs healing as much as the body."

I open the door and then stand aside for Chris, but he gestures for me to go ahead. The sound of movement in the kitchen alerts me that Mom is awake and probably getting ready for work.

Stopping in my tracks, I turn around and whisper, "She doesn't know anything. I want to keep it that way, okay?"

Chris's blank face doesn't agree or disagree.

"It's just easier this way. Follow my lead," I hiss.

"Jules? Is that you?" Mom calls from around the corner to the kitchen.

"Yeah, it's me. I'll be in my room," I call back.

"Not your bedroom," Chris says.

"Why?" I ask.

The look he gives me should be a no brainer, but I'm choosing ignorance. His face is either saying, "you're not serious, or get a clue."

"Come on," I whisper as I take a couple of steps toward the stairs.

Chris shakes his head once, his feet planted squarely on the entry floor.

"Oh, hello there," Mom says, as she walks out of the kitchen. She stops, takes a look at Chris and then at me, waiting for an introduction.

I can't, I mean I really cannot tell my mother about being possessed or being exorcised.

After a silent pause, which is becoming uncomfortable — at least on my end of things — I say, "Mom, this is Chris Abeyta. Chris, this is my mom, Diane."

"Nice to meet you Chris. Abeyta? Are you related to Sherman White Wolf Abeyta, out on the rez?"

"My father," Chris answers. "It is also nice to meet you, Mrs. Crowson."

A strange look passes over my mom's face when Chris says "my father," but she hides it quickly and says, "Please, no formalities. Diane is better. Mrs. Crowson makes me feel old. I think we've met before when you were, well, much younger."

"A definite possibility, Mrs. Diane. My father knows your late husband's family well."

"Um, we were about to go upstairs, but I think we'll go out back instead," I say before either of them get into some long-winded conversation about whose family is doing what and what's been going on out on the rez.

"Oh, okay. I'm off to work soon, too. Hey Jules, did your brother just leave?" she asks me.

"Yeah. Why?"

"He left me the sweetest note. Will you tell him thanks, if you see him before I do?"

"Sure, Mom," I say. Then I walk straight for the sliding glass door to the back deck, hoping Chris will follow me without any more protests or words with my mother.

Chris sets his medicine bundle on the patio table and opens it. "I brought you a few things."

"You didn't have to do that," I protest.

"I know I didn't," he says curtly.

Sitting quietly in the chair to his right, I watch as he removes the implements of his trade from the fur bag. Chris has accused me of talking too much, so this time I wait and hold back the hundred questions that are already beginning to form. He places a leather pouch, some feathers tied together at their shafts, and two glass bottles filled with a clear liquid on the table.

"Are you willing to continue my treatments?" Chris asks.

"Do I have to give you an answer before I know what the treatment is?" I ask. "I mean, I can't agree to something as painful as what I've already experienced. No one in their right mind would volunteer to go through that again."

"I understand. No, the follow-up consists of food, rest, protection, and some medicine. I don't want to waste my time is all. I have never had a patient disappear in the middle of recovery before."

With this last statement, Chris gives me what I think is a pointed look, although his expression really didn't change much. I can more or less feel the exasperation coming from him.

"It wasn't entirely my fault — leaving your house. I had something come up and I...had a bad reaction. Then Jared overreacted and took me to the emergency room." I try to explain my abrupt departure without having to really explain about Jared's situation. "Then we came home and I slept."

Chris's face actually shows expression as his mouth turns down and his eyebrows dip in concern. "Reaction? Were you ill after I left the house? Please tell me everything. I may need to change the medicines I brought for you."

"No. I just passed out. It was nothing," I say. I rub my temples with the pads of my fingers. "Jared wanted my mom to check on me. That's why he took me to the hospital. She works there."

"But why did you pass out? Did you fall, or hit your head? Did you vomit again?"

"Chris, no. I was upset and really exhausted. It was all too much, I think. Don't worry. It hasn't happened again. Actually, I feel tons better today. Maybe not perfect, but a lot better."

Chris stares at me. His focus moves from my face to a spot higher and then lower, as if he inspecting me inch by inch. "This is about your brother," he says with certainty. He frowns and then continues. "I can see the energy around you is healthier today. Your normal purple and green energy is brighter than the last time I saw you but there is a new cloud hanging over your head. I suppose you met the other Shadow."

I take a deep breath and as I exhale I say, "His name is Marcus." I run my fingers over my scalp and through my hair. Of course Chris knows. He sees spirits and ghosts like I do. A sigh pushes itself out of my lungs and my shoulders droop. "I had a little talk with Marcus on your patio. The truth about Jared hit me like a sledge hammer. I'm not sure if I can talk about it right now," I say as emotions begin to rise.

"The one you called your friend, with the brown hair, he was also following your brother? Not you. Am I correct?" Chris asks.

"Yes." *Chris had it figured out. Why didn't I see it before?*

"You need to protect yourself, Miss Crowson. The Creator's Shadows cannot make friends with the living. They take away life. Do not be confused by their disguises."

I don't care for the turn in this conversation so I move on. "Will you drop the Miss Crowson, please? Really, Chris, I thought we were past formalities. And what's with you not coming upstairs anyway?"

Chris blinks and says nothing else about Angels of Death. "Jules, in case you haven't noticed, I am a male," Chris says as if this should explain everything.

"And what? I'm a girl. Is that it?" Instead of waiting for his answer, I make one more point. "In case you didn't notice, I live at home with my mother. If I want any privacy I have to go to my room."

"You're very attractive and young, and I am a professional of the opposite sex. It is not appropriate for me to be in your bedroom."

He says this with his usual straight face, although possibly frowning at me, it's hard to tell, but I can see a change in the color of his aura as this subject progresses. Chris's aura is very earthy looking, with a lot of oranges and browns, some yellow and some greens. Looking at him is like seeing a vibrant semi-translucent haze of fall colors that follows him around everywhere he goes. Except now that we're talking about him coming upstairs to my room, the colors around his middle are condensing, darkening and changing to reddish. The meaning of this doesn't escape me, but I wish it would. I don't have any feelings for Chris that aren't completely platonic. Although, in all honesty, I do find him oddly curious and extremely intriguing but only in a friendly way. How *does* someone end up being so serious all the time?

"So, you're a professional, and you're also kind of old fashioned," I say.

Chris narrows his eyes at me. He knows I see people's auras. He's the one who helped me develop the ability. So, he also knows I can see his aura right now. Who knows what mine looks like? I'm sure it's mortifying.

I scan the yard and fix my gaze on my little garden, avoiding eye contact with him. The garden is in full bloom. The chamomile has outgrown the boundaries of the raised bed and is migrating along the fence row. I can also hear the weeds calling my name from all the way over here.

"Let me get this straight. You and I are having a strictly professional relationship, right?" I say, trying to clarify because I'm sure we're both feeling the uncomfortable honesty in the air.

"Yes. Since you showed up at my door and I worked on you as a patient. I do have integrity and morals, Jules. Something humans are sadly lacking these days."

"Yeah," I agree. I glance back at him wearing an apprehensive smile, hoping we can still get along even though I know he's attracted to me. "I hope I'm not one of them, but I probably am."

Images of the dream flash inside my mind. Nathaniel's description of what Travis Dawson was doing at the cemetery replays in my head. There are no morals in that evil man.

"You have more integrity than most people I've met, especially for your age," Chris says.

Evading his compliment, I shift the focus of the conversation. "How old are you?" It's something I have been wondering for a while.

He's definitely frowning now. "You may have integrity but you lack tact. I am twenty-five," he says through tight lips. "I don't think age matters. I've always been the same."

I smile unwillingly. He's so funny when he isn't trying to be. "Born an adult," I say and then add, "I can believe that. So, can professionals be friends without everything getting weird?"

Now Chris looks away, not meeting my eyes. He stares across my backyard, "Right now, you are my patient. Then we will have to see," he says noncommittally.

"Okay, Chief." I notice his aura returning to normal. "Then tell me what I have to do to feel like myself again."

From somewhere in the trees behind my house I hear the raspy squawk of a Steller's jay followed by the false scream of a hawk call. Power and imitation. Should I be learning to use my power, or is someone using theirs against me?

Chapter Nineteen: Unfortunate Events

Nathaniel

As far as I can tell, the only benefit to losing my angel powers is Travis has no effect on me. He's aware that I'm lingering in the foreground. I caught him looking at me more than once, but he was indifferent to me being in his house and made no move to send his demon slaves after me. I think he knows the damage is already done. The man is less worthy than maggot food. Although, if it were possible to feed him to the nasty little worms, I can't think of a better place for him.

While contemplating how I might be able to help Corrine leave this nightmare of a house, I saw a wraith of a man float through the living room. The ghost was unresponsive to me. It drifted through the house looking tortured and in a serious amount of pain. It couldn't be described as anything other than a ghost, but it was unlike any lost spirit I've ever seen. It was barely visible for one, and its behavior was too remote, expressing only agony as its entire spectrum of emotion. I have a strong suspicion one of the demons kept in the mirror downstairs is the corrupted soul of this man. I'm starting to believe Travis is so used to having the spirits of his demented labors hanging around that he's past the point of doing anything about them. Then again, maybe he finds perverse enjoyment in it. Either way, I never want to fully understand what makes him tick.

Travis is a neat and tidy little freak, but the longer I'm here, the more I notice how little he does to keep the house the way he expects it. Corrine is expected to cook for her brother and Travis and keep the kitchen and bathrooms spotless. She's currently ironing Travis's shirts and pants. The bedrooms and living room are so sparse of personal items that there is almost no picking up to do. The only effort I've seen Travis make to help out, other than order his stepdaughter around, was to pick up a pair of Patrick's shoes off the living room floor and put them in the trash. Corrine retrieved them for her brother when Travis was busy in the basement.

Corrine doesn't clean the basement. In fact, I've never seen her or Patrick go down there at all.

"Hey Corrine, phone's for you," Patrick says as he walks into the kitchen.

He holds out the phone to his sister. Corrine looks surprised and not a little confused.

She doesn't receive calls. In all the time I've been here, I have only seen her talk to her brother or stepfather on the telephone.

She sets down the iron and takes the phone then heads for her bedroom.

"Hello," she says quietly.

Corrine closes the door behind her and walks over to the bed and sits down. It's the only place to sit other than the floor. She hides her eyes as she stares down into her lap. Her breathing is shallow as she listens.

"I don't know," she finally says. Another silent pause, and then she adds, "I don't think that's a good idea. I'm not sure when he's leaving again."

There's some more talk on the other end and then Corrine says, "Let me check. Hold on a minute."

Corrine leaves her room, crosses the hall to her brother's bedroom and looks inside. I follow, wondering what the call is about. No one is in Patrick's bedroom. Corrine walks into the living room and out the front door. She stops when she sees Patrick and Jared standing by one of the BMW's parked in the drive.

She puts the phone up to her ear. "Yeah, Jared's here. Do you want to talk to him?"

I pull up short and hug the side of the house when I see Marcus across the treed yard. A familiar flash of green near him catches my attention, but I move before getting a good look at who is with him. I'm not sure I'm ready to face my mentor yet, or anyone else either. And who is asking for Jared? *Juliana?* Could it be her on the phone? Corrine hands the phone over to Jared. My eyes close involuntarily at the thought of her voice so close. It's an ache that has become my new normal. Knowing I have to be without her, without love, and without a life that has any meaning. Then there's last night. My God, what was that about?

She found me in her sleep. If it were a dream, then I could keep the memory to review, like watching a favorite movie over and over again, but I do not dream. She found me as I watched Corrine do Travis's dirty work, and I'm not talking about scrubbing the toilet this time.

Last night, in the hours when very few people are awake, Travis forced Corrine to go with him to the local cemetery. She put up little resistance to his unholy errand, but I could see the remoteness in her eyes and the dread in her heavy steps as she wandered from grave to grave searching for the pieces he wanted. Corrine has an unusual ability to find things. He makes her find raw gems in the earth, but also horrible things, like last night. His request was a silver watch, buried for at least a decade.

She had told him where to dig. Then he made her help him. In no way, to the visible eye, can I say how she finds what she's looking for, but Corrine can find anything as far as I have witnessed. The only thing that appears to limit what she can find is how specific the description of the item. I watched her thin little body and those tiny arms dig in the rocky soil, scooping away pathetic amounts of grave dirt with each heft of the shovel and it made me sick.

All I could do was try, with every ounce of ingenuity in me, to come up with a way to get her away from him. Unfortunately, the nagging uncertainties of my ability to be of any help at all kept picking away at me like a hungry vulture and a resolution to Corrine's problem kept escaping me. I have to figure this out for Corrine, even if I am a shell of what I once was. This was the situation when I felt, knew, smelled, sensed...Juliana come near to me.

How had she done it? She was there, and we were of our spirits only. Free and weightless, in the physical, but also free of the mental responsibilities that keep us bound in our daily lives. Amazing doesn't begin to describe what her short visit felt like. Her smile and her enthusiasm radiated all the way to the next galaxy. She made me wonder if I was somehow dreaming. When she began to fall, I knew it couldn't be a dream, because I could never watch her be in danger in any way inside of my own head. And how would a spirit fall? Does the answer matter? Juliana dreams about me. And the dreams are real. *She has to stop it. For all the ecstasy it brings, in the end it will only serve heartache when we part again.*

Now, she's calling Corrine. Doubt makes me second guess my assumption. Maybe I only want it to be her, and it isn't. I miss any words spoken by Jared. He turns and hands the phone back to Corrine and I hear confirmation that it is her.

"Jules, I'm really sorry about everything that happened. I needed to tell you that," Corrine says softly into the phone and then pushes the button to disconnect.

I walk away from the house, away from this insanity, away from my client, and away from the damned telephone.

Marcus must have seen me leave, but he doesn't approach immediately. Had I thought of it sooner I would have buried myself under a rock and disappeared, but I didn't, and now I'm staring straight up into the face of one of my only friends. There's no feeling of the grass and dirt under my back as I look at the blue sky framing Marcus's broad face. I'm little more than nothing. It's exactly what I deserve.

"I would be there for you, if I could," he says.

"I know."

"There are only so many laws in this universe and I'm not one for breakin' them."

"Please don't. I know you're not allowed to help me," I say.

"My boy's in that hell house again right now. I won't step a foot inside there. 'Specially after what's happened to you."

"Please don't," I say again. "Whatever Jared's doing, it's not worth going inside Travis's house."

"Buyin' drugs. He wants to get high before he no longer can," Marcus says.

I can only shake my head with pity. Jared is so talented and intelligent. He's wasting so much time and energy poisoning his body.

"He chooses to spend the last of his breath altering his reality."

"He's addicted," I say. The truth hits me solidly for the first time. Jared is an addict. I don't think he realizes it yet, or Juliana either.

"Some say it's a sickness, like catchin' a flu bug. But I never met a single person who went lookin' for a fix of the green apple quick step."

I sit up and Marcus takes a seat on the ground across from me. As large as he is, he still looks perfectly comfortable in his loose linen pants and shirt with his legs folded yogi style in front of him.

"No one wants to be addicted. It happens and then they realize it after it's too late. Jared doesn't know he has a problem."

"You could be right, but he keeps using and he doesn't have to."

"Addiction's the worst," I say and stare at the blades of grass growing beneath me. "The world is full of meaningless waste."

"Nathaniel, we'll figure this misfortune out. The universe always has a plan."

"Do you understand Juliana's role in this grand plan? Has she told Jared about you yet?"

"I'm fairly certain she told him everything. Jared keeps looking over his shoulder, like he's expecting to see the devil himself."

"Hmm," I answer. Of course Juliana would tell him.

Staring across the yard, I can partially see the muddy brown color of the house through the trees. The color mimics my disposition almost exactly, dull, uninspired, and depressed.

"Nathaniel, I may not be able to help you, but I can talk with you."

Looking into eyes that have witnessed centuries of human history, I can tell ideas are brewing inside my soulful friend.

∞

For the human experience, time is a limited resource. Since I became an angel, I've noticed most people pay very little attention to the fact that they have a limited supply of time. They go about their daily lives as if tomorrow is always waiting for them. Corrine and I have everything and nothing in common when it comes to the perplexities of time. She has an ample supply of it and doesn't want it, and I am stuck observing eternity but have no effect on it. We both want out of our miserable predicaments while time seems to laugh in our face.

Travis, Patrick, Jared, and Marcus left some time ago in one of the BMW's. He didn't make Corrine come along because she wasn't needed to go buy and pick up another used BMW. The minute the car was out of hearing range, Corrine went straight to the bathroom and grabbed a bottle of pills from the medicine cabinet.

Unfortunately, I've seen her with these pills before. Last time however, she didn't swallow them. I don't blame her for wanting to end her own life. If I were in her situation — even though it sort of feels like I am — well, I don't know what I would do.

Corrine walks out of the bathroom and down the hall to Travis's bedroom. The room could be any guest room in any average house from the sixties to the early eighties. A full size bed with a blue plaid bedspread, two nightstands, and a matching brown dresser furnish the room. But I know better than to think that an average man sleeps here. In the closet there are two safes, and in the top dresser drawer Travis keeps a gun, talismans for rituals, and drug paraphernalia. Corrine opens the closet door and steps inside. I watch as she opens the smaller of the two safes, surprised she knows the combination. She's quick about her errand as she reaches inside and grabs a baggie of some capsules.

Now, Nathaniel. This is the time to help her. But the only thing Marcus and I had been able to come up with was to try to reach her in her sleep. She has no idea I'm here. She can't see or hear me. *What can I do? This is really looking bad.*

She takes the bottle of pills and the bag of drugs to the kitchen and lays them on the counter next to the sink. Then she fills a tall glass with water.

"No, Corrine. This isn't your time," I say.

She starts with the drugs. I don't know what the capsules are, but I'm sure that taking a bag full of them will be hazardous to her health.

"Think about your brother. Patrick still wants you in his life," I say with some desperation. Corrine swallows three of the pills, one after the other, and without pause.

Reaching my hand out to grab the pills off the counter is useless, but it doesn't stop me from trying. My fingers pass straight through the gold speckled laminate countertop.

"Believe me, I know how awful it is here, but we'll figure something else out. Put the drugs down, Corrine."

I see her gag reflex kick in as she tries to swallow another one. *Good, her body is rejecting this suicidal mission.* The pill makes it down her throat as she forces her mouth to stay closed. *That makes four.*

What will happen next? She should be able to see me and hopefully speak to me, but I will not be able to take her the entire way to the afterlife. The path has been closed to me. If I can't show her the way, will she still want to go? Lost souls often want to stay on earth with familiar surroundings. I couldn't let her do that. If she is this determined to leave her life behind she must pass to the next level. Would Marcus take her for me? "Arrrrrhh," I groan, and rub my hands over my scalp. Have I ever mentioned how my afterlife didn't turn out the way I thought it might?

And then, as I'm about to face my fate, and Corrine hers, we both hear knocking on the front door. Corrine grips the glass of water. She doesn't turn around or make a move for the door.

"Go see who it is," I say, but she ignores it and the next round of knocking.

She reaches for another one of the capsules out of the baggie.

"Stop doing that. This is the universe telling you there are other options."

"Corrine? I know you're home. It's me, Juliana. Open the door."

Juliana is here! What is she doing? Has she lost her mind? My gaze is fixed to Corrine's face. After Juliana announces her arrival, Corrine squeezes her eyes closed. Her fingers turn white as she clutches the glass.

"I have something to tell you. It's about your mom. Come on, open up!"

Corrine's eyes quiver beneath her eyelids. She hasn't swallowed another pill, but she hasn't moved to answer the door either. My initial shock passes as quickly as it had come and I practically fly through the house to get outside. The walls mean nothing to me. I pass through them like gliding through the air. Startling Juliana, however, is a bit more dramatic. Albeit was not my intention to do so, the appeal of watching her jump has its own value. When she realizes it's me, her face morphs through a few different emotions. I don't have time to dwell on it.

"She's in the kitchen swallowing pills. Go inside and stop her," I say. I didn't realize it would be so difficult to speak to Juliana again. Two short sentences felt like being strangled while trying to talk. We're not supposed to see each other again. I swore to myself I would quit bringing her pain, and now here she is helping my client.

Juliana doesn't say anything, but I know she heard me because she immediately reaches for the doorknob. Her wrist turns and her body moves forward but the door doesn't give. It's locked. She slaps a hand on the weathered wood and her eyes close for a longer than necessary blink.

"Corrine, I have to tell you about your mom. Please open the door."

She pounds her fist against the door. Chips of the crackling brown paint fleck off and flitter to the ground around her feet.

"She's on her way here, Corrine. I talked to her and she's coming to get you."

"Her mom? You spoke with her? That's incredible." *This is the answer to Corrine's problems. Her mother is coming for her.*

My helplessness is a pitiful disaster. I feel like I can't do anything but watch.

"Is there another way in?" Juliana asks as she takes a few panicked steps back and looks around the side of the house.

"I'm sure it's locked too. Travis is a paranoid freak. Break a window if you have to."

Juliana looks down at the ground for a rock, or something else to throw. We're running out of time. It may already be too late. I don't know what the large dose of drugs is going to do to Corrine, but my imagination is scaring the piss out of me.

Juliana pries one of the stones loose from an old flower bed in front of the house. It's bigger than a brick and should do a good job on one of the front windows.

"I'm going back inside," I say.

Then we hear the doorknob. We both watch as the tarnished brass jiggles and then turns. Jules drops her rock and runs to the door.

"Corrine, what did you do?" she asks, as she pushes her way inside.

"My mom?" Corrine asks weakly.

"Yes, she's only a few hours away. What did you take, Corrine?"

"Take? I, uh...Oh, Jules."

Corrine is looking up at Juliana with fear and horror plastered all over her petite face.

"I don't feel so well," Corrine says as she sways dangerously to one side.

"The pills are in the kitchen," I say.

Juliana steers Corrine to the couch and then runs into the kitchen. "Where's your phone?" she yells from the other room.

"There isn't one," I answer. "Only cells. Travis has them. Are you going to call an ambulance?" I ask as Juliana picks up the baggie and the pill bottle on the counter. She shakes it lightly and the rattling sound seems to echo in the small room. Corrine only swallowed the capsules then.

"Darn! I don't have a phone with me either," she says. Then she looks at me and adds, "She has to vomit."

Juliana opens every cabinet. Standing in the doorway between the kitchen and living room, I watch Jules rush around the kitchen as Corrine begins to bawl her eyes out on the couch.

"What are you looking for?" I ask. "Maybe I've seen it."

"Ipecac? Or spices?" she says, as she continues to search the kitchen.

"Spices are above the stove and to the right, but there isn't much, and probably no ipecac."

Juliana halts, one hand floating in mid-air as it reaches for a drawer and her other hand is on a cupboard knob. Then without warning, she smacks her forehead with an open palm and a loud "thwap."

"What am I doing in here? It's in my car," she says as she spins on a heel and runs out of the house.

Confused, I shake my head and go over to Corrine. Tears stream out of her eyes. She lays on her side, curled up like a sad little hedgehog.

"Who are you?" she asks as I approach.

"Nathaniel," I answer slowly. This is it then. She sees me. She must be very close to death. It happens to many people. Their body is still alive but the spirit is beginning to vacate and becomes aware of other dimensions.

"I've got it," Juliana says in a breathy rush through the living room. She's holding her purple shoulder bag. The same one she takes hiking, or camping. It's not very large but seems to be a one-and-all, and everything in-between, multipurpose catch-all. She runs straight into the kitchen with it. "Keep her awake," she commands as if she's forgotten I'm invisible.

I hear running water and then a few seconds later Juliana is next to us, holding a glass of water and a small brown bottle.

"Sit up, Corrine. This is going to help."

"Can't. Too tired."

"Don't you dare fall asleep. You have to stay awake for your mom."

"My mom's alive? Are you sure?" Corrine asks through a series of sniffles.

"Yes. Now, drink this," Jules says as she pries Corrine off her side and props her up against the couch.

"Nooo," she moans. "Everyone will be better without me."

"Stop it. Open your mouth."

"She's not doing well. She can already see me. Do you understand what that means?"

"Is he your boyfriend?" Corrine says sleepily to Juliana. "Congratulations," she slurs. "He's super cute."

"Corrine, I mean it. Open up."

Corrine's small pink lips part as she sits staring at me. Her pale blue eyes go in and out of focus. Jules tips about half of the small bottle's contents into her mouth.

Juliana didn't answer Corrine's question about my status in her life. I can feel her purposely not making eye contact with me, but the slight flush creeping over her ivory face is telling enough. I don't say anything about our feelings for one another either. If things were less complicated, the answer would be easier than breathing, but I don't even breathe, so how can I claim a girlfriend.

"Now, swallow it."

She holds up the water to Corrine's mouth and lets her drink.

"That's disgusting," Corrine complains after taking about half of the water.

"Can you stand up, Corrine? We're going to the emergency room."

"No. I won't go."

"I guess I'll have to drag you then."

"No. Just let me sleep for a while and then I'll go."

"Yeah, right. If you fall asleep you're probably not going to wake up."

"Oh. Well, that'll be for the best, I think."

"No, it's not. Stay awake. Can you crawl? We have to get out of here."

"No," Corrine says. Then she moans and puts her hand up to her mouth.

"Don't let her sleep," Juliana says to me as she darts into the kitchen again.

"What did you give her?" I call out.

"Lobelia. Its other name is puke weed," she says as she returns with a trash can.

As soon as the bin is under Corrine's face, she heaves and an explosive geyser of liquid shoots out of her mouth and nose and splashes all over the plastic. I watch with amazement as the blood drains from Corrine's face until she is roughly the same color as snow. As she tries to catch her breath, a shaky hand wipes at the fluid around her nose and mouth. Her color is alarming but the swiftness of her hands grabbing the trash can in time for the ensuing torrent of water, stomach acid, and partially dissolved capsules is somewhat reassuring.

"Corrine, just get it out. Let it all go, and you'll feel better," I say trying to find any words of comfort.

An unearthly roar from depths I didn't know existed in someone so tiny wrench out of her again and again until the last bits of whatever was in her stomach comes up and out. Juliana keeps an arm wrapped around Corrine's back for support while also holding her gold hair to the side so it doesn't get wet.

"We need to get her out of here," Juliana says to me.

"I know, and before Travis comes home."

"I think she's about done. I'll drag her to the car if I have to."

"Shit! I hate feeling so useless. Juliana, I'm sorry, but you shouldn't have come here. What if Travis comes home and finds you?"

"I know it's bad, but I talked to Jared before I left my house and he told me Travis was going out. We need to get her in the car, but I want to grab her things."

"Let's go right now. Hurry," I say.

"Corrine, I'm going to take you to your mom. Can you try to stand?"

Her throat sounds raw as she says, "Yeah, I think so."

"Watch her. There are still drugs in her system, but I think most of it came out. Her pulse feels steady and she's breathing okay. I don't think she's in serious danger, for right now. I'll grab her stuff and then we'll leave."

"Corrine, is everything you own in your bedroom?" Jules asks.

"Yes, but Travis will never let me go."

"We're getting you out here," Juliana says. She takes the soiled can from Corrine's fingers and sets it to the side. She gently pushes Corrine back against the cushions and then stands up.

"I'll be fast."

Juliana dashes down the hall and returns with an armload of Corrine's clothes. She runs out to her car and then back into the living room. After a second trip, she says, "We're ready. Are you feeling any better?"

"I'm so screwed. You should have let me do it. Travis is going to kill me after he sees his caps missing."

"I don't know if she's tripping, or passing out, but she's higher than a kite," I say as Juliana leans down and tries to help Corrine to her feet.

"It's both. Travis's special blend. He sells them for thirty dollars a cap. I swallowed like," Corrine pauses as her jumbled mind tries to calculate. She gives up and says, "hundreds of dollars' worth. You should let me finish what I started," she says again.

She leans heavily against Juliana and the two of them make a slow trek toward the door. Corrine's eyes are closed as she continues to babble. "He'll murder me and steal my soul. Then use it to do wicked things."

Juliana uses Corrine's words as motivation to move faster. "No, he won't. You're getting out of here for good."

"He'll find another seeker. Poor thing, no one deserves to live with Travis."

"It's got to be the drugs talking," Juliana says and looks over her shoulder at me.

"I think so. We want her to stay awake, right?"

"Yeah, definitely. Talking is good."

"Why is your boyfriend so shady? He looks strange. Kinda see through. I think the pills are affecting my eyes, or something. Um, Nathaniel? Can you help us? My legs aren't working so great."

I stare right into Corrine's half open eyes. "I will do anything for you if I'm able. But we're both having a rough day."

"Yeah? Life sucks, doesn't it?" Corrine says, and then somehow the two of them have made it to Jules' blue Saab.

As she opens the door, Corrine nearly falls to the ground, but with a grunt of effort, Juliana manages to get Corrine onto the passenger seat.

Juliana runs around to the driver's side and it dawns on me that I may not be invited to tag along. Seeing her and being near her is a kind of agony I thought people made up and over exaggerated about. To have her this close and not be a part of her life anymore feels like I am dying all over again. I step away, not even realizing

I've backed up into and through the side of Travis's other BMW parked in the drive.

As Juliana is about to duck into the car, she looks over at me and frowns. "What are you doing? We have to go."

I break eye contact with her immediately. I don't want her to see my damaged ego. Then I'm inside the car before she realizes I've moved. *Stay with Corrine and worry about everything else later.*

We back out of the driveway and with every few passing yards, my anxiety grows that Travis is going to pull up and see us getting away. As I'm about to suggest I get out of the car and go ahead to watch for him, Corrine breaks my train of thought.

"He'll find me when he realizes I'm gone."

"He won't find you this time," I say.

"He will," she says with absolute certainty. Or as absolute as one can sound while high on pills. Then she continues as if she needs to explain something important.

"He always does. You know what? He forced me and my brother to move away with him. He said my mom died in the hospital after her gallbladder surgery. I didn't want to believe it. I tried to run away and find out the truth, but he always found me. I don't know how he does it. Then he called the succubus and after she was inside of me, I didn't have control of my body. He's coming. I know it."

My anxiety spikes as I listen to Corrine's garbled, slow speech. She may have vomited some of the drugs but a lot has made it into her bloodstream.

"I can watch the road ahead and then we'll know if he's getting close. I can move faster than any car. If I see him then I'll come back. Corrine, you should slide down in your seat."

She's so small that she doesn't have to move down very far to be almost completely hidden from passing cars. She rests her head to one side and her eyelids droop all the way closed.

"We're going to the hospital, first. My mom's a nurse there. She'll help us."

We both look over at Corrine expecting a protest, but she doesn't say anything. Juliana reaches a hand over to her shoulder and gives her a light shake.

"Corrine," Juliana says, jerking her with more force the second time, but she doesn't respond.

Then Juliana reaches over and slides her fingers under Corrine's jaw.

"How's her pulse?" I ask even though I'm not sure I want to know the answer.

"I think it's not so great," Juliana says. "Not strong enough."

"Corrine, wake up!" she tries again.

"Hey, we're about to see your mom, so wake up, sleepy head." My words have absolutely no effect on her. "Come on, don't do this." *She can't die now. She's about to see her mother again. This is the change she needs to get her will to live back.*

I take my eyes off Corrine for a second and notice Juliana is very pale and tight-lipped. Her hands grip the steering wheel as if she's holding onto the thread of Corrine's life.

We're on the highway and moving at the normally unacceptable speed of sound, but in this case, it seems reasonable.

"How much farther?" I ask.

"Two minutes," she says.

Juliana presses the gas pedal and the car speeds forward. Then she reaches over to feel under Corrine's jaw again. I can see Corrine's chest move with every breath, but the movement seems shallow. Juliana's tension is also easy to see. I wish I could help relieve some of her stress. If I was my old self I could use energy to calm her but I'm once again reminded how useless I have become. All of this is my fault.

I see the sign for the emergency room and the parking lot comes into view. Medical help is only seconds away.

Juliana breaks the sudden silence in the car. "Look behind us."

"F-ing crack head. How did he find us already?"

"This is bad," Juliana says, stating the obvious.

She whips the car around a turn and into the parking lot, speeding toward the emergency room entrance.

"I'll try to stall him," I say and then I'm instantly inside the BMW with Travis.

"She needs a doctor, Dawson."

I catch the slightest shift of a dark eye in my direction and then nothing. He doesn't say anything, or slow down his car. Instead he accelerates across the lot, taking the most direct path to Juliana's car. He races toward her, the engine revving high, the tires squeal as he jerks the wheel to miss a parked SUV.

"You insane bastard. Stop this. Corrine's sick." I grab for his hands, willing with all of my soul that I can actually get a hold on him. Of course I can't.

"I decide what happens to her," Travis snarls.

He narrows his eyes and makes a beeline for Juliana and Corrine. I have the instant realization he's going to ram Juliana's car.

"Stop!" I scream, as I appear back inside the car with Juliana and Corrine.

She slams on the brake and Corrine slides to the floor in a crumpled heap.

The black BMW skids to a stop in front of our car. Before Jules has a chance to unclench her hands from the wheel, Travis yanks the door open and lifts Corrine out. She whimpers in his arms and then I hear her speak.

"I'm sorry, Travis. I won't do it again. I'm really sorry."

"Get inside, Juliana," I order as she watches Travis take Corrine. The mask of shock on her face is startling. I don't think she even heard me. The entrance to the hospital is only yards away. She has to get to people, and she has to do it now while Travis is preoccupied.

"Corrine," Jules gasps.

"Run, Juliana!"

Her hands shake as she fumbles to open the door. It opens an inch then she slams it closed again.

The scream comes out of her quick and heart stopping. On the other side of the window is one of Travis's creatures. It's black, and faceless, and enormous. If you look at it too long, you start to see things moving inside. It's indescribable, and terrifying.

Juliana dives across the car to the other side. The door is standing wide open but as she gets her feet on the blacktop the demons move in to circle around her. I can see at least three of them. She scurries back inside pulling the door shut.

These soulless pieces of Hell are the ones that shredded me into lifeless bits. I fling myself at them like a madman, waving my arms and screaming at the top of my lungs. They ignore me completely. What they have done to me is history. I'm nothing to them now. They move to stand guard around the car. Juliana huddles on the passenger seat with her head buried in her knees.

"He's scaring you on purpose. Don't stand for it. He's a weak and pitiful person."

"I could feel them. I could feel them, Nathaniel. They're…"

She's talking about the demons. Her voice and body shake. "I know. I'll stay with you, Juliana. They're staying outside the car."

Travis walks up, opens the driver's side door, and positions himself behind the wheel.

"We're going for a ride. How's that sound, my Siren?"

He restarts the engine. Juliana doesn't say anything. I don't think she can. He shifts into first gear and we start to move. "I think we'll take my new car," he says conversationally. "After I park this piece of shit, you will follow me, and you will be quiet. If you do or say anything I don't like, I will give you to my Night Terrors. Do you understand, Siren?"

She still doesn't respond. I'm afraid her silence is going to anger him further. I'm not exactly sure what that may do to him, but none of us want to find out.

"Answer me," he commands with chilling calm.

"Yes," she chokes out.

He parks her car by a van and some tall shrubs where it is mostly unseen from the hospital entrance and turns the key. "My Night Terrors are wonderful pets. If you like, I can make you one of them. Don't forget. Let's go. Wait," he says, pausing, "one last detail."

With this last statement, Travis reaches into his pants pocket and pulls out a small vial. He uncaps it and pours some gritty substance into his palm. "Your nuisance of a friend can stay here."

Before I realize what is going on, he blows what looks like dirt at me. It falls through me and scatters over the leather seat.

Quickly and calmly, he releases a spell onto me. "A prison's a prison. In life, or in death. You will stay. Where I know it's best."

And then, as if I'm chained to the car, I'm unable to move.

"What is this?" I yell, as I struggle at invisible restraints. I try to vanish and reappear outside of the car, but nothing happens. I'm glued to the seat, helpless and exploding with rage.

"Prison grave dirt. It's hard to come by, but it's useful for unwanted pests," he says.

Juliana looks at me from the front seat, biting her lower lip, and then her green eyes meet mine. Her thick black lashes, which normally enhance her emerald and gold eyes, now only serve to frame the fear and the tears threatening to spill over.

"I'll find you. I swear."

She looks away without saying anything and then with a trembling hand opens the door. I watch in utter disbelief at this current turn of unfortunate events. Travis and Juliana walk toward his *new* pristine looking classic BMW. She clutches her purple bag in one hand, holding it close to her side. The black shadow demons circle around them like body guards from the depths of Hell.

Chapter Twenty: Terror's Turn

Juliana

How do you find your voice when fear is strangling the life out of you? How do you know if you'll ever have the chance to say what you really wanted to? What if this is the last time we'll ever see each other? My brother, my mother, Nathaniel? Why am I so freaked out about Nathaniel, when I really need to be worrying about myself and Corrine? And where is Jared? Is he still alive?

I couldn't speak. I wanted to say something, but I was incapable. How am I supposed to leave him there? I guess I just did it, but I don't know how it was possible. My mouth knew to stay quiet. Travis's energy has the force of a hurricane inside the skin of a rabid wolverine. I couldn't be the one responsible for releasing any more devastation on Nathaniel. Still, the look in his eyes was enough to shatter me into a million shards of guilt, remorse, misery, desperation, and wretchedness. It was perfectly clear he was thinking all of this was his fault, when actually, it's mine. How could I have let this happen? I wanted to make things right for Corrine. I was hoping that if her situation improved then it might have a chain effect on Nathaniel's predicament. All I've accomplished is to make everything worse.

"Get in the back," Travis says as he grabs my arm and steers me roughly into the back seat of his car.

I clutch my hiking pack with an iron fist, but to some little relief, Travis doesn't seem to even notice it. I scoot across the seat, as far away from him as possible. Corrine sits in front of me. Her pale blue eyes are bloodshot under heavy lids but she's awake. I imagine the look on my face is much like hers, afraid to speak and yet silently screaming some important piece of advice to run, or call for help. Anything to get us out of here, but there's no one. The teeny mountain hospital parking lot is as quiet as a church at midnight. The towering nightmares Travis called his "Night Terrors" stay just outside the car, but still easily within range to come torture me.

"What the hell is the matter with you?" Travis says after closing the door. He starts the car and drives out of the lot before Corrine answers.

She shrivels back against the charcoal colored leather. Her voice cracks and she has to try a couple of times before any understandable words form. "I, it's, I took some of your special blend."

"Damn it, Corrine! Is that it?" he says, as if he can't believe he's being bothered with something so trivial. "Did you give some to this piece of trash?"

Travis shoots me a glaring look and then he turns back to the road in front of him. He turns left onto the highway, heading west, and out of town. I watch the distance grow between me and my car with Nathaniel sitting inside helpless and trapped. And then stare at the hospital where my mother is until all hope fades from my view.

"No," Corrine says. "But, I think I took too much. I'm so tired."

Travis scowls instead of answering her. His already coarse face hardens and his eyes become pinpricks as he drives straight into the harsh sunlight of late evening.

"How could you do this to me, you ungrateful little whelp? You knew that I needed you tonight."

Travis leans forward and reaches for something under his feet. I have a fleeting urge to jump on him while he's distracted. Then I realize that I'll probably end up killing Corrine and myself by crashing the car, so I sit and watch from the back seat. He hands Corrine a small black case.

"How many caps did you take?" he asks.

I don't know how she's able to do it, but Corrine shrinks even further away. "A couple," she lies.

"Swallow a pink one."

"Are you sure?" she asks, hands unwilling to open the case in her lap.

"Do you think I spent all those years studying pharmacology and learned nothing? Do you think I'm as stupid as you are?"

"What's it going to do to me?" she whines.

I can hear the choking sob in her voice and can easily picture the tears welling up. I want to cry with her. Her drug induced fog is causing her to struggle to find and pronounce her words correctly. Serious doubts that she may not have survived her suicide attempt didn't escape me when we were headed for the hospital. The vomiting had to have helped.

"Pinkies wake you up. You have to be alert tonight. Do it now, or I'll force it down your throat," he says, leaving no doubt he'll do exactly that given the first opportunity.

"Okay, I'll take it. Just let Jules out. I got really sick and she was trying to help me. Please, Travis. I'll do whatever you want but she doesn't need to come with us," Corrine pleads.

I knew there was a sweet and thoughtful girl inside that tiny messed up shell. Her circumstances and her family members shouldn't be held against her. That's another reason I had to come save her. Unfortunately, things have gone terribly wrong. *How am I going to get us out of this?*

My heart pounds as I wait for his answer. Would he really let me walk away?

"I have a special job for your friend," he says, his eyes never leaving the road.

The malign smile lifting the corners of his mouth, the confidence and satisfaction in his tone, and the ever-present black void of his aura, terrifies the life out of me. Unable to think clearly, I ride along, digging my nails into the leather seat as if I can claw my way out of this moving prison. It doesn't work.

∞

"Get out," he orders.

Corrine had already climbed out of the car and is standing nearby hugging herself, misery written all over her face.

Travis pushes the seat forward giving me room to slip out. His soul-sucking demons are back, but they keep their distance, hovering near the trees like hungry wolves. Their presence alone is enough to keep me doing whatever Travis wants.

We're in the old mining district. Where he parked the car may have been part of a camp once, but all that remains are the partial walls of a cabin and some heavy timbers, strewn here and there, and decaying like the memories of the old days. The drive had taken a couple of hours. I know roughly where we are. Not that I've been to this exact location before, but I have been in the area. Silver was the reason for the destruction to the mountains around here and apparently it's the reason we're here tonight.

"Find me a piece of ore. The highest content of silver that you can. Raw silver, or the ore, and any crystals you can find. Tonight is the only time in Cancer that the moon is right. I will get this done tonight, or you will suffer."

"It's almost dark, Travis."

"You better hurry then."

"Jules can hold a flashlight for me," Corrine says as she moves in my direction.

Travis doesn't respond verbally, but the withering look he gives her makes her step back.

"Can I take a light, please?"

"Trunk," he says.

Corrine finds the flashlight and hikes away from us. The mountainside looms in front of her, deep in shadow, but I can still see the streaks of yellow and rust, gray, black, white, and even some purple where different minerals are exposed to the air and the weather. Piles of old mine tailings cover acres of ground, and I can't imagine how Corrine will be able to find what she's looking for. She disappears into a nearby stand of blue spruce and then I'm alone with him and his demons.

I stare down the trail, looking back from where we came. Could I make it back to the paved road on foot? How far is it? Five miles perhaps. It's hard to gauge the distance, mostly because we were moving at a snail's pace over the rough road. All the way Travis pissed and moaned about every rut or pothole hurting his precious new car. Then he kept glaring at me or Corrine after any bump as if it were our fault somehow. I'm not sure what's so new about it. The BMW looks pretty old to me, but he seems obsessed with these cars. If I could get away from him, I wouldn't be able to follow the road anyway. He would find me. No, I would have to go through the woods and stay out of sight.

"There's no going back for you, Siren," Travis says as he takes a backpack out of the trunk of the car and slips it over his back.

"What did I do to you? Let me go and I won't turn you in for kidnapping."

"What did I do to you?" he mimics in a terrible impersonation of me. "Why do you even try to lie?"

His black eyes narrow as he glares at me. He's a little shorter than I am but I feel like the smaller person, wanting desperately to cower or at least take a step back. Better yet, run away as fast as I can, but I hold my ground afraid to move and unleash the lurking Night Terrors.

"You lack respect for important rituals. You have no idea how hard I worked to bring the succubus to me. Tell me what you did to her, you brainless tramp."

Fear and disgust are at equal measure as tiny bits of spittle hit my face as he talks. I shift my gaze away from his evil eyes and refuse to answer him. I refuse to cooperate in any way with this demon-loving scumbag. He can threaten me all he wants, but this pathetic little man is getting nothing from me. He grabs my arm and yanks me to the side. The toe of my shoe catches on a rock and I stumble and go down. Landing on my one free hand and both knees sends a jarring shock up my arm to my shoulder. I try to ignore the impact. I twist to the side and decide to plant myself on the ground, rather than stand up and take more of his crap. He relinquishes my arm after a painful tug. I hear his boots scrape across the gravel and then the car door opens. I stare longingly across the clearing at my envisioned path to freedom. That's when I see her.

She's keeping her distance and I'm not totally sure what or who she is. I can't see her face beneath the shadow of an oversized hood, but I'm not completely freaked by her like I am of the Night Terrors. My instincts are screaming that she's not alive, but also not a threat. *Could she help me?* My gaze flicks over to the opposite side of the clearing where the soul-sucking demons are still hanging around. They've moved out of the trees and are a few feet closer. Instinctively, I know they're watching me and a grip of icy steel wraps around me like shackles. Travis's Night Terrors are more horrific than anything I could conjure up in my worst nightmare. Indescribable pain, anguish, and horror are what they infuse into your being just by being near them. Quickly, I look for the lady. At first, I don't see her, but then I get a glimpse of dark green moving away through some tall shrubs.

Travis backs out of the car and closes the door. I watch the pointed toes of his cowboy boots walk up next to me and stop.

"Stand up."

When I don't move, his left foot kicks me hard. Something in my hip tweaks and a shot of fire zings down my leg. An involuntary scream escapes from my mouth. I scramble to my feet and make a run for it. My feet slip on the gravel and loose dirt but keep moving forward, clawing at the earth to get away. A shriek of terror escapes me as two towering black shadows slip in front of me, blocking my way. Making a quick attempt to go around them proves totally useless, they move faster than any human. At any cost, I can't touch them for fear of disappearing into their black depths. I spin around and see Travis watching me. His face is hard and angry as he takes the few steps needed to be in my face again.

He reaches out and grabs my hand. I try to yank it back but he's squeezing the bones so hard I think he's going to break me. Lifting my hand up to chest level, he inspects the fingers of my right hand. Repulsion and creepiness add to the fear swimming through my body at his touch. Travis repositions his hold so he's gripping the edge of my hand with my pinky finger sticking straight out. I'm positive he's going to break it, and I feel a wave of nausea roil inside my stomach. I look away, unable to watch the mutilation of my own body or see the seething hatred on his pointed face.

My little finger nearly snaps as he yanks my hand down and to the side. As my knees are about to buckle, I feel an almighty slap across my face.

"Look at me, stupid girl."

Instant tears spill over my burning cheek as intense pain radiates into my brain from the impact. I keep my head turned far to the right, refusing to look at him. He raises my captured hand, holding it between us, like some sick and twisted proposal.

"The back seat of my new car was absolutely perfect. Now there's a tear in the leather. And scratches," he says with icy calm.

The pain in my hand, the instant migraine, and the demons standing behind me are making my heart race and skip and my lungs unable to function. The world begins to spin and all the edges are turning black.

"How dare you," Travis roars in my face. "I've been waiting for a car like this for years and in one ride you've ruined it."

With those final words, I feel him fumbling with my finger. Part of my consciousness wonders if he is going to tear my pinky off. I'm mostly numb by now and am beginning to feel distant from my body, as if we are two separate beings. That is, until he rips my fingernail off.

Hysterical screams tear from my throat. Falling to my knees, I cradle my bleeding finger against my stomach and scream and scream and scream until I feel something being shoved into my mouth. Reaching up, I grope for the dirty tasting thing, but he stops me. While he squeezes my wrists, I spit and push the rag out of my mouth and let fear choke back any remaining cries.

He yanks me back onto my feet, holding me by both wrists.

"Have you forgotten my Terrors already, Siren?" he asks with his frighteningly calm self-assurance. "They like to devour souls one small piece at a time until there's nothing left."

How could I forget them? They're looming a few feet behind him, eight feet tall and blacker than a bottomless pit. They have a distinct maleness about them even though they're missing any real facial features, and they're curious about me — or more like savagely hungry for me.

"Keep your mouth shut and do what I say or I'll give you to them. Do you understand?"

I nod and he lets my hands drop.

"Walk," he says and nods his head in the direction Corrine had gone.

I move mechanically only changing direction when Travis says to.

"Stop," he orders, and my footsteps halt instantly.

We have only gone ten feet or so and I dare a look over my shoulder as I hear Travis moving away from me. The demons stay within a few feet, leaving no chance for trying to run again. Walking back toward his precious car, Travis stops and picks up a hunk of granite from the ground and then wedges it behind the back tire. I turn back around, not wanting to be caught watching him.

"To those bushes," he says as he moves back into step behind me.

The sun has dropped behind the mountain peak to the west but for now there is just enough light to see where I'm going. We head across the small clearing away from where the car is parked and across the narrow 4x4 road toward the scrub. It's a gradual downhill trek, but the farther we walk the steeper it gets. I think

Corrine is off to my right somewhere, amidst all the old mines and piles of rock, but that's only a guess. I'm not sure if I want her to return safely or not. If she comes back quickly, then Travis will have what he needs for whatever terrible plans he has, but on the other hand, her company and knowing she is safe would be somewhat relieving. Maybe she went to find help?

A light breeze blows down from the mountain side. Strands of hair tickle my face. I want to brush them away, but I don't want to make any unexpected movements and anger Travis. Besides, I'm not sure if I can unglue my hands from each other. I've been gripping my injured hand, afraid to let off the pressure and now I'm not sure if I can let go. My pinky throbs and I feel the sticky blood drying on my hand. I shift my head slightly letting the next breeze move my hair away from my face. That's when I hear the water.

In front of me is a wall of willows, tall with age and dense with summer growth. Their familiar leafy scent hits me and makes me want to weep for another time and place, when being by a river was fun. I stop not sure where I'm supposed to go next.

"Right," Travis directs.

I walk along the bushes and when there is a break in greenery he says, "Find the river."

Pushing my way through the dense brush, I head straight for the water. I can tell it's close, but I can't see it. The sound of rushing water over rocks grows louder and the air is crisp. The shrubs thin out onto a rocky patch of ground. I pick a careful path across the loose river stones to the next group of tall bushes and squeeze myself into a narrow opening. Reaching a hand out to spread some of the branches and thinking that the water should be visible, I'm not mistaken. Unfortunately the ground also drops away a foot in front of me. It's not a very high cliff, but higher than I would want to fall off of. It's too steep to climb down in the dimming light. My right foot is close to the edge so I take a step back.

"Keep moving," he orders.

"There's a drop-off," I say.

He pushes past me and spreads the screen of branches. As his eyes narrow, I get the distinct impression he's considering pushing me over. I move a couple of steps to my right, wedging myself into the branches of a dogwood. I can tell by looking at the land that the riverbank is not as steep upstream as it is down. Corrine had also gone that way. Travis stands still and silent for a minute as if he's considering something. I swear I can feel his menacing thoughts shift. He's not happy about changing direction, but he's going to do it anyway.

"Move up river, wench."

A distant memory nags at me as I push on through the next cluster of bushes. The feeling is like a tap on the shoulder. I try to dissect what is needling its way into my head. I just felt his shift of thought. *Why is that important?* I always know when people have direct thoughts about me, not that I know what those thoughts are exactly. Is Travis like Chris? My shaman friend has the uncanny ability to read my mind like an open book. And he told me I can shield myself from it. *That's it!*

Chris was trying to teach me how to protect myself, how to put up a mental shield to keep him from reading my thoughts, and to protect myself from evil. *Like from Travis and his Night Terrors.* A twinge of hope surges through me at the idea that I can do something to help myself. My little boost is instantly followed by a dose of fear and doubt. Will Travis know what I'm doing? Will he punish me for trying to block him? *No, Jules. Don't go there. You have to try anything.* Chris also said the Steller's jay may be telling me to use my power or watch for someone using it against me. Even if Travis does know what I'm doing, it may still help. And any help against him and his demons is better than nothing. Timing is another thing. The jay bird was also pretending to be something it's not by screeching like a hawk, to fool and distract its rivals. This detail seems important, but I don't understand why or how I can apply it. Then I hear my teeny-tiny inner voice say, *"Trust yourself to know when to use your power and when not to."* I take a deep breath filling my lungs with the cool mountain air. *Trust myself.*

After trudging farther upstream the ground levels out. I push my way out onto a stone covered beach and wait for my next order. It takes him only a second.

"Strip. Then cleanse yourself in the water."

I don't follow his orders. There's no way in Hades I'm going to take my clothes off for this psycho. My soul may suffer and my life may be in jeopardy for refusing him, but isn't it anyway? He's going to have to kill me. Then it won't matter what he does to me, right? *Or, will it. Look at Nathaniel.* Goose bumps ripple over my skin.

"You will obey me. Take off your clothes and clean yourself in the river."

Turning very slowly, I'm ninety percent certain I'm about to commit suicide, but the other ten percent is stubborn enough to stand up and refuse. "No. Kill me. Then do what you want."

He takes a step forward as if he's about to make good on my suggestion and I take two steps back. Movement catches my eye. The woman wearing the dark green hood is in the willows behind Travis. I suck in my breath. I think I know who she is. Her long blonde hair shines around the edges of her hood and her profile looks familiar. It has to be her. Travis spins around and the Angel of Death, Harmony, disappears into the night.

Travis turns back to me and his searing anger is enough to make me cringe. I think I can hear the blood vessels bursting with the rise of his blood pressure. His hand reaches around to the side of his pack and he grabs the handle of a silver dagger. It's not long but very sharp, and his intent is clear.

"Undress and get in the water," he says. He sounds calm, but I can tell he's starting to lose it.

"I'd rather die," I say as my feet stumble backward over the rocks toward the river.

"You must be clean for the ceremony," he says. His Terrors are practically on his back and look like they are a second from coming around and attacking me.

"You wash or I'll make your boyfriend my prisoner for all eternity."

A flash of Nathaniel's gorgeous face, pained and miserable with helplessness as he sits in the back seat of my car floods my mind. He's more precious than the air I breathe. *I know* he would never want me to give in to this bastard. My doubts suddenly slip away with the current flowing behind me. The night becomes perfectly clear and I see myself standing in the middle of the mountains next to a river with a warlock and his Night Terrors. An Angel of Death wearing a green cloak waits nearby. A Steller's jay flies by screaming like a hawk on a kill. I suddenly know exactly what I have to do. Be a great pretender. Play along. And when my opportunity comes, grab it by the horns and ride like a bat out of Hell.

Chapter Twenty-one: Soul Stealing

Juliana

I slowly reach for the hem of my shirt and pull it over my head. Travis quits advancing on me, so I continue and unbutton my shorts. Stepping out of them, I leave my shoes on and hope he doesn't insist on taking them off as well. With my shirt and shorts in a heap on the ground I back into the river until I'm up to my ankles, underwear and bra securely in place.

"Surround her," Travis says in a hiss to his Night Terrors.

They're quick to move in and then I have nowhere to go.

"Scrub your body with the sand," he says while brandishing his dagger at me. "All over," he adds.

Backing up to my knees first, I try to ignore the ice cold temperature. Middle of summer or not, the runoff up here is still snow melt. I scoop handfuls of water over my bare skin until I am wet from shoulders to toes. I follow this with handfuls of the sandy river bottom, letting the larger pebbles and stones filter through my fingers and rub the muck over my skin while clenching my jaw and trying not to scream, cuss, or cry.

"Wash your hair," he demands.

I was trying to avoid this. The tips of my waist length hair are already wet from bending down, but it isn't soaked by any means, and I really wanted to skip getting my head wet for the sake of freezing to death. Dipping low, I let the mass of my hair fall into the water. It flows with the current creating black ribbons among the stones. I give it a few good swishes, making a show of my effort.

Standing up, I wring it out, holding it away from my gooseflesh covered skin.

Travis stands three feet in front of me watching my every move. I look him directly in the eyes and think, *Am I finished, you crazy freak?* Then I brace myself for the order to remove my shoes, socks, and underwear, but he doesn't say so.

"Get out."

Stepping out of the river, I try to make as wide a pass around Travis, but he grabs my arm, and squeezes it hard enough to bruise as he pulls me close to him.

"Don't move until I say to," he says and then drops my arm.

My clothes are almost within reach. All I would have to do is take a giant step to the right and bend down to get them, but I'm sure he meant not to even move that much. The Night Terrors stand close enough that I can feel their misery and pain. It seeps out of them like vile fumes. Holding the frayed ends of my sanity together is becoming increasingly more difficult, especially since I'm freezing, but I will myself to keep it together. I have to. Jared needs me. My family needs me. I need me. And for the suffering Nathaniel has endured, I won't give into this S.O.B. If only the demon wasn't blocking my way to my shirt and shorts, then I could at least have a chance to escape death from hypothermia. It currently seems unavoidable, so I wrap my arms around my torso and shiver through the numbing cold.

The daylight has left us behind. The shadows have turned to black and everything else is shades of gray beneath the stars and the moon. Travis's movements are swift and purposeful as he takes off his backpack and removes a square black cloth. He spreads it on the ground and then lays out a couple of bottles, the dagger, and a silver lighter. His eyes dart every direction like startled minnows in a stream. He's keeping watch but he obviously isn't letting anything stop him.

Standing up, he quickly undresses, boots, socks, black pants, black button-up shirt, everything except his briefs. He glances around our beach, stares at the screen of willows, and then grabs one of the bottles from the ground. Facing the water, he seems oblivious to my presence as he begins his maniacal ceremony.

"I ask for protection. In return I will honor thee," he says in a deep monotone.

He pumps the spray bottle quickly, covering himself in the mist. He spends extra time covering his face, head, and underwear. It takes only seconds and then he grabs the second bottle. He sprays only his chest, back, arms, and legs. A chemical smell fills the night air. I hold my breath, afraid to inhale any of the vapors.

"For fire shall cleanse me of all impurities and water will wash them away."

The next thing I know, Travis flicks his lighter. A tiny orange light in the dark becomes a raging whoosh of flame as his entire body lights up. I jump out of the way, feeling the wave of heat hit me. It's a mistake because I accidently touch one of the Terrors. An icy burn seers my shoulder and I reach up instinctively to cover the spot with my hand. My shoulder feels intact.

Travis growls like an unearthly wildcat. I hear the tink of the lighter as it hits the rocky beach. Then Travis walks into the river. He holds his arms out, parallel to the ground, and looks like a burning cross. He seems to vanish into the flowing depths of the river, the fire dying with his disappearance.

My heart races and my breath is thready. This is my chance. I throw an invisible shield of steel walls around myself and picture the inside of the walls filled with the brightest white light I can imagine, brighter than the sun at mid-day. But before I can take one step toward freedom, an extraordinary thing happens. The angel, Harmony, appears from the bushes. She looks me right in the eye and winks.

"Come and get me," she says.

It takes a millisecond to figure out she's not talking to me. The Night Terrors fly passed me so quickly that I'm only partially aware of their absence. Then I make a run for it in the opposite direction.

In the distance I hear a female scream, loud and piercing, and so terrible that my heart clenches into a rock inside my chest. I rip a path around, through, and over the willows and rocks and then I am stopped short as I feel my head jerk back in an agonizing whiplash.

A scream tears from my throat and then I feel his hand over my mouth.

"Nice try, Siren," Travis says as he yanks even harder on my hair.

His breath is hot on my ear. His body is cold and wet and I feel an oily slick rub off him and onto me. I want to cry and give up, but I don't have that luxury as he drags me by my face and hair back to the little rocky beach. I realize I hadn't even made it twenty feet. He must have been coming out of the water before I took my first step.

Travis jerks me down to the ground as he kneels next to his backpack. I fall down on my knees and hands panting, my insides roaring with adrenaline. As soon as he releases me I scramble away from him, but it's a weak attempt. He reaches out, snagging my ankle and pulls back hard so I land on my stomach, rocks digging into my body.

"If you would behave yourself, I wouldn't have to tie you. Why don't you make this easier for us both?" he says.

"Screw you," I say as he wrestles my arms behind my back.

"Every time you resist, I will take another finger nail. If that doesn't work, I will start taking toes. They're useful, so don't tempt me."

I feel the rope he's using dig into my wrists. Then he is off my back, putting his clothes on, and packing up his things.

"Walk back to camp or lose your toes," he warns.

I turn my head, looking away and wishing for something, anything to make this all go away. My limp concert T-shirt lays five feet away. The name of my favorite band glows under the light of the moon. Almost exactly one year ago Jared and I had driven to Red Rocks to see the show. The tickets were his graduation present to me. It was one of the greatest nights of my life. Could that girl be the same person I am now? *Yes, definitely, yes.* I roll over onto my side, pull my legs up, and stand. Without a single look at Travis, I walk straight to the car. I will see my brother, and I will listen to my favorite band again. Over the sound of rushing water I hear a Steller's jay squawking. *I will get through this.*

∞

Travis ties my ankles together when we get back to the car. On the ground, miserable and cold, I have nothing better to do than watch, listen, and plan my escape or attack — whichever is needed first. I desperately want to know where Harmony and the Night Terrors are? Is she all right? What if they got to her too? Travis starts a fire in a circle of stones about twenty feet from his precious car. I continually work at freeing my hands but it doesn't seem to be making any difference. No matter which way I twist or pull, the rope doesn't give. He lays out the contents of his pack again. I can see the shift of his concentration as he begins his heinous magic. He doesn't look over at me at all and I know this is the time, if any, that I have to get away or try to help myself, but I have no idea how to do it. I couldn't squirm away fast enough or even run before he would have his grips on me again. I hold the circle of protection around my body like a force field, but apparently energy has no effect on rope or cold.

He unwraps small boxes and bottles and lays them out on the same square of cloth he used by the river. The blade of his dagger flashes metallic orange in the light of the fire for a second before disappearing in the shadows of the night. He walks over to me and squats down. My insides curdle with his nearness. *This can't be happening already. Where's Corrine? Will he go through with any of it before she comes back? He said he needed silver to do the ceremony. No, not yet.* Travis reaches down and yanks on the rope tied around my ankles and then gives the one around my wrists a tug.

Apparently satisfied with his findings, he kneels down and lifts a lock of my hair.

"Stay still, Siren, and I'll use your hair. Distract me and I'll take something much more painful."

Then his dagger is next to my face and in the blink of an eye, Travis is walking away with a long tail of my hair.

Breathing fast, I suppress the rising panic and reassure myself that he only took a small section, not all of it, and no other body parts. *I have to get away.* Quieter than a slug, I begin to inch away from the scene before me. If nothing else, some distance feels like a safe plan.

Travis adds my hair to his makeshift altar and then picks up one of the bottles. Next, he draws a wide circle around the fire, counterclockwise, and using whatever is inside the bottle. As he completes its circumference, he makes some sort of flourish with his hands.

"I seal the circle with a knot in time. All who enter will be hidden from the eyes of death."

He reaches for one of the boxes. Most of what he does next involves the fire. His words are lower in volume, either that, or in some other language, because I can't understand any of it. At one point the flames turn green and yellow and the smell of the smoke makes me gag on the noxious fumes. Then a hissing of liquid sizzles in the heat reminding me of my night with the snakes. I shudder. Travis moves away from the flames and picks up my lock of hair. In the low light it's hard to see, but I think he divides it into two. With one section, he appears to tie my hair around some small round object. There is something already dangling from it, like the chain of a pocket watch. He carefully puts this back down on his altar. He then ties the remaining strands of my hair to his own.

A shiver like a thousand centipedes racing down my back makes me want to escape the confines of my body. *A knot in time, hidden from death, tying my hair to his, and an Angel of Death hanging around, God, what does he have planned for me? It's definitely not going to be a picnic beneath the stars.*

After he finishes with his hair, he holds his hands to the fire and I imagine the last few loose strands singeing in the flames. He turns to the mountains behind the car, looking over me, looking I suspect, for Corrine.

Travis stands motionless for countless minutes and then without warning, he steps out of his circle, waves a hand in some cryptic pattern, and then walks away from the camp. I listen to his diminishing footsteps and want to cry with relief. The Night Terrors haven't returned and this is my only chance. I wiggle to my feet with the hopes of hopping away and then fall down again hitting the hard earth and suppressing my cry. The knife? Is it still on the ground by the fire? I'll cut my ropes. That is the focus of my next move when I feel someone grab my hands. They're soft and very warm.

"Quiet," she says. "I'll free you."

"Harmony?" I whisper.

"Yes. Now go away from here," she says as she unties me. "I'm here for him, not you. Fast, be gone. It is not your time."

"Corrine? The demons?" I ask. I can't leave Corrine with him. Could I go get help and then come back? Would she be alive?

"The demons are gone. Go. Find assistance."

I stare down the dirt road. Only the moonlight to guide me. I could make it, but if he comes after me, I'll have to hide in the forest. The BMW is right next to me. Did he leave the keys in the ignition? I have to look.

I reach for the car door, multiple thoughts racing through my head. Travis could be back any second.

"Harmony, the angel Nathaniel is trapped by some spell in my car at the Springs Medical Center. Please send help."

Her eyebrows crease with concern as she watches me. "I'm looking for the keys," I explain.

They're not there, but then I remember my bag. I stuffed it under the seat so Travis wouldn't take it. I reach into the back and grab it. It's my all-purpose take everywhere pack that has saved me more than once.

"Juliana, he's coming."

Panicking, I back out of the car but the strap of my little bag catches on the gear shift knob. I yank hard, not willing to give up something which may save my life. It pulls free, but I also hear the shifter jerk out of gear with a low thunk. Turning to run, I see Travis and Corrine step out of the trees. Changing directions, my foot pivots slower than my body and I trip again falling against the side of the car.

"Stop!" I hear Travis yell and then a gunshot reverberates through the air, temporarily deafening me. I drop to the ground, afraid of being shot. As I'm about to make another attempt at escape, I see the stone behind the tire. I watched Travis put it there. Propelled by an unmistakable inner voice, I push the rock out of the way. The tire moves. As fast as I can, I jump to my feet, grab the doorjamb of the still open door and push the car backward with all my strength. Another shot blast is immediately followed by the window exploding next to me. I keep pushing, now bent over, trying to hide my upper body behind the car.

The sound of Travis's boots pounding into the ground overshadows the sound of the tires as it rolls away. He's too close. I dare to look and he's right in front of the car's hood. I let go, jumping away from the open door and run as fast and as hard as I have ever run away from anything, but neither footsteps nor gunshots follow me.

Seconds later, scraping and snapping sounds of branches against metal rolling through the willows blend with Travis's string of curse words as he tries to rescue his precious Beamer. His shouts are suddenly silenced as a mighty screeching crunch replaces all other sounds. The picture of the BMW going over the small cliff on the other side of the brush is perfectly clear in my mind's eye. Where he is, is not so clear.

Corrine runs passed me and heads straight for the wreckage. I run after her, intending to grab her and get us off this nightmare of a mountain.

"Let's get out of here," I say as she scrambles over flattened willows.

She doesn't answer me as she continues farther into the shrubs.

"Come on, he could be coming back for us right now," I say to her back.

"I have to see," she says.

There's panic mixed with determination in her voice. I stop my pursuit for the briefest of hesitations. I can't live through any more of Travis's torture. He was going to kill me, I know it. But, I can't leave Corrine out here by herself, or with her maniac stepfather.

Holding my breath, I listen to the night, trying to pick out any boogey-men in the dark. I don't think I hear anyone but my paranoia has instantly been ignited with the idea, and I catch myself looking all around the moonlit clearing. No one lurks behind me, but I feel my feet moving toward Corrine anyway. Safety in numbers, right? Fear and adrenaline pulse through my body, keeping time with my heart, until I see her standing as still as a porcelain doll, overlooking the river.

I rush up next to her and peer down at the accident below. The car is upside down on its roof. I'm pretty sure I see Travis's legs sticking out from under the car, but in the shadowy light and the dark water, I can't be totally certain.

Unfortunately, there's more going on that I don't think Corrine can see.

"We have to get out of here," I say. I grab Corrine's shirt sleeve and tug gently. She takes a step backward, her eyes never leaving the wreckage. Maybe she does see it. Tearing my own eyes away from the fight below is taking every last ounce of my reserve.

Harmony, and two other beings, are wrestling what I think is Travis Dawson's soul. The struggle is awesome in the most dark and disturbing way. He's liquid and smoke, twisting and coiling like a flying serpent. There are other beings helping — I think they're helping — but they are cloaked and even more agile. They have some kind of semi-translucent net or rope to wrap around his spirit and hold him. Tiny winged fairies, like the ones I've seen near rivers before, dart around the scene holding the rope or diving in and out of the fight. They appear to jab, or bite, or pinch at Travis with their teeny hands and mouths, causing him to pull away in the opposite direction from their touch.

I grab Corrine's arm and force her to move. She snaps out of her trance and runs with me. Before we make it out of the broken bushes, I hear my name being called.

Whipping my head around I see the angel, Harmony, standing near the cliff edge. She looks as fierce as a hurricane, and yet so beautiful.

"He fights us, but we'll take him," she says in rushed words. "He meant to use your soul to take the place of his. Destroy what he has started. It will help protect you. Then be away from here. Quickly, Juliana."

The angel had shown herself in a physical form. Corrine's slack jaw and wide eyes confirms it.

I bend down and grab a leafy branch from the ground, my actions coming from somewhere instinctive. I know what I have to do, even if I can't explain it. Then we run away from the car crash and the battle between the spirits, and toward the glowing embers of the campfire.

"Who was she? What was that? What's going on?" Corrine spits out in an agitated string of babble.

I don't answer her as I start my disassembly of Travis's dangerous ceremony. Moving to the exact place I had seen him seal his circle, I stare down at the ground. I see the faint line of powder. Before I move forward I quickly increase the mental shield of light and the walls of protection around myself. In an instant it feels more powerful than ever before. Then I take my branch and start to erase the line on the ground, moving clockwise, and sweeping away

Travis's marks. A strange break in the air happens around me as I complete the first task, like the crisp feeling just after a lightning strike. Next, I move to Travis's makeshift altar. The repulsion in me to touch the implements of his sorcery is as strong as putting my hand in the fire, but I force myself to do it anyway. Squatting down, I grab the four corners of the cloth and lift them altogether so the bottles, jars, and boxes crash together in the center. With my branch in one hand and the bundle in the other, I step over to the fire. I jab the end of the willow branch into the coals and stir until they glow red hot and the flames dance. Holding the bundle over the rekindled fire, I release a corner and let everything spill out, hoping most of them will break. Something clinks and falls short of the fire pit, but I ignore it. We have to get out of here. I can hear angry bellows and piercing screams from the direction of the river. The sounds urge me to move faster.

Corrine comes up next to me and throws a stone at the jars and boxes. I follow her lead, smashing the glass and cracking the boxes with rocks. The flames sizzle and flare, changing colors from green and black to blue and yellow. A small explosion happens and sends Corrine and me ducking, but neither of us are hit with debris. I kick and throw dirt and more rocks onto the fire, making an attempt to smother the remains before running out of these mountains. The glint of metal catches my eye and I see what it was that didn't make it into the fire, Travis's dagger. On a whim, I bend down and grab it. The handle is warm, but not too hot to hold. I don't like it. I don't want to be near or touch anything of his, but as I'm about to drop it into the center of the fire ring, Corrine reaches out and takes the handle from me.

"Just in case," she says.

I nod in agreement. A weapon, especially a knife, could be helpful in a situation like ours. "You carry it," I say.

"Okay," she agrees. "Do you know how to get out of here?"

"Yeah, I do," I say, and it's true. Even in the dark, I could walk straight home and never get lost. Freezing may be another issue though. I push the thought aside. At least it's summer. How cold would it get? Low forties probably? Surely not below freezing. *I will get through this.* It's my new mantra.

We start for the road and then I stop mid-step. "Wait, one more thing," I say and then backtrack over to the last place I thought I had my hiking pack. I see it on the ground, a dark lump on the road. I pick it up, grateful to have it back, and thankful to my grandmother who always insists I keep the bag close to hand.

"Let's get out of here," I say. Then Corrine and I run.

Chapter Twenty-two: Finding a Bear

Juliana

"How long will it take to get back to the pavement?" Corrine asks after stumbling over something in the road for at least the tenth time.

"Not too long," I say even though the truth is, we have a long walk ahead of us and when we get there, the chance of seeing any car in the middle of the night on the mountain pass is slim.

"I'm not sure if I can do it, Jules," she says through chattering teeth.

"Here," I say as I pull her shirt over my head.

We've been sharing her shirt. Her pants would never fit me but having a turn at wearing anything other than my bra and underwear is helping way more than I thought it would. Corrine somehow isn't holding up to the cold as well as I am, even with her pants and dry shoes. It could be her size, she is tiny, or maybe it has something to do with the drugs in her system, but she's freezing worse than I am.

She takes the shirt and puts it back on. Corrine has long since passed the small dagger off to me and I placed it in my bag, neither of us wanting to hold it in our hand, but not wanting to discard a possibly useful weapon either.

I wrap an arm around her shoulders and we walk like this, sharing our body heat. How does someone find strength when there is none? Is there some secret reserve that is only accessible when needed? Does everyone have this reserve? Do I have one?

"Will we be eaten by a bear or cougar if we stop and wait until morning?"

"I don't think so," I say and take a deep breath as if breathing will help me be more understanding. "I want to get farther away. Then I can build a fire if you can't walk anymore."

"A fire, really?"

"Yeah. I have a lighter in my bag."

"Jules, please. My legs don't want to move. I climbed all over the mountain earlier, and just everything today. I have to lie down."

Her chattering teeth and the tears I can hear in her voice should be enough to make anyone give her anything she wants, but the fear of what is behind us overpowers everything else.

"A little farther, okay. I know you can do it, Corrine. We can't rest until there are miles between us and him. Do you understand me?" Honestly, there's nowhere on earth far enough away from Travis Dawson, and the angels trying to capture him, but I don't say it aloud. Instead I send out a silent prayer, something I never used to do but find myself doing a lot lately. *God, Angels, Michael, Mary, whoever may be listening, let Travis be far away from this earth, forever.*

"Let's sit down, please. Just for a couple minutes."

Corrine stops walking and sinks to the ground pulling me over with her. With my arm wrapped around her back, I heave her up, not letting her give in yet.

"Not here. Not on the road. Come on."

"I'm so tired, and thirsty, and cold. I'll feel better after a nap, I promise."

She stumbles a few more steps forward because I refuse to let her stop. We ran for a while, and we walked even farther. I know a decent amount of time has passed because the moon is high overhead. It's completely full tonight. Travis wanted to use the power of the full moon to assist him in forcing my soul to take the place of his in the afterlife. The thought that he nearly succeeded sends shivers running up and down over my bare skin. But the moon brings me one comfort; we have enough light to see as we make our way off the mountain. We can also see if anyone or anything is coming.

"Over here," I say, trying to lead her in the direction of the deeper shadows.

Corrine doesn't whine anymore and she even walks somewhat on her own as we move away from the small dirt road and into the trees. I have to find a place with some cover if we're going to stop. And since I'm planning to start a fire, we need to be hidden from the road completely.

I don't think Travis is following me, but Harmony's advice to get away was clear as crystal. Is it possible for a person to hide from an evil spirit? It doesn't seem likely. It would be like trying to hide from the ultimate assassin. How did Harmony get rid of the Night Terrors? Was she successful in capturing Travis? And what, or who, was helping her? Once again I'm under informed. I'm out of my realm. I see things I don't understand and I can't talk about it, because no one else sees it. So, here I am, mostly naked, in the middle of the forest, at night, running away from spirits, Angels of Death, and with a girl who's about to collapse. The best I can do is refuse to be a duck out of water. Protection and willpower are my only answers right now. We'll rest under cover and I'll attempt to keep a wall of light around Corrine and myself until, I don't know...after tonight, probably forever.

My ankles and calves keep getting alternately scratched or tickled by the underbrush but I do my best at ignoring it and continue moving always into the shadier places until there is virtually no moonlight filtering through the trees overhead. I hold one arm up and out, blocking unseen branches, and one arm around Corrine. She snuggles in close to me, staying quiet and trusting my direction. I hope her trust is well earned, because at this point I'm really only moving by instinct. It's slow going and our feet are constantly catching on roots or stones. Finally, when I feel we are a safe distance from the road, I pull out my lighter and hold up the small flame, looking around for someplace level. I see the spot quickly, not by my miniature light but by a ray from the moon.

"Over there," I whisper, nudging us forward. "See it?"

When we get to the place, it's even better than I thought. The moon was shining on a boulder the size of a Volkswagen beetle, which isn't great, except on the other side is a perfect campsite for two people. It's completely hidden from the road, and there's even an old fire pit against the backside of the rock.

"Sit," I say as I ease Corrine to the ground.

She immediately lies down on her side and curls into a ball. I hope she's not worse off than I think. There must still be drugs in her system, but how bad is it?

"I need firewood. Will you be all right for a minute?"

"I'm okay, Jules. I just need to rest my head."

I squat down in front of her and place my hand on her forehead and then check her pulse. She feels normal to me. Then I grab her hand, feeling for temperature. She's cool, but not life-threatening. Should I even build a fire? The warmth would be nice and the light too, but is it too much risk?

Waving my lighter close to the ground, I look for small twigs to add to the dry pine needles needed to get the fire started. That's the easy part. But I also need larger pieces of wood to burn and keep the flames going. There's nothing burnable larger than my finger within the small oval clearing. Maybe this camp has been used more recently than I would have guessed.

Moving farther away, I feel with my feet and continue to wave my tiny flame out in front of me. I resort to breaking some of the lower dead branches from the trees. After each loud crack I hold my breath and listen to the surrounding night, wondering if I've awakened some unseen predator.

When an unfamiliar sound answers back, my heart leaps into my throat and threatens to erupt in a gagging retch. I force the muscles in my throat, and the rest of my body, to freeze as I strain to hear more.

Laughter? Deep and chuckling, and definitely male. Something in the air tingles inside my nose. I sniff cautiously. Wood smoke and...food. Not just any food but the distinct smell of popcorn. As silently as possible, I creep closer to the sounds.

"Hey, Crash. Quit fondling that bottle and pass it over," I hear through the trees.

"I'm not givin' it up, man. This is the curviest thing we've got up here," another male voice says.

"No, it ain't. Hey Butch, lift up your shirt for Crash."

A low voice, thick and gruff answers, "For fifty bucks, I'll give you a private tour of my moobies."

"You're both sickos, you know that?" one of them says.

There's a few seconds of silence and my brain races through the possibilities. Should I walk into their camp and beg for help? What if they're perverts, or criminals? The conversation starts up again and I listen some more, trying to narrow down my opinion of these strangers.

"Awww, Butch, go sit your fat ass down and get those hairy boobs away from me."

Gruff voice says, "Don't be a tease. You know I can't take rejection."

"A woman. I was talking about finding a woman."

"Now you're just insultin' me," the one with the rough voice says. "Best give me fifty dollars so I won't flatten your face."

"Touchy old broad isn't he?" one of the others says.

"Expensive too."

So far, I can distinguish three voices, maybe four. I decide to go tell Corrine we have campers near us and ask her what she thinks. In light of the fact that I couldn't hear a single female voice, and I don't have clothes on, I'm definitely leaning toward staying away from them, at least until morning. Daylight provides a certain level of false security the dark of night lacks.

Taking cat-like steps back to where I'd come from, I suddenly find myself shrieking with surprise.

"Who's out there?" a man asks.

Where had he come from? I hadn't heard him at all. My firewood falls to my feet in a jumble, all but one long branch. I brandish it out in front of me like a sword.

"Who are you?" I ask in an accusing tone.

"Uh-huh, I asked you first," he says.

"I was collecting firewood," I stammer. "My friends are waiting for me," I add.

His voice seems to be coming from the ground, but I can't tell for sure, or he's very short, like a child, but he doesn't have the voice of a child. Then I see is his outline under the shadows of a tree. My heart thumps inside my ears. I know how vulnerable I am right now. He doesn't make a move. Neither do I, and I don't want to give him any advantage over me, so I hold my ground.

"In the dark? In your skivvies?" he asks.

I can hear the skepticism in his voice.

"That's right," I say curtly and with as much confidence as I can.

"Well, you have a real nice night then, ma'am," he says, still not moving away from his tree.

Why won't this guy just leave? I don't want him to follow me, and or jump on me, and I can't see his face. What is up? And why is his voice so familiar?

"Who are you?" I ask again. The perturbed sound coming out of me is more annoying to my own ears than anyone listening, but I can't get past the fact that I know who this guy is.

"I'm afraid you've caught me at a real disadvantage. If you wouldn't mind takin' up your firewood and moseyin' on along the way, I'd be much obliged."

I digest his words and can hardly believe it. I'm in my underwear, alone in the dark, and he's telling me to scat. I bend down and grab a couple pieces of the wood from the ground, intending to make a break for it, but my brain can't stop wondering what this guy is doing? The next thing I know, the phrase, *"Does a bear shit in the woods?"* plays like a recording only I can hear. I feel my face flush with heat as embarrassment sends me scurrying away like a startled mouse.

Then, like a brain fart letting loose, it hits me, a repulsive bubble of stench, but also, oddly relieving. "Oh God, you've got to be kidding me," I murmur under my breath. I don't turn around, but I know he can hear me. "Is your name Eli?"

The unmistakable sound of his fly zipping makes me want to bite back my words and take off. What the hell am I doing? This couldn't be the same group of bikers that rescued Corrine and me before. Even as I deny the possibility, my gut knows it's them, the deer killers.

"It is, Ma'am. And you are?" he asks, his southern accent more clear than ever.

My eyes close for a brief moment. *Of all people, why this guy?* I silently ask the mysterious universe. I hadn't exactly made the best first impression and Corrine had all but put her hand in Eli's pants at our last run-in. Oh hell, how many levels of embarrassment can there be? A sigh of disbelieving resignation escapes my lips and then I answer him. "In desperate need of your help. Again."

∞

Do I dare try to come up with the right adjective to describe the mortification of walking into Eli's camp partially dressed in the middle of the night with a story no one would ever believe? There isn't an appropriate word. Thankfully, Eli saves my nearly naked butt some humiliation by giving me a shirt to wear and a camp blanket before his fellow bikers see me.

"Are either of you girls hurt?" Eli asks.

"No, nothing serious." My little finger isn't throbbing as bad since I wrapped a crushed plantain leaf around it. Even at night the herb wasn't too hard to find. It grows just about everywhere. I also know that my nail being torn off isn't life-threatening. I wish I could just forget about it, but at some point I'm going to have to look at the damage. My other bruises, scrapes, and sore parts are numb. All I can feel right now is relief at finding help in the middle of the night.

"If ya'll can wait 'til mornin' then we'd be happy to give you a ride to town," he says as we step out of the trees and walk into the circle of light cast from their fire.

All eyes watch us enter the campsite. Bandanas, facial hair, and leather are apparently mandatory to be a member of this motorcycle crew.

"If you want to shed a little light on your situation, we could get you out of these hills tonight."

"Morning's fine," Corrine says before I have a chance to say anything about our *situation*.

"Our car's broken down, that's all, so we decided to try to walk out."

I see Eli eye me up, down, and back up again, but he doesn't call me out.

He's more friendly and personable than I remembered him. In the firelight, he has a soft golden and white glow around him, which instantly comes across to me as feeling safe. Which is completely opposite of how I thought of him from before, with a handgun pointed at an innocent deer. I push the memory aside — he's offering his help now — and I don't have many options.

"See, Crash, ask and you will receive," one of the bikers says.

Crash, a man with a narrow nose, and a thin mustache and goatee, stirs the fire with a long stick and answers back. "Those are girls. I said I needed a woman."

"They look of age," the other one says back.

"Cut it out, Mike. You're makin' them nervous," Eli says.

And he is. I can't spend the rest of the night here wondering if we're about to be manhandled at any second.

"They're harmless," Eli says to Corrine and me.

I wish I could believe him, but then Butch, the hairy giant, spots me and any trace of reassurance is snuffed out like a dying candle.

"Hello there, Dolly. Eli said we'd meet up with you again," Butch pats his rotund middle. "I'm a big ol' warm bear and you look like you're in need of some warmin' up."

"Thank you. No," I say, and grab Corrine's hand and then turn to leave this less than desirable camp.

"Butch, you stupid boar," Eli swears. Then to my back, he continues, "We've all sworn an oath to Christ. We're not your typical bikers, Jules. I swear on the Bible, you and Corrine are safe here with us. No matter what those fools say."

"He ain't lyin'," one of the others adds. "Eli's even ordained. If you don't believe it, just look at us. We all wear the patch of The Savior Rides MC."

MC, MC? I try to work it out quickly. *Master of ceremonies? Motley crew? No silly girl.* My brain slaps me a big 'duh' — *motorcycle club.* I had seen the patches on Eli's vest. I stop my retreat. Corrine hadn't really moved anyway. I had been tugging at a motionless blob.

"Bet y'all could use a bite to eat," Eli says to my back.

My shoulders sag with resignation and the two tons of responsibility weighing me down. *Do we have any choice?*

Corrine eats a hot dog, but I decline, and instead, eat a cookie from a bag, and then share freshly popped smoky flavored popcorn with the whole lot of them. When Crash hands me orange mango pineapple juice in a smooth curvy plastic bottle, I decline, remembering what I overheard in the woods about fondling. I gratefully accept a brand new unopened bottle of water from Eli.

Shortly after our midnight snack, Eli insists Corrine and I take his tent as he was planning to tend the fire all night anyway. Corrine doesn't hesitate as she climbs into the tiny space and lies down. I crawl in next to her, seriously doubting I'll be able to get any sleep at all.

I listen to the night, the strange men, the crackle of fire, and refuse to sleep, even though lying down does feel like a sudden exotic luxury. A need so desperate I almost cry as my head touches the ground. I keep up my energetic wall of protection like encapsulating Corrine and myself in a vault. It helps, but fear lurks around the edges and weakens my confidence. There's a few hours left until the sun comes up so I vow to stay awake. I'm not willing to let my guard down. Too much has happened. Before I finish counting to ten, Corrine's breathing slows to a heavy rhythm and she's sound asleep. I roll over onto my side clutching my hiking pack tight in my hands and try not to be envious. I can't relax here. I don't know how Corrine is able to. She's the one who lost her stepfather after all. The smell of Eli's bedroll is strong and all male. It's a musty mix of cologne, campfire, motorcycle exhaust, and a hint of gasoline. This is the last thing I remember before the nightmare starts.

Chapter Twenty-three:
The Dark and The Light

Juliana

"Nathaniel, where are you?" I call out for the fourth time. It's completely dark. I have no idea where we are, but I know Nathaniel is close. I can hear his perfect smooth voice and I can even smell his clean fresh smell, but I can't feel him or see him. Where had he come from? And better yet, how did I get here? I blink my eyes a few times trying to figure out if I'm blindfolded. Nothing brushes my eyelashes. Everything is pitch black.

"Where did you go, Juliana? I can't see you either."

"I'm right here," I say frustrated. "What's going on?"

"I'm not sure. Keep talking and keep moving. I think you're getting closer," he says.

"I don't like this, Nathaniel."

"Neither do I. You're close. Say something else."

I say the first thing that comes to mind, a poem from a favorite book. "How doth the little crocodile improve his shining tail, and pour the waters of the Nile on every golden scale. How cheerfully he seems to grin. How neatly spreads his claws, and welcomes little fishes in..."

"With gently smiling jaws."

Nathaniel finishes the poem and then I feel him. There is something like webbing all over him. There's some kind of tool in my hand and I cut very carefully at the gauze-like film until he reaches out and wraps his arms around me. He's solid and warm and so real feeling that I could lose myself forever in this unexpected gift.

"You know the poem," I whisper into his chest.

"We're all mad here," he whispers back, continuing to quote one of my favorite books.

A tiny smile lightens my heart in this black void and I can't resist playing along. "Curiouser and curiouser," I say with a very bad British accent.

His arms tighten around me for a second and then he moves us one slow step at a time.

"Where are we?" I ask.

"I think you need to tell me," he says.

"What do you mean?"

"I was trapped in your car a minute ago and now I'm by your side."

"You're saying I'm doing this," I say in disbelief.

"I think so. Maybe I have something to do with it. Juliana, I haven't been able to stop worrying about you since you were taken, but look down at your hand. I know I don't have anything to do with that."

My right hand rises in the dark. I can feel it, but I can't see my own hand. I can only see Travis's dagger. The metal blade catches a light that has no source. "I cut you free. I was so worried about you. He said he was going to enslave you for eternity." My mouth stops talking as my head tries to put it all together. "Nathaniel, how is this happening?"

"I only have theories, Juliana. Are you sleeping? Are you safe? Where is Corrine and Travis?" he asks three fast questions as he holds me almost painfully next to his side.

"I don't know," I say. "Maybe I'm asleep. But don't worry about Travis. He's dead."

Silence fills the black space around us while I wait for Nathaniel to respond. He stiffens, holding me tighter. His chest doesn't rise and fall with breath, but there is life in him. There's a soul inside him. It's heartbreakingly pure and precious, fragile but unbreakable. I want to reach up and touch his face, ease the worry lines I imagine are creasing his brows as he broods over my last words. I don't get the chance.

A hand clamps down on my shoulder and something smothers my face before I can scream.

"I am not dead, Siren," it hisses in my ear. "My blade is part of me, you stupid girl. It pulled me straight to you the moment you used it."

Chaos turns my world inside out and upside down. I thrash and kick against nothing but blankets, yet something is being pressed over my face and I can't breathe. My feet hit someone and a yowl of pain pierces the night. This is quickly followed by Corrine's hysterical screams, one after another. I rip at the fabric over my face, fighting for air, but I'm unable to pull it away or make any difference at the unbelievable weight holding it against my nose and mouth. My hands grope in all directions. What is on me! I feel the hilt of the dagger. I grab it and swing wildly. On my right, I feel and hear the tent shredding with my madness, but there's no contact with anything more solid. Blackness creeps in around the edges of my unseeing eyes as I begin to suffocate. Then suddenly, and with a rush of air, the blanket is flung to the side. My burning lungs fill with air and I flail to get out of the confines of the shredded tent.

Landing hard on the ground outside, I see the invisible monster, Travis. He looks like a warped version of himself. He's still small and wiry, but he's not in a body like mine or anyone else who is alive. His spirit is loose and it's a darker adaptation of his physical self. Nathaniel has Travis in a full body hold with his arms locked around Travis's throat and chest. When Travis sees me on the ground, he lurches toward me and starts to break Nathaniel's grip.

Nathaniel yells over the ensuing chaos. "Harmony Allistair, over here!"

A rush of shadows appear from all directions and head for Nathaniel and Travis. I think I see a flash of Harmony's green cloak.

Then a body jumps in front of me blocking my view. I can't see if Travis has broken free. My hand reaches forward to push whoever it is out of my way, but he won't budge. I lean to the side and see Travis coming for me. Supernatural beings surround him, but he manages to slip from their grasp. The murderous hatred in his eyes and the snarl on his lips causes me to panic. I push myself off my knees ready to run, or hide, or fight.

Men yell and Corrine's screams overwhelm my ears, but then what happens next stops everything.

"In the name of Christ, I command you to be gone from here. Lord protect us from this evil and surround us with your light!" Eli booms over all the chaos and instantly we are engulfed in a glow of golden light. Eli stands in front of me holding up his arms as if he is holding up the sun itself. When Travis doesn't tear through Eli and begin to devour my body and soul, I dare to look at him. Travis's face is turned away from the glow but his body is still leaning in my direction as if he's going to pass through the protection anyway. He appears to be in terrible pain and yet he still won't back off completely.

Nathaniel tackles Travis from the side, knocking him over. Travis roars with anger and turns to his attacker. Nathaniel grabs his arms and pins him down on the ground. Travis warps into liquid smoke, attempting to get away but Nathaniel does something similar, distorting his shape to keep his hold, and doesn't fall for Travis's trick again. Then I see Travis open his mouth and lunge at Nathaniel's face with his teeth. Nathaniel sees him coming and twists his head away before being bitten.

In the next second, hooded shapes swoop in and surround them again. Travis's scream is blood-curdling as they wrap him in the strange netting I had seen earlier by the wrecked car. Nathaniel helps restrain the spirit of the dead warlock and then I clearly see the green hood of Harmony.

She calls out, "Double up. We can't let him use sorcery and mischief again."

Nathaniel takes some kind of ethereal chain from one of the other hooded figures and moves with lightning speed as he wraps it around Travis. He makes sure to cover Travis's eyes and mouth and then binds his wrists and arms. The others form a tight circle, holding the netting taught. When Travis is completely bound they take him quickly away from our camp, disappearing into the night.

Eli spins around and grabs me by the shoulders. "Holy smokes," he exclaims in a whoosh of hot breath. "Let me see you."

He turns me so the firelight shines on my face. "What was that?"

Numb with incomprehensible fear, I stand and stare at Eli, unable to speak or move.

Without waiting for an answer, he drops my shoulders and grabs Corrine by hers. Looking her over and apparently finding her satisfactory — she somehow avoided the dagger I was swinging — he half drags her over to me and wraps both of us into the protective shield of his arms.

He doesn't let go and I can hear him praying over us, repeating verses from the Bible over and over. We stay that way for so long I lose all focus, mental or physical. Finally, Eli unwraps his arms from around us, but only long enough to drag blankets and his sleeping bag from the remains of his tent and pull them closer to the fire. He nudges us down onto the blankets and then sits next to us. The other bikers all bring something to sit on and make a circle around the fire. No one speaks. I look down at my hand, noticing for the first time I'm still holding Travis's dagger. Eli looks down at it too and in one quick movement he reaches over taking it from me.

"This thing is evil," he says, and then unfolds himself from the ground and disappears into nearby shadows.

Eli returns within seconds holding a bottle. "This water is blessed," he says. He steps up to the fire, unscrews the cap of the jug, and then holds up the dagger. As he pours the water over the blade and handle, I think I see a stream of inky black leave the dagger and hiss into the coals. He says another prayer, this one too low for me to hear the words and then drops the dagger straight into the flames. Corrine flinches slightly at the sight and then leans into me. I close my eyes and lean against her. I can only imagine what all this has been like for her. Her own stepfather had kidnapped her and used her for whatever he wanted and then was killed in front of her eyes. Could she see any of what just happened? Is she relieved he's gone, or is she sad? Maybe she's too shocked to feel anything right now. That's how I feel. When I reopen my eyes, the first hint of morning light brightens the eastern sky above the black ridge of mountains. Somehow I managed to live through another day. Did Jared?

∞

"Jules, is that you?" my mom calls out as I open the front door.

Crap. I was hoping she would be asleep or better yet, not home at all when we got here. "Yeah, it's me," I say, and make a run for the stairs. If she sees me, I'm done for.

I hear her footsteps coming from the kitchen so I take two steps at a time.

"Honey, there are a couple of strange messages on the machine. Can you come down here, please?"

"Sure, just give me a second," I call over my shoulder. I'm sure I look worse than one of my cat's special presents. The last thing Ariel brought me was a half alive rodent, bedraggled, gimpy, and covered with unknown filth. *Yeah, worse than that.* I have Eli's shirt on and Crash's dirty jeans which look like they haven't been washed all summer. If Mom sees me like this...well, she just can't see this.

My bedroom door swings mostly closed behind me as I throw off the biker's clothes and grab anything within reach, then I rush across the hall and close the bathroom door. Moving through the motions of cleaning myself and dressing with ultrasonic speed, I'm back downstairs before my mom has a chance to chase me down and interrogate.

"Is Jared home?" I ask.

"No. You two think you're all grown up, but you're never too old to let your mother know where you're at. I was really starting to worry. No message, no note. It's not like you. I almost called the police." Her eyebrows are raised so high on her forehead in an accusing and questioning stare I wonder if they can actually touch her hairline.

She's not done. "And these messages. Who are Corrine, and Laura Petit?"

Her piercing gaze doesn't waver an inch as she waits for me to say something. As casual as possible, I walk over to the pantry door and open it, grabbing a plastic bag. As I stuff the biker's wadded up clothes inside I give a very careful answer. "Umm, a friend and her mom."

"She made it sound like she was supposed to meet with you. Are you all right? Have you been camping again? You smell like smoke. You need to tell me if you're out in the woods. What if you didn't come back? How would anyone find you?"

"I know, I know," I say, as I try to slip out of the kitchen.

She blocks my exit. "If you know, then why didn't you—"

"Mom," I interrupt a little too harshly. "I'm fine. Please, believe me. I know I screwed up. I'm sorrier than I can ever say, but right now I have to return this," I hold up the bag for her to see. "Did Jared leave a message?" I ask, letting my tone come down to the level of my distress.

Her brows dip and her mouth pinches at the corners. Her concern is equal to mine. "No, I was hoping you knew where he was."

"I'll find him this morning," I say, and grab the phone from its cradle on the counter.

As I walk out of the kitchen, Mom asks, "Are you going to tell me who the man on the motorcycle in our driveway is?"

"No."

∞

"How did you know we would run into each other again," I ask Eli as I hand him the bag of clothes.

Eli insisted on following Corrine and me safely home from the hospital where my car was still parked. His motorcycle friends had not come with us, saying they were after some hot breakfast.

Eli sits astride his Harley, face grizzled and hazel eyes serious. "Inner guidance told me we had unfinished business."

"Are we done now?" I ask, wondering if his sixth sense is telling him anything else I need to know.

"Almost," he says, and settles back on the leather seat as if he may be here awhile.

"I'm really grateful for everything you and your friends did to help us, but I don't think I can handle another run-in like last night."

"I don't think somethin' like last night happens twice in a lifetime. At least I pray not. No, I was thinkin' there's words left between us that haven't yet been said. Somethin' you're wantin' to ask? Go on then, and I'll do my best."

Is there something I want to ask? I stare down at my Mary Janes and tuck a lock of my grimy hair behind an ear. "Do you know my brother?" I ask the first thing that comes to mind. Jared. I have to know if he's still alive.

"Can't say I do," he says.

Is this some sort of riddle? Are we suddenly playing some ridiculous game? I look over my shoulder at Corrine. She sits on the front steps, running her fingers through her own messy blonde hair. She looks almost as bad as I feel. How had we survived last night? How had Travis gotten away from the angels? How had he been able to smother me with the blanket? Where is Nathaniel? And then it comes to me, clicking into place, like finding the right key to a lock, questions for Eli. Information he's supposed to share with me.

"How did you do it last night? Why did your prayers protect us?" I turn back to meet his gaze, remembering how his shield of energy was so bright and how it kept Travis's evil spirit from attacking me. "I've been trying to use energetic protection like a bubble or a wall around me, but the way you did it, was so much stronger. I could see it. It was unreal."

"It's really something that you can see the Light of Christ. It's a rare gift. Let me ask you this. Do you belong to a church?"

I shake my head. Is he going to start preaching at me? I'm not looking for a lecture. If I wanted one of those, I'd be inside with my mother.

"Don't shut down now," he says. "I was only askin', so I can give you an answer that will make sense to you. Whether you believe it or not, there's a phenomenal amount of love available to all who ask for it. I called for help and it came. It was some strong evil last night, but it couldn't stand up to so much love. That's all I did. Anyone can believe in love."

I digest his answer, letting it settle deep inside. He obviously believes it. I could too. Belief is a strong thing. That much I understand. "Thank you," I finally say. "For protecting me and for telling me how I can use such powerful protection in the future." I pause and scratch the top of my nose. It's suddenly tickling like a bug is crawling inside. *Is someone thinking about me?* I believe in superstitions. *Is there a church for that?* I don't ask Eli aloud. He has a different idea about what church is. "Why do you call it a gift? Being able to see spirits and energy? People tell me it's special, but it doesn't feel good. It scares me and I don't even understand most of it."

Eli looks down hiding his eyes from me for a few seconds before answering. "Whether you believe in God, or Great Spirit, or in nothing at all, here's what being on the road for so long has shown me. You ain't never gonna be someone else. You were born you, so be at peace with it. And if you're unsure, then go learn about who you are. Findin' some peace and happiness can make life a whole lot more enjoyable."

I'm not sure if I will ever find peace with seeing ghosts and demons. "I'll think about it," I say and step back.

His hand moves to the ignition switch and the motorcycle wakes up with a roar. Heels digging into the ground, he backs the bike around. Before he takes off, he calls out, "Be thankful you have angels watching over you."

He gives a knowing nod of his head to somewhere over my left shoulder. His scuffed and worn boot moves to the gear shifter and he clicks into first. Eli's camp-smoked tinged hand lets out the clutch and the bike rumbles out of the driveway.

Spinning around, I see Nathaniel standing by the corner of the house, forlorn and serious as ever. And God, so beautiful, I almost weep with relief just seeing him again. He survived last night as well. Then an unexplainable jab of insecurity makes me look away.

With the phone still in my hand, I dial the number to retrieve messages and then walk over to Corrine. Her pale blue eyes droop with exhaustion as she watches me. Even her head looks too heavy for her this morning as she rests it against the deck railing. I listen to the recordings and then commit a phone number to memory. Next, I hang up and dial Jared's cell phone. It rings and goes to voicemail.

"Jared, I swear, if you don't return this call I will bury every one of your CDs and your MP3 player and your wa-wa pedal and everything you own in the middle of the forest where you will never see them again, until you convince me that you deserve to be my brother. Call me, I'm home, and I'm freaking out."

I hang up again, and dial the number I just memorized. As soon as it rings I hold the phone in front of Corrine.

"Here," I say.

She gives me an uncertain look but takes the phone.

"I'll be in my garden." I point a finger in the general direction around the side of the house.

Then I hear a muffled voice as someone picks up on the other end.

"Mom?" Corrine says.

I turn and walk past the garage, past Nathaniel, and straight for my flowers.

Chapter Twenty-four: The Lumps

Juliana

Stampeding wild horses across my abdomen would be more comfortable than what I'm feeling right now. My insides do flip-flops while I wait for him to say something. Did I really free him from my car last night? And if so, how had I done it? How am I traveling in my sleep? He was there last night, I reassure myself. I saw with my own eyes as he kept Travis away from me. Why is he here now? Because of Corrine?

"Travis is gone. I wanted to be the one to tell you. He's dead forever. You never have to worry about him coming back," Nathaniel says.

He stands by the garden fence, leaving the thin wire as a boundary between us. Kneeling in the dirt, I choose to surround myself with yarrow, wild geranium, coneflower, and chamomile. Their smells are bright and so are the blooms. It helps me stay grounded, but barely. Keeping my fingers connected with the earth also helps, so I pull any and all intruding blades of grass as if it were a life mission.

"Juliana?" he says in a low voice.

Hearing his voice causes a warm whisper of sensation to run over my skin. I'm not sure what to say. If I open my mouth I may barf all of my uncertainties on him in a gush of girlie blither-blather. Instead, I stare at my oriental poppies, their vivid red-orange petals catching and holding my gaze.

I see him move over, positioning himself to be able to see my face better.

"I heard you," I whisper.

"Why won't you look at me?" he asks.

I turn to face him, but I don't meet his eyes yet. He looks different. Not his clothes, he still wears jeans, T-shirt, and tennis shoes from a different decade and his shirt is a dark heather gray, so similar to his eye color. The eyes I don't want to see right now. No, he's more solid, not the ghost-like Nathaniel he had been only yesterday.

"Something's happened to you," I say as I spot another weed needing expulsion.

"They gave me some privileges back, after last night. I'm not completely my old self though. Harmony gave me more credit than I deserve. And you helped too."

"How? I didn't do anything, other than almost suffocate."

"You did. The knife you were holding. You cut the bonds that were holding me. And you hurt him enough so I could pull him off of you."

I give Nathaniel a disbelieving look. "The dagger? How? I didn't..." I say in denial.

"It worked. I saw it. He felt it cut him. I don't understand it either, but the dagger worked in the spirit realm. Travis must have done spells on it."

Looking away, I can't accept any acknowledgment right now. "You're waiting for Corrine? That's why you're here, right?"

"I needed to see you. Your dream. Do you remember any of it?"

Not answering, all I can manage to do is bite my lower lip.

"Juliana, what's going on with you?"

"I can't talk about it right now. Please, Nathaniel. I...just everything." Silence weighs heavily until I finally say, "Corrine's mom is probably going to be here any second."

The lines on his face mirror the grief on my own and the hard edge of his jaw mimics the tension in my shoulders. I will myself to not collapse in a sorry heap. I take a tentative step around the artemisia. "I need to find Jared," I say, letting my first priority have a voice.

He swallows, then looks out across the yard, not pressuring me.

My eyes flicker over to the house as I hear a car pull into the drive. Nathaniel looks over toward the sound as well. In silent agreement, we leave the garden and walk around to the front of the house, leaving everything unsaid and unresolved hanging over the flowers like a cloud.

Corrine and her mother's embrace is so personal I look away feeling like an intruder. Their reunion is powerful and I can feel it standing twenty feet away. My eyes fill with tears as I watch the quaking leaves of the aspens in my yard. He may not have the ability to form a body yet, but I think I feel a hand stroke my hair. I must be imagining it, and yet I would swear I can feel him. My complete and utter breakdown is too close to the surface. I can't look at him right now because I refuse to break right here. Later, in private, I can let go of the terror and the heartache, but not yet.

Corrine sobs into her mom's shoulder. I hear a bit of what she says. "Travis is dead, Mom. His car. It was an accident. It was terrible."

"Everything is going to be all right. Shh, shh," Laura soothes into Corrine's ear.

After countless minutes, or seconds, I hear Corrine say, "You have to meet Jules. She's the one who called you."

They break their hug and Corrine turns to me. I wipe my eyes with the back of my dirt and grass stained hand and walk over to them. Laura wraps her tiny arms around me in a fierce hug. She is the older version of Corrine, thin and lithe, with golden hair, and the same powder-blue eyes.

"Thank you. I've tried everything in my power to find her and Patrick. Thank you so much. I owe you everything," she says.

"You're welcome," I manage to say past the lump in my throat.

She releases me, looks up at my swollen eyes, and then leans in again for another quick hug.

"Do you guys want to come inside? I can make some tea, or some breakfast?"

It's Corrine who answers. "No, thank you, Jules. You've already done so much for me," she says as more tears leak down her face. "It's more than I deserve, especially after what I did to you. You have no idea how sorry I am."

She has to be referring to the succubus. "I know it wasn't you," I say. "If anyone's to blame, it's Travis."

Her shoulders heave and then release with a deep whoosh of breath. I actually see a massive weight leave her. A darkness around her, a part of her aura I didn't realize shouldn't be there, lifts and evaporates into the air. She practically jumps on me with an even tighter hug than her mother's.

"I think everything is going to be better," she says.

My eyes close and I can feel the love in her spread like an encompassing warmth. The change in her is almost overwhelmingly beautiful. I squeeze her back with the knowledge she has just overcome an enormous hurdle in her life.

"We're going to get Patrick and then we're going back to New Mexico," she says. Then she whispers so only I can hear, "Your boyfriend is here, my witch friend."

As they pull away from the house, I walk over to the front porch and pick up the phone again. I dial Jared and listen as the recording tells me to leave a message. I look at Nathaniel as I hang up. He's watching me closely, but staying silent. He's solid. *His body is as real as mine.* Corrine had found her will to live and he was restored to his previous state of being. Everything I had planned worked. Somehow it had all worked out. Corrine was back with her mom and Nathaniel was an angel again.

"You can come inside if *you* want," I say leaving the decision up to him. He did dump me after all.

Without a moment's hesitation, he follows me into the house.

Mom comes around the corner from the kitchen as soon as the door closes behind me. The expectant look on her face immediately changes to questioning surprise when she sees Nathaniel standing behind me. Her eyes flash back to mine for a second and her face morphs again, this time filled with motherly concern.

"Good morning," she says to Nathaniel.

"Mom, this is Nathaniel Evans. Nathaniel, this is my mom, Diane," I say, making the introduction short and sweet.

Nathaniel moves around me. I try not to breathe in his sweet ozone smell, but some of the fragrant molecules tickle my senses anyway. *Why does he have to smell so good too?*

"Nice to meet you, Mrs. Crowson. I hope I'm not disturbing your morning," he says as he sticks out his hand.

"Not at all. I have to say I'm surprised Jules is up so early," she says as she returns the handshake.

"They had a little car trouble last night. I think Juliana and Corrine wanted to get off the mountain as early as possible."

My molars clench as I will Nathaniel to shut it. Mom doesn't need to know about last night.

Her polite smile turns upside down as she addresses me. "Is your car okay? I saw you pull in. What happened?"

"My car's fine, Mom. I didn't get much sleep last night though, and I'm really tired." If only she knew how exhausted I am, then she would send me straight to bed.

"But, *are you* all right? Who were you with?" She looks over to Nathaniel as she asks this last part.

"Please stop with the twenty questions," I beg of her. "I just need food and sleep right now."

Her lips pinch for a second and then she seems to come to a decision. "Fine. I'm dying to know what happened, but I can see you're not in the mood to talk about it. I could use some sleep too."

She's still in her work clothes and her hair is up, albeit loosely with stray strands falling down around her face, no doubt from a long shift at the hospital.

"Get some food, and some rest, and then you're going to tell me everything later," she says in her perfect mom voice.

I nod in silent agreement, and so grateful she isn't trying to pry answers out of me.

"Are you sure I shouldn't be worried about something?" she asks again, her green eyes penetrating my soul, looking for some clue.

I sigh heavily. "Only death, Mom. It comes around for everyone, you know."

"Not funny, Jules." She scowls at my bad joke. "I'm going upstairs. Nice to meet you, Nathaniel."

I wish I was being funny. I walk into the kitchen, not really caring if Nathaniel follows or not. Mine and Jared's survival seem like the only important thing in the world at the moment.

As soon as I hear Mom's bedroom door close, Nathaniel steps up close. So close we are almost touching.

He whispers, "I'm sorry. I'm sorry about Travis, and for causing you any pain. You've done everything. You saved Corrine, Juliana, and I wouldn't be back to normal — if you call this normal — without you. You're amazing. I don't deserve to be here with you. And you still let me in."

His face is a mask of torture and I want to erase all the terrible things we have been through, but I can't. All I can do is stand here, surrounded by his warmth, his smell, and his caressing voice. It's the most comfortable place I've ever known, and the most agonizing. I have to work at forming any words at all.

"I had to do something. If it wasn't for me, you wouldn't have been killed in the first place."

"I don't want to start arguing again, Juliana. I shouldn't even be here now. You should run away from me."

"If I do, if I leave you now, you know I'll find you when I sleep. I don't mean to do it, Nathaniel. It just happens."

He lifts a hand, but then stops himself from touching me.

I look down, staring at nothing, and whisper, "I'll be with you as soon as I fall asleep."

"We're connected spiritually."

"I can't seem to break the connection. I don't know if I want to."

"I don't want you to. It goes on our inexplicable list," he says and I see his chest rise and fall in a heavy sigh. "I won't pretend I'm a good thing in your life. You're the most unbelievably beautiful and amazing person I've ever met. I was such a fool to think I could walk away. Juliana, I'm here now and I want to be with you. I want to know you and if it's only in your dreams, then I'll take it."

A shudder passes through my soul. Every instinct in my body is telling me to melt into his arms and never let go, but my head is resisting. How can I fall for someone who isn't even alive? How can it ever work? How can I be thinking about any of this when I don't even know if Jared is alive.

"Nathaniel, I need to find my brother," I say in the darkness of closed eyelids. "We have time, but Jared doesn't. I'm leaving to go look for him."

"No, you're not," he says ever so gently as he shakes his head. I take a step back and look into his heart-meltingly gorgeous face.

Every second could be critical. A tight knot in my chest clenches. "It could be too late already," I say.

"Juliana, you can go. I won't stop you, but I can find him faster, and be back to tell you in minutes, or even seconds. I can move with my thoughts, remember?"

I stare at him like he's a godsend. I hadn't thought of it. Of course he should go. "Really? You'll do that?"

I move in close to him and rest my cheek against his chest. His arms wrap around me and he holds me tight against his solid body.

"I'll be right back, if it's what you want."

There are no words to express the feelings of relief and the comfort of his touch as they wash through me. He'll find Jared for me. All I can do is nod and attempt to swallow the lump in my throat.

I take a deep breath and look up at him. His pewter colored eyes search my face. His gaze lingers on my mouth and then slowly lifts back to my eyes. "I'll find him, Juliana," he says, and then he vanishes from my arms.

Chapter Twenty-five: Saving a Life

Nathaniel

Jared Crowson isn't difficult to find. What is difficult, is explaining to my mentor, Marcus, why I'm still interested in my previous case, what I'm doing there, and most of all, telling Juliana what I've found.

I recognize the room and Jared's company instantly. Patrick Dawson sits on the floor of his bedroom hunched over a pad of paper. His drawing resembles some sort of medieval monster, but I don't have time to study it. I shut down my empathy for Patrick as I realize he's completely unaware of his father's death, and turn toward Jared. He appears to be asleep on the bed. Marcus takes one look at me and then looks down at Jared. His knowing eyes and his somber face leave no doubt as to what is going on in here. Without saying a word I understand the situation. One look at Jared is all it takes for me to see he is too still, his breathing is too shallow.

Marcus walks over to me by the door. "I wouldn't have believed it, if I wasn't seein' you with my own eyes. I knew you'd figure it out, my friend."

"I had some help," I say, acknowledging his statements about my transformation. "You probably haven't heard, but the warlock passed."

"Oh, I've heard. It's the only reason I'm inside this house. Harmony has a way about her. Travis escaping would have been devastating."

I nod in agreement then look over at Jared. "He's close?"

"It's what I was expectin'. He likes to escape reality too much," Marcus says. "They stayed awake all night on some kind of speed and then when they got back here, he swallowed some pills to bring him back down. He isn't going to wake up this time. His heart is barely beatin'."

"Excuse me. I need to check in with someone. It can't wait," I say and then leave the room.

∞

"Juliana, he's at Corrine's house. I'll drive if you want."

Her exhausted eyes meet mine as I tell her I've found her brother. She bites her lower lip and then tucks her hair behind an ear. Then as if her switch had been flipped, she jumps out of the kitchen chair and rushes toward the front door.

"Is he..." She grabs her keys from a hook on the wall and digs in a brown leather purse hanging from another hook. Cell phone in hand she heads outside without finishing her question.

"Here," I say, and take the keys from her.

"Are you sure? I mean, can you stay like that long enough to drive?" she asks, referring to my physical body.

"I'm strong right now, so don't worry about that. You shouldn't drive. I'll tell you everything while you tell me how to get to the Dawson's, by car."

∞

As we pull into the driveway, I see Juliana stiffen, if that's at all possible. She already has so much tension, I'm afraid she might shatter if I hit a bump in the road.

"Travis is gone for good," I say.

She looks at me and her face is paler than normal, and so sorrowful I wish I could hold her right here in the car and tell her everything is fine and right with the world. But holding back reality doesn't change anything and it certainly doesn't help either. I wonder if she was even thinking about Travis at all. She doesn't respond with words, only turns back to the approaching house. We both see Corrine's mother's car parked in front of the house, but again, neither of us say anything. So they had made it here before us. Does anyone in the house know Jared is on the brink of slipping away? Are we too late already?

Behind us, I hear the wail of the ambulance Juliana had called. As soon as the car stops she jumps out and runs inside. Because I can, I meet her in the bedroom in my spirit body.

"Jared, wake up," she says, as she shakes her brother's shoulder.

Laura, Patrick, and Corrine rush to the bedroom behind Juliana and now huddle by the door.

"What the hell?" Patrick says.

"What's wrong with him?" Corrine asks.

The three of them wear matching looks of confusion. Juliana ignores them as she tries to rouse Jared.

"Did you go get her, Nathaniel?" Marcus asks me.

"I did," I say.

"You're disobeying the rules for no reason. He just passed," he tells me.

"He's still in his body," I argue.

"He's hangin' on, but his heart's not beatin'. Maybe he knew she was on her way."

Just then, Jared sits up, moving out of his body. He looks so surprised I almost laugh out loud. If this were a typical case for me, I would introduce myself and ask if he understood what was happening. But nothing about this day fit into any category that includes the words typical or normal.

Seeing her brother move away from his physical body startles Juliana and she jerks back a couple inches.

"How did you get here?" Jared asks.

"Jared, no. Don't do this," she cries. Tears begin to stream down her cheeks.

"You need to get out of here, Jules. You shouldn't be here."

"Jared, look at yourself," she says, gesturing to the body on the bed. "Go back, I need you, J. Please not yet, please."

He finally notices he's not with his body. "Oh crap. Are you kidding?" he says.

I hear the ambulance crew moving into the house. Laura calls for them to come down the hall to the bedroom. Two EMT's rush into the room and move quickly to Jared's supine form on the bed.

"I love you, Jared. Please don't leave," Juliana sobs and lays her hands on his body.

"I don't want to, Jules. Shit, what did I do? So this is what idiocy looks like?" he says as if he can't believe what he's brought on himself. "I swear it was an accident. I'm sorry. God, I'm so damn sorry."

He can't stop looking between his spirit self and his physical body on the bed. Then something seems to click and his brown eyes widen as he shifts his focus to his sister. "I should have been a better brother, Jules. Forgive me? I love you sis." He chokes a little on this last part.

"Wake up, Jared. Get back inside and wake up."

With a look of mixed astonishment and shock Jared lies back down, disappearing into his body.

"No pulse," the EMT says to her partner. "How long has he been like this," she asks anyone in the room.

"I don't know, I don't know," Juliana says, her head shaking with panic. "Help him, please."

The other tech squeezes in next to the bed with more equipment and Juliana moves out of the way. One EMT starts unpacking an AED as the other one begins CPR. They're going to shock his heart, I realize.

Juliana begins to sob uncontrollably. Her pain is unbearable. I knew it would be like this from the beginning. I can't see her this way. I'm unable to standby and do nothing. It's not a choice for me. There's something inside I can't control when it comes to Juliana.

It's a frightening realization, but I can't watch her suffer. When Travis attacked her in her sleep, I've never felt stronger in my entire existence. I thought I had been able to grab Travis because we were both dead, but maybe that had nothing to do with it. Seeing her in pain makes me react. Maybe I can understand Jared's addiction after all. There are forces inside all of us that are uncontrollable.

I pull energy from the universe and form my body, not caring about the fact that I just materialized from thin air. Marcus shakes his head at me, but I ignore him and move to Juliana. Wrapping her in my arms, she falls against me, completely overcome with despair.

I hear Corrine's mom gasp, "Where did he come from?"

No one else in the room appears to care or notice. Everyone's focus is on Jared and the EMT's.

"I'm sorry, love," I say.

"I can't do this," she says. "This isn't happening."

She pushes me away, almost in anger, and falls down next to the bed, crying on the covers and pleading to Jared to live.

I move up behind her and lay my hands on her shoulders, channeling the same energy I use to form my body, only this time, I send it through myself and into Juliana. This is how I'm able to help people feel better, or even heal small wounds. She doesn't shrug me off, but instead reaches forward and places both her hands on Jared's legs.

I think we both feel it happen. The surge of energy increases as if she's tapping into the same source as I am. I feel it pulling through me and passing straight through Juliana and flowing into her brother. It grows and becomes so strong I'm alarmed and almost pull my hands back. Then I see the expression on Juliana's face shift as she realizes what is happening. She can feel it too. It encourages me to keep going.

The paramedic on our side of the bed barks at Jules, "Hands back. Right now."

Juliana breaks the connection with Jared, but I feel her hesitation. She looks up at me with so much pleading and vulnerability I react without thinking.

Relinquishing my body, I move quickly around Jules and the paramedic and place myself closer to Jared's head and shoulders. I reach over, placing one hand on the top of his head and the other one on his chest. With every ounce of my will and focus, I pull energy from all corners of the universe and send it into Jared. The commotion around me becomes less significant than a whisper of breath in my ear. Nothing matters now except my focus.

I catch some words that should mean something to me, "You're making a huge mistake, Nathaniel. Stop what you're doing." But I ignore Marcus and continue this unexpected mission.

"Clear," the EMT orders.

The pull of energy moving through me is electric, like white fire shooting down my arms and into Jared. Will this work? What am I doing? I question myself, but I don't want to stop. The force is like supercharged magnetism. I've started something and I can't let it go now.

"Come on, Jared," I hear the EMT say next to me.

Then with a surge, like the sun exploding inside every cell of my being, the energy takes over and the room and all the people around me disappear. Only brilliant light, whiter than a star and completely blinding surrounds me. It's similar to when I died in the basement of this same house. Only I have no pain this time, and the energy is moving in the opposite direction. I hear faint traces of sound from someplace I can't locate.

"He's back. Hang on there, buddy."

"Jared," I hear Juliana's sobbing relief. Her voice carries above the rest, like pitch perfect notes above a drone of chaos.

Chapter Twenty-six:
Taking Things Slow

Nathaniel

My heart races inside my chest, which is surprising, considering I'm not in possession of a real beating heart. She's inside the small building. It's an old house that has been converted into an herb shop. The painted sign says Native Naturals, Herbal Medicine and Private Consultations. As anxious as I am to see Juliana, I can feel myself stalling. How long have I been gone? My rest period was longer than normal this time, but has it been two days or five? She had come to visit me once in her sleep, but it was a different experience than before. Whatever I had done for Jared had drained me to the point of near total oblivion. When she had found me, I was unable to even speak. I could only be with her in a way like having a strong memory of someone. It was intimate and personal, but quiet and nearly without shape or form, and very different from our other dream-time encounters. Now I'm back, and I have no reason not to run inside and whisk her away. Except I can't make myself move forward. The way things stood between us the day Jared overdosed wasn't ideal. Would she be happy to see me? Should I be here at all?

I swore to her I would stop all this madness. Angels and people don't have relationships, except that we do all the time. But not the way it is with her. I'm unseen ninety-nine percent of the time. My relationships with the living are mostly one sided. Until they pass away, that is. No, this is not the same. She's not like anyone else. There's no comparison.

I move closer to the glass door, wanting a glimpse of her, wanting to see if the shop is busy. Maybe I should wait until she's finished with work. I peek inside and see orderly shelves and a long counter with a cash register, a scale, and small baskets filled with dried herbs and packages of herbal remedies. I don't see anyone, but I know she's inside.

Then she walks straight out in front of me, apparently coming from a room I can't see. She doesn't notice me by the door as she turns her back to me. Her hair hangs loose, shining all the way down her back. It guides my eyes to keep going over other curves and down long legs causing stirrings of warmth inside me.

She sets down the bottles she's carrying and then brushes her hair over her shoulder as she looks over at the door. I move out of sight. Did she sense my eyes on her? Juliana sees and feels more of the supernatural world than any other human I've ever known, except for maybe Chris Abeyta, the shaman.

I'm being ridiculous and letting my nerves control my actions. Stepping to the door, I push it open and do what I came to do. Visit Juliana. Moving faster than a living person could — before I change my mind again— I stand in front of the counter and wonder where she went. Then I see her, bent down organizing a shelf. She rises and turns.

"Boo," I say. How can one look at this beautiful girl reduce my intellect to that of a lumpy bowl of mush? *Boo – is that really the best I can do? I'm a total imbecile and now she knows it.*

I see the immediate start I give her but she's quick to cover it up. She narrows her startling green eyes at me long enough for me to know she didn't appreciate the surprise. Then her face changes and she looks down, hiding under her lashes.

Her chest rises and falls in one of the long steadying breaths she so often takes. I give her an uninterrupted moment. *Will she banish me from her life? I wouldn't hold it against her.* Then she looks up at me.

"So, you're really okay?"

"No, not really."

"What's wrong?"

Her concern is etched around those precious eyes, and I almost give in, but not yet. "I messed everything up. I want to fix it, but I'm not sure if I can."

"Maybe I can help," she says.

After everything she's been through, she's still offering to help me. "Do you have a death wish?"

"I didn't think I did, but I owe you, Nathaniel. You saved Jared's life...again. Do you have any idea what that means to me?"

"You owe me nothing. I wouldn't be standing here if it weren't for you. You're blowing my mind, Juliana. Did you know that? No one offers to help an Angel of Death."

"I don't think of you like that," she says, and lays her hands flat on the counter in front of her.

"I don't think of myself like that either," I confide. Stepping forward I raise my hand and lay it lightly on top of hers. She doesn't pull away so I tuck a small gift, a charm I made for her, into her palm and take a step back.

She turns her hand over and looks at the four-leaf clover. I found one for her and cast it in clear resin so it would last forever. I even put a jewelry finding in it so she could wear it or hang it on her keys.

Juliana flips it over in her palm to look at both sides. She hides her eyes from me again, but I see the small smile take hold of the corners of her mouth, and my heart.

"Thank you," she whispers, and closes her hand around the charm.

I hope the clover reminds her of the one perfect night and day we had together on the mountain. "How's Jared?" I ask, as I stare at her long pale fingers. Her nails are neat, nicely curved, and not short or long. Natural and authentic, like the rest of her. Her pinky finger is wrapped with gauze — *I'll have to ask about that later.*

"He's mostly recovered. And still above ground."

I lift my gaze to hers. She's watching me now. The need I experience from being near her can only be described as an obsession. I need to know her, to protect her, to give her my soul, my life. It scares me, but I couldn't imagine walking away again.

"I did come here to ask you something. If you say no, it's all right."

Is it worry I see, or curiosity? Am I imagining her hesitation?

"I'm not sure if I can deal with another Travis this soon. But, I'm always open to new things." She adds a qualifier, "I think."

"Yeah?" I ask, feeling a minute amount of encouragement. "You told me once that you wanted to take things slow. So, I was wondering if you would like to go out with me, on a date?"

She looks down again, breaking eye contact. Her hair slips forward covering half her face. When she looks up, she brushes her hair back with one hand. The shy smile she gives me almost sends me over the counter to wrap her in my arms and never let go.

She bites the edge of her perfect lower lip and then after an indeterminable length of time she finally answers.

"I'd love to go on a date with you."

Other Works Available

An Angel Falls series

Death Lies Between Us #1

Haunting Me #3

Book #4 coming soon!

Historical Time Travel series

The Night Medicine

If you enjoyed reading *Angel Dreams*, please help spread the word. The greatest compliment you could give is to write a review at your favorite online retailer, share with a book club, or recommend it to a friend!

About The Author

When Jody isn't navigating the terrain of her imagination and writing it down, she can be found exploring the wilderness of Colorado with her family, or in the kitchen baking cookies & brownies - and then trying not to eat them all. She's passionate about continuing to learn and reads anything and everything that catches her interest. Jody is a full time mom, a Reiki master, and has taught Hatha yoga for over a decade.

Death Lies Between Us, book one in the *An Angel Falls* series, is the winner of RomCon's Readers' Crown award for best Paranormal Romance in 2014.

Jody A. Kessler invites you to stop by her website and see what's new at: www.JodyAKessler.com. You can also connect with her on Facebook at Jody A. Kessler, or on Twitter @JodyAKessler.

For updates on future releases you can sign up for her newsletter.

From the Author:

I would like to say a special thank you to my family, friends, beta readers, and fans for their continued support. I couldn't do this without you.